when i argue with myself
how is it i never win?

when I argue with myself
how is it I never win?

a coming-of-ages story

by earl grenville killeen

This volume is dedicated to the memory of John P. (Hobby) Miller who, through example, provided me with the Light which has illuminated the darkness of his shadow where, through my many shortcomings, I have resided.

My undying gratitude to Leah Raechel Killeen, who lent me more than her expertise as an editor with her many contributions to content and word crafting which, in turn, contributed to my inspiration; her devotion to both me and the task of writing makes this volume possible. Many eternal thanks for her steadfast encouragement and friendship.

contents

1 ~ Uncle

1.

Everything is good. Then evening comes. That's expected. What isn't is the orders that come down. We're told that martial law has been declared and that we, as Security personnel, are to join ranks with the Shore Patrol for shore duty. Two men to one Petty Officer. That is, two billy clubs to one .45 per squad. Duty: to stop all public and/or private transportation that is used by or conveying black persons; search and confiscate any drugs and/or weapons. It's 1966 and civil unrest is rocking the nation's boat. Who thought this one up? If this isn't a bad idea, then there's a good chance that it could become one very quickly.

My unit meets up with another on the strip just outside the base as a train is rolling up from the south. We, the four clubs, are told to board the train and hold it. They, the POs, will be with us shortly. A bad idea getting worse by the minute. We board the train, looking for the conductor. We walk through one car and enter a second, two by two, shoulder to shoulder, with me being the left lead. We spot four black men sitting together at the far end of the car near the exit, with two of them facing us. My attention falls on the one seated on the aisle. The oldest, he seems, if not the ugliest. He looks to weigh a shriveled hundred pounds at best. To my keyed-up senses, he looks like a giant deranged shriveled peanut.

1

As we draw nearer, I'm painfully aware that they are painfully aware of us, as demonstrated by their shifting about and whispering. The hair on the back of my neck is standing on end. I think half of me — who am I kidding? — all of me wants to turn and run. Or at least do the smart thing and wait for armed backup. But I'm junior in the pack and have to abide by those who are more experienced in not thinking for themselves, as they were trained. I take comfort in the fact that Mr. Peanut is staring at the man to my right, who is also black. Maybe that will defuse the contempt that distorts his features. I try my best to keep up my manly face. I'm scared to death. This is the real world where real people do real things and they ain't necessarily good things. You know, the kind you read about. The kind that happen to other people.

What the hell am I doing here? I never imagined myself landing the role of *the other person*. As we come up on the group I see that Mr. Peanut's eyes are aflame with malice. I feel my mouth fill with pain from front to back, right to left. I'm clinching my teeth so tightly that they might explode any moment.

BAM! They do!

No – that was the shotgun that Mr. Peanut whipped up from beneath his trench coat. Out of fright or the shock of the wind that presses my sleeve to my arm, I drop my club. My peripheral vision catches sight of a giant red blossom on the gut of my shipmate to my right. As if propelled by some great unknown force from the rear, I spring forward with all my kinetic energy channeling into my hands, which wrap around the shooter's head and, jerking it, snap his neck like a crisp stalk of celery. The light in his eyes goes out but his face refuses to relinquish the strain of demonic loathing. In a millionth of a second his face, like the suction cup of an octopus's tentacle, attaches itself to mine and melds into my brain. In the latter portion of that same second I turn my head to the left only to have my eyes fill with a muzzle flash. I never hear the shot. For all I know, I'm dead.

- - - - - - - - - - - - - - - - - - -

I stare at the white square tiles of the ceiling. There are dull sounds of activity somewhere around me. As it turns out, I'm alive; if I hadn't turned my head when I did to confront the man to my left, I wouldn't be. Instead of taking the bullet directly, I'm only stunned when it deflects off my forehead. After being treated for that minor wound, a few bruised ribs, contusions, and some pellets my right arm took, I am held for a day and a night in the detention room at our headquarters. Normally, prisoners aren't allowed to talk or smoke, but I'm one of the in-crowd so allowances are made. I had sat that watch myself a couple of times -- the most boring duty you could pull. It is odd to be on the other side of it but just as boring. I am numb, in limbo, and still scared to death. It feels like this isn't my house and I don't know the rules. I am preoccupied with the face of Mr. Peanut. His dead red eyes, his clenched teeth that lock onto my nerves like a steel leg-trap . . . an image that runs through the defense of my denial like water through a sieve and stamps itself into my subconscious where it could safely hide for the life of the mind and, whenever convenient to its muse, pop up like a Halloween mask. Boo!

All a nurse will tell me about the part of the action I had missed is that I was found (by the POs, I guess) unconscious on the tracks. I ask her about Gamble, the only one of the foursome I care about, and I'm told that the blast to his gut bled him out. The other two, white trash identical twins from Georgia – the scuttlebutt had them both alive or both dead. I can easily imagine the world without them.

When I'm released, I'm escorted to a Board of Inquiry. What inquiry? I'm not allowed to give testimony or ask questions. I answer to the facts: yes; no. Any defensive posture I may take is made null and void by reason of my arms being pressed against the glass wall of the test tube they stuffed me in for examination. Now they lay the tube on the bed of a guillotine and read me the riot act, which is composed of veiled threats. Yeah, I get the point. It's all a lie, just our little lie. That's all. I sign some papers I'm not allowed to read and I'm then dismissed with all the courtesy one pays a pawn as it's swept off the chess board. But I have it easy. The entire chain of command that had been involved with that little fiasco are shipped off to Nam faster than you can say *fragbait*. They can't send me because I'm not of age. Yet. They'll have to wait another year. Meanwhile they have something else in mind.

2.

I quit! I did not buy into this shit! Sure, the duty I did sign up for had been tough at times -- but it had been real. Now somehow I'm adrift in a backwash of bullshit. Two days after the inquisition, the shipping orders to Nam came down for our CPO -- and they appeared to cripple him. A big burly black Boatswain's Mate -- his usually stoic face instantly contorted as though he'd just been read a proclamation reinstating slavery. Gone was any trace of his endearing smile that beamed like a rainbow when humor moved him. No trace of humor in this moment. I was near brought to tears, losing yet another parent-I-never-had in this man, Boats, who had seemed to take a shine to me and had taken me under his wing from my first nervous moments on base.

Now I find myself waiting for the next "really big shoe" to drop.

The day after Boats got his orders, an hour before taps, I'm transferred out. My walking papers, though, send me only a walking distance away. Not across the world, just across to the other end of the base. Galley duty. That's a whole lot like Latrine duty except you wear your whites instead of fatigues. Fatigue's an apt word. Up at three forty-five a.m., taps at ten p.m. -- and you don't dare give in to exhaustion and try to hit the rack before taps. Misery loves company and no one is going to let anyone get away with catching an extra half hour of sleep. Such violations will be met with vengeful practical jokes. Maybe not so much practical as sinister. One such lesson-teaching prank is Stacking the Racks. When someone is discovered surreptitiously asleep in a lower bunk, the rack is disassembled and restacked, with the dozing occupant now three bunks high. Then reveille

4

is called. Jumping from sleep to a floor suddenly three bunks down makes for a rude awakening. My favorite trick, though, is when everyone bunking in close proximity to a sleeping beauty goes through the motions of rising and readying for duty, while gently nudging the victim awake. Pitch black is pitch black no matter what the time of night, so there's nothing to clue the sleeper that it's ten p.m. and not a pre-dawn hour. The dummy readies himself and reports to the back door of the Galley, waiting just long enough to fully wake and realize he is alone; not to mention, he's been had. It makes for some really pissed off – and tired -- sailors.

I soon find that inflicting discomfort isn't restricted to the boundaries of the barracks. It is the bread and butter of the Galley's POs -- the Loser Brotherhood, the bottom of the barrel stenciled LIFER. The Galley POs find themselves there because it had at some point become evident that they couldn't hold their own in their chosen striking. We have a house full of ex-Machinist Mates at the kitchen's helm. If they knew how to turn a nut they wouldn't be here. It's ironic, though, that they show a marked ability for twisting another type of nut. Nobody but nobody enjoys Galley duty, but a fair's-fair thirty days a year is mandatory for all hands. So we Scrubs grimace through our month, sharing our misery during the countdown to release. For these guys, though, the lifers, it's forever-after duty. Are they happy with that fact? Well, let's say that they give life to the well-known rule that shit runs downhill – them being the wielders of the shitcans, and us being at the receiving end of the hill.

When I first arrive at the barracks, I get the disconcerting impression that I had been transferred to a sleepwalker's version of the Navy

Me: "Hi, how ya doing? (I find myself looking into blank faces.) How's the duty? (I'm guessing I've boarded the *U.S.S. Wax Museum*.) What time's reveille?"

Other Scrub: "Early."

At least it has a pulse. Most of the other bodies just turn away. I just know there are better places-to-be and things-to-be-done; joining the Marines occurs to me. Damn if this doesn't remind me of when I had to change schools as a kid, six times in eleven years. That inescapable first day when I had to face those menacing silent stares that caused the floor to fall out from beneath my feet. Now, at least, I'm mature enough to not feel that terrible overwhelming sense of embarrassment.   Nonetheless, it's uncomfortable enough.

   Reveille – my first one here -- comes soon after I hit the rack. Like, in the middle of the night. This isn't the movies, there's no bugle in the distance. Just a Coke bottle rattled around the innards of a shit can. That's first call. Second is being tipped out of your rack. This is worse than Boot Camp. Deader. I'm not hearing a word out of anyone's mouth. Showered and dressed, I just fall into the ranks. Not unlike being on a chain gang. I find myself waiting for everyone to break into musical cadence: *Raise 'em high! Umph! Raise 'em high! Umph!* But no -- I join the funeral procession to the Galley's back door. Still not a word. Not a ray of light to breach the silent darkness. The sun still has some hours to sleep yet. Never have I encountered a more somber crowd. I'm still waiting for a noise that hangs social, never mind friendly. After inspection, duty starts and there's little time from this point on to even hope to be social. There are four thousand waiting for breakfast, then four more thousand for lunch, then dinner, then breakfast . . . . I quickly acclimate myself to the whole zombie thing. There's safety in blending.

   Now it's the second day -- or is it just the end of the first? I'm told to report to the Chief. In the normal scheme of things, it isn't anything I'd feel I had to be apprehensive about. But yesterday I noticed the Chief and his circle of cronies in a tight group, all whispering while staring at me. None of them was smiling. I've been waiting for that second shoe . . . up my ass. Let us not disappoint. I report to The Office. Entering, I find the Chief and (no surprise) his right-hand right hand – First Class PO Mr. Wood. The Chief looks like every other Navy Chief. Grey, tired, and grumpy. He's about two weeks from retirement and doesn't have the appearance of being a drinking man. Which explains a few things. Facing his future cold sober will make any old man grumpy. His goon, Mr. Wood, couldn't have been more perfect and well-starched if he had been a 2x4. His fatigues, right

6

down to his squivies, are pressed. Every hair on his head is glued down to its appointed station and was probably cut individually, one and three-sixteenths long. He's handsome enough to be a recruitment-poster poster boy, sporting a pleasant and permanent smirk that dresses his face like a suit of tails. Whatever is about to happen, I'm feeling well inadequate for it.

It hadn't got past me that I'd found the Office door closed when I got to it – I had to knock. That automatically put me in the position of being subservient. Getting permission to come in and all. Yeah, this is going to prove to be some kind of power trip, I'm sure.

"I understand we had some kind of problem at inspection this morning."

"I'm sorry, Sir, I wasn't aware of one." *Dickhead.*

"Mr. Wood here tells me that your uniform was dirty."

Another dickhead. "I'm sorry, Sir, all my whites are stained from Galley duty in Boot."

"I was told that you had dirt on your trousers. What are you, some kind of fucking scrounge?"

"No, Sir, I don't think so."

"Well, you look like a scrounge to me. Come on, we're going to inspect your locker."

Wait -- I was only kidding about the whole dickhead thing!

The corners of Mr. Wood's smirk perk up to a new level of smugness.

The sun is barely up, but I'm sweating bullets anyway. Hell, I haven't been on duty long enough to have anyone know me, never mind dislike me. Be that as it may, I can see a Court Martial coming. The closer we near the barracks, the further my heart sinks. Any lower and I'll be stepping on it. I'm trying to strategize which second-story window I can jump out of, and will the fall be far enough to put me out of my misery. And, if I survive, is there anywhere I could hide for the next sixty years or so where they couldn't find me. What the hell, who's shitting who? How mad can they get about an ol' eight-inch folding knife? At least this ordeal will be over quick because that little unauthorized item is going to be the first thing they see on the locker's top shelf when they open the doors.

Now at the locker, the Chief and Wood take up their positions, locked and ready. Apparently they, too, gave some forethought to the windows -- I quickly notice that my avenue of escape is blocked. Okay, what's done is done. I open the lock. I open the doors. I close my eyes. I click my heels. *There's no place like home, there's no place like home.* After a few moments of not breathing while listening to various objects being rustled about without consequence, I slowly allow my eyes to open and my teeth to unclench. Maybe they're overlooking the knife. Maybe they're looking for something better -- like drugs. Maybe my comeuppance will only amount to a Captain's Mast. Maybe I'm still in the hospital and this is just a bad dream . . . . *Holy – what? There's no knife? You gotta be screwing with me.*

This has to be the biggest freaking miracle since . . . who the fuck knows? Can God possibly love me that much? Because shit like this doesn't just happen by itself. Right. I'm beginning to suspect there was a little help from the wings, but we're not talking angel wings here. It's dawning on me that I had probably been visited by the House Mouses, as they're affectionately known among the crew. They're a two-man team in charge of keeping the barracks clean. It seems they're also into locker-tipping. Tip a locker forward enough and the doors will open just wide enough that anything on the top shelf will slide off and out. Like money, cigs, or even a knife. Gotta love them House Meece. Curtain, please.

But wait – now what? Oh. Yeah, right -- I forgot. I'm a contestant in that old-time favorite: *This is Your Life!* The Chief continues to rifle through my stuff, all the while straining under the effort to not repeat himself as he growls out a collection of insults calculated to abash and belittle me. He comes now to the point where he appears to be frustrated. Then, *voila!* As he plucks the last vestige of my laundry off the locker floor, there it is! *A knife!* Suddenly, my inner glowing smirk, that a moment ago had rivaled Wood's visible one, sinks into my socks to keep my heart company. Yeah,

8

there it is. But not a measly eight-inch folding knife. Not some under-the-radar jack knife. No. It is a motherfucker of a switchblade such as any felon would be proud of. Circumstantially, that would be me, I'm guessing. The Chief instructs me to pick it up and give it to him. I do. As he opens his big mitt to receive it, the long blade suddenly flicks open. Great . . . now I can be charged with attempted assault with a deadly weapon against a superior officer. As Mother often told me: "Always make sure you're wearing dirty underwear -- you never know when you're going to shit your pants and there's no sense in soiling a perfectly clean pair."

And for a moment there, I had thought there was a God.

I know the drill. I know it too damn well. I'm looking at serious Brig time, and Brig time of any length is serious. Especially for a sailor. The Brig is the exclusive house of the Marines and they hate squids. Although they don't mind entertaining them. I got some hint as to the quality of that hospitality when I was in Security and had to escort prisoners from the Brig to court. My mind is racing. I'm starting to panic. I want to be somewhere else. I want to be nonexistent!

I'm feeling just like I did that day when I was nine, which seems about a century and a half ago . . . . *It's a beautiful day, fresh and new. Sandy's yanking on his leash, can't wait to get to the wooded lot where he knows he can run free off lead. The woods are my fantasy world, my home away from everything my home isn't. A reprieve from the daily brutality. We reach the trees and Sandy is quick to disappear. Suddenly there's vicious growling coming from a depression in the land that was formerly a crawl space to a now-absent house. Running anxiously to the knoll at the rim of it, I see a cat and several kittens hurriedly exit over the opposite rise. In the pit I find Sandy, otherwise the sweetest dog, tearing apart a squealing kitten. I quickly take it from the dog's mouth. The mangled creature is beyond hope and repair. With my heart in my throat and what's left of my mind in the blackout of denial, I lay the thing down on a rock and, with another stone, crush it to death. As I strike it, I turn my eyes away so as to not witness that which I'm doing, only to have them fall on the line-up of mother and offspring who are now staring at me accusingly from across the pit. Suddenly there's a black*

9

hole where my stomach used to be. I start to be sucked into it. I feel my body shrinking inward as it's being pulled into myself with a power greater than gravity. In another instant there won't be anything left of me but a small black hole suspended in midair where moments ago I had been standing.

Where the hell is a black hole when you need one? It's the end of the world. Yeah, the end of the world, for me. The Chief takes the knife and gets in his Jeep and merrily drives off to Security. Um, leaves me in the dust with Mr. Smiley-Face, who escorts me back to duty. That's odd. I guess Security will come to the Galley to pick me up. I guess the Chief is too close to retirement to chance handling a murderer like me. An eternal hour passes. I swear to God, I'm beginning to believe I'm not even here. The vacuum of time sucks me back again. Again, not so much an escape as a sort of reverse déjà vu . . . .

My friend Doug and I are arguing, as usual. Always about army stuff. His father had been a Private and Doug believes that rank to be something higher than a General. Naturally, just like his father, he knows everything there is to know of war and combat.

But I'm not backing down on this one. I say, "Here! Give me that grenade. I'll show you the way it's supposed to be thrown."

Doug hands me the dummy-explosive reluctantly. I throw it in the direction of our front lawn from the street. I throw it too goddamn well. My guts jump out and fall on the ground as I watch the grenade sailing over the fence, over the yard, exploding the picture window of our brand new house. Before I can say "oh shit!" my mother rushes out of the house. Grabbing me by the hand, she whooshes me into the house, past Go, and straight to Jail – that is, my bedroom closet. Not as a matter of punishment, but rather protection. The blackness in the closet is blacker than anything I've ever known. It exaggerates the sound of my bones rattling. An hour passes. The longest hour I've ever had to try to breathe through. The void between life and death. The waiting place; anticipating the battleground-to-be where the two goliaths would meet head-on for the sake of me or the death of me. *My stepfather the potential executioner. God knows I've been beaten for far less. Like, close to nothing.*

The hour passes again; the difference this time is there's no Mother Protector, just the pathetic motherfucker, myself, my own worst enemy. At last, I see the Chief coming and going straight in to conference with his stoolies. I'm waiting. I say again -- I'm waiting. The clock face no longer has twelve numerals on it, more like six hundred. The end of the day just plain ain't gonna come.

Well, someone, I guess, pulled the wool, because, just like yesterday, at the appointed hour, someone pulls down the shade of darkness over the face of the day. With it, the sound of taps.

3.

I think everyone in the world slept that night. Everyone but me. It's amazing how many things you can think about when there's absolutely nothing to think about. There's nothing more painful than the anticipation of pain. I'm guessing that the professional pain-givers of the world are keenly aware of that fact.

An arrest never comes. No formal charges ever brought against me. Nothing ever said. Gee, does this mean the Chief really likes me? I'm keeping my mouth shut. What am I going to do? *Excuse me, Sir, are you ready to screw me yet?* No, better to suffer in silence. In wait for falling shoes.

Well, it doesn't take long. These suckers are real professional mindfuckers. They have the program down pat. It's called: bad cop/worse cop. I'm ordered to do one thing by one PO, only to find the action wrong in the mind of another. Of course, that always gives rise to punishment duty, usually lasting until taps. My personal favorite -- and I'm sure one of theirs -- is scrubbing the perimeter sidewalks with a toothbrush. On

11

extra special days, I also catch mid-watch, 12 to 4 a.m. There's a two-hour gap between taps and duty, permitting me my one hour of guaranteed sleep in a twenty-four-hour period. Thus, it's all kept legal. Which is great -- it's one hour more than I would have been afforded in the Brig. But I don't bother. It all seems more trouble than it could be worth, with undressing, dressing -- and who am I going to get to wake me? I'm stacking up a whole lot of sleepless nights.

I think the POs are happiest when I stupidly apply for liberty. You know, the stuff this country's made of. Any way you want to look at it, I'm under house arrest, but no one is saying so. I just never get liberty, because my right shoe is shinier than my left. The square knot in my kerchief isn't square enough, I have dandruff, etc. The POs can hardly hold back their laughter each and every time they refuse me. Eventually, I just stop trying. That must really hurt. Them. But if I had thought about it a little longer and harder, I would have gone along and let them have their fun. I learned as a kid, when someone kicks you, act hurt, otherwise they're going to kick you again and harder.

No, don't listen to me. I'm ready to fight the good fight. *Yeah, good luck with that.*

I don't know *which* way the shit is flowing now. Every which wrong way, it feels like. Things are getting a little out of hand – I mean, impossible to deal with. I get the concept of crime and punishment. But – the locker, the knife -- why the plant? Why the games? Why is this whole stupid travesty being conducted outside the code of military justice -- where's the trial? What the fuck's up with this puppet-theater bullshit? The sardonic jerking of my chains has me ready to spill my guts to JAG in hope of getting out of this purgatory – a misguided hope, no doubt, that would more likely send me straight to hell than reprieve. But what I find most intolerable is the *insult* of the thing! The slap in the face. The blatant betrayal of my trust. The progressive disintegration of my faith in a higher order of things presumably more valued than *my* skinny little ass. I joined this Mickey Mouse outfit to serve my country honorably. I had high expectations of coming up to the measure. However, I was thinking more in the dimensions of a yard stick as opposed to a pocket-sized ruler, measured in feet rather than inches. I expected to be schooled by men, not children in adult bodies.

Now, I'm as young and resilient as the next guy; maybe, with my background, more so than most. But after months of this crap, I find the limits of the elasticity of the rubber band that keeps my sanity contained within the bounds of my brain being severely tested. Someone for some reason has pulled the rug of reality out from underneath my feet. I can no longer rely on my perspective on things. I'm no longer trustful of *anyone*.

I can remember when I was hook-line-and-sinker trustful, way back when. I also remember how that callow trust was broken. *Snap.* It was a time when I trusted adults because it was their world. I was small and lived with the hand-me-down values and rules that were deemed by my elders important or necessary. Adults understood what was right and had the power to act on that knowledge. Could be depended on to evaluate the options and reassuringly choose the good. Could fix things. The breaking of virgin trust is more traumatic than finding out that Santa Claus doesn't exist . . . .

It's a normal day -- not that there are any days on my calendar that would be considered normal by the standards of a normal child. Sandy and I are walking along the edge of the river. No more running off lead, no more getting out of my sight. Suddenly, the dog begins madly digging into the side of the river bank. I think nothing of it, digging is one of his favorite things to do. Laughingly, I egg him on with the innocent tease: "Rats! Rats, Sandy! Rats!" Oh-oh -- suddenly the earth opens and out spills a mother rat and her six offspring, rolling down the bank to my feet. The mother is horribly disemboweled and, equally frightfully, alive. Please, God, this can't be happening again! Although it seems impossible to summon the capability to deal with this wrenching horror, I somehow find the means to tip the scales toward mercy. Raising my foot so that the top of my shoe acts as a blinder, I stomp the suffering remnant to death. The repulsion I feel slithers up from the bottom of my foot and causes my own bowels to want to evacuate, against my will. Ignoring myself as best as I can, I find a discarded paper cup and hurriedly gather up the new orphans, still in a more panicked state than they probably are. I'm frantic in my futile effort to exonerate myself from this crime. Now I'm faced with the only recourse I can think of -- a pet store, two miles away.

I'm keeping the dog safe from speeding traffic on the narrow road. Keeping him on the other side of the wood-pole-and-cable guardrail. There's not room for both of us there, as the land abruptly falls from the road down to the river. I'm hot, tired, guilt-ridden. All I want to do is sit down and cry, but I know I have to rise up to accomplish that which needs to be done. Doing nothing just isn't a choice. Each car that speeds by us reminds me that no one else cares; I'm alone. My burden is my burden exclusively. All other people are in a rush to be somewhere else doing something else. Each post in the guardrail becomes a milestone. Exhaustion, guilt, and fear tug at my feet with every single effort to move a foot forward.

At last I'm here. Perhaps now I can come to some sense of relief – or, at least, release. I tell my mournful story to the kind lady behind the counter as she stares at me with a quizzical look on her face.

"Can you take care of them?" I ask in the quivering tones of a beggar, holding out my cup with the mixed hope and reluctance of a mother giving up her children for adoption.

She takes the cup from my hand and disappears momentarily behind a curtain, only to return empty-handed. She cuts off my last anxious query about the well-being of my little parcel --

"Don't worry," she tells me. "I took care of them alright."

"?"

"I flushed them down the toilet."

I'm instantly reduced to some shrunken alien form. The blood drains out of my veins. I become so brittle that if I were capable of taking in a breath, I would crack and shatter into a million pieces. She flushed something else down the toilet that moment. I would never trust anyone again; at least not from the station of being a child.

4.

Four months now in the Galley, and feeling like a potato in a pressure cooker. Trying to hold myself together inside my skin, but things are starting to take their toll. Even a pimple can grow only so big before coming to a head and bursting. So it seems only natural that, having little more sense of identity or rights than a pimple, I feel my own head is ready to pop.

This evening I dare to risk a head-butting with fate and hit my rack early. I really have little choice. I've been suffering an excruciating headache for hours and finally have to surrender to it. My head is throbbing, ready to burst. *And it does!* Suddenly I'm jolted awake. The lights are still on. All I see is red everywhere. I recognize it to be blood -- something I'm still wishing never to see again – and now there is much more than I've ever seen before, I mean it's everywhere. I think someone has split the front of my skull open. I'm almost overwhelmed with the smell of copper. I look up to the fellow in the upper bunk of the rack next to mine, who's reading a book. I have just enough time to murmur "help". He looks down at me and his face goes white. I hear my own personal taps. Everything goes black . . . .

I stir to consciousness. There's the reflection of a red light in the space around me; I conclude that I'm in an ambulance. There's the blackness again . . . . Waking, I find myself in the hospital, again. My head is killing me, again. They give me a shot, hook me up to an IV, then stuff about two yards of cotton gauze up my nose and secure that by wrapping up my face with another four yards of gauze. Back in the ambulance, again. Back to the barracks, again. There's over a foot of snow on the ground and I'm dressed in nothing more than my skivvies and my newly-acquired mummy face. The Medic turns to me and in a dour tone inquires: "I suppose you don't have any shoes." I think his tone is more in response to his own situation than mine. He, a very large black man, probably doesn't

15

care much for the idea of having to care for a white boy, the times being what they are. *Excuse the hell out of me, I really didn't set this whole thing up. Not to mention, it's not my fault I'm not black.* He wraps me up in a blanket and carries me to the barracks. Actually -- real or not, whether a product of his head or mine -- in those moments of being carried I perceive some small note of caring. God! How foreign is this?

Back in the barracks, I'm confronted by an empty rack. I mean, not even a mattress. I guess they thought I wasn't coming back. I'm informed that all my bedding was so blood-soaked that it had to be discarded. I empty my sea bag to cover the springs with my uniforms and use my pea coat for a blanket. I've had better nights' sleep.

This morning I report for duty as normal, although I certainly feel less than normal, with my head still feeling split open, and at least as dizzy as I once did as a kid when I was harboring a one-hundred-and-four-degree temperature. After inspection, I'm approached by one of the POs, who is relieving me of my normal duty on the chow line due to my mummification. I'm told to report to the Spud Locker until further notice. The Spud Locker – sort of a little suburb of the Galley. This is heaven! My guardian angels have at long last rediscovered me. I'm back in the Real Navy. The PO here is actually a Cook and has nothing to do with the Front Office. Or its pirate crew. Better yet, I'm now out of sight of their eagle eyes and, even better than that, out of range of their talons. Maybe, just maybe, they've become bored with the game. For me, it's a new lease on life. I'm not in the Locker but two days when my new PO recognizes my leadership qualities and makes me honcho. But never count your chicks before you have the eggs. Come to think of it, you shouldn't count your eggs before you have the hen.

So today, while quickly and violently having my way with some vegetables with the help of a very large and sharp knife, I cut one of my fingers to the bone. Actually, right *into* the bone. It takes some effort to extract the blade. I report to the Office to request that I might get permission to report to Sickbay.

"Suck it up, you're not going anywhere!"

That's the problem with galleys -- there are no hens to be had, they're all in the oven. For three days, I live with my finger wrapped up in a piece of sheet, leaving a trail of blood wherever I go. The blood flow, along with the throbbing, never stops. On the fourth day, I request Sickbay once again. I'm once again refused. Brother, this time they're pushing it a little too far. Legally, they can't refuse me medical treatment, which I remind them of, with the kicker that I'm going to go to the Chaplain. That they can't prevent even if they declare me AWOL. It won't fly. That puts them in a position of being powerless -- something I'm sure isn't sitting well with them, something they're not going to soon forget.

"Alright, go! You fucking hypochondriac."

They just have to get the last knife in.

You gotta know they're not happy, and you don't win arguments with people in power who aren't happy. While I'm at Sickbay, they find out that I had been made honcho, and, brother, does the shit hit the fan. When I get back, I find that most of the flying shit is coming my way. And I find my PO also taking some crap flak; he's in charge of the Spud Locker but not the Galley, and, besides, he is lower in rank than the other Lifers. There isn't a damn thing he can do about my abrupt transfer out of his domain other than to be mad as hell. Once again, I'm shipped out. I'm re-assigned to the lowest rung: GSK. That's where you spend most of the duty day with your head in doody, washing out shit cans. He who has the last laugh, and all that. It sure as shit ain't me.

There's two crews in GSK, the unlucky and the luckless. The indoor losers and the outdoor losers – one contingent, at least, dry and warm, and the other wet and cold. Befitting my station, I'm assigned to the wet and cold. There's nothing to compare with working in steam all day in subzero temperatures, given that steam is generally wet. Of course, there's also the smell to contend with, but that's only half as bad now as it'll be in the summer. It's the kind of stench that, once you get it in your nostrils, you never get rid of it, no matter how many times you shower. Our PO, though, appears to be a regular Joe, despite the fact that he is another born-again lifer, another erstwhile Machinist's Mate. To his credit, he seems to avoid the company of the Office jokers and their nonsense ways -- but that's not to say he isn't in some way under their thumb . . . which, I think, explains what happens next.

Naturally (as it seemed to me), after just a short time of doing my excellence, I'm made honcho. Given indoor drinking-coffee duty. God knows, this ain't right. And *I* soon know I'm right about that. I'm walking past our wing; I happen to glance in. Our PO is taking a paint brush, dipping it in a can of varnish, then laying it across the top of the can and walking away. The moment passes into some hours, and we are then called to assembly. Our PO points at the varnish can and, turning to me, he spouts: "What the hell is that doing there!" What am I to say? *I don't know, asshole, you put it there -- you tell me.* No, I know better.

"I don't know, Sir."

"Well, sailor, you're shit-canned!"

I knew that. Now I find myself out in the cold again and duty is only going to get worse.

 One of the more fun duties is clearing the ice off the street that fronts the steam shed where we wash the cans. There's never a shortage of four-inch ice sheets to break up because of the fact that the boys in the Office don't allow the trucks to plow there. With the daily ritual of steam cleaning, the frozen build-up becomes eternal. But even more backbreaking than chopping ice with a hoe is the labor involved in the daily dumping of our leftover shit into a dump truck that is owned by a pig farm. Our rotting food scraps are the pigs' dinner-to-be; the pigs, our dinner-to-be. And so on, in a kind of cyclical food chain. It's enough to make you think twice before eating pork. As they say: "You are what they eat."

The truck shows up on schedule -- I've been looking forward to it all day. I'm carrying a shit can of salad dressings weighing well over two hundred pounds. The fifty-gallon can is boiling, probably the combined result of a chemical reaction and the immense pressure the rancid slop is under by virtue of its sheer weight and volume. It's like a can of hot lava. As I'm approaching the lift gate of the truck, I naturally slip on the ice. I'm still holding on to the can; hence, when it hits bottom, the applied force of my arms translates into pulling. Yeah, pulling *me* head-first right into the bucket of shit, right up to my waist. I come out of the immersion totally blind and on fire. I helplessly grope the air with my extended arms, searching for where the Galley might be. Out of nowhere, someone grabs me and rushes me indoors and straight to the head. This someone forcefully plunges my head into the toilet and flushes it. I remain there for some minutes, continuing to flush -- you can't get enough of a good thing. I don't know who the merciful soul was, but it was the kindest act extended to me during my tenure at that shithouse.

- - - - - - - - - - - - - - - - - -

It's now coming up to the six-month mark in the Galley. That's two months beyond what's demanded of me for the entire duration of my four-year enlistment. It doesn't look like I'm going anywhere soon; somebody likes me right where I am. I can only suppose that my drop sheet, which I fill in every month requesting duty in Nam, isn't dropping any further than the Front Office's round file. If anyone bothered to ask me why I was so keen to go to Nam, I would have told them. Simply. I'm getting ready to kill someone.

I had become a victim of my conditioning -- actually a round-robin version of it. When scientists want to study the effects of who-do on the human body, they use the flesh of pigs. Appropriate. When they want to study the effects of you-do on the *mind* of man, they use mice. Even more appropriate. In studying the effects of conditioning, they took a mouse and put it in a bell jar. They then rang a loud bell unceasingly for twenty-four hours. After letting it rest in silence for a day, they put the mouse back into

19

the jar and turned the bell on once again. Within two seconds, the mouse keeled over dead. It committed mental suicide rather than living through the torment again. You might ask if the experiment is viable -- are men and mice comparable? (Don't ask a woman.) After all, many men survive wedding bells several times over. Perhaps some bells are more lethal than others. But the theoretic principle is solid. All nervous systems are wired the same. It was noted, for example, that captured North Viet Nam soldiers would soil themselves when an American bomber would fly overhead.

Whether it was by design or not, the powers that be that are in charge of my fate put me smack into that bell jar. Everything that I had managed to survive in my past is now being shoved right back at me in spades. That sense of unescapable enslavement is being revisited on me. I am shackled and brainfucked by the best in the business. I'm riding the razor's edge . . . .

I am caught in a great gulf. My stepfather taught me dignity and how to stand up for your rights. How to fight back by means of who you are and what you stand for. This was not a pedantic education insofar as my stepfather had little to impart to me verbally. He let his hands that were half the size of the continent of Africa do the talking. No, I learned by his example, and he was unshakable in all things. He never lost an inch of ground in a dispute.

While in fourth grade, I'm grievously assaulted by a leather-jacketed punk, a classmate who's fresh out of a one-year turn in reform school for having killed a kid. He had split the boy's head with a pipe. Now he's working on splitting mine by using a cement gutter as a backstop for the ball of my head. My stepfather comes home and learns of this -- but first things first. Dinner. Then he packs us up in the car and we go to the assailant's house. Leaving me in the car, he gets himself admitted inside. The living room is brightly lit, enough to cast very visible shadows on the pulled shades. Suddenly those shadows are traveling through space, from one end of the room to the other. Loud words can be heard that morph into screams that abruptly end with a resounding thud as those shadows are introduced to the opposite wall. My stepfather soon exits the house with a shit-eating grin on his face; and that's that.

Okay, I've learned my lessons well. The master taught me. Now my

20

new masters are teaching me that when you're nothing but a nigger, you're not entitled to fight back. Fuck you if you so much as try. My pain, my anger, my frustration, the whole total sum of my despair has no outward means to vent. It can only implode. I am about to become the enemy within.

I wake up seething. Why should this morning be any different from any other morning. *Hey! When did I start referring to the middle of the night as morning?* Only cows think that four a.m. is morning. That's it -- I'm identifying with cattle. I've lost the sense of who I am because I've forgotten who I was. But I know one thing for sure, the I of me doesn't feel very good. This thing I'm living in, trying to survive in, just isn't right. Not real. But in any case, it's sure as hell inescapable. *Okay, shut up now. You know, there's no time for this shit. Stop talking to yourself and get ready.*

Standing inspection. The Petty Officer -- and I mean petty -- pauses in front of me.

"What's that on your hand?"

"What?"

"That wound on your hand."

"Oh, that. When I woke up this morning I found chicken tracks on my sheet. Then I realized they were blood. I followed them to the bottom of my bedding and found a wart that I must have scratched off in the night."

"Holy shit! Why didn't you get up and report to Sickbay?"

"For one thing, I didn't wake up when it happened. For another, I wasn't bleeding to death like I was the last time, when you wouldn't let me go to Sickbay."

"Well, now you're on report, wiseass!"

You forgot to notice my socks are inside out, you . . . . Same ol' day, same

21

ol' shit.

Evening finally comes. No verdict on my punishment duty yet. After waiting on line, I finally get to use the phone. Oops, someone forgot to take my barracks privileges away. I call Jo Ann, my love-want, both past and present and one and the same. With the call concluded, I'm not feeling much better for it, maybe worse. I step out of the booth and try to light a cigarette. I'm shaking so violently that the match goes out. Then someone turns on the faucet and I'm blinded by my own tears. I turn about and out the door I go, down the stairs and walking across the snow-laden lawn. I'm going home. I'm going to reunite with my loved one.

No . . . I'm being arrested. Back to the Security Building. Again. I'm read the riot act. Again. Now not only am I accused of being AWOL, but naked to boot. Come on, are you freakin' kidding me? *Naked?* I'm explaining that the only thing I did wrong as far as being undressed was to go outside without my cover on. Okay? The Security Officer isn't buying it. I see three silhouettes behind a one-way mirror in back of the officer. *You think you might want to bring the President in on this one?* All this crap is way too much like the last time I was here. *Gee, you think they'll hang me this time?* You hope. La-di-da, la-di-da, it's off to suicide watch we go. This time around I'm an outsider, so no talking or smoking allowed. Well, *there's* a good reason to commit suicide right there. Morning comes and I'm released -- I was a good boy. No ramifications. Again. What the hell is up with this shit anyway?

This time around I'm not bothering with going through the chain of command. What are they going to do -- punish me? *Hey, boss man, I'll catch you later, I'm off to see the Chaplain. Bye. I'm outta here.*

- -

"Excuse me, Sir, but I have to ask you this: Are you an officer first or a man of God first?"

The Looie leans back in his chair and displays a smug smile of confidence. "A man of God, of course."

"Good, I'm glad to hear that, because I'm here to talk to you about my spirit -- or the loss of it, due to the treatment I'm undergoing."

In answer, his smile retreats and, with not another word, he gets up from his desk and walks over to the door, opens it and stands there. I'm not so

stupid as to not realize, my work is done here. It may be a little thing but, while in his office, I peg him to be of the Catholic faith. If I remember properly from my childhood, the Catholic church has a crucifixion as its center-stage. My Protestant church was a little more benign when it came to its decorations, with the centerpiece of their altar being a large stained-glass window depicting Jesus welcoming lambs and children with open arms. I guess I put my faith in the wrong faith by coming here. I'll try again tomorrow.

I do, this time with the Protestant officer. He's far more accommodating and gives me privileged access to the next step in seeking mental health assistance. That turns out to be a screening interview with a Machinist's Mate PO. They must have had a run on them this year.

"What's your problem?" he barks more than asks.

"Well, the other night I was arrested for taking a walk in the snow . . . ."

"So you want out of the Navy!" Now he's lost the bark and is showing his teeth. I pause in shock, trying to collect myself and square my shoulders.

"No, I'm trying to find out what's wrong with me so I don't get arrested again."

He calms a little and types a little, while keeping an eye on me; I must somehow look suspicious. He tells me to take my paperwork to Building Three, hospital side, and that's that. For now.

5.

This is my sunshine. My whiff of fresh air. Or maybe just a tease or, more perturbingly, a big "but" waiting to be spoken. Such little things (like dropping shoes) are known to be game changers. I'm on my guard as I enter the room. It's my introduction to Dr. Clark, a Lt JG.

He is indeed a breath of fresh air. He looks to be a nice enough guy. At least he looks nothing like a Machinist's Mate. Actually, stereotype-wise, he looks just like a psychiatrist. Thin, thinning hair, thinning eyesight. I like him immediately. I almost feel bad that he's in the Navy; he looks as though he deserves better. At last I have a time and place to vent, although I fear it may be too little, too late. It certainly isn't going to change my status in the Galley, other than to provide my keepers with yet another dig for their bag of razzes. I get to suffer that bonus once per week as I leave the Galley for my one-hour teaspoon of sanity or, at least, logic. So here I am.

----- Mr. McByrne, it's important for me to understand where you were coming from in joining the Navy. What were your intentions and desires? What was your general background?

----- Are you kidding me? Where the hell do I begin? When the world first wronged me or when I became wrong with the world?

----- Start wherever you're comfortable starting. At what point did the world around you start changing?

----- Well, I guess I'd have to start with my childhood, at age four -- but my childhood was textbook as far as abused kids are concerned. I wouldn't want to bore you. I guess my journey down the slippery slope started the first time I decided, consciously or not, to fuck up my own life . . . . I was living with my godparents in Pleasantville, NY. If they hadn't taken me in, I probably would have been homeless, so I guess you could say they rescued me. This was a very different world from what I had been used to at the hands of a very sick stepfather who had no desire to be a father and a mother who had no clue about how to be a mother. My so-called mother -- she was far more preoccupied with her own security than she was with mine. Now in my third relocation – in my godparents' care -- I found myself "living the life of Riley". Although I never did get over feeling guilty for not deserving it, somehow. That world, which was one of having-it-all, just never felt real to me. Or at least not like anything I was going to be able to hang on to. It didn't belong to me. I knew I had no real claim to it all.

----- That's interesting. Why did you feel that way?

----- Well, I wasn't blood and I certainly didn't pay for any of it. I was there only by the whim of my godparents' generosity. That could end any moment. In fact, it did, after the close of my first academic year there. They only took me back in at the last moment before the start of my second year of high school.

----- I see. Please, go on.

----- I guess it was a matter of being haunted. I just wasn't feeling in control of my own destiny, and I so desperately needed to. To make things worse, I was spending far too much time thinking that my guardians' son was some kind of demi-god. He smoked, drank, wore Levis, drove his own car, and was sexually active. What greater God could there be except the one that changed the water in your bowl, if you happened to be a goldfish. I was only fifteen and he was eighteen. And oh how I needed to be eighteen right then and there.

25

----- I can sympathize. It's a tough age to be.

----- I have to say, my godparents were very liberal-minded. They knew I was kicking back a few beers on weekend nights but said nothing. Even when I started smoking, although they weren't happy about it, they didn't give me a lot of static over it. For me, the ax fell when I returned back to their care after a summer break to find they had switched high schools on me. That really pulled the rug out from under my feet. That wire noose I had worn for ten years prior was back around my neck and tightening. I felt desperate to escape it, again. It was a mini-bell jar for me and so I committed suicide -- after the first quarter of my sophomore year and turning sixteen, I dropped out of school. That equated to me being dropped out of the family. That was the fourth time I found myself homeless in three years. I'm guessing that my godparents thought that I would magically disappear or, even more miraculously, that my mother would take me back. Are you kidding me? She didn't get rid of me three years prior for no reason. Besides, she had been paying my guardians a dollar a day for my keep. Now she'd be thirty dollars a month richer. Pennies from heaven.

----- What were you feeling? What were you supposing for yourself?

----- I was feeling free! I didn't see the future. I couldn't conceive of it. I just felt euphoric, as though I had discovered the greatest drug known to man. I remember walking down Route 22 in Armonk on the first night of my flight. I didn't know where I was going, because I had nowhere to go. All I was aware of was that I had a Tiparillo in my mouth and a good pair of boots on my feet. I couldn't conceive of the fact that tomorrow I might be in need of money to buy another smoke. I was just so totally lost in the moment of "coming of age." Or so I thought.

----- I'm sorry.

----- There was nothing wrong with that scene. It was what it was. I wasn't expecting it to be any different, and at least for that hour or so, I was happy, and that's saying a lot. For one thing, I'd shed the skin of always feeling younger than everyone else in the world. Always someone else having all the things in the world. All my life I wanted and wondered when and if it would ever be my turn. Now, I was my own world and it consisted of me and my boots. Beyond that there was little to worry about. I was just young enough to be stupid, I guess, and with that you can afford to be pretty fearless. I always managed to find someone to loan me a couch for the night. There were always odd jobs here and there and, when not, there was a local priest who was always good for a touch. I did alright.

----- You were what – sixteen? -- at the time, and you didn't join until you were seventeen, is that right? Did you just wander the streets for a year?

----- No, but that year certainly turned out to be an odyssey. As hard as it was -- and it was probably the hardest year I ever had to live through -- I have to say, apart from it being interesting, it probably was the best year of my life. I was in charge. If I didn't like something, I could walk away.

----- Is that what you want to do now?

----- Hell, no! I want to fight! Ha! But who? How? Besides, I couldn't walk away from this circus even if I wanted to. I know reality when I run headlong into it. I've got enough experience behind me. Way behind. Like -- when I was five, we moved into an old Victorian apartment building. I had to play out on the screened-in porch. Among the few toys I had were a couple of pot-metal soldiers, one a flag bearer. That particular one refused to stand up. I understand now that the porch was on a slant for rain runoff. But, at the time, I lost all patience with the little guy. I certainly didn't care for the smirk painted on his little face, little wise-ass that he was. I felt as though he thought it was funny that I wasn't getting my way with him. I decided to punish him, but good. I propped him up by means of using a small wooden block. Once I'd gotten him erect, I slammed my foot down on him just as hard as I could. I was wearing only soft-soled slippers. Did I ever get the surprise of my life.

--- Ouch!

--- Yeah, tell me about it. I couldn't wait to get out of the emergency room -- I knew exactly what I was going to do to that little so-and-so! When I got home, I got my stepfather's hacksaw out and cut one of his legs off. I was quite gleeful about it. "That will show you!" But, guess what -- the little son of a bitch never fell over again. I had unknowingly changed his center of gravity. The smug little bastard outsmarted me. I can't tell you how painful it was to be outwitted by that little hunk of tin.

--- And how does that relate to where you are today?

--- Well, I'm standing in a room barefoot and the exit is on the other side of the room. The floor is covered wall to wall with metal flag bearers that the big Admiral in the sky or in Washington or on this base has put there. Now tell me what my next move is.

--- I think we'll have to stop now and resume next week.

--- Great. If you're going to leave me stuck in the corner, maybe you could have some food for thought airlifted and dropped to me.

- - - - - - - - - - - - -

Walking back to the Galley, I notice something. I'm surprised at how surprised I am. Surprised that it's daylight out. The sky is blue. The sun feels good. The air is fresh and there are actually real people about, involved in real things. Some actually being nice. I'd forgotten. I forgot almost instantly when I transferred into the Galley; it was like putting a bag over my head. Back then it was still hotter than hell, and hell to work in that heat. I can remember going out for a smoke and crouching down in the corner of the building for support. Within minutes I would literally disappear under a layer of flies. I would look across the way at my shipmates and, although they were dressed in white, all the white I could see was their cigarettes and the whites of their eyes. I swear to God, we looked like a bunch of tar babies. I guess, if anyone else from the outside had seen us, they might have found the tableau comical. I think, for us who were under the layers of insects, we probably looked as pathetic as we truly were. So beaten down that we couldn't be bothered even trying to shoo them off us; would have needed a fire hose anyway. In a word, we were resigned. I guess you don't understand how rank shit is until you step out

28

of it and bathe. I wonder when my chance to bathe will ever come. Right now the stench seems eternal. I'm not sure that having been given a peek at the Real Navy once again is serving as any kind of favor. How the hell did I get into this quagmire? What did I do wrong and what the hell is this place anyway? It's like the B-29 dubbed *The Leper Colony* in the movie *Twelve O'Clock High*. A place to dump all the rejects. Is that what someone has declared me? *Hello -- is anyone there?*

Reveille. I don't even wake up anymore. I don't think I sleep anymore. I think I just turn off, then turn on again, as needed. There's a guy four racks down, every morning he sits up, throwing his legs out of the bunk and, putting his feet on the cold floor, he sits there and laughs. I think he knows something. I think he gets it. I think I want to kill him. Nah, I'm in enough trouble as it is. I wonder what the screw of the day is going to be. I get through the day and the next and the next and the next. "Dear Mom, have nothing to say. P.S. Thanks for giving birth to me." Oh, yeah! That was another screw. My mother writing my superiors, or so they claim, to complain that I don't write her. What the hell? I write her. The last time I wrote her was to get permission to join this outfit. We always lived quite happily with distance between us. Or at least I did. She must want something, probably to be put on my GI insurance. Now the assholes make me sit in the Office once a week and write her. They're probably enjoying the flattery I give them to lighten their mood while they're doing their censorship.

Thank God this week has passed. Now I just have to get through the parting shots – the Galley POs cracking wise when I show them my permission chit, my nut pass to get my head shrunk ha-ha. Just walking anywhere besides the hundred feet between the barracks and the Galley is like a stroll through heaven. It's a big base and it has to be at least a mile between points A and B. I used to run a four-minute mile, now I'm all the happier taking a half hour. All total, between the walk and the session, I get an escape time of two hours. Boy! The bastards must hate me for that little trick. It's okay, they'll find a way to vent. They always do. I just wish I wasn't the air duct.

----- Hi, Lt Clark, how are you?

----- I'm good. How are you doing today, Mr. McByrne?

----- Well, I'm glad to be here, although to tell you the truth, I'd be afraid to tell you why. I'm sorry to say, but after a bad experience I had with one of the Chaplains, it's hard to trust anyone.

----- Well, I want you to believe that anything you say to me will never be turned against you.

----- Is your night job being Santa Claus?

----- It's okay. I think I know where you're coming from. Why don't you have a seat and get comfortable and we'll get started.

----- God, I wish that didn't sound like I was about to get a rectal exam.

(He smiles.)

----- So last week you were telling me of your new-found exploits, free of parental guidance; do you want to continue from there? Or do you have something else on your mind today?

----- The only mind I have is the one I left behind in civilian life. In fact, things have been so different for me, just the fact that you're being civil to me is giving me the willies. I'm just not used to it anymore.

----- Has it been that hard on you?

I bow my head. I'm almost on the verge of tears. The Lt seems to catch on. He gets out of his chair and climbs up on his desk, putting his back to the wall. It's as though he's trying to demonstrate the fact that he's human. Maybe the secret hippie in him. I get it; he's indeed kind. Oops -- in the process, he drops his requisite therapist's pipe on the floor. Now he's done it -- blown his "cool" stature. I try to relieve his embarrassment by picking up the pipe for him and breaking the tension with, "It's alright, it didn't break." He thanks me and seems to return to his comfort level.

----- Well, I guess . . . going back to where I was . . . you first have to understand a couple of things about my godparents. Their home sat up on the hill. I guess that was supposed to mean something of a social order; all it ever meant to me was that the bird shit had a shorter distance to fall. Anyway, it was a big deal to my godfather, who was a doctor. Reputation was everything to him. It's funny how preoccupied he would be with my behavior when his own son had a terrible reputation. For one thing, when he graduated from high school, to celebrate, he and some of his buddies dropped a car engine through the gym window and destroyed the floor. That was a lawsuit that went on for years. That wasn't the whole iceberg, though. But there's no reason you need to know everything about that family's closet. Anyway, when I went to live with them, I had to be passed off as a nephew in order to have the right to attend school in their town. Now, being in the street, adrift, I was reflecting badly on the family, "*my* family". For my godfather, this was intolerable, you know what I mean?

----- If I can't see it coming, I can smell it.

----- Yeah, well, he wasn't exactly a cornerstone himself. But I'm not going to step all over his toes at this point in time. I wandered about in a tri-town area, but hung out in Pleasantville more often than not; it was the most familiar and I knew the most people there. The problem arose from standing too long in one place. One Saturday, I went into a diner that I used to go to back in my school days. My regular Saturday let's-go-drink-some-coffee-as-something-to-do days. I guess I was trying to recapture the moment. I sat down and waited for my coffee. I thought it was odd that, instead of seeing that I got it, the diner's owner went into the phone booth. A minute later, he came out the same way he was dressed when he went in, so I knew he wasn't Superman. Maybe my godfather was, because he must have flown down from off his hill. He was there before I was halfway

31

done with my coffee. "Come on, kiddo, let's go." And those were the last words he spoke in the next forty-five minutes. Silence has a way of belittling you more than words sometimes.

----- Did you pay for the coffee?

----- Nah! Are you kidding?

----- Where did he take you?

----- Rowayton, CT.

----- What's there?

----- The remnants of my mother.

----- Did he think she was going to take you back in?

----- Hell, he didn't care one way or the other. All he knew is that he was rid of me and probably figured that I got the message that he didn't want me in his town. Of course, my mother already felt rid of me for some time. Nothing was going to change – are you kidding me?

----- I'm sorry.

----- I appreciate that. But if you're going to continue in that vein, I have to warn you that you're going to end up as a professional mourner by the time we're done here.

----- So I'm supposing that the long and the short of it was that you were stranded. What did you do?

----- Well, I knew I had to find work and shelter. I had no money; it was nice of my godparent to not ask if I was flush. I don't know what he was thinking. I guess that great American standby: "It's not my problem." In order to pay for a place to live, I figured I better find a job first, but Rowayton was nothing more than a one-street town -- not a whole lot of pickings. Plus it was late February and I didn't have a lot of daylight left. I made the rounds in no time at all with no luck. There was one place I didn't want to stick my nose into. A seafood restaurant where my mother

32

worked one night a week, keeping the books. She had for some years, reaching back to when she was with my stepfather; so I was well acquainted with the owner. Pure sleaze. But with the end of the day coming faster, what the hell, any port, right? When you're homeless, tired, and hungry, sometimes you have to put your dignity and common sense between your legs. I went in and begged a meal and a job to pay for it. There was no way he was going to give up a free meal, so I got the job to boot. Brother, did he see me coming.

----- Did your mother intercede at all when it came to your future welfare?

----- I would love to say no, but that would make me a liar. She did highly recommend me. On what basis, I know not. Anyway, the nice son of a bitch provided me with a charming little unheated attic in a small apartment building he had down on the river. It had a toilet, sink with cold running water, a bureau, and a bed with one wool blanket. If I wanted to use the plumbing, I was going to have to supply my own icepick. There was one window that overlooked a frozen tidal river. I guess you pay for the view. It only cost me twelve hours of kitchen time per day with four hours off on Sunday. My benefits were a hamburger, fries, and a Coke per day. If I wanted anything more than that, it would be taken out of my fifteen-dollar-a-week paycheck. Does it get any better than that?

----- Sounds pretty rough around the edges.

----- It was rough everywhere. But it could have been a lot worse. So I'm not going to complain, no one owed me a goddamn thing. You have to be grateful for small favors, right? The one thing I can say is that I learned about loneliness real quick. The only close proximity I had with another human being was with the cook. Not that we were close. We never spoke. He was a big black man with deep razor scars on his face and neck. But he didn't appear to be the loser type in an argument, so you have to wonder about the other guy. He didn't seem to relish the company of white folk any too much, so I kept my distance and obeyed any orders with a smile and "yes sir." Kind of training for the future, don't you think?

----- Sounds to me like you pretty much had things in hand. How long did you remain in this situation?

33

----- Well, it wasn't forever, it just seemed that way. As it turned out I think I managed to survive a little more than three weeks. As exhausting as the whole thing was, it turned out to be the loneliness that was the real killer. It was like bedbugs slowly bleeding you to death. You know what I mean? One day it came to the point of seeming terminal. On Sundays I would sit on the small roof just below my window, air bathing. One day I was observing a group of seagulls out on the ice. There were two standing separate from the group. One was desperately trying in vain to get the attention of the other. The one ignoring the attention suddenly flew off. The remaining bird seemed dumbfounded. After a few moments, the bird let out with a screech that defined loneliness. The sound shot into my heart and spun around in it like a razor blade. I grabbed my chest and sat there crying like a baby. I couldn't have known it then, but it was the beginning of the end.

----- It sounds just terrible. I myself have not had any experiences quite like that. It's a little hard to relate to, but that's not to say I can't imagine the weight of it.

----- Well, it just got worser and worser. I don't want you to think I'm nuts or anything, but I was so starved for companionship that I started to name the lobsters in the cooler. Do you have any idea what it did to me when someone ordered a lobster and I had to choose who was to die? Yeah, maybe I was nuts.

----- Don't be so hard on yourself. Your feelings were completely justified. Loneliness is a hard bullet for anyone to bite.

----- Well, that wasn't the only burr under my saddle. I was kicking myself in the ass because I had looked the ultimate gift horse in the mouth, not to mention ass. I had gone from having almost nothing to having just about everything. There I was, with a room in that house on the hill in Pleasantville and all the privileges that might have come with it, if I played by the rules. I had the world by the balls, and yet there was a part of me that couldn't tolerate the idea. That part won the tug of war. I guess I had to go along as baggage. What the fuck could I have been thinking? How could I be so stupid? But, once you jump off the bridge, it doesn't matter how many times you change your mind on the way down. I was almost to the bottom. One Sunday mid-morning, I was in the kitchen . . . all I could feel was the tired weight my feet were holding up. The odor of myself was the only thing I could smell. You have to understand that the clothes on my back were the only clothes I owned. Working three weeks in a seafood kitchen without bathing or laundry makes for a scent you wouldn't find pleasant. I was just standing there staring out at the rain that was coming down in buckets. It was mild for March, so the door was left open. I can't tell you how refreshing all that water looked. Other than the thoughts of my exhaustion, smell, and that lovely water, my mind was a blank. Suddenly, for no reason at all, almost against my will, I bolted out that door . . . .

----- Do you need to rest?

----- Yeah, I think I do.

A few minutes pass, feeling like hours. It's almost becoming embarrassing. Then, as if to extend my relief, Dr. Clark changes the subject.

----- Are you alright? You said a moment ago that you went from *nothing* to everything. What did you mean?

----- Oh, well, my mother married badly and poorly – I mean, she married a working bum. A self-described artist. Con artist, more like. Also, he was my father. Until I was two. Once she got rid of him -- or should I say, once her father did -- she married the first security that came along. Great for her – but not much concern for *my* needs. That's something that would never change. She and my stepfather both worked for wages in the same factory, so that should give you some idea of the finances. I won't get into the squalor we lived in, I'll just say we started out in the lowest of neighborhoods and had little, although, in time, they both made strides to better themselves and our living situation. When I turned thirteen my mother dumped my stepfather for the promise of better security – a sugar-daddy she thought she had on the hook. She dumped me as well -- first into the hands of her brother and family, then her sister and family, and ultimately on the doorstep of my godparents with their son and daughter.

They were affluent, to say the least -- the top of the heap and all that. I wanted for nothing but, as I said, I never came to feel the sense of entitlement. I never got over the sense that I was just a bottle of vinegar in an elite wine cellar. So . . . .

----- I can understand your plight. That brings us back to your flight.

----- Yeah, what kind of asshole do I feel like. Like running out of a burning building and right into the swamp. You know, it's harder to talk about it than it was to actually live it. I mean, how can I possibly admit to being that stupid? At this moment, I feel like the regret of making such a stupid decision could kill me.

----- Which decision are you speaking of?

----- You see what I mean? Which one. Yeah, there were too goddamn many, weren't there? How stupid does that make me? Well, I guess I'm referring to dropping out. The decision to run wasn't a decision at all. Where the hell was I going to run to? The same place I was going to walk to a few weeks ago? What -- *home*? *What* home? A fantasy place. That could be anywhere. I suppose to my warped sense of imagination, that would be Pleasantville. Why? I guess it somehow represented life as it could have been. My first love lived there although she didn't love me. Go figure. If I ever get a tattoo, it isn't going to read: "Born to lose." It's going to read: "Born to be Earl."

----- Let me stop you here for a moment. Are you aware of how much time you spend beating yourself up? Do you derive any sense of satisfaction in doing that?

----- I hate to admit it, but I grew up with being beaten up, at home and school. I guess I've come to be comfortable with it. I've probably come to feel that somehow I deserve it.

----- Do you wish to talk about that feeling?

----- No, thanks -- I have enough on my plate for the moment, maybe we can save it for dessert. I'd rather deal with the can of shit I've already opened.

----- Okay, then, I'm not one to argue with the headwaiter. Why don't you continue.

----- As I said, I ran out the door. The rain was so thick that I thought I had run into a brick wall. The air was so dense with moisture I felt as though I needed scuba equipment to breathe. Sheer panic was the only motivation for my legs to keep moving. You know, I really don't believe in the devil, not really. But just the same, I didn't dare look over my shoulder for fear I would see him catching up to me. As exhausted as I already was, the idea just made me run all the faster.

(The doctor tries not to smile.)

----- I just became a ball rolling downhill. Four and a half hours and thirty-six miles later, I collapsed in the arms of Jo Ann. I thought I was going to die. It's too goddamn bad I didn't. I couldn't believe how glad she was to see me. It's almost like she missed me or something. We always had a thing for each other but it never developed into anything. Once, I asked her to be my girlfriend for the night on my sixteenth birthday; we went to a movie; it was fun. Oh, well.

----- So, now you're back in Pleasantville, what happened next?

----- Yeah, being there was not really an option. I'm not trying to be coy or anything, but, damn if I can remember that particular frame of time, I mean from point A to point B. I just can't remember. Maybe 'cause I don't want to, I don't know. All that I can tell you is that I had some crazy urge to go north. I had some need to find this plot of land in upstate New York where, a couple of years earlier, I had visited. While I was there I had – I guess you could call it a religious experience, or at least some sort of mental transition. But first on my quest I stopped off in Poughkeepsie.

----- Why Poughkeepsie?

----- A couple of reasons, like having to wait for the winter weather to break. The fact that it was a city, so finding work and shelter was a lot easier. And I suppose I had some small heartfelt longing for the place due to the fact that I had family there.

-----   Did you stay with them?

-----   I guess I should explain. The family was a lost uncle, my mother's oldest brother. Their father was a minister of the Victorian era and came into dispute with his son over the son's lifestyle and how it reflected back on the father's good standing in the community. The solution was simple. All things were simple in the good old days, weren't they? Good because you could pretty well do anything you wanted, I'm guessing. My grandfather had my uncle committed to a state asylum. I think it was in Poughkeepsie, I know it was on the Hudson. We used to visit him twice a year and we always stopped in that city for lunch. I felt very close to my uncle -- I think I related to him because each of us found ourselves in a state of incarceration. The fact of the matter is that when I got to the city, I made no effort to see him. I can't tell you why I didn't, any more than I can think now of a good reason for not doing so then. I suppose my visiting would have been nice for him, and I guess that should have been reason enough. But we're not dealing with someone here known for good decision-making . . . .

I just odd-jobbed my time away and built up a little bankroll. The Post Office turned out to be a dependable source of income. On weekends, when the Postmaster wasn't there, you could always pick up some good bucks throwing bags. The guys who were being paid too much for doing that job were always glad to part with a few bucks to hungry kids like me so they could sit on their asses. In late May, I made my break and headed north, but not before outfitting myself for the outdoor life, including a bow. I had gotten really good with the bow when I was living with my godparents. I had no idea where I was going but I knew that I would know it when I got there. I knew it. I ended up right in the middle of dairy country on top of a mountain that still had forested land, but close enough to farms for the pickings I was going to need. I had stocked an ample supply of canned goods, enough to give me time to scout out the terrain and lay of the land. I made myself central but not exposed. I found a farm with a whole lot of children -- that equated to a well-stocked root cellar. Take very little and it won't be noticed. You hope. I let my love of milk lure me into becoming an utter thief.

(The doctor lets my word play pass without comment.)

----- How did that sit with you? I mean stealing and all. I'm not hearing anything in your history that tells me you were ever in trouble for that sort of thing.

----- You know, I'd been acquainted with a couple of WW II vets . . . I won't trouble you with their stories, just their conclusions. "When you're at war, you forget everything you ever knew of morals, you just do what you have to do in order to survive." It was the same thing for me. I had to fall back on the powers of my lower self. My instinctive values. I'm not making excuses. I'm not trying to justify anything, not now anyway, but back then it was war, in a sense. I'm just not sure who the enemy was. Anyway, you replace the "I shouldn't do this" with "I hope I get away with doing this." That's all. When you're hungry, it's amazing how easy the transition is.

----- So how did you survive? What was the worst thing you had to encounter?

----- I don't know. Maybe it was loneliness, although there was little time to consider it. Maybe the killing. But, again, you give in to doing a lot of things you wouldn't normally do, when you're hungry. But it was never pleasant and, whenever possible, I would steal as much as I could from wherever I could. The best pickings were when the apple trees were full of fruit. Not to mention the corn. Meat was actually last on my diet. Apart from the act of killing, there's the rigor of the hunt. That's no walk in the park. You may go three to five days without getting a shot. Then there's the dressing, which can be a real pain in the ass. At the end of it all, you have to ask yourself if it was worth what you had to go through. What did you get out of it? I'll tell you, I only ate crow once. A crow consists of a lot of feathers, bones, oil, grease, a beak, and some feet. Squirrel isn't much better for the effort involved. Woodchuck, though, was high on the menu.

----- What about deer -- were there many?

----- All over the place, but not for my wants. Too much meat, too much waste. Besides, it would be the same as shooting a cow.

----- Well, I think we'll have to stop now.

----- That's okay, I was beginning to make myself hungry. I guess it would be a waste to go off base, even if I could get liberty. I can't think of one place that serves a good woodchuck steak.

- - - - - - - - - - - - - - - - - -

Walking back to the Galley and passing other sailors that I know to be in the Real Navy, I muse. What if I follow one of these guys . . . duck into their barracks and take a rack, fall in when they report to duty. Would anyone realize that I didn't belong? Would I be missed back at the Galley? Would I be considered AWOL if I were performing my duty elsewhere? Good for a laugh thinking about it anyway. That's the trouble with these little weekly breaks -- I get to see some of the real world and it gets me to thinking. Don't want to do that. It kind of spoils my ability to ignore things. It's just getting harder and harder to go back to those chains. Maybe I should bring the JAG thing up to Dr. Clark. Nah, I don't want to push it. He may be a nice guy and all, but he's still Navy, and I haven't gotten over that business with the Chaplain and his Open Door Policy: ruffle my complacency and I'll open the THIS-WAY-OUT door for you. People are sensitive about their bread and butter. I guess I'll have to bite my tongue and hold my breath, pretty much what I've been doing all these months. Just waiting for that final shoe to drop. The question is when and how hard. And the waiting is more tiring than a month of mid-watches.

Coming into the Galley, I go first to the Office to report in for duty and I meet once again with the same wiseass bullshit – the wisecracks alluding to my mental health, or lack of it. Who are these jerks? If they're so smart that they understand the power of words, then they surely have to understand their consequences. Consequences -- that's a good word. An outstanding one. How is it that it doesn't apply to them? I grew up in a world where there was nothing but consequences. Of course, they were a lot more pleasant when they fell on someone else's head. Sometimes entertaining. Boy, would I love to see something fall on the fat heads of these puffed-up assholes.

I don't understand this new world order. I sure as hell remember the one I had to learn to watch my ass in. Like when I was three and had just entered nursery school. You can't start your real-life education too early.

40

The school's owner and warden-at-large was a towering and formidable red-headed Irish single mother of two boys. She pretty much ran the place like a jail for miniature people. That was okay with me, I suppose, as I had no way of perceiving that it could or should be any different . . . .

I'm in the sand box, playing with some very tired little metal cars. I keep remarking to myself what a perfect day it is, due to the rain last night which has compacted the sand so as to allow me to dig tunnels for the cars' passage. I'm humming and happy in my little bubble. Uh-oh . . . here comes the elder boy -- at fourteen an adult, to my perception. One of the Big People. I'm wary of his company. A few days earlier he had invited me to witness "something funny". He brought me over to the chicken coop where I watched as he chopped a chicken's head off and then watched the bird running around in frantic pursuit of its lost head. I didn't find the "funny" in it. Now here he is again in his capacity as the executioner for the kitchen. He has in a bucket his three latest victims. He sets down the pail and then himself on the corner of the box. Still uninvited, he starts to engage me in conversation. He wishes to know the extent of my knowledge on the subject of the soul. I have some small idea, but I'm all ears. Whatever a soul might be, I'm going to hold on to mine tightly when he's around, especially when he has his hatchet with him.

He goes on at some length embellishing a visual description until I develop an image in my head of a soul that looks very much like a Brillo pad. Once he's satisfied that I've firmly got the picture, he levels me with the information that my soul is going to burn in hell forever. I become hysterical. In response to my anguished wails, his mother rushes out of the house with her hair aflame and her eyes blazing, as if looking for a good brawl. She quickly gets me in her sights, then she's looming over me, wanting to know what all the racket is about. I blubber out the reason for my distress. She rushes back into the house and then again appears, bullwhip in hand. She corners her son between a fence and the coop and whips the ever-loving clothes off him. This time it is his blood spilled. My horror gives way to a great sense of satisfaction. I wonder where the chickens' souls are right about now.

And now I wonder if that bitch is still alive and, if so, does she do freelance work? I can picture a few featherless bipeds I know being near whipped to death by the nursery warden, not to mention being sent off somewhere, as her son was. Don't these assholes-in-uniforms stop to consider consequences? If they really think I'm nuts, shouldn't they worry about pushing me over the edge? Maybe they should, because I'm really feeling my back to it. Do I dare to tell my doctor? What would he be obliged to do with that knowledge? Any which way, I feel like these Galley devils and Front Office Beelzebubs have their pitchforks stuck in my Brillo pad! I worry in the back of my mind that the day may soon come when I might ignore the idea of consequences myself. It's coming down to the wire. I have only to consider how my mindset changed when I was out in the woods. The swing into survival mode, forgetting the rules. God! I feel in danger of becoming dangerous. If I really did what I'd like to do, I wonder if JAG would see it as being self-defense -- you know, the Brillo Pad defense. Better bury it, it doesn't sound real even to me.

6.

Another week passes. All I can smell is the fuse burning.

----- Hi, Dr. Clark, I hope you're well and strong today.

(He looks at me askance.)

----- Hello, Mr. McByrne, the question is how are *you* today?

----- I'm holding my own for now, but I have to admit that things are getting awfully thin.

----- Well, I want you to hold on just a bit longer. I'm starting the wheels of getting you transferred in motion. Do you think you can hold on a little

42

longer?

----- If you're telling me that there's an end in sight, I can hold on with a hang nail.

----- Excellent.   Well, Mr. McByrne, the last time you were here, you had us roughing it in the woods, in survival mode, as you described it. How did that go?

----- Well, back in the forest primeval, things hadn't reached a downhill slope as yet, but I'd be a liar if I didn't tell you that I was constantly preoccupied with the thought of the coming winter. I'd spent a past winter about a hundred miles north of where I thought I was -- a stone's throw -- with my relatives in North Syracuse. I knew the weather wouldn't be survivable. On the other hand, I had no alternative plans. I tried real hard not to think about it.

----- That, in and of itself, sounds like a daunting situation to face.

----- You can believe me, it was. Even in warm weather, I suffered a lot from being cold. My use of fire had to be limited. When I did use it, I had to keep it very small and very hot to keep the smoke down. I also kept it up against a very large spreading tree so that the tree would basically eat the smoke -- the smoke clings to the tree, so very little, if any, ever gets to the open sky. Of course, at night I could be a little more liberal, and warm. Farmers go to bed very early.

----- Sounds like you know your stuff.

----- Well, call it the benefits of keeping your ears open. That's something I did all my life. If you don't know something, someone else does. But I can't say that being out there was any Sunday walk in the park. Actually it was so grueling that I've benefited by not remembering much of the experience. Partly because all the days blend into one another. It all just becomes one long day, and those things that want to take a peek out aren't necessarily things you want to remember. I'm not saying there weren't good moments. I think the fondest are of laying down at night feeling near death and witnessing the agonies of the coals of the fire on their deathbed as they struggled to stay alive. I felt a oneness with that.

----- Wow. It sounds rather Romantic.

----- Yeah, if you didn't have to be there. Oh well, it did come to an end. One morning I made my usual milk run. As long as the house lights weren't on, I knew I was safe. That morning, after gorging myself, I got stupid and gave in to my craving for warmth. I thought a short respite behind the haystack in the barn could take the chill off me. Suddenly, I'm aroused by the light reflected off the back wall. I panic. Stupidly, I rise from my hiding place. If I had remained where I was, I would have remained safe. I think, deep down, I wanted to get caught. You have to know when a thing is done. I think that was the message that was knocking at the back door of my brain three days earlier. I had surprised a squirrel that jumped up onto the side of a tree and froze. It couldn't have been more than ten feet from me. On any day before that one, it would have been dead at fifty. I raised my bow and took aim. I missed it by a foot. Yeah, you have to know when a thing is done, alright.

----- Do I dare ask what happened next? You left me on a cliff there, in the barn.

----- Well, I was almost blinded by the glare of the direct sunlight – though it was partly blocked out by a black silhouette looming in the East door. This dark figure seemed aflame, with the sun's rays shooting out around it. Was it a devil or an angel? Whichever, it was my worst nightmare come to visit me. My life passed before my eyes. Whoever he was – most likely the farmer, I realized -- he could have shot me right then and there and no one would ask any questions. Instead, he shot me between the eyes with a few words: "Wouldn't you be happier being honest, son? Starting with asking for help." I collapsed under the weight of shame. Sobbing like a baby. Everything I had ever learned of good came flooding back into me like a reverse enema. I couldn't hide any longer, enough was enough.

----- Wow. I don't know what to say.

----- It's okay, I didn't either. The short of it was that he was a fourth-generation American Swede with five children, the oldest boy in the army

44

serving in Nam. I'm guessing his wife was dead, I don't know, no one ever mentioned her. His sister, however, was taking her place. They took me in, almost as family. I lived there for two-plus months and worked off my debt, and made a little money on top of it. I've been quite a few places and known many people. I can tell you, people are definitely not the same all over. There are bad places and bad people. This proved to be a good place and he a good man. I was sad to leave, believe me. But I knew a future was out there, although I didn't know what or where -- I just knew this wasn't it. I caught a bus, then a train south. I returned to where my journey had begun. What happens when a dog becomes lost during the family move? It goes back to the last home it knew.

----- Pleasantville?

----- You know it!

----- Weren't you afraid of a reenactment with your godfather?

----- Yeah, it was actually a bigger concern to me than you might imagine. I had found out that, apart from his successful practice, he was also running women on the side. He actually offered my mother a position at a thousand bucks a night. She turned it down -- she was too proud of her virtual virginality. Anyway, it concerned me that he probably had some guys somewhere in his employ as protection for the girls. Why not for himself as well? Shit does happen, you know; and there has to be someone somewhere pulling the strings. I took my safety very seriously. Maybe that makes me a nut for being there – but, just like a dog, I couldn't conceive of anything else. Where the hell else was I supposed to be? I was going to have to make sure to stay out of sight until I could think of a better refuge. I found a place in a rooming house on the other side of the tracks, and I got a job as a packer at a small manufacturer in the same neighborhood. The diner where I ate was fifty feet from where I roomed. My godfather rarely ventured out of his house; his offices were downstairs in the home. Even if he did leave, he would never think to venture down to this part of town. Just the same, I stayed off the street. When I wasn't working, I was hiding out in my room. I got a lot of reading done. I read the Bible twice. All in all, I felt pretty secure.

45

-----   What about Jo Ann, was there anything going on there?

-----   No, not really. As reality goes, she was going to have to be backburner. But that's not to say she didn't remain a heartache. One of the problems was there was nowhere to see her. She lived right down the hill from my godparents, and I certainly couldn't have her in my room. Besides, I had Rita in my life now.

-----   Who was Rita? Where did *she* come from?

-----   You can picture the stereotype diner waitress -- you know, fat, bleached blond, bright red lipstick, cheeks to match, and thinks that your name is "Honey" -- well, Rita was the original model. Just the love of my life. Her company the height of my day. The Princess of the Canned Peas. Between her and the meatloaf, what could I be wanting? Yeah, I could get myself a Harley, she could plop her fat ass on it, and we could ride off into the northern sunset over Canada. Really?

-----   You mention Canada -- were you considering that an option? Were you concerned about the draft?

-----   You know, just like Jo Ann, it was in the back of my mind. By that point in time I was finally catching on to the fact that things weren't going to be the way I wanted. I got it that the very fact that I wanted something was pretty much a guarantee that it wouldn't happen. And, on the other hand, I had been living through things that, before they unfolded, I would never have dreamed of. My mind and fate were definitely at odds with one another. I just couldn't trust my perceptions any longer.

   With something as big and concrete as the reality of service looming over me, it was more a matter of which service and when than a matter of avoiding it. Canada didn't really come into the question. I guess I was just too patriotic. That's not to say I wanted to fight, but I'd be damned if someone was going to take my place. It's ironic, if not downright stupid -- I mean, it doesn't make any sense at all, but -- I had this buddy named Charlie. He was the nicest kid you could possibly imagine. He was everything I wasn't. I couldn't picture someone putting a gun in his hand. I couldn't picture his mother giving him up. Just by virtue of him going into the service, because I know it changes you, I saw how an American family would be lost. And Charlie, he'd be the first to get it. Bullets love the innocent. Like I said, it was really stupid thinking, but I felt if the country needed one hundred bodies and I jumped line, that would make Charlie number one hundred one and he wouldn't have to go. And you know what? If I ever go back to Pleasantville, I'm never going to inquire of him. I never want to know. Does it get any sillier than that?

----- No, I see the logic of it. I can understand your thinking with your heart. That sort of irrationality, so to speak, is part of being human – maybe one of our more admirable qualities. After deciding to sign up, what led you to choose the Navy?

----- Well, I always had a thing for subs, as long as I can remember. But, beyond that, I had been acquainted with two sailors, both Petty Officers. They were grown up, I wasn't. They were in authority, I was clueless. It seemed as though what they were doing just might be an avenue to use to get there from here. One of them was my godmother's nephew, the other their daughter's boyfriend, so I saw both of them whenever either was on leave. The boyfriend, in particular, tickled my fancy with the tales he told concerning his abilities to wield power over others. In retrospect, I see now that he really wasn't much better than the assholes I'm dealing with now. But back then -- I think you can understand how blind I was and the need I had to be one in power and control. It was all very enticing. If you don't know any better. So in the end, when I turned seventeen, I got permission from my bio-birth unit and joined. How could anything be worse than what I had already lived through? By the way, has anyone published the book yet? I've been waiting for it to come out -- you know, *The Answers to Stupid Questions.*

(The doctor laughs. I'm always pleased whenever I can get a rise out of him. I like him too much to want him to be saddled with a boring complainer.)

----- Well, I knew there was going to have to be a transition, and I was clued in to what Boot Camp was going to be like. In principle, I had no problem with what I was expecting. In fact, to some degree, once I got there, I found the process almost comical. Guess I always did have a dark sense of humor anyway. I lost it real quick, though, when they handed me a dummy rifle. I wasn't looking to play. I immediately tried to transfer to the Marines. That didn't happen, as you can see.

A lot of kids cried for their mamas those first nights. I wondered what the hell they were doing here. *Let's just get this shit over with* was my idea of things. Of course, my idea of things had nothing to do with reality; as usual. But not a whole lot bothered me. Not even when I had to do Captain's Chair – you know, sitting against a wall without the benefit of a chair and holding your piece out in front of you -- for having fallen across a rack instead of the deck as a result of having walking pneumonia. As did half the company. When I wasn't able to hold the chair, I was kicked until I resumed the position. Too weak to hold it again, I was kicked again, until the person doing the kicking himself ran out of steam. I didn't mind. I had worse. What really pissed me off is what happened to the next victim in line. When they were done kicking him, they must have brought in a fresh kicker. Finally, the poor fellow was physically escorted down the staircase because he couldn't hold himself up and was quivering like jello without the bowl. He was crying hysterically about I don't know what and was never seen again. I guess he wasn't Navy material. They couldn't see that at his induction? You know what – he looked just like Charlie. It was all just too stupid. Boot Camp -- I was glad to get it behind me. It gave me pause to think. I had put other things behind me. My childhood, my godparents, the farmer – all these things came to a conclusion. They died their death. Their time existed no longer. But now the end of Boot Camp meant the beginning of a commitment for four years of the future, and I wasn't going to be given the option of killing it off if I wanted to. That thought was truly fucking scary.

7.

When I get back to the Galley after my session, I go to the barracks to change into my fatigues. As I enter, I almost fall over a House Mouse who's stooped over on the floor. Well, if this isn't the picture of irony -- he's setting a mouse trap. After I stop laughing to myself, I get a brain freeze. It's as if someone just pierced my head with an icicle and caused a chill to run down my spine. It hits me – what about what *I* want, or don't want? This mouse trap is just a for-instance -- what if I don't want the cute little furry thing to die? The trap is just another slap-in-the-face reminder that, in this shit box I have to live in, I have no say at all, no control over anything. As small as this trap-setting incident is, in my head it's clanging as loud as the Liberty Bell and maybe – given that it's *my* head -- just as cracked.

Clang . . . Clang . . . . I'm still shackled in the same chains that I was in when I was five. Hell, that was thirteen years ago -- and I'm still stuck feeling what I felt then. That was right after we moved in to the Victorian, when my stepfather decided to evict the indigenous tenants.

I watch Jim set the mouse traps throughout the apartment. I feel almost panicky -- and powerless, as usual. The idea of killing anything breaks my heart. But, of course, I have no voice in the matter, no right to speak up. When Jim's will is set, it's a steel trap you don't want to spring by putting your foot into it.

That night, in my bed, I feel like I'm holding my breath. For hours, it seems like. It's so dark and quiet. And then – snap! -- right next to my pillow, which is separated from the kitchen closet, where the trap is, by a paper-thin wall of lath and plaster. The thunder of the trap, the lightning jolt of knowing it had done its job, nails me to my bed in horror. The darkness of night keeps me there.

The light of dawn gives me hope. I can now get up and do something. I sneak out of bed and into the kitchen. The pity I feel for the mouse, lying so still in the trap, is a lump in my chest. I take the mouse, and a piece of cheese that I steal from the refrigerator, back to my room. There are things in my head, some of those hand-me-down notions and laws gifted to me by my elders, that encourage me to believe that, by the diligent performance of faith and ritual, I can get a miracle to happen. Using the cheese as an incentive, I try to get the mouse to wake up and live again. Yeah, -- in my as-yet-unobliterated trustfulness – I earnestly try to resurrect the lifeless little thing in the name of Jesus Christ. It doesn't seem to be working, but I haven't given up.

At this moment – in walks Jim. Through my bedroom is the only passage to the bathroom, where Jim is headed. It's obvious that he wasn't expecting to witness this voodoo ritual or to hear the name of his Savior taken in vain. This is obvious

to me because of the coal-red fury that comes over his face. The revulsion and
condemnation in his burning eyes freezes me.

How many times as a child did I freeze when it occurred to me that something I had thought of doing might be WRONG? How guarded did I feel whenever I found myself on the verge of taking some initiative? And now . . . if the Navy has a Secret Police, I imagine that my stepfather is their Führer. Once again, I'm cornered in a house where any attempts at independence of thought or identity are dealt with like varmints – *snap!* Kaput. And yet – I joined up. And yet, on the other hand, I have recurring impulses to think for myself, to become me.

Like the night of the mousetraps, the days of Galley service drag on, the weeks pass in a blur, running on a treadmill. And then – *splat!* -- it happens. I'm transferred to the lightest duty ever devised. Personnel Office. Typing, stamping, filing, in all its cushy glory. What? What bag of fairy dust did this fall out of? I'm out of the shit can and into the padded desk chair . . . but I can't relax. I'm waiting for the shit to hit the fan . . . or -- not? I'm waiting for that other shoe to drop. It will, right? Sometimes the question hurts more than the eventual answer. And sometimes I think fate is a centipede.

- -

----- Hello, Doctor. I'm supposing you know of my transfer.

----- Yes. Good. How are you feeling about it?

----- I'm not really sure. How good do you feel after you wake up from a nightmare?

----- I know what you're saying. I want to reassure you, though -- you're in no danger of having to end your work here. We'll stay at it until there's some resolution. And, uh . . . I have to ask you at this point . . . . there has been some talk in the Psych Office of having you discharged. How do you

50

feel about that possibility?

----- Believe it or not, without thinking about it, the first thing that pops up in my mind is fear. I'm so used to being confined and being told when I can breathe, and being punished when I do. And keep in mind that's all I've known for the last nine months. I'm not sure what the hell the real world is all about anymore. I don't have the slightest fucking idea who I am anymore.

----- Every person who's discharged goes through a similar quandary. There's always a period of adjustment. It's just something you'll have to confront, either now or later down the road.

(The doctor is wearing an expression of concern that I had never noticed before. He seems preoccupied. This just adds fuel to the fire of my paranoia.)

----- God, this whole thing has awakened a memory that's been asleep for a long time. One of my first, I think. At least one of my worst. My first encounters with the outside world . . . .

----- And that frightened you?

----- You better believe it. It happened as soon as my mother married my stepfather; I had just turned four. Until that point, the only thing outside my home and nursery school I knew was the grocery store. I wasn't in any way ready for the outside world that I was going to be exposed to. If you ask me, it was criminal.

----- What could have been so bad? Your parents didn't take you to a public execution, did they?

----- No, actually, something like that would have seemed like a puppet show compared to what I saw.

----- Why don't you tell me about it.

----- Well, Day One, my mother marries Himself, Day Two, we visit my uncle on the Hudson, Day Three, we go down to New York City to visit my

51

mother's aunt who's been a street person most of her life. She was at a women's shelter down on the Bowery. Brother, what a couple of days that was. It would seem that my new father was heavily into family obligations or something.

----- I see.

----- My mother had told me of my great-aunt's story. She'd been thrown out of a very privileged home onto the street over lying about the purchase of a dress. The long and the short of it was that her father at first defended her in the matter and ended up being made a fool of. I guess it all came down to that old Ancient Roman law: If your son disgraced you, you -- the father -- had the right to take his life. I'm supposing that my aunt's father's actions were more in keeping with the modes of his day – which were Victorian. Out she went, exiled from the family -- that was satisfaction enough. By the time of our visit, she had been an outcast, a nomad, for about forty years.

The place where we found her, on the Bowery, wasn't much better than a stockyard, except indoors – which, in a way, made it worse. The stench was overwhelming – it made me feel like I'd been punched in the stomach and smacked in the head. I was four. It was hard for me to understand why we were going into this place.

We found my great-aunt in a black pit of a room with I don't know how many other lost souls. It was hard to recognize these once-human beings as ever having been women. I remember being terrified. By what – I didn't have a name for it – I guess it was the misery, the hopelessness. Imagining being stuck in that place. That place sure stuck in me – it's the image that comes into my head when I hear the word 'hell'.

I didn't get much of a chance to feel relief when we finally left. How was it that we had gone to visit a person and had then left her in that sad and stinking hole? That thought was still troubling me . . . and then, as we walked back to the subway, my innocence was blindsided by the filth and garbage that seemed to be everywhere, and the humans I saw seemed to be part of the trash. I didn't have a label for what I saw, I didn't know from 'Bowery bums' – I just worked myself into a sweat wondering where are the parents of these creatures? Why aren't they being taken care of? Who's in charge of this mess? I guess, in its quandary, my little brain had to conclude that God had at some point tired of managing his creation and said: "That's it, I can't do anymore." And maybe took a shit before walking away -- and this was it. I can tell you that all of this didn't leave me feeling any too good that day.

Well, the terror and despair that I was feeling in those hours is now revisiting me with the prospect of having to set foot in a foreign world. Even if I might imagine getting a discharge as being released from purgatory and set down on a new road, I guess I can still conjure up the idea of hell as a destination. Not so sure about the supposed alternative. Anyway, the Galley goons did their work. I am broken.

(The doctor remains silent. He lets out a heavy sigh and just stares at me.)

8.

But here I still am, two months later. With Personnel duty comes nine-to-five hours and liberty. Someone, I guess, left the barn door open and the horse got out. Free time equates to pool, both in the barracks and out on the strip. I find I have a knack for it, and it isn't long before I become a great cheat. The money is certainly good and I only hustle the suckers -- that somehow justifies it. Almost immediately, I buddy up with a barracks mate named Bob, who dubs me with the nickname "Duke" because I own the table. He's the first friendly relationship I've formed in the last eleven months of active duty. My paranoia hasn't lessened any, though, so I'm more than happy to take a room off base. Bob's joined me, so it cuts the rent in half, six bucks per man per week. We have staggered duty hours, so we aren't bumping heads in bed. It's an interesting house. Three floors, four rooms to a floor, one bathroom for all, and two floating whores that are optional. Most of the tenants are retired dropouts from life, on Social Security. The place is a real education. If the school of hard knocks has an address, this is it. The whole new gig is lending me some sense of a return to normal. What the hell is normal?

Therapy goes on. The one thing I never dare to bring up -- the one thing I keep waiting for Doctor Clark to bring up -- is the train thing. What happened on the train. *The red bloom, the dead red eyes.* The Holy Grail of secrets. I can't figure out what he might know, if anything, and is this all a test to see if I haven't learned my lesson and might be willing to spill my guts. That unanswered question makes my burden all the heavier by tenfold. There's no relief or release from the pain, anxiety, and guilt about what happened, coupled with the fear of being found out and punished. To yak or not to yak -- that is the question. It's the kind of goddamn shit that keeps you awake at night; makes you sorry you were ever born. The paranoia just keeps building and building, feeding on itself like a shark eating its own entrails.

So today the Doc lays it on me. The ultimate threat of knowing the unknown.

"In two weeks, you'll receive orders to ship out -- or be discharged."

All I can hear is "ship out". Discharged? No. Uh-uh. I signed up for four years. It hasn't even been sixteen months. Yeah, I knew I'd be Uncle Sam's property for four years, but I also figured that would give him enough time to make a man out of me. With the added benefit that I'd know where I was supposed to be and what I'd be doing for the next four years. My discharge date when I joined was set to be the day after my twenty-first birthday. I'd be a man, and I'd have had plenty of time to figure out my next move. That's the plan. So I'm waiting for my shipping orders.

- - - - - - - - - - - - - - - - - - -

Dr. Clark is a man of his word. Two weeks later, almost to the day, my orders come through. Hawaii. *What?* Hawaii – duty: Auxiliary Oiler. That means three days at sea, four in port. A sailor's dream – some might call it Paradise. It's the skatingest duty you could pull – if Personnel was cushy, this would be a feather bed floating on a cloud. But I want no part of it. I don't want to sail. I want to ship out -- to Nam! Not so much feeling my nerves on a hair-trigger now, as I was a few months back; then, I figured that, when I reached the point of exploding, or bashing someone's brains in, it might as well be someone my country regarded as an enemy. Now what I'm thinking is, if I'm set down in a real place, on a mission – a mission more serious than peeling potatoes, a function calling for more initiative than filing papers – I might get a chance to take my courage in my hands and serve my country honorably, to come up to the measure like I saw myself doing when I joined up. And if I get blown up in the process – well, at least it's a better way to go than what could befall me on that Oiler. Unwanted commodities on those vessels have a way of disappearing at sea during night mid-watch. I once overheard a discussion between two Southern boys about how they overcame their prejudices in that manner. This prickles my paranoia. I'd prefer to be fragbait than ballast. To at least have my boots on my feet and my feet on the ground when I go down.

So I run to Dr. Clark. I'm ranting between pleading and demanding that I get new orders. He's not saying much and his demeanor isn't giving much away either. I feel like a rat. The lighter side of my mind has to wonder if the Doc hadn't pulled some strings to get me out of harm's way. Maybe this is some kind of reward for hard time served. But paranoia runs in all directions. So, on the other hand, the thought that I might be wrong in imagining Dr. Clark's protective involvement leaves me feeling empty. A perverse kind of empty – a void that's filled to capacity with a blackness. Not a lack of light, but a goo. Dark, and sticky as flypaper designed to hold onto everything that is wrong. What the hell happened to the me of myself? Seems like someone raped me and I didn't know it. I find myself limping along in the ranks of the violated – a club I never wanted to be a member of – the losers, the downtrodden. I'm one of *them* – one of the brainless that walk around with something up their ass. But – have I been fucked, or am I fucking myself?

I'm overwhelmed with a sense of betrayal . . . by who? by what? Myself, the Navy, life, maybe even – God forbid – Dr. Clark? I thought I had gotten past expectations of beneficence, of some kindly guiding hand, or divinely-lit inner spark leading me in the right direction. I thought that, over the years, I had developed enough scar tissue to protect myself from such nonsense. From any of that shit that smacks of "poor me".

The first open wound I can remember . . . . *I'm four. Too young to understand, really. My grandmother is fifty-two. Too young to die . . . or, at least, what I do understand, too soon pulled out of the sphere of my life. I'm standing at the bottom of the stairs that lead up to her bedroom in the home where she lives. This is the home where I know I always feel safe, where I feel her gentleness and warmth. I feel that when she looks at me, she really sees me. And, in her goodness, she sees me as good. Now I see her being carried down the stairs on a stretcher. Her hands are being pried loose from the bannister. She keeps trying to clutch onto it as the stretcher moves down step by step. She's crying and begging to be allowed to die in her own bed, in her home. The home where she had spent her life devoted to the comfort of her husband and five children. Now none of them is going to sacrifice their peace for her sake. I don't know why the Good Humor men in their white shirts, pants, and caps are taking her out of the house. But I do hear her cries and pleas, and I do feel something in my heart and my little mind breaking. I don't have a word for it then . . . but it's the first seed of betrayal. Hers at the hands of her family; mine at the whim of everything bigger than me.*

That was four years into my untried life. Somehow, thirteen years and a lot of shit later, I manage to arrive at this Naval Base with still enough green around the edges that I can hope to make a new start in a new season. I can plant myself here and sprout. I'm hopeful, but also apprehensive. What's going to happen here? What do I know about the Real World of Men in the Navy? I'm pretty much a scared kid trying to keep my manly face up. The first minute of the first day – I'd just got off the train – I'm told to report for active duty on base. I'm told to report to my CPO, a Boatswain's Mate. This imposing black man in a uniform right away starts telling me about my assignment, which I'm starting immediately: Gate Duty. Security. *What, right this minute? I just got off the train.* Without reflecting on what the protocol might be – without a clue, really – I blurt naively and sort of pathetically, "Can I get lunch? Is there time to eat . . . ?" I gulp and wince as it hits me that I might have put my foot in it with my first step in this place. Then this big man, Boats, chuckles and his face breaks out in a rainbow smile. He gives me a reassuring shoulder hug with one of his brawny arms. He seems amused by my innocence.

I did get lunch.

And now I'm not much older . . . but I'm feeling the weight of time. That's about all I'm feeling, though. I'm on automatic pilot, waiting to see if the worm of my fate will turn. I do my work. I breathe air in and out. I eat and shit. Without much commitment to any of it. I don't see Dr. Clark again. I guess he concluded that things were as concluded for me as they were going to get. His work was done.

How much he might have continued to work behind the scenes I don't know. But somehow the worm has its day. My new orders come down. Nam. 86th Battalion, Seabees. Report to San Diego for Special Forces training. *Now* someone's talkin'. It's enough to make me feel religious again. I almost feel like skipping and smiling in my heart, like I did as a kid when the box I opened under the tree had the very set of replica mounted deer heads – a boy and a girl – that I'd been longing for. There was a real moment of joy . . . for a moment. Which came to a quick end with a smack from the back of Jim's big hand across my face. And my brief bubble broken by his voice: "I was never happy at Christmas – I'll be damned if he's going to be"-- followed by his perversion of a satisfied laugh as he pointed his Christmas-album Brownie at my teary contorted face to capture the magic of that Kodak moment.

No, but that was then, this is the Navy. This is Real. And these are the orders I've wanted. *The orders I've wanted* – aye-aye, there's the rub. The smack from the ghost of Jim's other hand. I see that other shoe coming at me fast. This time it's on the Navy's foot. Or God's. Maybe they're all in cahoots. First thing I'm going to do when I get off this base is get myself a pair of boots. Good big ones. I've got to figure out how to kick some ass, not just my own. Damn it, yeah, I will.

Meanwhile, that government-issued shoe is still airborne and I'm still on desk duty pulling files. I pull one that's getting stamped with an award. *The Medal of Honor.* I feel a twinge of awe. The subject of the file being awarded is *a sailor.* Wow! Some guy who's s*till living* – a bigger wow.

In the middle of this moment of wonderment at Some Guy's achievement, my CPO calls me into his office and tells me to go to the barracks and pack my sea bag and report to Building 34. Okay. I don't have a clue what's up. Must have something to do with getting shipped out. I guess.

I'm directed upstairs. A Yeoman behind a desk instructs me to take off my uniform and put some civvies on, then starts to type. He says, "We're giving you an Honorable Discharge. What do you think of that?"

What do I think of that? *I think I've been shorted two and a half years of indentured security. A minute ago I thought I knew where I was. And one sentence later, I suddenly have no job, no home, no bed, no food.* What are my thoughts?

"Does this mean I don't get lunch?"

2 ~ Jo-Jo

Shit! What the hell was that? God, I hate this crap. I'm asleep and now I'm awake but I'm really not awake. I have to move, but I'm not back in my body yet. Still somewhere out there in dream space. Now I'm being evicted from the shelter of sleep where I don't have to suffer the pangs of consciousness. I'm trying . . . but semi-conscious is as far as I can drag myself. Maybe because more than half of me doesn't want to go. The smarter half, no doubt. I'm still drunk. And just moments ago I was sublimely unaware of that fact.

RRIIINNNNGGGGG

Jee-zuss. *Shut up!* I'm doing the best I can to get myself out of this bed without killing myself. I can't see through my sleep-sodden eyelids, but I'm far from blind to my simmering anger at being rousted out of my numb mindlessness. I'm stumbling toward the kitchen where I seem to remember the goddamn phone is.

RRIIINNNNGGGGG

I'm not thinking yet, just reacting robotically to the blaring summons. But I've had so many different residences in the last twelve months, I'm not even sure where the hell the kitchen is. And it doesn't help that it's part of a great-room, so there aren't even any walls I can use to guide me along.

59

RRIIINNNNGGGGG

Alright – *I hear you!* And now I hear a thick squelching sound and feel – *what the fuck?* – hot fresh shit oozing on up through my naked and unsuspecting toes. If my toes don't know for sure it's shit, my nose does. I'm about to retch. Sonofabitch. *Now* I'm awake – and seething with anger at myself. I drank too much. I fell into bed too early. I caused myself to be incapable of hearing the dog when he scratched at the door because he needed to go out. I feel the punch of guilt at the guilt my dog must be feeling through no fault of his own.

RRIIINNNNGGGGG

Now I'm infuriated! I'm in no mood for this crap – and I just know this has to be a wrong number. Why else would God put that pile of shit there for me to step in?

RRIIINNNNGGGGG

All I want to do is to stick my dogshitty foot in a vat of scalding water – along with the head of the asshole on the other end of the line . . . who's probably going to hang up before I can find the friggin' phone.

RRIIINN--

Got it!

----- Yeah?

My what-the-fuck-do-*you*-want tone is answered by a mild "hi."

God -- it's Jo Ann. Just "hi" and I know it's her. For the last three minutes, I thought that damn RINGING was jangling every raw nerve all over my body and making mush out of my brain. Now – her voice, her "hi" – now my nerves are numb and I've got a skullful of scrambled eggs. Damn. Why the hell is she calling me? This year had been one of the long offs in our on again-off again . . . relationship? Is that what you'd call it?

60

Jo Ann. Numb is where I try to go when she gets into my head. The times I've risked being all fired up have always gotten me a good dousing. It's been ten years since the first time. Don't know that I've learned anything. I do know she's never been chit-chatty. I doubt she's calling me now to tell me her parakeet died. Whatever her reason, or whim, it better be good – it's got me standing here with shit all over my foot. Then again, when have I ever had a meeting of minds – or bodies – with her when I didn't find myself standing in shit.

All she said is "hi". She knows I know it's her. She's in no hurry to tell me why she called. She's letting her "hi" sink in, waiting for my response. What is she expecting?

All I say is -----   Jo Ann.

All she says is -----   I want to have a child by you.

Now I say -----   Jo-Jo . . . .

I very purposely call her that because I know she can't stand that handle. It's the name her father always called her. I don't really know what was up between the two of them, but it's enough that it pisses her off and I'm just in the mood to piss on her. This mood might be a long hangover from our last meeting. That meeting left me thinking there wasn't much chance or reason for us to be having another. Yet here she is on the phone saying "I want to have a child by you." I say

-----   I heard the words 'I' and '*by* you', but I didn't hear anything that sounded like 'us' or 'ours' or '*with* you.' As usual.

There's a long silence on the line. She's better at long silences than anyone I have ever known. This silence causes the darkness around me to become darker, the shit-smell ranker, my aloneness more lonely. I have to suppose that she knows exactly what she's doing and that she's deriving some warped sense of gratification from her cool control. Yeah, I got it. Well, let me speak on your behalf. I mean, on mine, in your stead. Just to hear a voice of some kind.

----- Look, Jo Ann, you're rocking my boat here. I guess you know that. Having a child with you – I say *with* – would be an answer to a dream for me. What can I say? I could say, what the hell took you so long? I've wanted that, wished for that, for years. Did you know that?

----- I guess I don't know what you knew. Or what you felt. What you did with me, what you said to me when we were together . . . I kept thinking it meant something. And every time you dropped me and I waited and you picked me up again – maybe I was a jerk for believing . . . for believing what you told me. So was there ever really any love there? What should I believe? You're calling me now . . . . Is there a limit you could maybe set on the number of times you break my heart? Or would that take the fun out of it for you?

----- Goddamn it, Jo-Jo. What the hell's up, anyway? What the fuck-over? Have a child by me . . . there's no way I'd ever agree to being an absentee father, a sperm donor. That *is* what we're talking about, isn't it? Forget about that. That's for damn sure not going to happen.

I can't help myself, not even in my want-to-punch-someone's-lights-out state. I love her and, like a dope, I'm seeing her naked in front of me. It's easy – I've been doing it for years in the absence of her. The image of her is ingrained in my heart and soul. Her body voluptuous, with just enough baby fat to give her unclothed charms the pretense of innocence. Her breasts round and full. Her deep brown eyes peer through the center part of her long straight black hair. There's a twinkle in her smile that always means something is up.

God, what the hell is wrong with me? I can't let her realize that I'm starting to cry. I can't give her to know that she has that kind of power. Her image is so real to me. I remember the first time I ever saw her naked. . . .

62

She leads me into a stand of pine and lays me down on my back. This isn't a bad thing, seeing that, between the drinking and the shit that just an hour ago unfolded, this night has pretty much left me a cripple. She's standing over me and, as she pulls her shirt up over her head, one of her breasts is silhouetted against the full moon, almost eclipsing it. I think this is supposed to be one of those once-in-a-lifetime moments. Funny, it doesn't feel that way. I know something's up, but I don't quite know what's happening or why. I'm still very much in the surreal aura of the scene we left an hour before. Now, in the tense hush of the woods at midnight, with a radiant goddess haloed in moonlight, I should be feeling some kind of thrilling sensation, I'm supposing, but the only thing erect around here are the trees. Maybe it's a combination of the events and the God-awful pin pricks of the pine needles in my ass that I'm finding so distracting. In any event, this isn't playing out like anything I would have imagined. I'm in no mood to enjoy the scenery, not Nature's or hers. Apparently, she wants to make love. Where the hell's this coming from? Not only is this something that was never ever going to happen, but didn't she just share the same experience that I did an hour ago? Where the hell is her head? She must be nuts or something, because the only thing I'm ready for is a good belt of booze and a few good belts that come with a straitjacket. I mean, you gotta be shitting me.

Yeah, I remember that night. We had been out and about, drinking, as usual, which is about all our relationship had boiled down to after our time in high school together – about a year and a half -- came to a close. Back in those days, she and I and a couple of other friends would hang out together in her basement playroom. She was a bit of a tomboy back then. Regardless of that, at some point a kind of passion started to rise in me, although it wasn't really sexual in nature, at least not in the nature of sex for sex's sake. It had a lot more to do with love, whatever *that* might have been. We tried the boyfriend/girlfriend thing, in title only, but that lasted all of two weeks. That didn't mean that I didn't remain smitten. What is it about first love that makes it so hard to get over?

I remember that I wasn't really feeling any sense of sexual frustration, though. I really didn't want much to do with sex at that time in my life. I was looking for a bond that went deeper than skin. Besides, hanging out with my godparents' older son and his gang, I was made aware of the darker side of sex. No one but no one was making noises like it was a really great thing. I heard girls ranking on the guys and regretting that they had become disrespected whores. The guys seemed preoccupied with whether they knocked someone up or not. It all just sounded like more of a hassle and embarrassment than it could be worth. Who needed that kind of shit? I was happy at the idea of waiting for a more meaningful and mature relationship. Happy little moron.

Then, after we both dropped out of school, independent of one another, we went our separate ways. I went to do my military service thing in North Chicago, and she, in Pleasantville, NY, took the fork in the road to drug addiction. For her, it ended badly. She had to be committed. For me it ended just as badly. I *should* have been committed. That aside, after getting out of the Navy, I took a good job as a manager of the Officers' Club back on base. With that and a good apartment in the next town, I couldn't say I really wanted for anything. But then again, I had always been such a good liar. Other than on the phone, there was no Jo Ann in my life. Bread without the butter. I made the attempt to be blind to myself but it really wasn't working all that well. There's no ignoring it. When your heart aches, it hurts. I didn't need much of an excuse to drop everything I had in hand in exchange for everything I believed I might have and hold, and so desired.

Jo Ann, on the phone, began hinting temptingly at what might have come of her desires for me had I only been there. At the same time, somehow, life on the base began losing its luster. My shiny future there as a manager dimmed in my mind as I observed what I could become in the two senior managers – fat, bald, single, and stuffing their faces with slabs of steak every night. Besides, my roommate's pool hall tussle with six low-on-scruples characters, ultimately involving guns and cops, added some urgency to the idea of getting away from that town. The idea of getting back to Jo Ann got the better of me. I threw caution and common sense to the wind that carried her siren song to my ears – I vacated my life as I knew it and flew to her side. Actually, given my fear of flying, I took an immeasurably slow Greyhound, seated with a mother and a child that never stopped bawling. It was the longest twenty-four miserable hours I ever spent. What the hell, though – what price love?

I might very well have saved myself the trip, not to mention the trouble of disrupting my life. The measure of one's sacrifice does not necessarily balance someone else's books. Apparently, my desires and expectations far outweighed and exceeded the reality of things to come -- or not to come. But, then again, I always had been a dreamer. Nothing to show for it, but what the hell. Is it possible that one man's dreams can be another's nightmare? Ask a stupid question.

I get off the bus in Pleasantville. At the very first sight of Jo Ann, I'm immediately propelled into sexual lust. That very thing I had always prided myself in avoiding. But I had been primed. While in the service, I had taken my first lover. In fact, I had come very close to marrying her. That's a little nugget that I use to tease Jo Ann with. Sort of a revenge/jealousy thing. Kind of a juvenile thing. Not unlike joining the Navy, taking a lover was calculated to somehow magically propel me into manhood. Both failed to produce the desired outcome and I came away from both failures as just an older kid. On the better side of things, I'm now less naïve and no longer a stumbling virgin. With the gate now open, I'm ready for the next giant step in my relations with Jo Ann. In typical male fashion, though, I never pause to measure the depth of my potential partner's want, or lack thereof. I don't bother to take the time to check to see if our timing is in sync.

There's a vast tract of land up by where she lives. A defunct estate where a new school is being erected. It's far out of view of the public eye. It's a perfect venue for what young people do when they're alone together in the dark. I have the whole in-the-dark thing down and I'm about to sharpen my alone skills as well. Jo Ann leads me there. This is my first dark-fall with her and I couldn't be higher if I were on drugs. As we're kissing, I start to thoughtlessly but passionately grope her. I'm meaning no harm, just riding on automatic pilot. Observing her reaction, I realize that she is considering this to be less than romantic. Her response is almost immediate -- she shuts me down on the spot, in the moment. I understand "no" when it hits me in the gut. You might as well tell a four-year-old that there will be no Christmas this year. Boo-hoo. Ain't that the shits. I didn't put all my eggs in the wrong basket, I missed the basket completely. I couldn't see this coming? Is this turn of events a temporary misstep or is it as permanent as my love lust for her? I'd given up everything in trade for this moment. It was supposed to be sublime, the first chapter in a tale that you know is going to end with happily ever after, with a feeling of finding home. Instead, I'm feeling lost and betrayed. I'm empty handed and broken hearted, a childless story book, a fairytale never to be

65

read. What could possibly lay before me?

Finally, now, Jo Ann speaks.

-----   I really wish you would reconsider. I really want to have your child. There's only one other person I would consider doing this with, so if you're not willing, it will have to be with him; but you're my first choice.

Oh brother! She's appealing to the old male ego thing. The old squeeze play to boot. I'm not buying into this shit. For the sake of the feelings I have left for her, I'm trying desperately not to let on to my fury, much less release it on her. Boy, am I burning! Somehow I need to put this back on her, where it belongs, before I explode.

-----   Jo-Jo, do you really imagine this thing you think you want to do is a good idea? Have you bothered to consider the amount of drugs you've done? And how many times did you drop acid? Do you think this is fair for the potential kid -- or monster that it might be?

-----   I know, but this is really important to me.

-----   And my child would be important to me as well.

I'm thinking of that other night, back in the pines. That shared experience should have been important -- to someone. Now it's dawning on me that I have to entertain the idea that the seduction that night might have been the first attempt at pulling off this bullshit. I guess that it was all about something that I had no idea about, and not at all about what I had passionately hoped and imagined was taking place. Something to do with actual love. Of *her* loving *me*. Wanting *me* – not something *from* me. I'd give anything for that night to not have happened at all. Hell, a million bucks for just being able to forget it, the final curtain on a really bad play gone worse.

After having had our little night out drinking, I'm driving her home, to her own bed, as usual. I'm feeling wanting for her as usual. The fact that I'm the conveyor isn't softening my disappointment any. It feels just like a trip to the vet when

66

you're putting a pet down. Never in my life have I ever been so tormented in the want of anything. Why can't I just make love to her, like I want to? What the hell is wrong with me that I'm so undesirable? How long can I endure these feelings?

It looks like I'll get a reprieve, of a few minutes anyway, when she asks me to take a detour to one of her friends' house. It's not anyone I know and she'll just be a minute but she asks me to come in with her anyway. It's a big lavish Westchester County antique home. A rich people's house. Nice if you can afford the trouble of it. Coming through the front door, we enter an expansive room with a large dining table centered to it. Around the table, like so many knights, are half a dozen teens, all staring across the table at one another like turkeys in the rain. Apparently they're not coping very well with the problems that come with being overly wealthy. I guess it's a good thing that they can afford the drugs to help them with this dilemma. They're stoned out of their collective gourds. Only the rich can afford to indulge in this shit as a sport. It beats watching football. I suppose.

Jo Ann takes me upstairs to one of the bedrooms and introduces me to her friend Collin. He appears to be our age and I figure he's the oldest brother to some of the floaters downstairs. Just as junked up, though, and probably just as depressed as I'm feeling. Maybe more so. He's fully dressed and languishing in his bed. The room is committed to darkness, which does little to disguise the disarray everywhere. It couldn't have been a more depressing scene. If I looked the way he did and was living in that shambles, I would kill myself, it was that depressing. I'm not sure how, but I'm drawn into having some few words with him -- or at him – not sparing the cruelty that is no doubt stemming from my self-loathing which I'm probably recognizing in him as a mirror image. I'm so totally devoid of mercy for the funk he's in and tell him so. A pleasant guest, I'm not. I'm uncomfortable as hell and can't wait to get out of here.

Now back downstairs and reunited with Jo Ann, we're ready to leave. She's probably procured her drugs. I'm sure, judging by the company, that's why we came to this particular house. As we're finally leaving, my attention is diverted by what I perceive as faint cries of distress. Although the murmurings are almost inaudible, there is something in the air and tone of them that sends a chill down my spine and causes the hair on my neck to stand on end. It's a pleading that evokes a sense of panic in my heart. As though I haven't been given any choice, I am picked up off my feet as if by a great vacuum and sucked up the stairs which lack any gravitational pull on me. I'm thrown into the bathroom where, to my

67

horror, I find Collin kneeling over a bathtub that is engorged with his brilliant scarlet blood. He had evidently sliced his forearm from wrist to elbow right down to the bone which now shines like a brilliant white neon light. Its immaculate gleam is in stark contrast to the deep red swelling evictions of flesh. Every red bloody fiber is unbound from its anchorage and spilling outward like a freakish tangle of snapped rubber bands. Suddenly there is only himself, no me; if I had been there I would have peed in my pants. This is one of those things I could have very happily gone my entire life without having to experience.

I'm outside my body. It's the only way I have of dealing with this horror show. I have to put my brain's air conditioner on high. It's imperative that I'm cool. I've already, without emotion, resigned myself to his loss due to the massive amount of blood loss. My sense of helplessness is not improved by Collin's repeated and wrenching cries of: "I didn't know it would be like this!" Well, ain't life just full of surprises. If he doesn't shut the hell up, maybe I'll let him bleed to death. This is hard enough without all the caterwauling. Any feelings aside, I have to be about the business at hand, but there is little hope or comfort in the knowledge that we are in the middle of nowhere and miles from anywhere; the chances of timely rescue seem remote, even if someone were able to locate our obscure address to begin with.

I scream for someone, anyone, to bring me the elements I need to make a tourniquet. Whoever is doing what, they aren't doing it goddamn fast enough. After an eternity of seconds, I take the fingers of Collin's good hand and press them down on major veins. I then run to the top of the stairs and peer down. Everyone is still waiting for King Arthur to show up. I return to Collin's side as Jo Ann meets me with some torn sheets. Using a toilet brush, I devise the tourniquet. Jo Ann goes and calls the cops.

As I busy myself with Collin's welfare, I desperately try to not see what I am seeing, while trying also to fend off his cries with the comforting thought that none of this is going to make any difference, that this whatever-portion-of-hell will probably not last much longer. One way or the other. As I escort Collin downstairs, a young officer comes through the front door. The kids seated at the table, if not still in another world, take no notice of either the cop or the bloody spectacle. However, the cop does, and faints dead over backwards, probably in an effort to not see what he was seeing. I scream to Jo Ann to call another cop and to be sure it isn't another rookie!

68

The ride to the hospital is better than any ride you could find at a carnival. My heart is in my throat the entire time; I keep asking the cop what time it is, I'm paranoid as to the length of time I have the tourniquet on. God, don't let us get this far to lose him now, I'm thinking to myself. I've had better nights than this, right? This can't be real. I just know I'm going to wake up any moment. Please, God.

We rush through the doors of the emergency room. Sitting in it is a mother and her young son; they look at us and turn white. I turn and look at Collin and down at myself -- it's hard to tell us apart and who's in need of attention. We're both just as blood-soaked. Judging by their faces, I'm thinking I don't have to apologize to the mom and kid for cutting in line. Next to review the incoming are a nurse and doctor, and they don't look any happier at seeing what they're seeing than that rookie cop did. I gladly hand off Collin and declare that I myself don't need treatment despite what I look like, unless this is a branch of Bellevue.

Jo Ann and I are taken to the police station where we have to relive our experience of the night on paper. Judging from Jo Ann's cool demeanor, I'm supposing that she's writing about her evening relaxing at the beach. As for me, the shock is finally wearing off and the jello factor kicking in. There were no allowances for falling apart in the real time of the event, but that's all changing now. I'm shaking so badly that I can hardly write. The police report to us that Collin is fine. He's conscious and even laughing about the experience. Laughing. Well, I'm glad he's over it. As for me, it's going to be a damn long while before I'm able to laugh about it. Centuries.

It is in this state of being emotionally hung over, not to mention suffering the effects of boozing most of the night, that I discover that Jo Ann considers this to be a good time to make love to me for the first time. I'm wishing that I could in some way take part in this plan, but that would mean being there and I just am not. I missed my birth as well. I surely hope I'm around for my death. I wouldn't want to be a three-time loser.

I tell Jo Ann

-----   I am just thinking about the night Collin tried to do away with himself – or, rather, what happened afterward. Where the hell did that lead to? After that night ended, you left me out in left field. I was left to marry someone who wasn't you. That wasn't very fair to my wife -- but I have to admit, that's on me. That marriage lasted all of a year and, if I remember correctly, we – you and I -- never even spoke to one another in that time. Did I ever tell you that she thought that I had cheated on her with you? I even admitted to it when she threw it in my face. It was a perfect excuse for ending a marriage I never really wanted in the first place because it wasn't with you! Do you have any idea how painful it's been to be in love with you? Ten years of first love. What's *that* about?

----- I'm sorry, it wasn't my fault.

----- Yeah, I know, but don't get the idea that you were totally guiltless in all this. When you heard my marriage broke up, you knew exactly what I wanted from my new-found freedom and you were just Johnny-on-the-spot with an invitation to come and spend the weekend with you. For what purpose? Sightseeing! According to you, that weekend was so heavenly that you demanded the next one as well. What did that do to my mind and heart? Did it ever occur to you to wonder, to imagine? Well, I'll tell you. You wanted me, and then you wanted me again. All I could conceive of was an eternity of weekends. But at the closing bell of the second, you kicked me in the balls. I was out with the trash like yesterday's paper. No reason, no fanfare -- just nothing.

----- I didn't mean to hurt you, I'm sorry.

----- Sorry, my ass!

I'm thinking of the passage of that next year. The one that came, the sun still rising every day, after those two weekends. Nights spent drinking excellent red wine and writing really lousy poetry about love lost. Shit, to lose it, don't you have to possess it first? Oh well, I guess a whipped dog just can't get enough of a good thing . . . .

Something is dawning in my head like the sun I've been ignoring – something about the passing of years and the holding out – or holding on – in the belief that this perseverance will be rewarded. I'm remembering . . . when I was a kid, I put a tooth under my pillow and the tooth fairy left me a silver dollar. If I had spent it then, I could have bought ten candy bars. But I was so in love with the coin that I'd held on to it all these years. Now, if I were to spend it, maybe I might be able to get two bars out of it. I'm pretty sure there's a lesson in there somewhere. I'm just on the cusp of figuring it out when she decides to stir the pot again. She doesn't have to exert a lot of energy, I'm waiting just below the surface of the skim. As some wise person said: "Beauty only lasts for so long, stupid is forever."

She calls and I answer. She's still in upstate NY so it's still quite the haul, eight hours' worth, but who counts the cost for a second chance of heaven. All my dreams come true again. The sex is great again. This time, I'm not going to make any mistakes. Maybe last time I appeared to her burdensome with the degree of devotion I showed. Perhaps I came across as being too needy of her. I'm a year older and wiser. This time I'm going to allow her her own space.

Jo Ann takes me to a wonderful park, just beautiful. I'm being very cautious not to crowd her. As much as I want to be forever near her, I give her as much space as possible. I let Jo Ann wander off by herself. I wander off myself, nearly off a great horseshoe cliff. It's a sheer drop of about two hundred feet -- no pauses no stops just straight down. I jump a split rail fence which is the only barrier, a poor one. I walk over to the very edge and plop down and swing my legs over the brink and dangle them into eternity. I know no fear; nothing can hurt me now. The world is my heaven, Jo Ann my Goddess. Luck my lady; no one arrests me. Besides, if something happens, like the earth beneath my ass giving way, this will be the last thing I see and, brother, what a view! I'm never going to see something this beautiful again.

That night we go to a bar. I'm shooting pool while on the juke box John Denver is belting out "Rocky Mountain High." Yeah, like being on top of that mountain, I am. Sing it, John! There's some dude trying to pick up my woman -- good luck with that. I know she knows she's got the best. It hits me then that, given what my life has been up to now, I have to figure that in reality I must have fallen off that cliff and now I'm getting to live my eternal reward. But what the hell do I know?

Now the second day of the second weekend of the second year comes to a close. The dawn comes. The cock crows. I'm vanquished with the rays of the new sun, like any other vampire. I'm dismissed. Again. No explanation. Again. I'm dazed

71

and confused. I cry to the point that the soles of my feet are drawn up to my mouth, having expended the entirety of myself. There are so many tears but they're all mine, none are hers. Can she be so heartless? What is this insane yo-yo type of love all about? What cruel game is being played out here? It's too otherworldly. It's like a nightmare I can't wake up from. It's too painful for even me -- I thought I had already experienced every pain conceivable. But what the hell do I know? It's too absurd. Someone has got to be yanking my shank!

I'm speeding down the NY Thruway just as fast as the traffic around me will allow. There are large mounds of snow roadside and high gusts of wind. Suddenly I'm enveloped in a whiteout. Minutes ago I couldn't see the end of the hood of my car through my tears, now I can't see beyond my windshield. It's okay, I don't need to see where I'm going anyway. There's no point in going anywhere anyway. Just as suddenly, I come out of the blind, just in time to see a bridge abutment dead ahead of me. That's okay too. I can die with that. I guess my car has other ideas - - I miss it by that much. Would you believe, THAT MUCH. Shit happens. Or not.

----- Yeah, I'm sure in your own way you're sorry. But I don't know where it can be coming from. Your heart is as cold as steel, your breasts as hard as cement. In fact, you could enter a pageant for the heartless and win the title of Miss Cement Tits of 1973.

Now there's a long silence. I'm hoping I said something to hurt her. As if she was movable. She never gives anything away, not through facial expression or voice inflection. I never saw her come close to shedding a tear -- or breaking out in laughter, for that matter. She was always even-tempered and cool under fire. Even during the episode with Collin, when I yelled for the things I needed -- even though she was looking right at what I was looking at, she handed me what I needed as though she was passing me a tray of cookies at a high tea. She is a great steadfast unmovable rock. A stone which I can't seem to remove from my shoe.

----- I'm sorry, Earl, I guess there's nothing more to say.

The hair on the back of my neck is standing on end. I still feel as if she is in total control. Don't I even get the last word? Can't I even insult her well? Above all the blathering in my head, *I finally get it!* I've been had. All those times together -- they were nothing but opportunities to get herself pregnant. To her, I was nothing more than a rooster to fertilize an egg. Next time I'm invited into the hen house, I'm going into it as a fox. I guess I don't have anyone to blame for my blindness but me. The crimes have been self-inflicted. Knowing that doesn't make it sit any better. Right or wrong, I'm still seething at her. Why did she allow me to struggle in the quicksand of my fantasy of her for so long? Where was the mercy?

----- No, I suppose not. I guess everything that can be said has been said. I guess everything that needed doing is going to be left undone. I've had it. I guess it's time to say good-bye. Good-bye.

I hang up the phone. The silence hangs over my head like a suspended anvil. The emptiness enveloping me is so vast and dark that I'm terrorized to move an inch this way or that for fear of disappearing into the void. Is the finality of it worse than having lived through it all? That will have to be answered another day, far, far away. I'm guessing I have to stop being in love with pain. I've gotten too used to it, rejection too. I'm guessing that the sick portion of myself was actually fooled into thinking that that was my health. Maybe loving her was just a symptom of my illness. Maybe the cure was not in obtaining her, but not wanting her in the first place. I guess she was the cherry on top of the ice cream soda that a diabetic has no business even thinking about eating. It's hard to admit, but I guess I trespassed on another's life with my own agenda as my supposed rights of passage. Lesson learned.

Oh! Shit! I can go wash my foot off now!

3 ~ Home is Where Your Feet Are

I shift my weight slightly to allow my back to conform to the contour of the deck chair, putting my feet up on the deck rail. The setting sun is looking very much like a giant glowing pumpkin suspended in the retiring sky -- just hanging out a little longer, like a kid on a summer evening pleading for just five minutes more after being called in. All the same, the sun's looking forward to a well-earned rest after a good day's work and a job well done. I share in its euphoric surrender. *I'm digging it, man. I'm with you, brother.* I reach down to grasp my evening scotch on the rocks, my reward for a day well spent. That is to say, I got through it, as boring as it might have been. The setting of the sun marks a new epoch of time. Time to drink. The glass is dewy with cold sweat; it feels good to the touch as well as to the taste. Lately, the glass is the only thing around here sweating, life is oh so – well, too goddamn comfortable. *God, if this isn't home, then I don't know what the fuck is.* Anyway, it damn well took enough time to get here. Let me see . . . in my childhood, I had four different residences. In my teen years, three. And after the Navy, seven. Now I'm damn well not going anywhere! Life in East Hampton is going to be the death of me. This is where they're going to have to bury me. After all, it doesn't get any better than this. It's the perfect place to be perfect in. Perfect people whose shit doesn't stink because no one around here shits. The land of the rich and beautiful. California can keep their forever young.

What is stupid good for, anyway? I've never known anyone who was young who wasn't stupid. Well, if I gave it any consideration, I guess I would have to say that, at my age of twenty-four, *I'm* young; but then, that's what the scotch is for. It allows me to not have to consider just about anything.

Thank God for my landlord, Hobby. Without him I would most assuredly be out on the street, again. I suppose in some small way, in some prior time that I've lost in the shuffle, I might have done some small good deed that kismet is now returning on me through the compassion of this man. No matter how self-impressed I feel or what I think myself entitled to, I'd be hard pressed to find myself on the better side of the cusp of bad alternatives without it. Being that I'm probably not the nicest guy in the world, I can thank my lucky stars that I'm here due to the thoughtfulness of someone who is. After all, if I ask myself what this man owes me, the answer would come up a lot shorter than the question.

I remember the first time I ever laid eyes on him. I have to say, I was immediately impressed. Some people, good or bad, just have an aura about them; Hobby's was more like a mini-universe -- and all good. If I didn't feel ashamed in that micro-instant, I most certainly did in the next full second. . . .

That was almost two years ago, in this very same house, when I was shacked up in it as the house pet of my then-current lover, Shari – who just happened to be Hobby's most recent ex-lover after a twelve-year co-habitation. *Just happened to be*, that's rich. Shari only operates by design. That night, her design was for me to be useful to her in her scheme to show the man up by showing me off. Off is exactly what I was -- really pissed off. About the show. Like if someone takes you to a burlesque theater, which you think you might enjoy – until you find yourself being shoved out onto the stage. No, I was not enjoying the show. It was called *If You Show Me Your New Lover, I'll Sure as Shit Show You Mine.* I sort of felt like the shit that was being flung in the face of a man I was just meeting. Meeting, yeah – but for Shari it wasn't an introduction she was arranging, it was a flaunt.

But it *was* my introduction to how crazy – and crude – Shari could be. How she could throw the unexpected at you in a way that could be really scary. At that point, I was thinking I had really stepped into it. Yeah, I was hungry, and it was her table. I was smart, I thought, but she was twice my age and twice as experienced in the game, and we were playing with her dice. The house always wins.

It was Easter Sunday and Shari had decided to hold court. The honored guests: all the exes with all their currents. Sounds like some kind of freaking game show. To Shari, it *was* a game. I was seated next to her on the couch when she spotted Hobby coming up onto the deck with his newly-acquired -- and, I guess, enviably exotic -- Chinese gal, Joan. Shari was quick to grab me by my hair and unceremoniously thrust my head into her lap where she kept it restrained, with some force, from raising. Maybe this was the natural place for me, being the pet I was. And this was the position I was in when I was presented to Hobby. In that instant, my mind's eye took in the benign radiance of the man. And the bizarre and pathetic picture I must have made (God only knows what expression of astonishment and shame my face was showing, sideways). And the black-haired spawn of Marlene Dietrich and Count Dracula who was pressing my noggin against her thighs. The rest of my mind could only grasp at the thought: *What the hell am I doing here? How did I get myself into this freak show? Am I a man or a* . . . even an organ-grinder monkey has more dignity.

Next in the receiving line came the queen-of-the-night's millionaire ex-husband (the one before Hobby), Hans, with *his* newly-acquired, young-enough-to-be-his-granddaughter trophy wife, Camille. A real blonde's blonde. Showing as much breeding as Shari is accustomed to keeping under wraps, she comes running over and, without need of an introduction, plops her ass down on Shari's other side and starts right in with *her* version of show and tell. Pulling up a showy pendant from its berth on her generous chest, she spouts: "See what Hans gave me for Easter?" Shari smiles back smugly. Then, reaching down to the coffee table, Shari picks up the identical piece of jewelry. Almost identical, Camille's piece consisting of one jewel-encrusted half-moon, and Shari's of three. The queen of the house now spits back, in a regal voice with overtones of cat-call: "See what *Earl* got *me* for Easter?" Now, I'm secretly laughing up my ass. That very morning, I had ducked into the local pharmacy for some cigs. The shop also served as a kind of general store with a lot of shit you wouldn't expect to see in such a place. I spotted the jewelry at the last moment. The first piece I picked up was the single-tier piece; then I reconsidered and bought the high-end version out of the three

76

designs available. Brother, I would have given anything to be the framed first nickel he ever earned hanging on Hans's wall when Camille got hubby home that night.

That was the first, middle, and last ha-ha-ha moment I had in my tenure as court chimpanzee. Mostly, I was feeling very much the thrall -- not a sexual one, as I had reason to believe I would be, but rather more in the role of a band-aid for Shari's bruised ego. Of course, having a second source of revenue available to her, from my fast-emptying pockets, gave Shari an additional motive for keeping me around. It would have been nice if I might have received some small benefit from the use of my own funds, but what Shari didn't drink went for food and drink -- mostly drink -- for the neighboring clan of Bonnakers that passed through our twenty-four-hour revolving door.

A few months into this co-habitation . . . then a few months more . . . I was feeling like a one-trick pony in a three-ring circus stuck in a long engagement at a funny farm. The pervading lunacy was kick-started, like clockwork, every morning at 4 am, with the shrieked command: "Get up! Get up! I'm not going to have any fucking dead bodies laying around the fucking house all day long!"   And that was the bright spot of the day, the sunrise over the land of quicksand and lye where it rained shit. *What in the Sam Hill did I get myself into and where the hell is the exit?* Oh; that's right. That's the way I came in – on the exit ramp from my life-so-far. The life that, at least, used to belong to me. As scruffy and aimless as it was – at least I didn't have to take cover from incoming barrages of loony flak or unpredictable assaults with a deadly sewer-mouth. A three-bedroom asylum was proving itself just too small to hide in. One nut per shell; that's all God ever intended. I really needed my own shell.

What the hell happened? The move-in with Shari was supposed to be a move up and onward. If there's a big brick wall across the path, why is it so hard to see before we bash our skulls against it? In my life-before-Shari, I was just minding my own business, living my life as the loser I thought I was. All it took was a blindfold, a few steps . . . and here I am. As long as I've got the blindfold, is there anyone around who can shoot me?

My friend George used to try to drive the point home with me that it's alright to run away as long as you know where you're running to. Running out of a burning house and straight into the swamp hardly qualifies, I'm thinking. Isn't it ironic that this mad dash into quicksand all started at George's house, and it wasn't even on fire.

At the time it all started, I was adrift from my short stint in the service, my misguided and dragged-out attachment to my first teen-aged crush, and, most recently, my divorce from a marriage that had lasted all of a year – after which I had remained in the shitbox home I had bought for the purpose of living happily ever after in with my new bride, in a shithouse town in Connecticut where I apparently was never destined to find a comfortable footing. That misfortune made itself known right off the bat when I first moved in and invited the neighbors over for a friendly let's-get-to-know-one-another drink and/or dinner, and they RSVPed, "Sorry, we don't do that kind of thing around here." Yeah, this *here* sure as hell wasn't anything like my previous *there,* a happier Connecticut town where I had last parked myself. Shit, I was just trying to be friendly. Back in Norwalk, whenever I wanted to have a party, I just went out onto the main route and flagged down Volkswagons. I invited the occupants in and we had some great times.

Now the only good times to be had were at George's house, in Norwalk. One night he was throwing a small party, with some of his NY friends and colleagues as well as neighbors invited. It must be nice to have neighbors who don't swear at you on sight, I thought. Not being the biggest social bug when it came to a room full of strangers -- especially ones of evident means, unlike myself -- I was happy to be relegated to the post of chef for the evening. In this simple and innocent act, in agreeing to participate in a social gathering, how could I possibly have understood that I was actually applying for a passport to a place where sanity is considered excess baggage. That is, Shari's world . . . .

Happily alone, downstairs, slaving over a hot stove, I'm tending to my white sauce when I begin to get the skin-crawling feeling that I am being stared at by a middle-aged vamp. She is spending an uncomfortable amount of time posing there, with her nose pointed in my direction. I'm pretty sure a white sauce isn't all that intriguing and starting to feel that it isn't just the skillet that is getting over-heated. Trying to pretend I'm not aware of this femme fatale's presence is becoming ridiculouser by the second, but I still do my best to not make eye contact with her. The Medusa legend is slithering up my spine.

Then she speaks, pointedly: "Do you really think that sauce needs so much attention?" I may be stupid when it comes to the way women think, but that line pretty clearly translates into: "Pay attention to me." Uh-oh. Where's my mirrored shield?

Even in my peripheral vision, I could see that that throaty voice was coming from a woman who was used to being paid attention to. She vaguely carried off that slink that models display while, unlike their sister snakes, remaining upright. It seemed like second nature – maybe first nature – to her. As I was to learn shortly, thirty years earlier she, at sixteen, had been the highest paid model in the world as well as, reputedly, the most beautiful. What the Lord giveth, time and ouzo will take away; which is not to say that she still wasn't a good-looking specimen in the Audrey Hepburn mold. Anyway, she made quite a first impression on my impressionable state of mind. Her thin but shapely form was disguised by a long-sleeved red pullover and blue overalls that were anchored by subtly stylish brown boots. She was capped by short jet-black hair which looked as though it was in search of a style. But, I suppose, in the eyes of some, that in itself was a style. Her sharp black eyes were sunken but had not surrendered their dissecting ability. Whatever she *had* been, she was no ingenue, and her life-worn voice was low and gruff with self-importance and the memory of adulation. She certainly was the whole package – delivering itself to my doorstep. Damn! Nothing was going on, as far as I was concerned, but just the same I was feeling way in over my head. Kind of like falling asleep on the beach and having the tide come in over you, and you don't have a clue how to swim.

Taking a hint from my own premonitions, I sought cover by engaging the lady-chigger's best friend, Annie, whose presence seemed more astral than physical in nature. At any rate, I spent the rest of the evening keeping myself out of Shari's claw-length. Boy, was I callow. While I was busy avoiding Shari's frying pan, Annie was measuring me up for her fire. With the dinner party ending, most of the guests left, with the exception of the two ladies, who were planning to bunk at the neighbors'. Having finished the last of the booze in the house, the merry quartet of George, Shari, Annie, and my laughably ingenuous self decided to go out and close a few bars. We lost George in one of the gutters, and the two ladies turned to me for their solace. I obliged them both for some hours until my solace-ability ran dry. Now I had done it. I had sown the seeds of my new identity. I would become Shari's official boy-toy – innocently enough, you could say. Yeah, innocent, as in clueless.

What I didn't know at the time – well, one of the things I didn't know – was that Shari had her sights set that night on snagging a prize catch that she could trot out when it came to that inevitable showdown featuring the exes and their current trophies. How she lured me in to become an unwitting player in her little production was by suggesting that I would be far better off moving in with her in her East Hampton home, sharing the Artist's Life together, than gathering moss where I currently was, which was: stuck in the muck like a rotting log. With Shari, of course, this wasn't exactly a suggestion – more of a pronouncement. I couldn't disagree – with her, or with the fact that I was miserable. Whatever turns I had taken along the way, my life had become, it felt to me, a dead-end road, and I had come to a stop in a blind alley. The view outside my window, on my wooded lot in Bushy Hollow, Connecticut, looked to me like a brick wall.

I wanted to get back into the real world, my world, as I remembered it. Or, at least, the parts of it that I wanted to remember. It hadn't been all that long ago that I had been living in Fairfield County and working in NYC as an executive. *How* I came to be there doing that is another story. . . that I don't want to think about right now. And I'd begun to get the lay of the land in the NYC art scene. I'd been painting since I was a little kid; in my teens I'd found my canvases were selling – maybe in a small-town way, but I saw – or, at least, envisioned – my path ahead. And then my feet took me one way and another – into beat-up woods-wandering old shoes, Navy boots, polished wing-tips – until they stumbled into this stinkhole closed in by a brick wall. So, now barefoot, I saw where I had ended up: during and after my short-lived marriage, I had blossomed into nothing but a country-bumpkin artist – if, under that label, I could call myself an artist at all. That was my hat, though, and I couldn't even find a damn hook to hang it on. Now, I had seen a painting hanging on Shari's wall, evidence that she had, in fact, wielded a brush and palette. She *looked* artsy. And, clearly, she was worldly, and knew her way around – and people in – more than one city out there. I could put in with her. I had heard of young artists coming up by this route. Sharing her house sure as shit beat holing up by myself in Bushy Hollow. What did I have to lose? That answer seemed obvious. The more interesting question was – what did I have to gain?

BOB: Alright, Jack, let's tell Earl what we have for him behind Curtain Number One!

80

JACK: That's right, Bob! It's what we like to call The Whole Package. No one has seen a deal like this since – who was that gal, Bob?

BOB: Pandora, I think, wasn't it?

JACK: Right you are. And Bob, I was told that this package has some brand new items that weren't even *in* Pandora's box. Earl is in for some exciting surprises when he gets home with this, don't you think?

(The audience roars. Kind of like the old crowd at the Colosseum.)

And so it was written. And God spake unto the lamb and said: "Go forth into the land of the insane and know that the purpose of your blood- and wallet-letting is for the sake of the manic-depressive, and that your sanity, money, and life have not been taken in vain." At least that's probably the view Shari was taking when I put my ass in her hands. And her middle name wasn't All-State.

What was her story, and how would my chapter in it fit into the plot? These were naturally questions that occupied my thoughts during the lulls between Shari's employment of me as her pillow, to weep on or knock the stuffing out of. These lulls occurred mostly when she was sleeping. One question that kept needling my brain was why someone of Shari's evident wealth and worldliness would be interested in a sprout like me. I put the question to George. He had known Shari forever.

Disappointingly, he took no time to ponder. He answered on the spot: Shari was not interested in me. What? I wasn't a diamond-in-the-rough, a budding artistic talent she could cut and polish and introduce to the world? No, the world, in Shari's book, was about Shari. That was a world in which Shari, as Coco Chanel's favorite model, had once been a figure of some fame. She had jet-setted and soiréed, George informed me, in circles that included such notables as Robert Graves and Vladimir Nabokov (like those names rang any bells in my little closet of a universe). No, I wasn't being groomed by a discerning patroness to make my debut in society's ballroom. George seemed to get a kick out of letting me know this. Any fairy-godmother-type scenarios, evidently, were being plotted only in my imagination; I was beginning to perceive myself as a pair of brown loafers trying to crash a black-tie world.

81

And it got even more pathetic as George assured me that my only function, for Shari, was to keep Hobby from thinking he had one-upped her. Shari, I was pretty sure, was the only one who would imagine that Hobby would expend any time thinking that. But if that really was my only function, why was I still here? And why would I want to be?

It was too late to second-guess my decision to throw in my lot with this crazy bitch. Sometimes I felt as though I had spent my last dollar booking passage on the *Titanic*. Sometimes I felt like I wanted to yell down from the top of the roller coaster, "I changed my mind – I want to get off!" I had nothing like a parachute, so I was stuck on the ride – up and down, up and down – absolutely fucking nuts. Strapped in with Shari, screeching around the track at manic speed.

The only reprieve from this surreal and maddening monotony was the occasional visit to the homes of other people who were more normal, or when we went out in public among the more normal, or when we had the occasional guests who were more normal – though few ever stayed overnight. Most were well-seasoned acquaintances with good memories, I'm guessing.

One brave soul was a city dweller and longtime friend by the name of Don. He seemed normal. That was a good start, and I welcomed the fact that he would be staying for at least a couple of days. Maybe he and I could take turns keeping the lid on the can of shit. We'd be the odd-couple partnership, though. He looked to be in his mid- sixties. He was so trimly-groomed and well-spoken that I felt embarrassed at my own sense of not measuring up. It was kind of like having a conversation with someone from England – afterward, you come away thinking: what the hell have I been speaking all these years? Overall, he seemed imposing, but not at all intimidating. He was a very large man – *very* large, without seeming obese. He had a full head of silver hair which he wore slicked back. But it struck me that there was something youthful about him, a boyish quality that twinkled in his ingenuous smile. Like most good and faithful drinkers, he was led about by an oversized red lantern, a W. C. Fields proboscis. This didn't seem to bother him. In fact, he seemed very much at ease with himself and, therefore, with the world in general. I found myself liking the man, despite my sense of feeling inferior. I knew that he was far more accomplished in everything than I was – including drinking. Where he was a card-carrying union member of the Happy Drunk Club, I was a measly scab.

82

As it turned out, though, my enthusiasm for this gentleman's visit wasn't very long lasting. The problem was, he was quick to get a snootful. Although he never lost his pleasant demeanor -- in fact, being snookered seemed to heighten his congeniality -- it wasn't long at all before Tinkerbell came flying out in search of a playmate. Normally, I don't give a shit as to what people are – as far as their sex or sexual preference, that's their business. But it really pisses me off when someone tries to envelop me in it, especially when I've spelled out the word "no" -- and politely at that, such as in "no, thank-you." I didn't really care if he was as gay as a football bat or related to Walt Disney; but his behavior was stretching the limits of my tolerance. Really, my coping abilities were being stretched from both ends. I don't like being put upon and I don't like being rude. The more Don cozied up to me, the more I struggled to keep my teeth-gritting attempts at polite responses from sounding curt. I was bristling; Don was chuckling. The more frustrated I became in my efforts to keep him at bay while yet not offending him, the more funny he thought the whole thing was. While I was thinking I had been reaming him a new one, he was evidently enjoying it. Well, yeah, I guess that would be right up his . . . alley.

Then, as roller coasters eventually do, the joyride I was on did a quick loop-the-loop and came to a screeching halt. One day, Shari decided to move to Spain. She had friends there who helped her find a house on Mallorca, and I was expected to trot along with her. Thinking back on it now, I suppose the house didn't come with servants, and I would do until she could hunt some up. But it sounded like a good idea at the time. Compared to my other options which, as far as I could see, were . . . going back to my house in Bushy Hollow. I figured I was young and resilient and ready to try anything. Why not Spain? A new and different experience. Cosmopolitan. A budding artist on the world's doorstep. I sold my house. I could pay my way to a new life and, I figured, maybe the crazy bitch would drop dead once we got there. Instead – *screech* – she showed up one day with a smooth-faced fourteen-year-old boy. He got the ticket to Spain, and I got the boot in my withered twenty-four-year-old ass. So now what? Only the final scene had to be played out before I was no-ifs-ands-or-buts cast adrift.

The stage-set and props were ones Shari had used before – the ones that brought down the curtain on her cohabitation with Hobby. I heard the story from Don, who had been there for the act. One day, Don said, Hobby woke up and saw that all the knives in the house had been laid out on the nightstand next to the bed. He asked Shari about it, and she told him: "I was up all night, thinking of killing you." Hobby casually lifted his morning glass of scotch, toasted Don with it, and asked him: "So, what do you want to do with the rest of this day?" After which, Hobby packed his bags and left. Don never said what Shari was doing when he and Hobby walked out the door.

I guess she'd had time now to work on her act. She did like knives. She had no shortage of them and, at some point every day, could be seen, in evident orgasmic pleasure, cutting up lemons or limes – *whack, whack.* Practicing castration, no doubt. So now it was my turn to exit stage left. Shari was at the ready. She let loose with a shrieking rant of unkind epithets, backed by her steely ordnance. When I was about fifteen feet from the door, she screamed: "Get the fuck out of my life!" and, to make her point clear, threw a kitchen knife at my back. I obliged her fury by turning to face her. I'm not one to carry scars on my back. Once she had depleted her arsenal of twenty-something knives without succeeding in doing me more harm than hurting my feelings, I bid her adieu, and my dog Jocko and me, myself, and I strolled off into the September fog. No sunset included. No luggage. A scrap of dignity. Screw the bitch.

After a mile or so walk to town, I paused in the center, on the East Hampton green. It was the first moment I really had to think, or react to what had just happened. The rain was light, but steady; so was the temperature: cold. I have to say, my mind's temperament was a little bit warmer, like the heat that emanates from hell. At that moment, I could well understand why people kill one another in domestic disputes. But I had more pressing issues that over-rode any emotional quandaries, like getting my ass out of the rain. And then – what was I supposed to do? Where the hell was I supposed to go?

I looked down at Jocko, who didn't appear to be suffering to the same degree I was. In the immortal words of Hobby, I asked him: "Well, what do you want to do with the rest of this day?" Jocko looked up at me quizzically. I hated like hell to have to admit it, but having the company of my best friend of five years made me far worse off than I'd have been on my own. This wasn't the first time I had found myself in no-man's land,

84

but it was the first where I was saddled with an impediment in the search for food and shelter. It didn't help any that I was in a totally foreign environment. Knowing my brain could only follow my feet, and seeing where my feet were, I had to consider the idea that I was in a world of shit.

What the hell, let me bury reality and just take a walkabout and enjoy the scenery; maybe I'll trip over a solution. That stroll didn't last long. I decided that something a little more in the way of concrete planning should replace my water-soaked wishful thinking. I just happened, then, to stroll past Hans's house. Oh! There's a nice enough fellow, I'm sure he'd be willing to help me out. *Are you shitting me?* What was it? How had George described him? A German Jew who wore leather underwear and was an international gun runner who sold arms to the Arabs because they paid more than the Jews. *Yeah, I'm sure that's the right door to knock on . . . .*

At least he let me get as far as the kitchen table. While I sat there crying, Camille caressed my head with her hands almost lovingly, while Hans grabbed the phone as if the house were on fire: "I'll call Shari's mother, she's a good Catholic woman, she'll know what to do with you." He packed me into the car and brought me to her house. It was odd, I thought, that after almost two years of living with Shari, I'm just now hearing that not only is her mother living but in the same town. Or the fact that she even *had* a mother. The only time she mentioned a parent was when she repeatedly conjured her father: "I'd like to dig him up and kick him back into his grave!"

It was an odd way to be introduced, if not downright embarrassing. Yeah, she was a good Christian, one of the first I ever met. She was actually willing to go out of her way for a total stranger. She gave me a warm bed. I got under about six blankets, trying to shake the goddamn chills. It wasn't enough blankets. My body was shaking so badly that I couldn't bring myself to cry. All my energy was in the shaking and all my thought processes in the toilet. Anyway, my respite didn't last very long. Soon Shari appeared at the bedroom door: "Get the fuck out of my mother's house!" I knew, from sad experience, she was not to be trifled with. Out I went, back into the unmerciful wet and cold world.

What the hell -- what worked with one good Christian should work with another. I decided to put my wet agnostic tail between my shivering legs and proceed to throw my fate into the winds of Christian charity. I set out to make the rounds of all the churches that surrounded the town green.

The nice thing about living in an exclusive town: they don't have any needy people. I guess that's because they don't go out of their way to welcome them. Either that or they don't have a clue as to what needy is. No one was looking to be educated. I found no food, shelter, or absolution beyond one clergy member letting me borrow a cot in a garage for a half hour. *Gee, are you sure I didn't overstay my welcome? I'd hate like hell to put you out.* So, I'm turned out, back into the rain again, empty-handed, stomach empty as well, and blessing-free. I mean, no one was giving anything away.

And so it came to pass, with Shari having made sure she had utilized my last dime before turning me out, that I found myself, like all beggars, at the back door of a likely place to beg for a scrap of food – which, in this case, was a pizzeria. Casting off the very last vestiges of dignity, I knocked at the door. A young Hispanic man answered the call. I was thinking to myself, how lucky. *He'll* probably have some understanding of my displacement, since he probably feels like an outsider himself. Always ask a poor person when in need, I say; they know what trouble is and are far more likely to help. Still, it never hurts to look respectable. So I pulled myself up and put on my best manners. I humbly explained to the young man that my dog and I were homeless and hungry; that I was endeavoring to procure some small amount of sustenance for my dog: "Perhaps you may have a meatball that fell on the floor?" While the pizza lad went back inside, I assured my salivating companion that I would naturally give him the lion's share of the hoped-for morsel.

When the kid reappeared after a small eternity of time, he was holding the biggest goddamn meatball grinder I had ever laid my eyes on. To my voracious peepers, it seemed to hang out a foot in each direction from his hands. I was ready to fall down on my knees and kiss his feet, when he bent forward and let Jocko daintily glom the whole freaking feast from his mitts. As I stood there drooling, and the damn kid laughing, Jocko made not the slightest effort to save even the smallest crumb of bread for me. I can remember murmuring something about *man's best friend.* I think I murmured for some hours to come. There's an old saying in Germany, George told me: "Hat in hand and a smile on your face, you can cross the land and never be hungry." Why the hell don't more Germans own pizzerias?

Now reckoning that I'd pretty much exhausted all possibilities -- in a sane world, anyway – I started thinking along the lines that I might very well have to do something illegal. But what? *I know -- I'll go ask a cop.* I remembered when I was a kid and used to watch the Abbott and Costello show. At the end of one of their skits they said that a policeman is your friend; never run away from one, always run toward one, he's your friend and he's there to help you. *Well, right about now, I'm not feeling much larger than a kid.* Besides, all that Christian bullshit I learned, about extending a loving hand, sure as shit didn't pan out. *What have I got to lose?*

I walked into the police station and approached the desk sergeant, wearing my best humble face. I inquired as to what minor misdeed one would have to commit in order to secure some city-subsidized housing. Either he thought I was fucking nuts or he didn't know what the hell I was talking about. Maybe it was the language. I was just making an effort to sound East Hamptony. Frustrated with his lack of a response, I started looking around for a brick that I might throw through a window. He finally got it and offered me the free use of the phone. That was the most generous offer of the day. I called George, George being the only person I knew who might give a shit. As I was pleading my case, I got the distinct sense that he didn't. In typical George fashion, he was merciless, and the only help he could offer was the suggestion that I call Hobby. I didn't say a goddamn word in return. That idea was about as good as the notion of standing in front of The Wall and screaming out that the Viet Nam war was a crock of shit. See what that will get you.

For God's sake, how can I be so lost? I'm twenty-four, the oldest I've ever been in my life -- at what point do I reach manhood? I wasn't this fearful when I was six months old; when I cried, someone came. Well, that's the only thing keeping me from being hysterical now -- I know goddamn well, no one will come and I would just drown in my tears. What the fuck am I supposed to do? No one trained me for this shit, and how is it that, after all these years, there's no one who can help me. In point of fact, if I'm supposed to be such a man, why do I need help from anyone in the first place? Is family the only friendly thing out there that anyone can fall back on? In that case, good fucking luck to me on that score. Ain't got it, never had it! What the fuck-over, I guess I'm just supposed to lay down and die. If I do, I wonder if anyone will take notice. Okay! I give up!

I brewed. I simmered. I stewed. I procrastinated. When you get hungry enough, you just take your shoe off and eat it. Why wait? Why put yourself through the discomfort of waiting for the end. Just bring it on and get it over with. Close your eyes. Shoot your wad. How painful can it be? *Maybe I should call George back.* Maybe in my telling of the tale, I was too vague.

Maybe the tone of my plea was too disguised. Maybe I was right, maybe he just doesn't give a shit. Yeah, maybe I *should* call Hobby. It can only lead to nowhere and I'm already there. In the middle of it. What's the worst that's going to happen? He's going to hurt my feelings?

After all, all I'm really doing if I place this call is admitting to being a bigger asshole than he already thinks I am. Is there really any true harm in truth? Well, no matter which way I might look at it, it's going to be a shameful call. Maybe I *was* feeling just a little too big for my britches. It's okay to be taken down when you deserve it. If I'm a pathetic asshole, then I'm an asshole. I've got time to get over myself.

Hello, Hobby, this is the big screwed-up asshole. That's about all I can remember of my abhorrent self-abashment. What I will never forget is Hobby's shockingly unhesitating response to my plight. He welcomed me with open arms and a safe haven in his own home. I was seized with humility.

Prior to all this shit unfolding – I mean before I physically moved in with Shari -- when I told George of my intentions to do so, the first words out of his mouth were: "You'll like Hobby." *Who the hell is Hobby?* Now I know. If you think of humanity in the form of a hand, then Hobby's the thumb. Stout, strong, and industrious. A retired Marine Captain and then a business and building developer while actively avoiding retirement. His graying hair speaks of his accomplishments, not the least of which was raising five children, before the one he had with Shari. His charming smile expresses his good humor, which is more tolerant than imaginable when it comes to overlooking the intolerable and non-sensible. *Oops, no egg on my face.* I guess, in my eyes, that makes him one of the most accountable and steadfast souls I've ever encountered. When I grow up, I want to be just like him.

Of course, not having a dime to my name and Hobby living an hour away was some little impediment. I wasn't going to stretch my impudence with *can you come pick me up? Hello? Hello?* No, even I wasn't that goddamn stupid. Fortunately for me, the cop behind the desk overheard the problem I was hashing out with myself and was able to set me up with a loan of fifty bucks for cab fare. Sometimes, just sometimes, I think that people just might be alright. Maybe from now on I can be a little more comfortable in the space where I am, which is not to say it's where I'm supposed to be, but it may be a good starting point.

An hour in traveling time. Didn't seem like much time when it came to counting my fucking lucky stars. But way too much time to have to wallow in regretting the goddamn mess I'd gotten myself in. A really hard balancing act to pull off. For every good thought I could come up with, a bad one would pop up and try to castrate it. How big was the man Hobby to take in not only a total stranger that he really didn't know from Adam, but an asshole whose very appearance in his life had been for the purpose of somehow showing him up. Rubbing shit in his face. And what the fuck was I? How small -- a defrocked lover begging on his doorstep. Life as I had known it, or expected it to be, was all but over. Just waiting for the funeral. During this very long and shameful ride, the constant ringing in my ear woke me up to the reflection of just how ego-laden I'd been, how wrapped up in self-involved fantasy. What a smack in the face. Hell, I wasn't anything near what I had imagined myself to be. Either I had spent too much time around myself or with the wrong people. I was beginning to realize just how defensive I had become and the false image of character I had built around myself in an effort to belong. To belong *somewhere*. I never bothered to ask myself if where I was was the right place to be, I just put on whatever necessary skin I needed in order to pass. What a shithead.

The wheels of the cab go 'round and 'round. Like my thoughts, spinning insistently, searching for something, like meaning, like purpose, but going in circles. A shithead on spin cycle. While going 'round in my head like this, I bump into another shithead. The last time I saw him was on a NYC bus, and now the scene replays in my mind. I give this film my full attention. It's a welcome distraction from the re-runs of myself I've been sitting here watching. Let someone else play the lead, it might be entertaining. The scene comes into focus . . . .

There I was, part of the audience, seated behind a teen-aged couple who were engaged in conversation. That is, the young lady was. I could instantly see that she might as well be trying to engage an 8 by10 glossy. I'm sure she had one of this guy at home; I'm guessing quite a few girls did. This girl was apparently hot to trot and this guy wasn't giving her the time of day in return. He was just all too satisfied with the attention she was lavishing at him. Just silently soaking it all in. Just too cool. God forbid, if he opened his mouth, he might let on to the fact that he was something other than what she thought he was. I guess there's something to be said for imagination. The poor young lady was bowing and scraping for some small crumb of recognition that evidently was not going to be in the offering any time soon. If at all. With every pleading for a future meeting -- whether in person or, at least, on the phone -- she was answered by his cool silence. *Better rely on the 8 by 10, honey,* I'm thinking. In his weaker moments, or maybe his magnanimous ones, the cool dude would answer with a "maybe" or "we'll see". His moon-eyed date's imploring went on forever – or, at least, longer than I could stand. Thank God, we came to his stop. He stood up without giving any further acknowledgment to his girlfriend and proceeded to take a step forward, right into some slush on the bus floor. *Whap!* Down he went on his ass. He spryly jumped up in less than half the time it took to fall. Maybe so fast that his partner never noticed the break in his iconic majesty. Either way, he carried on with his austere deportment as if nothing had happened. As he was exiting the bus, I could see the eyes in the back of his head searching the girl's face, trying to second guess his stature and standing in the eyes of the young lady. Did she see or did she not see, that is the question. Is it nobler to pretend, or should I just commit suicide?

And *whap* – here I am on my ass, wishing I could believe that no one had seen me trip over my own feet. What can I possibly say to Hobby? How can I even protect *myself* from the image of myself? I had thought that being caught with my head in Shari's lap was the most embarrassing moment in my life. How about having it up my own ass? I knew from past experience that eating crow was never a pleasurable howdy-do, literally or figuratively. Fortunately for me, while seated at Hobby's table of hospitality, no fowl was served. When it came to Hobby's manners, he was apparently a vegetarian. I guess I can live with that.

Talk about fitting into a world that you have no business in. I might as well have landed on Mars. This was Hobby's planet and I was the alien. I'm sure Hobby would have been entitled to feel guiltless in sticking me into the boathouse or attic or even a closet. What he did offer me, far beyond any of those options or my desserts, was normal space and socialization. My new situation was, in some ways, pretty close to heaven, although I wasn't in the frame of mind to fully appreciate it that way. I was gingerly walking on egg shells while in search of my identity. Was I a guest? A ward? A keepsake? A charity? Not exactly the kind of shit you want to bring to the dining room table as dinner conversation. So, not knowing what to say, I said nothing. That was like having an eternal gulp in the throat that I didn't know what to do with. It's not as if Hobby didn't know who I was or where I came from -- so what was I doing there? He didn't have anything better to do than put himself out? Hell, maybe he *was* just that kind of nice guy? That sure as shit was a nice I had never run across in my life before. I have to say that, even with the passage of time, I never was able to swallow that gulp. But the verification of his niceness was certainly forthcoming by way of the flow of humanity that passed through his door, both family and friends; lots of friends. It seemed all the world knew and loved the man. A nice planet to live on. Maybe someday I can work my way up from being an alien.

Perhaps Hobby saw some small thing in me and my situation that fit into his world-view, a test for his philosophy: "Nothing's never for nothing." I was quick to grab on to that one. I got it and I was going to keep it. That quip came to me as one of those gems. It was one of those brilliant light bulb moments that I only occasionally had. I may very possibly have already had the electricity, but Hobby supplied the bulb. Maybe Hobby was getting some little positive charge through keeping me. If so, the thought brought some measure of relief to me; but I never did fully get past that sense of overwhelming secret guilt. I felt as though I was playing the "innocent" murderer who was being questioned by the cops. Was I getting away with it?

I knew for sure that I didn't want to keep getting away with living off Hobby's hospitality. Now that Shari's hands were out of my pockets, I figured I should be able to pay my way. I had enough to cover rent and food every month from the physical/psychological disability compensation the VA judged it fitting to allot me since sometime after the Navy had sent me off, thirty-two months and twelve days ahead of schedule, with an Honorable Discharge and a few band-aids. And I could add to those funds by drawing or odd-jobbing for cash. Of course, I was once again, strictly speaking, homeless . . . though lucky, I guess, to come out of the sale of my house in Bushy Hollow no worse off than broke – but also out of debt and (thank You, God) out of Bushy Hollow.

I wasn't doing much except trying to figure out my next move, and somehow a week dragged by. With each day's passing, it became harder and harder to explain my presence in Hobby's home. What excuse did I have? Why didn't I just go away? I mean, what the hell, did I get adopted or something? Then I put it to Hobby. Shari would be leaving for Spain in another week, to leave her imprint there. Good luck with that. Could I possibly rent the house she had been using? It was among many properties that Hobby owned. This one had been provided for Shari for the sake of the son he had with her. Much to my surprise – and, again, owing me nothing and I owing him everything -- he agreed. If I wasn't actually living through it I would never have believed this fairytale. But here I was in the thick of it and it had been going on for far too long for it to be a dream. Besides, I would have woken up long before now, during the Shari episode of it. No one could possibly sleep through that nightmare.

With everything safely in place -- that is to say, with Shari now halfway around the world -- I took up residence in the old kingdom. This time around, I actually got to be king. As it turned out, the castle proved to be a little austere. Shari had tag-sold off everything but the dust. In fact, in typical Shari fashion, she had sold some of the larger items -- the ones that couldn't be readily carried off at the moment of sale -- twice. Now I was having to deal with an irate public looking for their stuff or their money back. Oh, yeah, the liquor store wanted their money too. I don't think she left many friends behind, with the exception of the cable company who got their three-month back payment from me, lest I not have any TV. Shit, I wasn't going to complain. Maybe it was an empty shell, but it was *my* shell. My snug and quiet shell. No Shari. This was heaven.

Yes, my slice of East Hampton Heaven. My own eternal happy haven home. *Isn't it?* I ask the glass in my hand.

tinkly tinkly tinkly I relish the sound the ice cubes make as I draw the empty glass down from my mouth. The sun is also moving more noticeably down as it starts to meld into the tree line of the hill across the street. *Shit, yeah, life is good.* I think I've got time for another.

A blue late-model Ford pulls into the driveway. There's a young blonde woman driving it. Blue Fords always look better when there's a young blonde driving them; but it's usually a disappointment when they get out. Their bodies seldom match their blondeness. *Oops -- this one is okay.*

----- Hi, are you are Earl?

----- Well, if you've got the right address, then I must be. Are you Gail? Come on up, I was just about to fix myself another drink, would you like one?

----- Sure, why not. What are you having?

----- Scotch, but if that won't do, I have some scotch or some scotch.

----- Then scotch will be just fine, thanks.

tinkly tinkly tinkly go the drinkless cubes as I pass from the outside world through the door and into the kitchen. That's where the phone is. That's the instrument I used a week ago to put an ad in the paper: Housemate wanted for open-air-plan house with three bedrooms, two baths.

When I moved back in after Shari's departure, there were neighbors I had met and liked still about. Now, with the onset of winter, with many of them being part-timers, they had migrated back to the city. To stave off loneliness, not to mention ease the finances, I had decided to look for paying company. Gail was the first to respond.

----- So, Earl, how long have you lived here?

----- Well, that's a long and convoluted story, so let's just say I'm a relatively-new-comer. And you?

----- Oh, I've lived here all my life.

----- I see that you're very well dressed. What do you do?

----- I'm with an insurance company here in town.

tinkly tinkly tinkly

----- I'm ready for another, how about you?

----- Yeah, that would be fine.

She's a good-looking gal with a body to match, although she isn't going to catch me looking. I have to say, though, she's not holding anything back in the way she's staring at *me*. I have to wonder.

The small talk goes on for some length; a lot of personal stuff unrelated to the rent. *tinkly tinkly tinkly* I glance over at the kitchen clock, backlit by the pitch darkness outside. She's been here for two and a half hours without so much as a hint of closing any sort of deal as far as renting a bedroom. I give it some deep consideration, and then chance the question.

----- By the way, are you intending to stay the night?

When I was in the Navy, there was a cheap paperback novel floating around the barracks. One night, with little else to do, I picked it up and read it. Yeah, it was cheap and boring. Page after page of a man getting all hot and bothered, working up a sweat with a woman, and then "the night passed in passionate rapture."

Well, in answer to my question, the night passed in passionate rapture. *tinkly tinkly tinkly* Ah, there's nothing like a glass of good scotch on the rocks in the morning. I've had a few now, since that night.

The following morning, she left without any commitment. Chalk that one up. Then Diane called, wanting to see the place. Better get another bottle. She came, she went, the night passed in passionate rapture. Are you shitting me? I must have accidentally fallen onto some secret E. Hampton sex cult signal coded into the wording of my ad. Either that, or everyone out here is nuts. I was just about ready to tell the next party who called to forget about it. I mean, this shit was okay as far as it went, but it wasn't going to pay the bills unless I started charging for the drinks. That's when a young lady by the name of Robin called. She got her foot in the front door because she was calling from the city, so I figured she didn't want my body. Well, not my naked one anyway. She says:

----- Hi, my name is Robin, I'm calling from NY, I was wondering if I could rent your house for a long Thanksgiving weekend for myself and a few other of my Park Avenue friends. We would like it if you could cook the meal and serve us as well, on top of the rental, if you'd be willing.

94

----- Say what?

This is a conversation that's going to last a lot longer than passing the night in passionate rapture, I'm thinking. I may be laughing on the outside but I'm starting to count the dollars on the inside. This could prove to be worthwhile -- not to mention I really do love to cook for others. I just have to get over this "service" attitude thing she's got going. *I don't live in the freaking servants' quarters back there on Park Ave., you know.*

After a lot of chit-chat -- some business, some social -- we finally come to an agreement as to the hour, fee, and menu. That last little nugget is shaping up to be the grocery list from hell. She's being absolutely insistent that this be bought there and that here. The melon balls must be of a certain diameter and color value. I wonder how much she values her life? I just can't wait to meet face to face. Perhaps we can pass the night passionately measuring melon balls together.

On the hour (being four o'clock), on the day (being Thanksgiving), I pass down the edict: the bird is done! I get only the lonely echo of my own voice in return. I'm playing to an empty house. There goes my passionate rapture along with my tolerance for Park Ave brats. By five-thirty, my curiosity outbests my anger and I give in and make the goddamn call.

----- Hello, Robin, this is Earl (quietly, politely seething).

----- Oh, hi. I guess you're wondering where we are (in a coquettish, innocent voice)?

----- I know where you are -- you just picked up the goddamn phone and it's not my bedroom's extension (holding back my true fury; I'm saving that to take out on the melon balls later)!

----- I'm sorry, the whole thing just became somewhat inconvenient for us.

----- Oh, well, thanks for the timely communication! I goddamn well appreciate it.

----- Yada, yada, yada.

I am seething! Any hotter and I'll burst into flames. I can't fucking believe her attitude. Like this is nothing. My time is nothing, I'm nothing. It's all I can do to hold myself back from berating her with a first class ass-reaming, but given her Park Ave frame of mind and isolation from reality, it would be like yelling at a retarded person. I guess, to keep this shit civil, I'm going to have to castrate myself, when all I really want to do is kick her in the balls, and brother has she got big ones!

----- Yada, yada, yada (she's still going on), why don't you call me back tomorrow at about four.

Oh, good; must be some kind of hook. Maybe she needs some time to think up some half-assed excuse for her behavior, because whatever shit she's been flapping about today sure as shit didn't cut it.

Tinkly. I shift my weight slightly to leverage my ass out of the sag in the deck chair, bracing my feet against the deck rail. I've just started to notice that, over the weeks of my habitation, the canvas of the chair has conformed to the habitual pose of my body. Is this some kind of rut? It's well into fall, and the sun might be going down. It's hard to tell – it's been gray all day, never really got light. My scotch looks gray, the ice looks gray. I'm lounging under a couple of gray blankets that maybe used to be white. Actually, *lounging* is a euphemism for what I'm doing. Dislodging my cramping ass has been my only act of rebellion against the deck chair in a couple of hours.

I'm thinking that my chats with Robin, which have become daily now over the last two weeks, are leaving me hung-over. Even the friendly *tinkly tinkly* from my glass isn't getting a rise out of me. What the hell – I must have some flies in my family tree, I'm such a sucker for getting drawn into a web. I just got out of a burning cabin – am I dashing off into a swamp *again*? What is it with these older gals?

I manage to get the chilly glass up to my lips. I need to clear my head. *Tinkle*. Okay, I see it – this is *different*. Robin actually *is* interested in me. I don't know why, but she seems to be making it a motherly mission to help me. I replay our conversation from yesterday . . . .

EARL: But where could I have it better than I have it here? I have the house, the deck, the chair, the scotch. Plenty of ice. Lots of quiet. And a TV too.

ROBIN: How old are you? It sounds like you're retired.

EARL: What's wrong with that? (She knows damn well I'm twenty-four.)

ROBIN: What are you retired *from*? What are you looking forward to – getting buried?

EARL: The people out here are nice.

ROBIN: What people? When they come back in the summer, take a good look – they're all old enough to *be* retired and sit around looking back at what they did in their lives. You have to get out of there and *live*. You should be in the city. You want to paint. Not vases of garden flowers. Not sailboats and seagulls. That's what you told me. If you're really an artist, you've got to come to NY . . . .

I sink deeper into the deck chair. She's right, I guess. I'm pretty damn sure. But so what? *Come to NY* . . . . It's not like she owns NY and she's handing me the keys to an apartment, or even a room there. What's the point of yakking about it? Sure, I'd love to get to NY. Just as sure, I'm stuck here. Stuck in this chair, anyway. Stuck stuck. I might not get out of it tonight. Just go to sleep right here. My fourth glass of scotch, I see, is empty. The ice cubes don't talk to me.

I guess I must have made it back into the house last night. Looks like I've been sacked out on this bed. I guess, sometime, the sun got itself up again . . . the air is yellow – kind of piss-yellow. Not sure if I feel like budging – what for? On the other hand, I'm feeling pretty crappy laying here like a rancid possum. Like some kind of road kill.

It's so damn quiet. I can hear the air in my nose. And my brain dripping like a leaky faucet. Wait – maybe that's the kitchen clock tock-tocking: tock tock tock tock tock . . . . I guess it's not going to stop. Nagging me about the seconds passing.

Now the screech of a seagull. That's a sound that cuts right through me. One gull, nearby. One call. Maybe I can hear others, in the distance.

Now I think of picking up the phone. And who do I have . . . who would I be calling? I better not ponder how nuts it is that I'm calling Robin.

----- Hey, Robin, it's me. How'rya doing?

----- Hi, Earl! I've been hoping you would call me early today – so glad you did. Guess what! I was at a thing last night, and I got introduced to a guy . . . a gentleman . . . his name is Milton L-something. He let me know that he's the (quote) Loft King of NYC. That's how he describes himself. He owns a lot of property around the city. So – I'm telling you this because I told him about you and – listen, this is really good, just what you need. He says he would not be averse to letting you have loft space in one of his buildings, in exchange for you running the freight elevator in the building during the day. This would be so great for you – loft space! . . . . yada yada yada . . . .

My head is kind of spinning and I can't quite follow her into all the nooks and crannies she gets into when she gets going, but after a while she ends with:

----- You will call him, won't you? Be sure to call me tomorrow and let me know what happens.

----- Sure. Thanks.

I think.

So, do I call some guy – some *gentleman* – named Milton L-something? Because Robin pulled this Fairy-Godfather out of a grab-bag at a *thing* and started pitching me to him and him to me? Could be another curve ball I should duck. And who's Robin? A voice on the phone, who stood me up and left me holding the grocery bag. Sitting pretty on her Park Avenue ass. Now she's making blind dates for me. Maybe I should call Milton L, just so I can tell her I did, and get the bitch off my back. What the hell am I talking about? *I'm* the one calling *her* every day. At her request. Because, I guess, I have to admit, she's the only show in town – or out. No . . . *she's in.* I'm out. If I want a shot at getting in, I guess I should pick up the phone. What else have I got?

East Hampton station, 6:23 pm. Here comes the train, right on time. I can't believe he's taking the time and expense to come to me. I'm the one with my hand out. Like Robin, he must have too much time on his hands. I haven't a clue what he looks like. I guess I'll just have to look for someone who looks like a Milton. I'm getting a picture in my head. That's scary. Do I really want to do business with a Milton?

Oh, shit, that must be him. Yeah, he can't be anyone else. He looks like a six-foot-something chicken, slim, sporting a full-length cashmere coat, topped off by a giant pompadour that he wears like a rooster's crown. Well, at any rate, there's nothing cheap-looking about this clown. I suppose the least I can do for him in recompense for all his trouble is to take him to the best restaurant in town. It's going to cost me more than chicken-feed, and I have to hope it will measure up to The Rooster's standards. Okay, it's not the Waldorf Astoria, but it's the best East Hampton has to offer.

Dinner with Milton L. III. How uneasy should I be? He's my senior, but not by much – except, certainly, our respective histories of invested wealth, as George would say. Milton wants to put pleasure before business, so we're dining before getting down to brass tacks. That's fine by me. I don't mind prolonging the opening scene, inasmuch as I feel like I've seen this movie before. That is to say that he's obviously gay, and I have a history, it seems, of being very attractive to that special-interest group. For the next hour, though, Milton does devote some of his attention to the young woman waiting on us.

"Excuse me, waitress, there's a speck in my ice cube."

"I'm sorry, let me get you another glass."

 . . . .

"How is everything?"

"Well, I found the salad to be a little gritty."

"Oh, I'm so sorry, sir."

 . . . .

"Is everything okay here?"

"Well, actually my green beans are ice cold."

"I'm so sorry, can I get you some others?"

 . . . .

"How are we doing here?"

"Well, I'm afraid the shark was a little too sharky-tasting."

"I'm so sorry, sir, I'll be sure to tell the chef."

Tinkly, tinkly, tinkly is my only comment. I guess I won't be coming back here again.

The table is cleared and Milton picks up his attaché case and sets it on the tablecloth. While he opens it, he gleams at me. Uh-oh, here it comes. When he gets to the small print of his contract – if the party of the first part (me) will sleep with the party of the second part (him), said first-part party will be favored with an additional loft, free and clear, for himself – I have to tamp down his dimmer switch with a polite turn-down. I'm not unfeeling when it comes to other people's sensitivities. I want to make sure the Loft King doesn't feel personally rejected. I explain that, over the years, I've received a number of generous offers by others with interests similar to his and I've turned them down as well. His thing just isn't my thing. In fact, I don't even want to see his thing. Thank-you anyway. Now with all matters of business said and done, we retire back to the house, where the rest of the evening passes without a speck of passionate rapture.

In the morning, I have a gentlemen's agreement that sets the date, time, and place for the commencement of my reclamation into the real world, the stream of the city. I must be out of my fucking mind. I'm basically putting my life into the hands of a total stranger who eats shark. Who does that, anyway? Another shark. I can't help but reflect that if I, in good faith, give notice to Hobby and remove myself and my sackful of stuff from his property, and then the bottom of this *thing* I've just jumped into falls out, I'm going to be in Shitsville, big time.

My last night in the bed, in the room, in the rented East Hampton house, in the neighborhood of Hobby's house, the kitchen clock is doing its tock-tock in the stillness: tock (shh) tock (shh) . . . . My brain cells must have counted a million measures of that beat. No other sounds except

tinkly

tinkly

Sounds I'm leaving behind.

I'm packed and ready. All I need is a good excuse for why I'm turning my back on Hobby's generosity, and a solution to how the hell I'm going to get to the city with my meager belongings and my dog in tow. George supplies the consideration that relieves my uneasiness about forfeiting the keys to Hobby's rental house: What happens if Shari shows up? She'd come storming in and kick me out in a heartbeat. And Hobby would accede to her, for the sake of Luke, their teenaged son. George also suggests that, as long as I'm going to probably piss Hobby off anyway, why not go the full nine yards and ask him for a ride. Hell, he'll probably be so glad at the prospect of ridding himself of me forever, he won't even charge me cab fare.

Hobby drives me in from the Island and leaves. Not much talking the whole way in the car. So here I am, on the corner of Park and 16th, with all that I need. My dog, my mattress, my hot plate, and my can opener. I wonder if I look as much like a pile of doo-doo as I feel. But why should I imagine there are any alternatives? There aren't any. I know this is America and all, and somehow that's supposed to make everything alright – or, at least, possible. I think that's something the rich are comfortable with saying, but the meaning gets lost somewhere between their mouths and the ears of the have-nots. The only damn economic reality I've ever known is that you are no better than what you own. About the only thing of possible value I'm still in possession of is what's left of my mind, and I can't remember the last time anyone gave me two cents for what I thought. Yeah, just a pile of doo-doo. I'm far from stupid -- well, maybe not that far -- but I do have some street smarts, if nothing else. I know right where I am. Almost sad to say. I'm standing on a street corner that, as far as I know, may be the last address I have, cold, tired, and hungry. Now I have some idea of that sinking feeling the Pilgrims must have felt as they watched the Mayflower sail off. At least they had the Indians' winter stores to steal in order to survive. That adventure probably gave rise to the grand old American epithet: Land of Opportunity. There's a lot here to steal, grant you.

A picture pops into my head – something I saw a few weeks ago while I was taking advantage of the opportunity to lay around watching TV. One of those *let's see how people in less-sophisticated societies manage the necessities of life* programs. It seems that in the Outback, when an Aborigine is thirsty, he reaches down into the parched sands and extracts a toad. He squeezes out into his mouth the amount of water he needs and then returns the toad to its bed, where it will resume its patiently-sleeping wait for the next rains when it will replenish itself and mate, producing little canteens. Unfortunately for me, I live in a more advanced society, where absolutely nothing changes hands without cost. If I don't pay the freight, or even if I'm late with a payment, they turn my toad off. What a country.

Well, let's face it, kiddo, your fate isn't about to change at the drop of a hat. But the drop of a dime . . . *Shit! I wonder if I have one.* Yeah, one little phone call is going to make all the difference in my life, starting with where I'm going to wake up in the morning. And it all hangs on the whim of a total stranger. *Are you shitting me? Aren't you getting a little too old for this*

102

bullshit? Apparently not old enough to stop asking stupid questions. It's time to search for some change, not to mention fortitude. You know, the kind you wrench out of your intestines and bring up into your throat just before you skydive out of a perfectly good airplane.

Okay, all that I have to keep in mind is the fact that I exist five feet above my feet, so I know exactly where I am. How can I possibly feel lost? God, I've always been such a damn good liar. Well, maybe not always . . . . As a child, I couldn't understand why I could never get my mother to believe me when she'd peek into my room to ask if I was asleep and I'd answer 'yes'. I guess I've learned *something* since then. Anyway, here I am. Stalling, instead of calling. Flapping the beaker between my ears, yakking myself silly with any distracting bullshit – and why? What if I dial, and the phone just keeps ringing and ringing? Or Milton picks it up and says, "Who the hell is this?" Then what? I'm too chickenshit to find out. So I'm still standing in the same spot, right over my feet. Not even so sure of that, either. I have to give the gnawing, buffeting cold of December's winds their due -- they can unroot the sure-footedness of any redwood goliath, never mind a transplanted sprout. I'm shivering, and an empty stomach isn't helping me feel any too secure right now. I wonder if there's a pizzeria anywhere nearby.

Jesus! Why the hell did I have to bring *that* up? God, that pizzeria's back door was only about two months ago . . . seems more like two lifetimes. I really don't need to go there right now. It's reminding me that in just two months I've managed to get myself from a street corner to a beautiful house, and now I'm back on a goddamn street corner again and the only upside is that this time it's not raining. That was well managed. How brilliant of me. Maybe what I should do is try to be more like my dog: don't make decisions, just lay back and enjoy the ride for what it's worth and where it takes you. I mean, right now, he's standing here thinking, wow, what a bunch of great new and different smells and look at all these new people to pet me and love me. Sure, what does he have to worry about? Fleas? I'm sure he doesn't wonder where the hell *his* next meatball grinder is coming from. Try being human for an hour and see what that feels like, *Jocko!*

Jesus (again) – did I think that too loud? Jocko's looking at me with something like kindly pity, with his eyebrows up and a sort of indulgent sigh. *Et tu*, you brute? Okay, Jocko, you're right. Your fate is hanging on this dime too. As I reach down into my pocket in search of change, I'm leaving my other hand free so I can stick my thumb up my goddamn ass to prevent my spine from falling out onto the sidewalk. *Clang* goes the dime as it hits the bottom of the phone's coin box. Or was that my spine? There's a lot of scary sounds out there in the world -- a dentist's drill, the screech of tires just before you're rear-ended, your wife announcing: My mother's coming for a visit -- but the one I just heard beats them all. Sounded a little too much like the trap door on a gallows dropping away. That's okay, I did put my head in a damn noose when I decided to travel down this deranged road. Whatever is about to happen, ain't no one's fault but my own.

With every molecule of my body vibrating with apprehension, I'm dialing the number that's supposedly going to change my life for the better, or perhaps, at least, end it more expediently. Milton picks up almost immediately. That's a relief. Sort of. His voice is shaky and his reaction to the sound of mine seems like shock or surprise. Apprehension is escalating to dread – but I quickly rationalize that I have awakened him. After all, it's only eleven o'clock a.m., an ungodly hour to call a New Yorker. That's just after bedtime for the party crowd.

But Milton doesn't grumble or sound half-asleep. He says: "Oh, I forgot all about you."

My ass is in trouble now. I wonder if two thumbs up it can do the job . . . ? After a terrifying pause, he reassures me: "Give me ten minutes and I'll be right down."

Okay . . . ten more minutes in purgatory. He's coming down -- but what does *that* mean? He's making sure that I'm not going to try to come up? I have no idea what's about to unfold. I'm starting to feel like a dribbled ball, bouncing, up and down, up and down, not really getting anywhere, not making any baskets. Bouncing out of a marriage into George's party scene . . . and then, with the steals and hand-offs, from Shari and her promised magic-carpet ride, to Robin and her pass-key to the palace, to Milton, keeper of the Treasure Room. Yeah, but I'm still standing in the street.

I'd really like to stop thinking now.

At last, Milton appears at the door of a building on 16th and waves me over. He's wearing pajamas and a neatly-belted robe, his hair is still perfectly coifed, just as I remember it to be two weeks ago when we met.

"You're lucky to catch me in," he says. "I'm usually not here. I forgot you were coming."

Are you shitting me or what? I can't believe my goddamn ears. *Are you telling me I could be standing out on the corner, having given up a perfectly good residence -- for what?! What is this -- some kind of fucking game?* What kind of shithead am I dealing with? What the hell would I be doing now if he hadn't been here?

Okay, okay – he *is* here. He *is* here, and he's taking us up in the elevator. *This is it. Get a grip.* We're going up . . . but, somehow, my heart is going down. What was I expecting? All I know is, this doesn't feel like *it*. The elevator stops at the 6th floor, but it sure as hell feels like the cellar to me. Are things ever the way you think they're going to be? My throat is feeling kind of tight. I hope he doesn't ask me anything; I don't think I'll be able to get any words out.

As we get off the elevator, Milton continues informing me: "I only use the office portion of this loft, so you can set up house wherever you please." The office portion occupies about 1/32 of the loft space, a 10-foot strip that runs the width of the building, overlooking 16th Street. I spot a cozy-looking area a half mile away overlooking 17th. Perfect, right next to the fire door for a quickie escape, should I ever come to my right mind again. Jesus, what a disgusting dump, complete with wall-to-wall horse manure, I shit you not. No one would believe it if I described it. *Who the hell kept horses here? When? What the hell . . . where am I?*

I'm having a flashback to a time when I had occasion to grab a couch or floor at a friend's down on the Lower East Side. Those cold-water flats were like palaces compared to this shithole. At least in those apartments you could control the roach population to some extent through selective breeding techniques. You simply drew a chalk line dividing the room in half. Any roach who crossed the line was awarded a lesson in birth control by means of the business end of a hammer. Only those roaches that didn't have the wanderlust stayed alive and bred more of their ilk. Here in this godforsaken joint, it looks like the little buggers have declared manifest destiny.

105

The loft, apart from the small finished office area, is a black cavern with only a single fluorescent lamp that hangs over a six-foot sink. The sink is what loosely defines the kitchen facility, which Milton offers freely to be at my disposal. With its jumble of pots and pans and plates all covered in an inch of green mold, it looks to me as if someone else had already disposed of it. If I get up the courage to serve myself a meal here, I'll use paper, thank-you. The only real other point of interest to break the floor's bleak horizon is the brooding hulk of two thirty-foot printing presses. But beneath the stretch of the fourteen-foot ceilings, even they appear to be dwarfed. As for me, standing in that darkness – not the kind, warm, encompassing type that comes with night, but the type that comes with human decay and forgetfulness -- I'm feeling very much like a tiny insignificant shrimp that has been swallowed by some great sea creature larger than any whale. Here I am, in its stomach, and it can feel me walking about. Knowing my helplessness. Aware of my hopelessness. That is more than I'm willing to admit to myself. But this great foul thing knows all of me. I'm not feeling like a grain of sand on the beach, I'm feeling like a grain of sand in the universe.

Other than the scant distant illumination coming from the galley, the only other hint of light struggles through the opaque windows that front 17th Street. Is this the space promised me? Before I can ask, with no other words spoken, Milton disappears. With his exit, the rude companion of solitary depression announces its presence. I am now nothing more than an orphaned child with nothing more than the great blackened walls to serve as overseers and parents. More unyielding, less forgiving and less caring, if possible, than the ones fate had me born to. I want to cry out ma-ma, to grasp out for some warm presence to suckle me – but, at the thought of it, the walls recede from me. They become distant and offer me no support. The hulking blackness is interrupted only by the presence of a little metal box over the fire door and my bed. The neon-lit EXIT sign. It seems to be the only human touch in this abandoned hell. It has a message. GET OUT! In bright red letters. And a brain-grating voice that never ceases: *AEAEAEAEAEAEAEAE.*

It's been the passage of a week now. Still haven't lost my mind; not all of it, anyway. Don't know why, don't know how. I occupy myself as best as I can with walking Jocko through Union Square as often as possible, but

106

that's getting thin, along with side-stepping all the narcs sitting on the benches trying to bait me with a score. Maybe if they left the park to real dope dealers, they might actually find someone to bust.

George just blows into town and takes a loft down in SoHo. I guess I don't have to worry any longer about Jocko's future if I happen to rot in this soul-crushing rat hole. With three Great Danes of his own, George would never tolerate a good dog to be out in the street. Me, that's another matter. Besides, at this point, he wouldn't touch me with a ten-foot pole if I was dead. When he decided to make the move to SoHo, he had asked me to go in with him half. After knowing him for six years and having worked for him as kennel boy for several of them, I knew better than to think half about anything. He wanted a full-time slave, for both his dogs' and his own wants and gratification. Knowing him as I do, I know now that, in refusing him his desire, I'm probably going to be on his shit list for next to forever. Still, I have somewhere to periodically visit. For whatever that's worth. Foundering in a desolate expanse of ocean, it's like groping for a lifeline, a thread of sanity, and grasping onto a shark.

Marooned in the middle of eight million people, I'm still finding so little to grasp onto that even a piece of flotsam looks good. When it comes bobbing into view in the shape of Susan, a coconut who was my old table partner in high school art class, I let it snag me and take me in tow for a short haul. Back in our school days, I would have steered clear. She was a boatload of over-nuts, over-sexed, over-the-top, and I pretty quickly see that she's still carrying the same cargo. I run into her across the street from Union Square. The temperature is sub-zero, so it's only polite, once she finds out I have digs in the neighborhood, to say it's fine if she wants to come up – which she does. It's not all that warm inside the loft, but there's steam rising up from under her parka, which she doesn't wait for an invitation to remove – along with everything else she has on. I'm sort of a spectator here as, within the same minute, she has all of *my* clothes shucked and dropped. She hasn't stopped giggling since we got into the elevator. At that time, it was still my intention to keep her at arm's length. But good intentions litter the road to passionate rapture . . . and I guess she has longer arms than I do. I sense how deep I've sunk into the pit of loneliness when the words *any port in a storm* start pulsing rhythmically through my head.

Now the days are creeping by at the pace of a funeral procession. Tomorrow night is New Year's Eve. A new year. What's going to be different? I look at the floor and the walls and the ceiling that contain my little corner of hell, and I figure that nothing has changed, nothing has happened, in at least a hundred years. But tomorrow night I'm going to meet the angel who worked the miracle that got me into this loft. She lives, I guess, in heaven which, it turns out, is only a few blocks from here. Yet for all our hours of ethereal communion, she's never contrived an in-the-flesh meeting. Our first encounter will take place in a crowd, at a holiday bash. Is she eager to show off her protegé, to introduce me to whatever circle of luminaries she revolves in? Or, maybe, will this crowd provide cover for her to disappear into in case she doesn't like what she sees when I walk in the door?

Well, this must be the place. Yeah, it figures -- a vacant storefront right on the corner of 15th and Park. All the better to be seen. A great venue for those people, all admiring themselves, to be admired. The crowd is looking a little too glitzy for me. I'll fit right in with my jeans. I should have brought Jocko with me; being a flashy Harlequin, he could be my bling. Anyway, I can use him as an excuse for not staying long: can't leave him home alone for too long, and all that. Out of the crowd, Robin walks over and introduces herself to me. I'm even more underimpressed than I thought I'd be. For all the months we yakked on the phone, I can't think of a goddamn new thing to say. Before finishing my one drink, I make my excuses and depart the phantasmagoria of glitz in trade for my more-than-real and tangible dinge. *There's no place like home, there's no place like home.* Ain't that the depressing truth.

Thank God that's behind me. The only regret I have is not grabbing that exasperating bitch by the hair and dragging her up here to see the royal circumstances she feels so self-congratulatingly responsible for. I'm sure they fit right in with her Park Ave. sensibilities. Brother, what I wouldn't give to laugh in her face and then kick her in the ass. One of life's little regrets that I'll probably carry to the grave. Ah, what the fuck-over! On the bright side, I don't ever have to call her again. And judging by her demeanor when I last glimpsed her, and her well-established you-call-me protocol, I don't think I'll ever hear from her. Thank God.

The sound of the elevator rudely shakes me from what I used to refer to as sleep; lately it's been more like a very uncomfortable suspended animation. The cage stops on my floor. What the hell? The light that's emitted from it is just enough to allow me to recognize Milton as he hurriedly exits and runs into the office. Still not sure of the world I've just awakened to, on automatic pilot, I yell out: "What's up?"

"I was just mugged, I'm calling the police."

His tone is panicked. So would mine be if I had the opportunity to ask him, while he's here, just what the hell am *I* doing here. But as quickly as he came in, he's twice as fast gone. *Shit, you mean to say someone mugged him and they didn't kill him?* I guess they didn't fucking know him. Maybe next time. Being between sleep and consciousness, I find myself out of my body looking at myself. I, as the viewer, begin to move away from myself, seeing that person of myself growing ever smaller with distance. Spotlighted in that little corner with nothing but the overhead EXIT sign shining and buzzing and buzzing. There is nothing else visible through that relentless and merciless blackness than that tiny little lit stage with that helpless, skinless little boy afloat on that stinking life preserver of a mattress.

God help me, I've never felt more like a pure bag of shit in my life. I think I'm dying. That little sizzling malignant box never shuts the fuck up! That unrelenting buzz sits on my brain like a wet bag of sand. Those deviant red letters never cease to scream at me: "*GET OUT! GET THE FUCK OUT!*" It's not a friendly voice. This is not a friendly place. I feel as though the very walls desire to close in on the kill. But there's no place to run and hide except further into the bowels of this monster. That's just what it wants me to do – all the work for it. To abandon whatever shred of strength and will I still have. And I am near the point of surrender; I can't take this shit anymore. I am dying. All this time I've been balanced on a sharp pinnacle, and the only safety net protecting me from the abyss was the unknown. Now that unknown is known. I'm yesterday's fodder. I no longer even have the strength to give up.

It's been some weeks now, I think. I think I'm not sure of anything anymore, I think. My routine hasn't changed. Nor my sense of isolation. My being is still suspended between who I was and who I am to be. In fact, who I was doesn't even exist any longer. I'm like one of those rope bridges hanging between two cliffs – but one of the cliffs is missing. Now what?

The sound of the elevator stopping on MY floor startles me. It's broad daylight this time, but hearing the sound of Milton's voice, I'm suddenly seized with terror, not even knowing the reason why. Except, I feel my world being invaded.

Milton steps off the elevator with a young couple and starts to show them around. I try to hide the emotion of being violated. I try to gather myself, to at least stand and tuck in my shirt, to be ready to face these people. I'm totally ignored for my efforts. Apparently Milton is showing the loft for sale. The three walk past me several times without so much as a nod of acknowledgment. I can only assume that I come with the space as one of the fixtures. The yuppie couple finish the tour and leave. Milton suddenly realizes my presence. He politely, and with some cool distance, informs me that, unless I have ten thousand dollars with which to purchase the space, I have to be out by tomorrow. Sheepishly, I venture to ask why our supposed agreement of occupancy has vanished. Milton makes reference to having met George who, at the time, told him I had a drinking problem. I doubt that George clarified that my problem was that I hadn't had more than one drink in the last two months. I already had figured I was on George's shit list. Typical of him, this was his childish way of getting even with me for not playing ball. Of course. According to *George's Rules for the Universe*, why should I get a loft four times the size of his, for nothing, while he himself has to pay inflated SoHo money.

So much for the gentleman's word. Milton. If that cocksucker isn't related to Shari, then I don't know. Both are adept at floating illusions, with a chaser of oasis-destruction. As for me, what little floor I had been fantasizing that I had beneath my feet is no longer there. Going down. The elevator bottoms out. Jocko and I step out and walk over to the same corner where we began this freaking farce. Minus the mattress, the hot plate, and the can opener. Don't need no excess baggage where I'm going because I have nowhere to go. I'm knocking on every door in my brain. Let me see . . . . There's George – yeah. Thank you. There's Susan – no, no, no thank you. Besides, she's full up now, with two roommates. The only other person I know in town is Shari's gay friend, Don. Yeah, that's a great fucking idea. I really hit it off with him the one time we met. Yeah, a real kissy-huggy relationship that was. Do I really have any goddamn choice in the matter? Who else can I call? I mean, I know God has an unlisted number, so what the hell am I supposed to do?

Then again, what the hell am I afraid of? I've already been stripped of every thread of dignity. When you're crawling, it's not like you can crawl any lower than you already are. Besides, the only alternative is to go down to SoHo and drop the dog off with George and then walk off peacefully into the sunset. If I remember correctly, the sun sets over New Jersey, as well it should, and if I set my aim correctly and keep walking, that would put me right on the end of one of the West Side docks. Need I really give it any further thought?

What the hell, we're already crawling – why not make the best of it while we're down here. What can happen? Just tell him you're in town and would like to drop by for a beer for old time's sake. Right. *Look on the bright side, someday you'll be dead, maybe sooner than you think, and you can look back on all this and have a good laugh.* That's funny, because for the first time in two months, I actually feel like laughing, but I'm not sure why. Maybe because I'm so pathetic.

I drop a dime into the same phone where this all started. The falling dime makes the same goddamn world-shattering noise it did last time. It's a beautiful day -- no reason for him to be home, I'm quietly hoping. After all, if you're calling someone, you really ought to have something to say. *Jesus! He answers. Well – speak!* That's pretty hard to do with your heart in your throat and the pain in your ass from having your tail stuck up it. Somehow, I get my story, short and sweet, on the table. Smells like broiled crow to me. But just as Hobby had, Don totally ignores the menu and, with friendly sympathy in his voice, says: "Come on over." I'm theorizing that those in my world who aren't related to Shari are kin to Hobby.

I find my way to the apartment building on the corner of Christopher and Bedford Streets. Don lets me in and gives me a seat at the kitchen table. Knowing he's a full-fledged drunk, I'm sure looking forward to that ice cold beer. First one of the year.

"Oh, coffee? Yeah, that will be fine." Well, I'm glad to see that, at least, I haven't been stripped of my lying facility. I wasn't going to complain about shit at this point anyway. I'm telling Don of my hapless adventure and cluing him to the fact that I'm now homeless, as he sits with his head bowed in what seems deep contemplation. Miraculously and almost instantly, Don thinks maybe, just maybe, there might be a solution to my quandary. Dare I even hope? The idea seems almost cruel. Yet another cliff to dangle from? Another dead end? Is there enough room left on my body for another "Born to Lose" tattoo?

Don goes on to tell me that an elderly gentleman downstairs had passed away two weeks ago and that he had been a sublease. Don knows the original lessee, but not his current whereabouts. He thinks, if we hit the local bars, he might be able to garner some information. Thank God. I just knew there had to be a blessed beer somewhere in this ludicrous story. Being that the lessee, Don says, is gay, we set out to hit all the gay bars in the Village. Hopefully this is going to amount to quite a few beers.

It does.

Quite a few.

About sixteen bars later, the mounting desperation (in my mind, anyway) of our quest sure could use some comic relief, and I think I see it coming through the door. We're in an S&M bar called Boots and Saddles – the bold lettering on the sign over the entrance says so . . . the door opens and in walks this young, blue-eyed, blond-haired, rosy-cheeked, tall glass of water in full cowboy regalia. I'd say he was made up for a part in some corny skit – but it's clear in a moment that he's the genuine article, from his open-faced grin to his tooled-cowhide feet, when he lets out with an earnest and friendly, "Howdy, y'all. I'm from Amarillo."

The chap looks pretty knocked back by the clenched teeth and hard stares he's getting from the leather-and-chains crew around the bar. I'm close enough to see his smile fall into his boots and hear his bewildered murmur that sounds like: "There sure are a lot of strange-lookin' fellas in these here parts," as he makes his exit, wobbling his head.

No harm done, except maybe a crack in the young poke's innocence. I think I know what that feels like. I have enough beers in me right now, though, that I can wink at the ceiling and murmur something myself, that sounds like: "Please don't break a sweat in my direction – there are other lost souls wandering around out there, maybe in need of more immediate attention." Besides, I've got Don at my elbow. And I've come to know he's not a quitter.

About eight bars back, this day was beginning to feel like the longest

112

day in my life. But now, what's left of it seems too goddamn short to end any way but badly. Hours of bar-crawling have succeeded only in making the beer taste sour (and that's something I never thought I'd hear myself say).

Well, wouldn't you know it, just like in all good melodrama, we strike gold at the eleventh hour in the last bar on our list. At this point, I can't be closer to being dead without being dead, so it's almost impossible to raise my spirit up from the coffin-in-waiting I have just about committed myself to. But our business still isn't over; all we have now is a phone number. If nothing else, I'm now ten blocks closer to the docks than I was this morning. Mercifully, it will now be a shorter walk out to the end. Thank God, because I'm freaking exhausted!

Don has to practically shake me to let me know that he's reached the lessee, a guy named Vincent. I have my good ear glued to Don's outer ear as if I'm going to hear the conversation pass through Don's head. My life is literally hanging on the whim of a single word. I hear it in Don's nod: "YES!"

All I want to do at this moment is to take a good one-hour piss. I do, all the while intoning: *Thank-You-God, thank-You-God, thank-You-God!* Physically and mentally relieved, Don and I start back toward his building. Even though I had been inside the place just hours earlier, I feel as though I'm entering it for the first time. Every sensation I'm feeling is new and fresh. In a don't-pinch-me-I-don't-want-to-wake-up trance, I'm heading for the super's apartment on the third floor, to receive from her the key to the empty apartment next to hers and a floor down from Don's. The key, I'm thinking, to my future – to my *having* a future. As I'm climbing the granite-and-iron staircase, the tile walls echo my footsteps to reassure me of my presence. The cooking aromas coming from the different apartments promise to assuage my hunger for security.

As real and concrete as these sensations are, holding the key in my palm is a different story. I can tell that it's a small solid piece of metal, but it exists in a magical dimension. It vibrates with arcane power. I can feel it. Or maybe that's my hand shaking as I insert the key into the lock. The tumbler falls with a loud clank. The door *e-e-e-ks* as I start to open it, with my eyes closed. I dare not look. Perhaps there's nothing on the other side. You know, one of those cosmic jokes that only the Gods get. I'm met by a whiff of stale air. That's alright. At this point, nothing is going to repel me from entering. I've already encountered all the demons this world has to offer. I open my eyes; I'm not exactly met by a vision of House Beautiful. The walls are painted in a putrid ocher under a drab coating of dinge. The wall-to-wall carpeting is running a close second in repulsive color and grunge. The hall from the doorway opens into two rooms which are actually one, intersected by two closets across from one another acting as a room divider. Each room is furnished with a daybed and assorted Salvation Army rejects. There's a typical Village bare-bones kitchen and a tiled bathroom. On any other day, my response to this eyeful of the apartment's interior might have been a resigned sigh, expressing: *it is what it is*. But today, to my eyes, it couldn't have been more beautiful if it were Gracie Mansion or more welcoming if it had smiled and placed a lei around my neck. Not to mention . . . as an added gift from the Gods, it's rent-controlled.

I step in and stand above my feet in the center of the stained carpet. *Home is where your feet are*, I say. Dare I put mine up? Yeah. Don set me up with a house-warming bottle of scotch, and I think I'll put it to a warming use right now. I pour myself a good shot and settle on one of the daybeds, adjusting my back against a worn bolster to get comfortable. I put my feet up on an antique iron-and-glass coffee table, take a sip, and gaze out the window. The sun is going down. I can tell by the shadows, but I have a back apartment so I can't see the sunset. As I slowly draw the glass down from my lips, I hear *cling-glang*. It's the sound of pots from the kitchen of an apartment in the building not more than fifteen feet directly across the alley from me. My view is of the brick wall, and I'm looking squarely at the kitchen window, like I'm at a drive-in movie. On the other side of the window, there's a gorgeous naked young woman preparing dinner and, like myself and most seasoned New Yorkers, she doesn't believe in shades. I don't have a TV yet, but people have to prepare dinner every evening -- don't they? -- and I could get used to this daybed.

What this scotch needs is a couple of friendly ice cubes. I'll get up in a minute and get some from the fridge. *God, if this isn't home, then I don't know what the fuck is.*

114

4 ~ Love on the Rocks
with a Splash of Vodka

I'm looking back at myself in the mirror over the bar at The 55. Behind me in the mirror, everything's pretty much where it always is, so I guess everything's where it belongs . . . except me.

My reflection in the glass is blurred – maybe by the ghosts of every reflection I've left there every day of my five years on this perch in The '5. Maybe because my eyeballs can't focus, with everything that's been hitting me in the head this past week – never mind the last five minutes. Maybe the mirror in this dive hasn't seen a washrag in twenty-five years. I don't know. I'll give this reflection one more shot: maybe it's because *everything* is blurry – what's in my glass, what's in my head, what's in The '5 – all sort of sloshed together . . . vodka, sex, drinking, love, art – my five years at The Art Students' League and the palette-full of lovers that place provided me – all mixed into an eye-crossing cocktail. Like a Molotov cocktail to my brain. I could use a hair of the dog right now. I think. Maybe I'm thinking this only out of habit. A habit I've been faithful to for five years.

For five years . . . it always went something like this . . . .

It's a bright beautiful sunny afternoon. As well it should be. After all, Saturday is a day of leisure. That means I can spare the guilt for heading out to The '5 two hours earlier than I normally do on a weekday. Yeah, two o'clock works for me. The perfect hour for the hair of the dog. I have to get my two heads back into one space. I shun the warming sun like a vampire and quickly descend the three steps down into my cool, dark sanctuary.

It's a shotgun space with a small barred window to the right of the door as you enter. My usual weekend station. I wonder how many snapshots of myself trapped behind those window bars turn up in out-of-towners' albums. I'm a real tourist attraction. Behind me is the bar, which runs the length of the room, with some small tables to the left. There's a little alcove in the rear with the only booth and one of the two light bulbs in the joint. Then, in back of that, the two bathrooms – although the ladies' room is unisex, among other things. It's an all-purpose room, an anything-goes kind of place: drugs, sex, and things I'm sure I don't want to even try to wrap my brain around. Kind of a Twilight Zone with plumbing.

The mirror over the bottles on the bar-back serves as a kind of pin-board for the book jackets of our renowned authors-in-residence. There's also any number of newspaper clippings – most, it seems, from burgs in Ohio, that spread the word of our existence to an otherwise happily-uninformed populace. They even name names – the more notable flukes of humanity, like Jason Holliday who's so famous he has his own movie, starring Who Else. All he does in the movie is to perch there and talk about Who Else. When I get tired of talking about myself, I'll have to get a copy of that film. No doubt Jason is a photo-worthy character, with his flouncy gestures and his fuchsia boa, although I can't count him among the professional drinkers, given that he never has money enough to buy himself a drink. I guess he's our token welfare case, among his other job descriptions. Me, I'm always good for a touch – a drink, that is – playing my part of keeping him in work. It's the least I can do for the man, since I just can't oblige his soulful plea of "Oh, Earl, I know I can't fuck *you*. But can I ple-e-ease fuck your dog?"

Apart from Jason, our cast of characters at The '5 includes our token drunken Irishman, Red ("Up the rebels!"). Our token Indian, who is a grim customer, to be avoided at all costs. Not to stereotype him or anything but, after a couple of drinks, the tomahawk comes out. He sure as shit is mad about something. I'm guessing he's too young to have attended the Custer party, so he missed his chance to work it out. Then there are the Three Witches – although a case could be made for them being one witch with three heads. They're a clump. They all wear floor-length capes, so you can't count their feet. Their grey hair is almost as long, and they glide as a unit – even floating in or out through the narrow front door, they do not separate. I've always wondered how the hell they use the toilet. But then again, I never have seen them enter the ladies' room.

It had been Don who introduced me to The 55. At first I wasn't at all interested, everyone there being too old and too drunk. Used-up souls who had retired from being sober. I needed someplace nearby that I could fall out the door of and fall into bed. I tried Chumley's, an old haunt where you used to be able to get a bowl of soup and a chess game. That had ended with a checkmate knife-stab to the heart from a loser who lost heart with the game. Now it was back to being a bar once again, as it had been during Prohibition. The only problem was, I was the only one who knew about it. I tried one other joint that everyone knew about, but I didn't want to know everyone. I acquired a taste for The '5.

If you drink enough, you can get used to anything. Almost. Susan was an overnight guest when she chose to be. There was more about her to drive me nuts than the sex could make up for. Like her fucking bloody British accent. Christ Almighty, she had only spent a year over there, she wasn't fucking bloody born there! As if her pretentiousness wasn't enough, she was always declaiming, "Ow, fuckin' 'ell" in a cockneyish voice, and I swear to God, every time she said it, I thought I heard "Ow, fuckin' *Earl*", which made her play-acting really get under my skin. She had made a stab at Shakespearean acting while taking up with a stabbing lover, a member of the IRA, and I suppose she was feeling all the more worldly for it and this fucking accent was supposed to give her some sort of international flavor or something. I don't know how many flavors women come in, but she seemed already everyone's favorite, without the need of hype. She came to my apartment one night, complaining that some dude had followed her for blocks; she finally turned on him with, "What the 'ell do *you* want?" And she tells me *he* says, "Oh, I'm sorry, I thought you were in heat." Yeah, well, whatever she had, she exuded it. Out of fear of feeling embarrassed or having her embarrass me – *"Hi, I'm Susan, fuck me, by the*

117

way, what's your name?" – I never introduced her to the 55 crowd. Despite some personal foibles, they were a pretty decent bunch. I guess I appreciated them because you'd be hard pressed to find a liar or, more importantly, a phony among them. I mean, The '5 was a pretty good measuring stick in that I could never imagine Susan fitting in with that crowd. Yeah, there was something wrong with that bitch.

The posterior of our relationship was almost as welcome as its beginning was regrettable. Either through some corrupt sense of kindness on my part or just my impatience with her whining about not being able to find theatrical work (although she had no shortage of theatrics), I decided – what the 'ell – to cold-call Shari's first born, Peter, who was a famed director/producer. Much to my surprise, he warmly replied with: "Sure, send her on by." Holy shit! Could a person like Hans L. have possibly fathered such a warm and generous offspring? Come to think of it, I have to wonder whether Shari could have been the mother. My last words to Susan, as she left the apartment to keep her appointment, were: "Beware the casting couch."

She comes back with, "What's a casting couch?"

"Holy shit! You call yourself an actress, and you don't know what the fuck a casting couch is!? What the *'ell* do they call it in England? Bloody *tea?"*

Well, Peter must have had an enormous casting La-Z-Boy, because Susan came back wobbly-legged and announced her lasting departure from my abode. *Honey, your ship can't set sail fast enough.*

But I have to be grateful for small favors. Susan had been modeling at The Art Students' League, and nagging me to attend classes there and get back into my art. I thought it certainly wouldn't hurt to take some courses and get out of the apartment to boot. I finally gave in and got the catalog of classes. Now I needed only to overcome my fear of perhaps seeing Susan nude again in one of them.

In any case, Susan's favor of prodding me in the direction of The Art Students' League would have taken me only so far if it hadn't been for another favor I have to be grateful for. This one came to me from my Uncle Sam, who was ready to pick up the tab for my enrollment in a course of study where I could pick up some employable skills to get me back to being a potentially functional member of society instead of the wrung-out dishrag of a shipless sailor the Navy had made of me in sixteen months. I signed on at The League.

I tried to not let my re-entry into art interfere with the time I enjoyed at The '5. Psychology had always been my second love and there's no better place to get your degree than a good gin mill, and The '5 was the Harvard of bars. I mean, there wasn't anything you couldn't learn about human behavior there. One day, for example, an Ohio type comes in, apparently slumming; wearing a jacket and tie and the attitude that comes with it. "Give me a scotch on the rocks with a splash of soda, don't worry about a glass," he quips. Wrong bar, wrong bartender. Pete throws some rocks on the bar, pours a shot over them, adds a splash of soda and throws in a swizzle stick, and then tells the guy: five bucks. The joker ponies up with a sheepish smile and a five-dollar bill, and orders another, in a glass this time.

A couple of weeks had passed after Susan's departure from my digs when, God only knows why, I had lunch with her at my favorite bar in SoHo. It was still a working-man's place, with truck-driver food not yet having been replaced by sushi. I was indulging myself with my usual diner-quality spaghetti and meat balls, which was almost as bad as the joint's diner-style meat loaf. But each was a dish I relished only in that they both reminded me of my early days of freedom, when a diner meal was the social high point in my day. As much of a struggle as that time had been, it was the happiest I can remember being since before going into the service. God knows, I haven't come close to that kind of euphoria since. Add some God-awful red wine to those meatballs and I was in seventh heaven.

As I'm busy dispensing with my fare, Susan is flapping her beaker about how much she enjoyed dining with Peter and his wife – I mean, she *really loved* the better half. I damn near choked.

"You mean to say you're fucking Peter by day and then sitting down and breaking bread at the wife's table at night? Is there something fucking wrong with you or what?"

Missing my point, if not my accusation, she gives me an unruffled, "Sure, why not?"

Yeah, I'm thinking, *Why not?*

My plate of spaghetti has never looked as appetizing as it does now, crowning that beautiful head of black hair. I'm enjoying the effect of those long red strands dangling around and over her face, setting off that alabaster complexion and that

119

pink-lipsticked smirk that shows no sign of anything like embarrassment or guilt. Man, that felt good. I think I've created just the right look for Susan. I've never liked her better (which, of course, is not saying much).

Shit. Fantasies just don't last long enough, do they. This really sucks. I'm used to acting on my feelings, but I'm not about to get myself eighty-sixed out of one of my favorite haunts over the likes of her. So – *bloody alas* – no spaghetti headdress for Miss Smug. If nothing else, I'll just have to satisfy myself with the prospect that she'll pass on the same infection to Peter as she did to me. That might be good for a laugh when Hostess Betterhalf comes down with it. Boy, would I love to be a pork chop on the plate during that dinner conversation.

In giving a farewell thought to my association with Susan, I have to figure that Peter had a bigger torpedo and that's why our love boat sank. But even weeks before that event, I was wondering why it was afloat in the first place. The whole relationship was a bit off key from the get-go. I guess it served its purpose while I was holed up on 16th Street, but now it was like sponge-bathing while standing on the edge of a lake. I mean, talk about other fish! Maybe it was time to move on to the open waters.

If I needed a no-doubts reason to cast off my ties to Susan, it came one night when we were in the apartment and a big fight broke out. In frustration, Susan began to cry, at which point I found myself fighting to hold myself back from smiling. That's when a little voice in my head squawked: "You son of a bitch, you've become Jim!" I was blitzed by an instant flashback of my stepfather provoking my mother into a state of hysteria and violence against him. She would beat on him with closed fists while he would just stand there laughing and egging her on. The question came to me in an instant: How and when did I become someone else's illness? In that moment, I put therapy on my to-do list. If my behavior was in answer to something, then I needed to know what the 'ell the question was. I intended to get to the bottom of it, some day.

Meantime, The Art Students' League proved to be a treasure trove when it came to providing a stream of potential cures for the afflictions of loneliness and sense of worthlessness that I was already aware of. I had some clue about the reasons for *those* feelings, though. My mother never liked me better – hell, she never liked me at all. At The League, there were countless young beauties who, if not into psychiatric nursing, were at least horny as hell. That was fun for as far as it went, yes; but my real wants and

120

needs leaned more in the direction of a life-mate. Surely there had to be at least one vindictive woman out there. I'm thinking of the saying: *Sex is the game; marriage the penalty.* I wonder what the byproduct – *offspring* – is considered. Oh yeah, that other pearl of folk wisdom: *Your parents ruin the first half of your life, your children the second half.* But I was willing to go that route, just as soon as I got over being a child myself.

As for the lovelies I was taking up with, it wasn't my world-view that women were Fords and Chevys. I didn't see them as something that one trades in for a better and newer model. But a natural pattern seemed to evolve over time, with each successive lover improving in quality. In some way a better and nicer person than the last. To put my progress in terms I can naturally relate to, I was slowly working my way up from Sterno to Chivas Regal.

These upgrades in the quality of my lovers seemed to run parallel to my drinking habits. I wasn't always the drunk that I wanted to be. I had my sober moments that could last as long as a year at a time, maybe longer. But there seemed to be some inside-out logic to my see-sawing between drinking or not. When I felt compelled to wallow in the depths of helplessness, I pulled the cork. When I wanted to move upward and forward, I abstained. This didn't play out as a struggle *to not drink*, though. It was rather the battle to survive the shit I was floundering in when I *did* drink. I wasn't getting drunk to escape the shit, I was drinking to throw myself into it.

My second year of going to the League, I entered into one of my sober periods. Which is not to say I forgot about The '5. I was in there on one of my usual Saturdays, sitting next to Dolores, one of the bartenders, sipping my Perrier, when she turned to me and pondered: "Is it true that when you stop drinking, you become boring?" I thought for a moment. "Yes. You have," I told her. She laughed and squinted at me with her one eye (she'd lost the other to a bar fight) before turning away and choosing to ignore me for the rest of the evening. It was true, though. Someone had become boring. Maybe everyone and everything. The place I was in sure wasn't the same without some scotch or vodka in me. Little was. I couldn't be sure that being straight-sober outweighed the benefits of being warped, in a warped world.

During my first year at The League, I always sat on the same bench out in the entry hall, to have my smoke. This year wasn't any different, with the exception that I was alcohol free. In the previous year, likely as not there was always the same young lady standing in front and just to the side of me, engaged in conversation with whoever. This year was no different; standing in that spot was as much her station as sitting on the bench was mine. Then one day she scared the shit out of me when she turned and started to speak to me familiarly, as though she had known me forever. Who was I, was I single, was I straight, was I boring? "I'm not going to let someone like you get away," she ran on. "I have a cousin who just got divorced; I have to get the two of you together. What's your number?" Why is it that married women can't stand to see a single man happy? It's like, you can't get away with that; you have to be as miserable as my husband. It's like their duty or something.

Well, being sober – which is to say, not in my right mind – I bit. This would be the second blind date in my life. We all know about everyone's first, which is why we never hear about a second. It's a part of the way things are, that cousin that everyone has, She's-Fat-But-She-Has-a-Cute-Face. The cousin and I arranged to meet at my favorite café in The Village; she would be coming from Queens. She didn't give me a description of herself except to mention she was Italian. So I was just keeping my eye out for a fat Italian with a cute face. I told her to keep a lookout for a guy who looked stupid and had some cheap flowers.

I'm seated in the window watching the snow coming down. Then – holy shit! This goddess in a hooded white fur coat walks by, looks right at me, and just keeps walking. I spring out of my chair, my eyes following her path as she gets further away. *Where the hell is she going?* I don't know how, but I just know that that passing vision had been her. And she must have known it was me because, when I laid eyes on her, my mouth dropped open, causing me to look really stupid. I'm beside myself with panic. A moment later, she reappears. Magic!

More magic: The night passed in passionate rapture.

Are you shitting me? What the hell did I get myself into? Way over my head, I would say. This woman not only *had* everything, she *was* everything. Everything, drunk or sober, that I wasn't. She was truly one of the Beautiful People. I was feeling very much the Ugly American, (minus the question of citizenship).

It was a lot like winning the Irish Sweepstakes and then being told you can't collect because you're not Irish enough. My new partner, Helen, held all the cards. Not only did she have the upper hand, she owned the casino.

And not only was *she* "all that", but she had a beautiful three-year-old daughter to boot. You could say she had a full house. A hard space for anyone to try to fit into. I knew, on a good day, the odds were against me, but I was naïve or wanting enough to think that I could just slip into a Robert Young skin when, in reality, my rough edges would have shredded it. Thank God, through Helen's good common sense, she ended the whole thing pretty quickly, giving as her reason that it was just too soon after the end of her marriage to jump in again. At least I have to give myself brownie points for effort, in spite of the stacked deck. Maybe just a case of dumb courage poured out in an attempt to make myself better than I could be.

I might have fallen short in my ability to measure my potential fit in the life of another, but I was pretty good at recognizing who wasn't going to fit into *my* version of the scheme of things. There were definite beds that I avoided. Top of my list were those of The Married. *That's your problem, Sister* was my take on such gals' predicament. And those of the very rich, because I wasn't willing to give up the frills that come with poverty, for one thing; or, for another, to fall under the entrapment and control I figured a rich bitch would feel entitled to put on me.

In any case, I'd found myself adrift in an ocean of women, and I needed some kind of compass to steer myself by. At first, I'd proclaimed myself a moralist. This was because I had no morals and, I reckoned, what better disguise? Now, navigating between The Rich and The Married, I had developed into a degenerate with scruples. What better game? I was fast learning the ropes: I could have many beautiful women in my life; keeping them at arm's length, I could enjoy their company without ever having to see them without their makeup on.

Of the women on my Do-Not-Touch list, though, I've encountered a few, from time to time, so alluring that I was willing to meet them half way, in the middle of no-man's land. They were among the ones with money (but not husbands), so I made it understood from the get-go that even if anything like feelings should occur between us, there would never be something called "us". *Us*, when only one of us has the purse-strings, amounts to the other one of us being kept, and I've had more than my fill of that. Women – with their apron-strings, their purse-strings . . . I'm still young – I don't know what other strings they might have hanging off them like octopuses' tentacles – but there's no way that any of them is going to end up as a leash on *me*. Not again.

As for The Married – they couldn't have been more off-limits if they had been nuns.

Messing around with women was daunting and intoxicating enough. Mixing women and drinking multiplied the chances for getting into trouble. How much of each to add to any scenario was a tricky business. I tried to get the measurements right and, by trial and error, I figured out a few things. For example, I found that being sufficiently boozed up was a comfort when I was getting fucked over. And when facing how fucked up I was, the right amount of booze also worked, as a passport to revisit my failings. On the other hand, what the hell, sometimes it was just fun to drink for drinking's sake – the rollicking lampshade kind. With my head under a lampshade, I might be kept happily in the dark about fucking of any kind. But, overall, I got the idea that thinking from the bottom of a bottle was just as dangerous as thinking with your sexual organ. In either case, it's doubtful that anything that could be called thinking was really going on. Anyway, if you're reckless enough to be stirring a glass of vodka with your dick – well, you're getting a double whammy at both ends that can leave you good and hung over and royally screwed.

There was that time, when I was suffering from the blurry vision that comes with appeasing both thirst and lust, that I made the acquaintance of a broad by the name of Helena at the local dog run. The commonality that brought us there was enough for us to become bed partners. At some point, Helena introduced me to Sarah. Both claimed to be artists. They left out the small print, though. Theirs was the art of vampirism. When they took to drinking, they got every drop of your blood. Sarah was a young lady who had been blessed by the gods with a body that borrowed the choicest assets from six other voluptuous beauties and configured them into something beyond the reach of ordinary mortals. She knew it. She knew how to play it. She had no problem gaily gliding through my apartment stark raving naked with the exception of her high heels. But, by her rules of the game, nothing was going to become anything in the bedroom without that marriage certificate on the pillow. The only way to survive one of her visits without my mental and sexual apparatus exploding was to douse both organs in enough booze to keep them flaccid.

Both Sarah and Helena professed to be print artists. It just so happened that, at the time that I needed my booze and my women, I also needed the services of a printer. I had a couple of pen-&-ink pieces that I wanted to make printed editions of. I picked Sarah to do the job. Was this because I thought Sarah was the more talented printer? I had no idea. But engaging her services was a way of getting to see more of her. Being a visual artist myself and being under the spell of her visual charms, I just couldn't get enough of looking at her. Unfortunately for me, my eyeballs were lodged in my organ – the one that has a little head with no brain in it. Not really surprisingly, I didn't see, until it was too late, the naked truth that, with my money in hand, Sarah had fucked me over by pulling only a quarter of the prints I'd paid her to produce, and cheating me out of not only the job but my plate and unused paper as well.

It was late December at the time and I was finding myself not much in the mood for caroling and eggnog. Not feeling jolly in the least. I was pretty damn pissed off – partly at my own dupability, sure; but this only fed into my flaming desire to see lumps of coal stuffing someone else's stocking. Or cascading over someone's gorgeous swindling head. My righteous anger, as usual, got no support from my stomach, and had to vent itself in these lame fantasies. Until one night when, with a snootful of the false courage that a fifth of vodka can give you, I called Hamp, one of my favorite bartenders at The '5. Hamp was an extremely large black man, two hundred forty-five pounds of muscle, who rode with a bike club of color. A mean-looking group. The timid of heart might very well find themselves frightened by this man's shadow.

"Hello, Hamp?" I boldly slurred into the phone, "I just got fucked over by this broad. I'd be willing to pay you five hundred bucks if you and a couple of your boys will ride out to her place in the Bronx and scare the living shit out of her. There's just two things: I don't want the bitch raped, I'm trying to keep this friendly. And she has a German Shepherd chained outside her door. I don't want that dog harmed in any way."

There was this long silence on the other end of the phone. Then: "Earl, Earl, Earl – I can't do *that*. Where's your Christmas spirit?"

I stood there dumbfounded, staring at the receiver, wondering if I hadn't misdialed and connected with a Buddhist monastery. Oh, well – have another freaking drink! *And Merry Christmas, Sarah.*

That left Helena – if I was still foolhardy enough to put my art and my money in the hands of the woman who had clearly been my second choice – and who therefore, it now occurs to me, might have harbored her own fantasies of payback. Helena assured me that, for a mere ('nother) four thousand dollars, she could see the job through. *Wait – what? Let me have another freaking drink.* Okay. I bit; and, in fact, she got the job done. She was awfully fast, too. Which made me uneasy, as I wasn't ignorant about

125

how much time is involved in the pulling of a print. It seemed just a little too quick. Sure enough, I later learned from the guy who burned my plates that the bitch had been bragging about the fact that she went to Jersey and had the edition run off on a high-speed press for two hundred bucks and pocketed the balance. *Hello, Hamp?* Never mind, I'll just have another friggin' drink.

By now, four years had passed. That was a lot of lovers under the bed and a lot of booze down the toilet. Going back to The League for a bonus fifth year, I decided to get into a class where I could sit off to the side and do my own thing, using The League as my studio. Soon after classes started, I was approached by this pretty little young thing who was admiring my artistic abilities. Normally, I might have wished in return to admire her aesthetic assets; but I did have my taboos. She looked to be sixteen and I had never resorted to being a child molester. On top of that, she also was sporting a wedding ring, which to me was an iron-clad impediment. A little band of metal that one could ignore as easily as a bear trap. Ouch. Where the hell's a friggin' drink when you need one?

It wasn't as though I hadn't experienced the overt or stealthy pursuit by married women before, but the truth is, I still remained a novice at avoiding them in a graceful, non-embarrassing manner. Luckily for me, just playing dumb worked more often than not. In Raechel's case, though, she seemed more willing to play dumb against dumb. In other words, she was ignoring the fact that I was trying to ignore her.

One day, while attempting to play hide-and-seek (me working on the 'hide' part), I'm sitting on the bench in The League's vestibule, trying to catch a partner for lunch out of a crowd of usuals, to no avail. The whole time, Raechel is seated next to me, and between us is the growing awkwardness of the fact that I am obviously ignoring her presence. Finally, she pipes up with the announcement that she herself is available for lunch. That's just a little like telling me the sky is blue. Short of dropping dead, what plausible maneuver can I come up with to sidestep my way around this snare trap?

With her eyes unnervingly fixed on me, I'm cornered, without space to turn around or time to think. The best I can come up with is choosing the uptown eatery I'm most comfortable in and hoping she'll be daunted by the number of blocks she'll have to walk to get there. She isn't. As we set off for Joyce's, I console myself with the idea that if I reveal enough of my history and proclivities to this Donna-Reed-world girl, I can throw a bucket of cold water on whatever fascination she apparently has with me.

I don't hold much back in painting an off-putting picture of myself, yet she sticks it out through lunch. The awkwardness is still hanging around too, and I still have to come up with what to do next. I grasp at doing the gentlemanly thing, and offer to see her to her train, her subway back to Queens. She's not getting the point I think I'm making, which, I think, is that she ought to be getting back to her reality and leaving me to try to put together the pieces of mine. Or, I guess, she's just got ideas of her own. *Premeditated* ideas, it dawns on me; and the next one is: to walk me to *my* train downtown. This is getting scary. I attempt to swallow hard and hope that I don't look too much like a deer-in-the-headlights. After she *gets on the train with me,* I keep up my attempts at swallowing. I'll have to speak eventually, though right now neither my throat nor my mind seems to be operational.

I muster a vague hope that as she finds herself walking toward the Bowery she'll get that smack in the face that will trigger *her* excuse-making mechanism and she'll hightail it outta here like any bona fide normal person from across the River. But no. Instead, she's taking in the sights along the way to my loft as though it were her first time in Paris. Decrepitude doesn't deter her and, evidently, the clues that I might be some kind of off-kilter Starving Artist character don't set off the alarm bells that her upbringing should have programmed. I have to count on what she'll encounter when we reach #334 and I open the outer door. If she makes it past the piss-smell and the broken-tiled floor and the tiny cage of the freight elevator, she's in for an eyeful of the menagerie I've been accruing. Her path will be crossed, and maybe impeded, by one Great Dane, two cats, and a rabbit that doesn't object to using the former-factory floorboards as a litter box. Her eyes will be crossed once she gets a load of the assortment of caged and terrariumed critters – the birds, the toads, the tarantula, and the pair of boa constrictors. My one apprehension in this meet-and-greet is the boas. In my experience, even those women who professed to have a fear of snakes instantly shed their clothes and jumped into bed with them. Maybe it's some kind of Eve Syndrome. As it turns out, Raechel isn't especially drawn to the snakes. But she manages the unfolding of the scene so that, in spite of my (mostly unvoiced) protestations, the afternoon passes in passionate rapture.

I have no freaking idea how I let this go so far. I've ended up seduced in the Garden of Eden, and I don't even care for apples all that much. Maybe it had to do with how beautiful she was and all. Maybe it just had to do with how stupid I was. At this point I can only hope that whatever had been going on in her head has now played itself out and that there would be no reason to carry this nonsense any further. The whole thing is ridiculous. She's been living the secure lifestyle of a Jewish Princess in Queens, and I'm living one mistake away from joining the denizens of the Bowery sidewalks downstairs. I'm not quite callous or selfish enough to consider laying back and just having fun for as long as it may last.

So much for my delusionary scruples. Who was I kidding? I did lay back a few more times that week, each time weakly struggling with my guilt and apprehension. What if she were *my* wife? Putting the shoe on *that* foot, I could practically feel it in my toes how unbefitting this all was. I kept wishing she would just come to her senses and run away. Or maybe *I* should.

Well, it's too late now, I guess. Last night, in an attempt to stop thinking, I had turned in rather early. The phone woke me. I wasn't expecting Raechel to be calling me, and I sure as hell wasn't expecting her to be asking: "When can I move in?" *Say again? What the hell just happened?* If this princess I've taken up with crosses my threshold with an overnight bag, by the next morning, I'm pretty sure, we'll find that the drawbridge back to her castle has been yanked up and guards posted by the moat – or maybe just Hubby with his arms crossed over his chest. I'll be stuck playing permanent host. Is that what I want? Is this my fate? Is this what I've been seeking and what the Higher Powers have chosen for me? Is The Force with me?

And now here I am. Today. Morning couldn't have come too soon. When a decent enough hour came, I stepped out into the day. I walked across town to The '5. It felt as though this journey took half the day. The sunlight was diffused, leaving me in a fog. It seemed the sun had gotten mugged on some side street or other. I finally got to where I wanted to be and, like any guilty blood-sucker, shunned the daylight and quickly descended the steps down into the cool dark sanctuary. On my way in, I couldn't help but notice a big blood stain at the top of the stairs. I asked the bartender what the fuck that was all about. It seems, the night before, someone got into it with Hamp and stabbed Hamp in the gut. Turns out, he was all right – but I was far from it. It just hurt me so deeply that some asshole could do someone like Hamp harm. To me, he embodied a gentle giant. I had come to feel an earnest affection for him.

As I was being told the story, I was staring at the Jason Memorial Cobblestone sitting on the bar-back. The stone commemorated the time Jason had gotten himself permanently eighty-sixed for having thrown it at Dolores when she refused to serve him a drink that he had no intention of paying for. Shit! No more Jason. Now someone tries to kill Hamp. This place can never ever be the same place for me. I can never come back here again. It's the end of an era.

I order a double vodka, neat. I stand there at the bar, staring back at the gaunt reflection in the mirror. We raise our glasses and toast: "So, what do you want to do with the rest of this day?"

5 ~ Absent without Malice

I'm blissfully absent from the Realm of the Conscious when some sort of racket erupts at my cave's entrance, shocking me back into the pain that rules my version of waking reality. The pain that clenches my lower spine and from there crawls out along the radiating nerves to pretty much everywhere in my body. The numbness of sleep, whenever I can fall into it, is my only refuge, and now, with that damn *rap-rap-rapping*, I'm evicted.

So – what? – I guess I have to contort myself up off this floor and see who's banging at the damn portal. There're probably only two things this can turn out to be: either some poor stupid Neanderthal who's lost his way on the path to humanity and is looking for a hand-out; or a hungry saber-tooth cat looking for a hand-and-arm. Begrudgingly, I erect myself as best I can, but without success at avoiding some extra stabs of pain. I take the first unsteady step towards the entrance, then the next, carefully navigating around the multiple stalagmites that clutter the cave floor at the head of where my bedding lies. I successfully make it around the dozen pill vials and the two jugs. One to drink from; the other to pee in. As dizzy as I am, this proves to be quite the task. There are those days I can walk and those I can't. It feels like there's no rhyme or reason to this debilitation, just the constant drumbeat of pain.

Man, I'm really not in the mood for this shit! I just know, when I open that door, it's either going to be the Jehovah's Witnesses, asking if I know why there's suffering in the world – *Yeah, because you continually knock at my door* – or it's going to be some inner-city black kid selling magazines. This won't be the first time either. He'll hand me a card that his new white masters wrote up for him. It will tell me that, while on his summer vacation from school, he's doing this as an alternative to throwing rocks through windows. I have to wonder if this isn't some kind of veiled extortion. On the other hand, maybe I'm supposed to buy into the idea that I'll feel good about giving this ignorant young savage a leg up by helping to redeem him from the lifestyle and natural disposition of a rock-chucker. Right. When the earnest-looking kid finds out he's not going to receive the thousand bucks he was promised, because of deductions made to cover his living costs while on this venture, I can only hope he knows which white man's window to throw the rock through.

I creak and creep toward the front door, while rehearsing the disdain I'm intending to show whichever salesman I find out there. I'm just not in the mood to be polite. I'm wishing it really were a wild beast on the other side of the door – anything that might help me out by depriving me of my fucking so-called life. I've lived with this shit for over a year now, and no doctor I've seen thus far has promised anything like the hope that there might be an end in sight. It would be nice if the medical practitioners would just admit that they don't really have a clue as to what pain is, where it comes from, and what to do about it. But that would put a dent in their God-like aura – and, in truth, we patients would like to hold on to the belief that our doctors have the answers. Hell, you might as well consult a woman about what the fuck love is.

Slowly I open the door, bracing for how I will manage the shoo-away. But – *oh, shit.* Was I just thinking this was going to be hard? Now I can only catch my breath and wish I *were* facing a salesman – or ten salesmen. But no. There, bigger than life, stands my step-dad Jim and his wife-after-my-mother, Anneliese. I can only respond to this surprise, like a scrawny wrong-again Ralph Kramden, with a stuttering: "Hum'na hum'na hum'na." I see the color drain from their faces, until all three of us must look like we're each staring at a ghost. After what feels like – no doubt, for all of us – a very long moment, I give them permission to come in. Jim and his wife can't seem to help themselves from eying me over and passing helpless looks to one another. I can't even guess what I look like to them,

131

barely able to stand, never mind up straight, never mind what I must smell like. I don't know when I bathed last. They scan the part of the room where I'm standing. What do they make of the pharmaceutical display on the floor? And the two jugs.

No doubt hoping for something that will place this scene into a normal context, they ask if Raechel and Jared are in the house or, maybe, in the backyard. My visitors, of course, are eager, if not anxious, to see my wife and, more importantly, my son, their sort-of grandson. What can I tell them? My family is not in our house here in Bushy Hollow, CT, not even in the backyard. Or running an errand in town and likely to return any minute now. What can I say?

I say, "Florida".

"Oh. Florida," say Anneliese and Jim, as matter-of-factly as they can, given how much shock and disapproval their eyes are signaling back and forth between them.

This short exchange is followed by a grim silence that seems much longer.

Jim is maintaining eyeball communication with his wife and, whether he intends it or not, the rest of him is communicating agitation, possibly fury. His comment to me comes out of the side of his face: "Do you think it's a good idea for you to be left alone in your condition?"

I guess he's made his own assessment of what my condition is. And his own judgment about my situation. There could only be one answer to his rhetorical question: *Of course not!* In spite of the mind-numbing effects of my pills, I surely know this; and now they know it. They walked in on me and let the deformed cat out of the friggin' bag: *Nobody Gives a Shit.* By 'nobody', I mean my wife. And my thirteen-year-old son. I didn't hear him ask his mother even once if she thought it was a good idea to leave his father alone on the floor for a week with his pills and jugs. So, yeah – nobody. Nobody whose shit-giving seemed to be implied in wedding vows and filial bonds. The bodies who live with me – I mean, reside in the same house as I do.

I guess I've known this for a while. You try to not know certain things, but eventually you open a door you can't get to close again. Behind that door, I'm seeing the day I collapsed in the woods. Not a day I *want* to remember, but there it is. That day in June of '93, I had decided to take my bow to the forested archery range in Wilford to try to resume my practice of target-shooting, as I was used to doing almost daily for three years. Until a slip and fall on some black ice put me out of commission for that activity along with other aspects of normal functioning. Like using my right arm, or relying on my right leg for walking – never mind moving, or not moving, my back in any way. I was used to traversing two miles through rugged terrain and shooting fourteen dozen arrows per session. After four months of waiting for my body to heal itself, I was fed up and decided to ignore the pain and debilitation. Just take up my bow and get myself to the woods. Mind over matter. Right? But matter won. This outcome left me on the forest floor with no feeling in my right leg. After spending some hours staring down a horde of hungry-looking ants, I managed to crawl out of there and back to my car.

When I got home, I had Raechel drive me to the doctor. As the doctor inserted the hypo into my spine to kill the pain – like the needle wasn't painful -- I rested my head down on Raechel's shoulder. I was seeking some touch of comfort, maybe a hint of sympathy. Hell, I would have been grateful for a grain of pity. But there was no one home. I might as well have laid my head on a cold marble tomb-stone. Maybe I had. Maybe that cold shoulder was the stone marker of our dead and not-yet-buried marriage. I sure as hell felt it, but how could I possibly admit to it? Just the same, the reality of the matter couldn't be ignored any more than if that stone slab had been dropped on my big toe.

Now that I've got the door opened, I'm rummaging further back into the closet. The truth is, I can't say I didn't feel apprehensive about our relationship from the get-go. After all, she insisted upon starting it up over my misgivings.

Maybe I was the one to put my foot in it first, by taking one little step in the wrong direction. Starting my fifth year at The Art Students' League, I had classes and lovers to choose from, as always. I should have known better when I laid eyes on the new young chick in Joe Kidd's drawing class. She was something to look at, there was something about her that drew me, but she was way too young. I did know better; but I didn't stop myself from coming up behind her where she sat at one of the long class tables and making a casual-sounding remark about Joe. If my cool delivery of that remark was supposed to be a lure and a hook, I guess it worked. I wasn't feeling so cool inside myself – more like, *Okay, I did it*, and happy to get back to my drawing board over in the corner.

But, evidently, she was reeled in. Before I could roll up the recently-pulled print of a pen-and-ink I had brought in to show Joe, this chickie had come up behind me and launched into admiring it. I was on my guard, keeping a close rein on my facial expression and a haiku-like limit to the number of syllables in my responses. I was also rolling up and rubber-banding my print, gathering my drawing materials, and obviously preparing to get myself out of there. First hint that I was in trouble: she continued to stand where she was, obviously trying to make eye contact. It seemed this chickie-poo wasn't shy about taking the reins.

Did I need this? My back was against the wall, between the rudeness of a quick mute exit and the awkwardness of mutely standing there avoiding eye contact. She had me by the bit. I had to bite. But I had no wits about me. I blurted a couple of questions that I had not intended to show any interest in, and that she answered without blinking. I think her lashes may have been fluttering, though. So, on the spot, I found that she was, in fact, thirty-one (one up on me) and not sixteen, so any protection I was getting from my taboo against robbing the cradle was blown away; and that she was, in fact, married . . . so up sprang my iron barbed-wire electrified taboo against entering into an affair.

She must have seen how, in an unguarded instant, the jolt of this knocked me back. But, evidently, she was not seeing marriage to some guy in Queens as a deterrent to putting the flirt on me. It seemed that she assumed her marital situation wouldn't be a deterrent to *me*, either – so I told her that it was. The fact that she didn't take me seriously on that point maybe should have been a loud warning siren in my head telling me that she would always expect outcomes to fit in with her designs and that, if I allowed myself to be drawn into her web, I could expect to be in a sticky predicament.

My security system must have short-circuited; maybe that's on me. But she was determined and persistent and, in less than six weeks from the first day I had laid eyes on her, she had managed to get herself into my loft, my bed, and my life. Things moved even faster in the next nine days – from me taking her to lunch (our "first date") to me handing her a pink-ribboned key to my loft (sealing my fate).

But during those nine days, I had another chance to glimpse what I was in for. At the end of a day spent together in all the expressed passion, doting, and mutual eye-gazing of new love, she would get on a train back to her twelve-years' love – if love it still was; and if it was, this was a hell of

134

a way for that lover she was married to to be treated. But for all the very present passion, doting, and gazing, I was feeling a kick in the teeth too. During our strolls on those mild autumn days, she would make a point of stopping to purchase a few pomegranates, a fruit that has a very short market season and was her husband's favorite. That bugged the ever-lovin' friggin' shit out of me. I don't know anything about the anatomy of a woman's psyche. Maybe the fruit was a guilt-offering, but I don't know what she could have been thinking, buying those big red balls for him in front of me. I do know that when *I'm* straddling a fence like that, I feel like *my* balls are being busted. Okay, a woman's anatomy is different. Are they built so that they're able to split themselves without so much pain? Even finding myself on one side of the fence *she's* straddling and knowing there's some (probably unsuspecting) guy on the other gives me heartburn. So what the fuck was I supposed to make of this? Which one of us menfolk was the chopped liver?

Jesus, that was fifteen years ago. A lot of meat and fruit has been on and off the table since then. Maybe there were two plates of chopped liver – but I was the one Raechel ended up with. *For better or worse,* I remember saying two years later. I'll have to think hard about the "better" part. Right now I'm thinking it would be hard to get worse. And I'm thinking . . . it's got to be time for me to take some kind of pill. One that knocks me out, I hope.

My eyes are open, I think. But it's dark. What time is it? Why do people always want to know that? Who cares? *People who have to take their meds on a schedule.* Right. My body and my so-called brain are pretty good timekeepers when it comes to that. One of them is telling me to take something now – it's probably what woke me up. But first I have to pee.

Did I finish my dream? I can't remember. Jim and Anneliese were here. I didn't dream that, did I? No. I can see him standing there, in a tie and jacket, typical Jim, always dapper. I hear his words: *Do you think it's a good idea for you to be left alone in your condition?* And Anneliese, a nice woman, his wife, I feel sorry for her – agreeing with him in her strong German accent. They were here. For how long? They drove all the way from Stratford. They didn't get much of a visit out of it. No one home. Even me – I wasn't entirely here. No idea when they left, or if I even offered them a

135

glass of water. It's pretty crazy, though, that they dropped in like that.

I've got boxes full of crazy in my attic. That old junk is what I was rummaging around in before the build-up of the pill cocktail in my system gave me some peace and quiet. I guess I'm still pretty zoned out. That's okay. At least I know I can blame the pain and the pills for putting me there. Not my fault. But fifteen years ago – what excuse for acting dopey did I have back then? I can't get myself off the hook by pleading innocence or ignorance. I damn sure knew better. By the end of Day One, I knew the chick was married. I knew she was a Jewish Princess from Jackson Heights. I knew she saw only what she wanted. Maybe she was breaking the Princess mold with Romantic fantasies about artists in garrets, but how would she adjust to the actuality when she found herself stuck in mine? She had standard-issue parents and six years of college, she was at The League on a whim, on a leave of absence from teaching at a junior high in Queens. That was her world. On a different planet from mine. Different universe. Worlds were about to collide, and when does that ever end well? So, if I opened my door, never mind my pitiful heart, it could only have been stupidity. Or willfulness. That ornery streak in me that makes me want to prove that I can do something just because I can't. That might be somebody's definition of crazy.

If it was crazy to let her move in six weeks after learning she existed, it was Twilight-Zone-level absurd to go out to dinner a week later with her jilted husband and the (also married) woman he'd been carrying on a three-year affair with. This woman and her husband had been socializing with Raechel and her husband during that time. They were all friends. (I'll have to check my dictionary on that concept.) So, minus the-other-woman's-soon-to-be-jilted husband and plus me, this little – as long as we're stretching the definition – friendly gathering was . . . I don't know, some kind of ceremonial changing of the guards. Proving to ourselves how sophisticated and comfortable we were. Everyone approving of everyone's choice, everyone wanting to appear at least as natural and relaxed as the next one, as if this chat-fest was the most normal Wednesday night activity in the world. If I were stoned now instead of just drugged, I might get a laugh out of it. At the time, at least, it seemed to bring the curtain down on something. After dinner, we exited, stage left – or stage right, if heading to Queens – and went home to start Act Two. In this act, my character would try to figure out his new identity. Was the drama going to unfold, as it always had, with me playing Earl and the rest of the cast being my current

136

lover; or would I have to learn a whole new role as part – at least half, I hoped – of a couple?

A couple. Earl and . . . ? This actually *is* good for a laugh. I not only had to learn my lines, I had to remember the other character's name. And for the life of me, *Lois* would not stay in my head. I'd be looking right at this woman who'd been sharing my bed for a week, and just drawing a blank. She'd be looking at me with her head tilted slightly and, as the seconds ticked by, her eyes semaphoring: *What the fuck – he doesn't remember my name??* Well, I admitted, I didn't. It wasn't a deal-breaker, though. When she got past wondering how awkward my inability to identify her might be in public settings, she decided not to leave the issue's management in my hands. She decided to change her name. She was never crazy about *Lois* anyway. Not attached to it. We tried a variation on her middle name and, when it turned out that I was able to call it to mind, she had her name legally changed.

The legal change, of course, took some time. But in our world she became Raechel as soon as she had decided to. She was acting pretty excited about it. The idea of starting a Whole New Life – which, of course, was a lot more true for her than it was for me. I only had to give up some shelf and drawer space (after acquiescing to her suggestion that I install some shelves and drawers in the loft), and half my bed – but that half was just going to waste and, like me, pining for a womanly body to fill it with her substance and warmth. She, though, was really taking a plunge, leaving a lot behind – pretty much everything – in her decision to jump on board with me. Which she envisioned as something like a donkey yoked to a grindstone jumping through a rainbow and touching down in Oz as the unicorn she was always supposed to be. Along with the yoke and the donkey-like view of life, she now had the chance to cast off her shame-laden name and leave all her Lois ways behind. *Jesus, Earl – listen to yourself!* I'm hearing my brain talking in her voice, and that's *not* a transformation I want to make. But the transformation that Lois-Raechel was promising herself and me – did I want that? Did I even know what it was all about? If it meant that she was changing into my Love-Woman, that sounded good to me. Did I believe it? The two of us were still telling ourselves the origin-story of our miraculous love, and in the story we were using names like Lancelot and Guinevere. We were mythical. So, yeah, I guess I was ready to believe in any kind of magic. Especially the kind that promised to make all my dreams come true. I was walking around like I was under a spell half the time. The other half, I would come out swinging. A dream-like change in your world can be strange and a little scary. I kept expecting to find pieces of pumpkin at my doorstep instead of a coach.

Well, it's not news to me that bubbles burst, is it. All those beautiful opalescent bubbles, blown from trust, from faith, or hope or desire . . . illusion, delusion, fantasy, or a bottle of pills – they don't let you live inside them for very long. Lurking reality is a cactus garden. The opaquer bubbles of memory, dreams, even daydreams come with thorns already poking through them – so I don't mind knowing, when I'm floating around in them, that they will pop and I can get out. The magic of meds is another story – when that wears off, the spiny needles are pricking not only my mind but my sorry-ass flesh and bones. Like now. The blankets and padding I thought I was lying on here have turned into corrugated steel. And the fairy tale of happily-ever-after with Lois-Raechel . . . well, I was never really so naïve as to believe that our marriage was going to be a bed of roses; but also not so fatalistic as to feel resigned to it being a bed of nails. But, in the end, I was only half of the partnership and had only half the say, at best, as to the crafting of the connubial mattress. I had less to say about how the bed was adorned. A nesting female wields décor to assert her presence. And, in case there were still any questions about the balance of power, at the foot of the bed Raechel installed her war chest. In that foot locker women keep their gender-specific weapons. Probably the most powerful, if not lethal, of these – above and beyond The Last Word – is the giant-slayer: Woman's Intermission. In man-speak: No Sex.

I've heard that this offensive piece of ordnance is often pulled out right after the slipping-on of the wedding bands; so I guess I can count myself lucky that Raechel held off on its deployment until after the by-product of our conjugality appeared on the scene. The appearance of that by-product, our infant son (combined with the new landlord's quadrupling the rent on our Bowery loft), was a swift kick in the ass that propelled me to figure out where we could afford to raise a child and at the same time provide him with a floor to crawl on that he wouldn't have to share with roaches and rabbit droppings. Never mind rabbit droppings – all kinds of shit was flying everywhere and there was no shortage of fans. There was no place we could afford to move to. We still owed money to the maternity ward at Mount Sinai, and we had no income except Raechel's severance pay from her ex-marriage and mine from the V.A. The worst thing about being in a tight spot is having to grasp at straws. Especially when the only straw in

138

arm's reach is my mother's.

Fuck it. *You weren't in enough pain? You had to get* that *image in your head?* Jesus. My mother holding out a straw to a drowning man – and the straw is her house in Bushy Hollow, CT. The house that she bought on the QT as soon as she heard that I would be settling in that town with my (first) new bride. Sally's response when she found out that her mother-in-law had moved to The Bush was: "I'm leaving." That was two days into the marriage. She hung in for a bit, but within the year she was out. I don't blame her. And it wasn't just on account of my mother; it was me, too. Even I found myself miserable to live with. And living in Bushy Hollow only made me and my life more unbearable.

Once I escaped, I was out of The Bush for ten years, living in the real world. How did I let myself get sucked back into this wasteland, this burg of the walking dead? Because my mother had me by the nuts. With piteous blubbering about her financial straits, she had finagled me into taking over the mortgage payments on her little shitbox house; my compensation was having my name added to the deed. After I'd been paying for years, she started in blubbering about how she couldn't afford the upkeep on the shitbox and was hoping to sell it and find a little rental to move into. If she sold the house, I knew that I would never see a dime back of my investment. I knew this because, when she sold my grandfather's house, her two brothers never saw a penny of the proceeds. Her brothers didn't need the money and, God knew, she did. Literally, in her mind, God knew, and it was God's intention that her needs be met. Once she learned of my predicament, God presented her with the answer to not one but two of her prayers. She could be relieved of supporting the house (while continuing to half-own it) by making it available for me and my family to move into. As a bonus, she racked up some martyr points by virtue of this sacrifice. At the same time, her wish to have me in striking distance was gratified. She'd never see me as long as I lived in Sin City, where a favored charity case of Jesus would never set foot.

I have such a fucking headache right now. The inside of my head is in NY, where all of me wants to be, in the loft I was ambitiously remodeling as though I had the deed to it instead of a month-to-month verbal rent agreement; the outside of my head is on the floor of this house in Bushy Hollow, CT – that I was ambitiously remodeling as though I had the deed to it instead of a co-signature on my mother's deed. In both cases, I was in

139

such a sweat to design and craft a dwelling so ingenious and perfect that it would ensure the enduring whole-someness of my family – and I was building this fantasy-world on quicksand. Fantasy and quicksand – a perfect combination for disaster . . . or, at least, deep disappointment. Well, I had that in spades – even though I tried to remedy the second situation by remortgaging the CT house so I could buy my mother out; and the first by letting the new landlord buy *me* out – that is, offer me pack-up-and-run money so he could get closer to his goal of the number of empty lofts he needed in the building in order to proceed with upgrades that would enable him to apply for a C. of O. so that the units could be legitimately leased and rents could legitimately skyrocket. The other tenants banded together, hired a lawyer, and put their monthly rent money into an escrow account, which we were invited to contribute to. Which, sadly, we could not afford to contribute to.

Acting like the rat I felt like, I was required to skitter, under cover of darkness, to a meeting point on the West Side, where I was scooped up by a limo containing the landlord and his lawyer and accountant. This landlord, for God's sake, turned out to be – like Milton 'The Loft King' L. The Third – too young to have amassed his evident wealth by virtue of his own labor. In a few years, I knew, I would catch up to his present age; but never – if I lived to be a million – to his present fortune and power. I was already daunted as soon as I entered the vehicle when I perceived that 80% of its occupants were the landlord, his two cronies, and their driver; and then, as these boys from Jersey took me for a ride to the West Side docks, I tried to be inconspicuous as I scanned the inside of the car for bags of cement. I only had to sign some papers, though – and agree to keep my mouth shut – and I was able to walk away with my life and $6,000. Enough to pay the hospital and the NY-to-CT moving company. That was great, I guess. But it's hard to say "Yay, I got away" when what you really want is to stay.

So moving here accomplished what? Yeah, the kid and the dog and the cats and the rabbits gained access to the world outdoors. I hope this benefited the kid; for the animals, what it added to the quality of their life it subtracted from the length of it. What other positives were there? Well, there was getting out of the line of fire of Lois-Raechel's parents. Of the four eyes they shared between them, not one of them looked upon me kindly. It's pretty discouraging when you rank lower in someone's esteem than the known (albeit Jewish) philanderer Lois would still have been attached to.   Her parents were savvy to his ways before their daughter was, yet they still found no reason to be pleased with my role in her seeing the light. And what I gained by putting some distance between them and me was reduced to worthless when *they* up and moved to Florida a year later. But in running from my in-laws' cold shoulder, I ran straight into my mother's Venus flytrap. I mean lap. Same difference. Once out of the city, with no moat of Sodom and Gomorrah around me, I had the woman right in my backyard. Fucking-literally. In my house. In my face. In my business. Again. All the time.

So what had I gained? A mortgage? On a house that fell on me like a weight around my neck, anchoring me to this purgatory of a place. Did I think there was pixie dust in all the sweat and devotion I poured into transforming this shitbox I was stuck with into a Christmas-card cottage? Did I think I could hammer-and-nail a Hallmark family into it? Maybe I did. Or maybe, if I just kept hammering, I wouldn't hear the foundation cracking.

But all this aside, the real boot-in-the-ass out of NY was the economics. Facing the fact that the city's cost of living has outrun your resources. Somehow becoming a chip that falls where it may – where it thinks (if a chip can think) that it may have a chance to reconstitute itself. I'm thinking of George, too – sucked out of NY by the undertow of insufficient funds, washed up on Virginia Beach like a fish out of water.   Suffocating. Heartbreaking – as insufferable as George can be – to see him closing out his life that way, trying to spruce up his facade and maintain his illusions. It's depressing as hell to think that I was in the same boat when I found myself cast adrift in The Hollow thirteen years ago. Except that I had no facade to worry about. And I was not so depressingly old. That, of course, meant that I'd have to face an unforeseeably long stretch of time in this joint, encumbered not just with myself and my dog (etc.) but with the weight of responsibility and anxiety for the well-being of my son. And, also unlike George, I had a wife. Along with all of the Big Three marriage underminers: disharmony in the areas of Sex, Money, and In-Laws. My wife had her take on each of these. (I had mine.) I wanted, she implied, too much sex. (Yeah – *more than none*.) I spent money too freely. (In practical terms, though, a zero bank balance made tedious record-keeping unnecessary.) It was uncomfortable having in-laws who mistrusted their respective offspring's partner. (A greater misfortune for *me*, I think, because the bar was set very low for coming across parental figures I might find more bearable than my mother.)

There was no shortage of parental figures – they were coming out of the woodwork. I think this expression suggests that, while *in* the woodwork, they were busy chewing away at structural elements. Like my backbone, and my feet. There I was, trying to stand my ground, straighten my spine, hold my head up, figure out how to function as an adult and whether any of my parental overseers was succeeding at it.

My in-laws, mercifully, are in Florida, but they can still transmit their disapproval, through microwaves or mental telepathy or something. My mother is in her own world, with Jesus, where she can play all day being Blessed Baby Gloria or The Blessed Virgin Gloria, and he's happy to be The Loving and Providing Daddy or The Loving and Providing Husband Who Espouses Chastity as a Virtue. She's all set – you'd think. What does it say for Jesus that she still needs *me* to be on board with all of it, especially her myth of Holy Martyr Mother Gloria. To get absolution for herself, she's always dragging me back into my childhood – the last place I want to revisit. And she really doesn't want to hear what I encounter there. Her awareness of the actual child in the room who is her grandson is overpowered by her insistent and rampantly verbalized vision of *my* childhood, which I'm still trying to escape, and her own, which she's still trying to get back to.

So now, today, I'm flat on my back, hurting, doped up, feeling frustrated and pitiful – kind of like a two-year-old about to have a tantrum. Which is what part of me would love to do. While part is trying to act like a grown-up. Trying to get a handle on what that entails – when my stepfather steps in. To all appearances, a manly man, always perfectly presentable, knowing what he's about. With his wife at his side. My wife is off in Florida, with my removed-as-possible in-laws. No danger of my ever-hovering mother showing up if she sees Jim's car in my driveway. But Jim is here, and he's a presence.

Jim's grim-eyed pronouncement, seconded by his wife – *Are you sure it's a good idea for you to be left alone in your condition?* – hit me like a slap, a humiliation, a condescending rebuke by an adult to a slow-witted child. But, then again, he had delivered it like a question. Did that mean that he was eliciting my opinion of the matter, as one grim-eyed adult to another? An astounding and uplifting possibility – but, in the end, only heaping

142

more humiliation on me, as I have no memory of what lame and infantile response I gave them, if any. But there's one more layer here I'm seeing under the haze. The haze of the present moment, and the haze that cloaks the past. I've had my glimpses, back then, behind Jim's hard veneer. I didn't know what to make of them then – they opened a peephole to a scary place where I only felt smaller, more helpless and guilty because – I think I get it now – that's how *Jim* felt. That was inside of *him*. I think maybe it was more horrible for me to see *that* than to see the back of his hand coming at me. Way more horrible for me to put my tiny useless hands on his shuddering back or bring him a cold cloth to lay on his forehead when he wept in the dark over laying a hand on me and choked out his fear of burning in hell. I don't know for sure if he felt any caring or remorse for me or my mother, or only for his own sorry tormented soul.

Old habits of the mind and heart die hard. Jim walks into my cave and I feel like a primitive child. But I'm a father. If I'm not a man now, what will it still take? God knows, the example of Jim schooled me well in what never to do. My son would never have reason to fear me. I've held true to that – but maybe I took it too far. Great, he doesn't tremble in my presence. And sure, there were plenty of hugs and happy smiles in his childhood. Now I'm just looking for a nod of recognition. I try to fathom this alienation, this withdrawal, this absence of my son's presence and affection. He passed through twelve and turned thirteen while I was on the floor and not able to be there to guide or support his transition. Transition to traditional manhood – yeah, we know how grounded in reality that premise is since at least the middle of this century. I guess, in the old days, a boy leaped into manhood without wallowing for seven years in entitled adolescence. If that's the threshold my son is standing on, good luck to me. Maybe there's something deeper than that . . . does he perceive layers in me that he can't comprehend, that he instinctively protects himself from by distancing himself? Or maybe it's shallower – a spin-off of the genes and character passed down the line through his mother. A congenital self-absorption.

God – talk about self-absorption. As if I wasn't feeling low enough, now I've plunged over the edge of a chasm filled with *me*. I should be in my own element here, but this black hole feels more inescapable than Bushy Hollow, and the air more unbreathable. The shroud of my whole life of bad choices smothering me. Depression. A familiar robe, I've worn it before. Sometimes you can get a few threads in the fabric to unravel, to give you some wiggle-room, maybe catch a breath of air with the wind blowing in a different direction. But with these mind-wanderings on my son, I feel the fabric tightening. I have a son. I made that choice – the one I can't walk away from. That's a gene I didn't inherit from my biological father – the gene that's cool with abandoning the child whose life you set in motion. Which the man – my mother's first husband, and previously and subsequently the husband of four other women – did five times. He didn't even ever wait to see if his kid would become an estranged teenager before making his decision. His escape. Whether anyone appreciates it or not, I don't take after him in that.

By 'anyone', I mean 'including me'. I'm so down the shithole now, I have to grasp at low-hanging bits of memory to find a time when I could say I felt well of myself. I try to think why I did then. Maybe it was nothing more than being sixteen. I don't know. But I was living off the land. Just me and what food and shelter I could muster up each day. Maybe my head was not in the right place at the time; maybe I wasn't doing the right thing. But one thing I wasn't was anyone's enemy. There was no one to dislike me, disapprove of me, or let me know that I was somehow responsible for their unhappiness. I had, simply, myself and the space I occupied. Shit, the biggest problem I had was at the end of the day, when it was time to sleep, deciding: Do I want to lay watching the fire, or do I want it to warm my backside?

Well, I'm not lying by any damn fire. The only fire here is in my nerve cells and bones. In spite of that, sometimes I have to stir these bones, and then go through the usual twists and turns to resettle them. I hear myself moaning and groaning as I ease myself down again onto the foam pad that doesn't do a hell of a lot to cushion my back from the floor. Now what? Oh yeah, there's that fucking ceiling again. I could be terminally sick of staring at it, except that I remember the barely-seven-foot-high acoustic-tiled atrocity that it used to be. Now, at least, it's a splendiferous cathedral ceiling, ingeniously crafted by me in the Tudor style. If I had not remodeled it and had to stare at that old oppressive perforated expanse looming over me, I think by now I would have shoved my vial of Vicodin down my throat and choked on it. I can stand being bored out of my mind for only so long. But, I have to admit, all these spatial divisions I designed, using inset dark-stained wood strips, make for a charming view, one that's easy on the eyes. With six major segments in the pitched ceiling and many smaller ones in the upper wall and little balconies, I count about forty wood-framed canvases of white plaster. It's too bad the scaffolding I used during the remodeling process is gone. As long as I have to be flat on my back in agony, I could be doing a Michelangelo. But even without egg-tempera frescoes, this ceiling is a work of art.

Yeah, and what a freaking battle-royal it was to get Her Highness's permission to undertake it. I'm betting Pope Julius II was a pussycat at the negotiating table compared to the rabid lioness I had to come to terms with. God, what a shithole this place was when we and our vanful of stuff were unloaded into it. Between the duffer who built it – a guy who didn't know the business end of a hammer from a soup ladle – and its subsequent owner – a woman who was waiting for Walt Disney to animate her brooms, mops, and scrub-brushes while she slept (my dear mother) – the house was a screaming announcement of failure. The embodiment of the failure I was resolved not to be, or to live in. Every bit of it – from its dingy aluminum siding to the cheap linoleum on the floor, the low-slung florescent lighting, tacky furnishings, and chain-link-fenced yard – triggered my freeze-fight-or-flight response. Running away, with no place else to run to, and no money, was the most tempting idea. But Raechel, the baby, and the just-uncrated menagerie didn't seem as daunted by their new surroundings as I was. They had no history of being swaddled in the robes of Saint Gloria, so were not driven to the brink of mental suicide or wishful matricide by finding themselves enveloped in her aura and décor. Also, they had no clue – or responsibility – regarding what the place needed just to be habitable. The snakes' nest of electric wiring, for example, that was not up to code. But we had four walls and a roof over our heads that we would not get evicted from. I remembered that there were times I was homeless. And those were feeling like the good old days.

After I got past the state of blood-freeze and conceded that flight was not an immediate option, I began making plans for the fight. I envisioned this as a fight with the existing structural and decorative elements that needed to be pried loose, and wrestling new materials into place with muscle and carpentry tools. That was definitely a battle I would have to gear up for, but I was up to that challenge. The killer was that, where I looked for allies, I got ambushed. By the woman I lived with, the town I lived in, and the fate that ruled my life.

Okay, Earl, that line sounds like something out of a trailer for a melodrama. I'm seeing Fate twirling her curly mustache. Yeah, very amusing. Not so amusing, though, packing marriage, parenthood, and moving to The Lost World into six months. Two mostly-mismatched souls and a baby, stuck in a cinder-block-and-pine-paneled box barely big enough to turn around in, with nothing outside its door to turn to. All we had was ourselves to rub up against. And neighbors who weren't even kind to stray dogs, never mind to outsiders like us. It hit home pretty quick that this place sure as shit wasn't NYC – and I guess, in some ways, I was no longer the person who had felt so at home there. But I didn't want to admit it.

Even now, I don't want to think about it. But, laying here, I have nothing to do *but* think. God! What happened to my life? It feels all but over. You pick a path – or maybe you go down one that you might not have freely chosen – only to find it a dead end. Oops. You want to turn back. That's when Karma slaps you in the face with the fact that the crows have eaten your bread-crumb trail. *Payback. All those crows – all those descendants of the one you shot with your bow so many years ago – have not forgotten or forgiven.* And I'd thought eating that greasy bird was punishment enough.

Yowch! I have to adjust my back a little more. Two inches of foam do next to nothing to soften the brutal hardness of the floor. My eyes scan the ceiling looking for a single canvas. A surface to paint an abstraction from my pain on. The pain in my spine is having a field day with my head. I keep thinking what a pain in the ass she was. The Mistress of the Purse Strings. It was always about freaking money with her. When I felt like I couldn't breathe in this stinking cave and broached the idea of putting in a cathedral ceiling, I was instantly hit with a resounding NO! God forbid we should spend a damn dime on our comfort – like we know what the fuck that is anymore. Well, I didn't deal with that two-letter word any better than John had. Besides, our marriage at that point was only fifteen months young. Certainly an inadequate time span for Raechel to have thoroughly blow-torched my old skin off. I was annoyingly persistent in pushing my plan for home improvement, presenting the argument that, since we had decided not to replace the furnace in the crawl space that the recent hurricane (absurdly, but aptly, named Gloria) had taken out, and had decided, instead, to install a coal stove in the living room, and since that would mean having to make a hole in the ceiling for the exhaust pipe, why not just make a bigger hole? *Well, I sense that I'm almost to first base; two more miles to third and then maybe I can steal home from there.*

She was equally persistent in her nagging. "How much is it going to cost? How *long* is it going to take? *How much* is it going to cost?!"

146

"No more than two weeks and two hundred dollars," says I.

She didn't acquiesce. But she didn't murder me in my sleep. I took it that that was her way of saying okay. When I set out to do my thing to the walls and ceiling, I was secretly smiling to myself. God only knows, I had to keep any small joy secret.

And then, like a crazy person, I went ahead and started the two-week project.

There I am. Standing in the pitch blackness and sweltering June heat of the attic which is all of four feet high at the peak and keeping me painfully and exhaustingly bent at the waist, I'm casting my gaze over the future of this space, and seeing the very now and the very present. A pink sea of insulation two feet deep. Half naked but fully covered with a sheet of sweat, I spend the day throwing the never-ending pink shit down the well of the drop staircase. Yeah, that fiberglass dust has to be great for everyone's health. Wonderful for the one-year-old I'm trying to make a home for. Now I stand here in the skeletal hollow. I'm alone and facing one terrifying fact: It's too late to turn back. At this point, I don't even have the space it takes to turn my *mind* around. *Do you have any idea of what you've just done? Do you have a clue as to what you have to do to make this thing right? And how much is this really going to cost?! In money, labor, aggravation, pain. And nagging.*

My mind is racing, but in that tight space it has nowhere to go but around, like a crazy vortex of sound, echoing the same questions that had raced through my mind at the conclusion of Raechel's short and sweet pronouncement: "I'm pregnant."

All my adult life I longed for a wife and son. Here I am, with an actual wife and son. Just like the poor saps who longed to invest in the stock market and got their big chance on October 28, 1929. Okay, what the fuck do I do now? I don't have a plan. All I know is that I have to get all this wood out of here, but I also need a platform to work from. Okay. A platform. Now all I have to do is engineer it. I don't want to paint myself into a corner. But, yeah, I'm feeling cornered alright. I've never had a relationship that lasted more than thirty days (if you don't count the travesty of my first marriage). Now I'm staring down the throat of the rest of my life – or, at best, eighteen years and nine months of parental obligation from conception to cutting the cord.

That's almost funny – nine months. That's exactly what it took me to craft this ceiling. Nine months and two thousand dollars.

I sure as shit hope Raechel doesn't think that I set out to purposely deceive her. I mean, things change. It wasn't until I got the attic gutted that I found that there wasn't a square angle or a level, plumb, or straight line in the joint. With so much out-of-whackiness, trying to create a simple clean-cut contemporary look was out of the question. I had to figure out a way to make some visual sense out of why everything looked off-kilter, askew, or misaligned. The pseudo-old look of the Tudor style worked for the house. What I couldn't figure out was why our *marriage* was sagging and otherwise out of alignment and running amok. Or how to fix it. I felt like I had been putting energy all my adult life toward my vision of having a family, especially being a father. As far as staying on course with a wife – after fifty lovers, I thought I had pretty much worked the bugs out. So why was the whole thing not working? I sure as shit knew what wasn't helping. The same goddamn thing that didn't help my first marriage: we were marooned in the town of Bushy Hollow – where the populace had apparently taken a breather on the evolutionary rung of village-centric, just one step up from the Bronze Age.

If the pressure got too unbearable inside our four walls, there was no respite beyond them. And that Beyond exerted pressure in reverse – a negative energy that pushed against our windows and seeped in under the door. We hadn't been in our still-alien home more than a few days that first time we ventured out to get a break and a simple meal at a local diner. One member of the group in the booth behind ours was entertaining the others with an account of his encounter the night before with a raccoon that had wandered onto his porch. An image popped into my mind of the raccoons I had enjoyed distracting from my garbage can with offerings of peanuts and other morsels. But I had the feeling that the rest of the story I couldn't help overhearing was not going to be about ol' Hank calling his kids over to the window to see a cute furry animal. No, it was about Hank getting his baseball bat and clubbing the critter to death. The crude laughter from Hank's gang made it obvious that getting the blow-by-blow on this turn of events added relish to their dinner. And made mine undigestible.

In the weeks and months that followed, nothing happened to reassure us that The Hollow, after all, had its redeeming qualities. I don't know which of us had it worse in facing the bleakness of this reality. Raechel had probably thought that The Bowery was the worst place she could possibly

148

have landed. (In Queens, the word 'Bowery' was always followed by the word 'bum'). She couldn't quite get it that, after what might seem like a reasonable period of adjustment, The Hollow would still be a soulless, unwelcoming place. As for me, I knew full well what a hell-hole this town was and would be again, and I couldn't believe I was condemned to another stay here. I guess I can say *good luck to me* again, if I'm still waiting for someone to commute my sentence.

We couldn't manage anything like a vacation or getaway to anywhere involving actual travel expenses. There wasn't even a friend or relative we could crash with – except for George, and that was only once – Papa, Mama, and Baby Bear bunking together in a twin bed in his Westport carriage house – when we were forced to evacuate during The Hurricane. What if we tamely ventured on a short outing across the town line? We tried that. Anyone tuning in to our serial misadventures might have found it kind of funny: In the Village of Hamilton, *we* became the yokels on the other side of the booth.

In The Hollow, they weren't quite sure what we meant when we asked where the bookstores were. We discovered that we had to go to Hamilton for anything so hoity-toity as literary matter. When we walked into J. R. Julio, Tome Purveyors, in the middle of Hamilton's three-block-long Main Street, we felt a refreshing breath of Manhattan air. There were two rooms of trimly-stocked bookshelves, and a sophisticated staff. Our repartee with Madame at the counter seemed to be going well. Raechel was an ex-English teacher with a Literature degree; she even knew where the commas and semicolons went and seemed to be holding her own with Madame, who was taking down our vitals for the bookstore's no-doubt-exclusive mailing list. The trimly-dressed woman was pleasantly recording our address until we hit the word 'town'. Writing the words 'Bushy Hollow' on a J. R. Julio registration card seemed to be taboo, as did smiling at a person who had uttered the phrase 'Bushy Hollow'. Madame turned her head. I heard Raechel murmur, "Did you just feel the temperature drop a few degrees?", and I observed Madame discreetly brush our card off her counter and into the shit can below. No explanation was offered for the abrupt ending of the interview, since we had become nonentities, consigned to the circular file under the heading GU (Geographically Undesirable). We left the store. I think we passed through the door without opening it, like ghosts. What existence did we have here? We couldn't manage to be either low-life or high-brow enough to fit in anywhere.

In the anywhere Out There, at least, we maintained a camaraderie, partners in a united front against the common enemy. In the space inside our home, we partnered like flint and steel. We were made of different stuff. Rubbing against each other sparked misgivings on pretty much a daily basis. And sometimes ignited hostilities that went underground as smoldering resentment. At least I know that's true for me. I don't know how Raechel would describe our life together but, if she were being honest, and in touch with reality, she'd have to admit that nobody was happy, and that it wasn't just me who needed to change. Maybe I could have taken it more in stride if she had come at me brandishing long, sharpened knives. Her m.o. instead involved persistent nuisance attacks by a molestation of mosquitoes – *zzt* . . . *zzt* . . . *zzzt* . . . she was slowly bleeding me to death.

Raechel had her share of shit to deal with when we moved here. I get that. She was the only one qualified to do the breast feedings at whatever hour of the day or night. She had been displaced from her accustomed people and surroundings. She found herself with no one to relate to or have a conversation with except a three-month-old baby and me. At times, I'm sure, it must have been difficult, in her mind, to distinguish between us. Her mind was having difficulty enough hanging on to sanity, given that conditions in both the Bowery loft and the Bushy Hollow shack had to be a neat-freak's worst nightmare. It didn't take me long to find myself at the receiving end of her compulsion for order and tidiness. I'll cut her some slack and say she couldn't help it. That's her nature, the way she has to be, no matter who suffers for it. Okay. But she seemed unable to deal with the concept that other people and things couldn't help it either. Shit happens. Sometimes it *has to* happen. That's the way things are. So when I'm remodeling the house, there's going to be plenty of dust and debris. She can throw guilt at me, The Mess Maker, in her insane efforts to sweep up every mote and speck as it falls, but there's always going to be more coming down. That's what happens during a building project. And is it a mystery to her that, when I'm cooking dinner, I'd like the stirring spoon and pot lid to be at hand, where I left them, not washed, dried, and put away while my back is turned? Can I help it if I express my frustration and maybe raise my voice a bit? Does she have any idea how much anger I'm holding in, how much restraint I'm using to keep myself from smashing the half-cooked dinner on the floor? I know she's been putting up with stuff – starting from the day she so recklessly planted herself in my loft. I was not unaware or unsympathetic, watching her valiantly sweeping rabbit poop off the 1,400 square feet of floorboards at least twice a day. It was a demoralizing chore – but what are you going to tell a rabbit? They can't help themselves.

I guess this shit is part of the answer to my question about what went wrong. What happened? The years passed, almost fifteen of them, receding like the tide, leaving us on shaky ground. There were no earthquakes, no floods or tornadoes. Just an almost imperceptible erosion of the common ground beneath our union, the way the ocean, over time, steals the shore. Grain of sand by grain of sand.

Or maybe all that sand went out the door on the bristle end of Raechel's broom – she'd never have left it on the floor. Yeah, well, it wasn't all that simple anyway. It wasn't just the two of us. It was also the Young One. And the Old Ones. And now the whole kaboodle of them are kaboodling down in Florida. Tracking in sand from the beach and sweeping it out. Who knows what they do down there. I know old people are dying to retire there. Me, I would rather die than set foot in the place. Of course, my in-laws would be fine with that.

But that didn't stop them from coming back to where I live – once a year, for two weeks, to see their grandchildren. The week they would stay in The Hollow Bush, whatever hours my son spent in their hands I spent dreading what might befall him and who I would have to kill if he came to harm, if I didn't self-destruct with grief and rage first. Maybe there's a gene for common sense that Raechel's parents were unable to pass down to her, since neither of them has it. My teeth and my fists are clenched right now – even my brain is clenched just thinking about it. How the three of them have a tacit conspiracy to ignore whatever Earl says and undo whatever Earl does. Maybe it's too late to protect my psyche from this family's rampant disregard and stupidity, but I was resolved to protect the welfare and safety of my son. The Little Pidge was the most precious thing God had ever created, and God help anyone who threatened his well-being. By 'anyone', I mean – well, his mother and grandparents top the list.

Am I just a crazy bigoted in-law hater? Is the danger to my child all in my whacked-out head? I think the evidence points to NO.

Jesus. Why am I dredging all this up? The truth is, I don't have to do much dredging – it's more like I've been holding the lid down on a volcano all these years, ever since there was a small vulnerable person in my life who called me Daddy. Who I gave my whole heart to. Who – *shit, just reliving those scenes of him in harm's way, I'm shaking.* I can't even get this

151

fucking match to hold steady enough to light my cigarette. I can't calm my mind, I'm ready to explode . . . . But what the fuck's the point of erupting now? Those three walking catastrophes who intruded into my life by way of a so-called marriage don't know how lucky they are that the idea of life in prison was a deterrent to me. So the shit all landed on Earl. Whatever molten anger I spewed at *them* rolled off the invisible shield of invulnerability that surrounds idiots. They did hear the sensible warnings I addressed to them just prior to each of the times that they put my son in danger. I know this because they proceeded to do the exact opposite.

There was the time I removed the empty Colonel Sanders bucket from the stove top, where one of the trio had idiotically placed it. I called their attention to this violation of common sense by simply stating: "Nothing belongs on top of a stove that's not a pot or pan." I left the room and, minutes later, the bucket was back on the stove and, sure as shit, it caught fire. *No harm done,* I suppose they thought, since I was quick enough to get the bucket into the sink. *I guess you were right, Earl* didn't seem to enter their minds. It certainly didn't come out of anyone's mouth.

During that same visit – Jared was about two – the Grandidiots had him at their rental cottage in the evening, so Raechel and I could get a break and go out for a relaxing dinner – or so they could try out some new way of exposing our child to harm. And I was supposed to relax? Before leaving the cottage, I did a safety scan. Grandma had started cooking dinner. There was a pot of simmering water on the stove with its handle jutting out over the edge. I turned the handle in, and made a patient observation that pot handles should never protrude from the stove top. I had misgivings about leaving, but I tried to tell myself that even the Grandidiots couldn't be so obtuse as to not pay attention now to where the pot handle was. But, no – it ended up in reach of little Jared, who wanted to be helpful in the kitchen. Unsupervised? When Raechel and I got back to the cottage, there was Jared with the front part of the top of his little red sneaker cut away and his toes wrapped in bandages. And his grandparents at least looking sheepish. They had taken him to a doctor and he had stopped crying. So I guess my relief and gratefulness to God pushed aside my outrage. As we left, Grandpa came as close as he could to mustering an apology. He told me that Jared kept crying: "I want my Daddy", and that that broke his heart to hear. *I should not like to tell you what I would like to do to your heart. A pot of boiling oil comes to mind.*

Okay, well, since my pain level now is already through the roof, and I was foolish enough to open the door to these memories, I might as well let the next one in and get this over with. Now I'm seeing the time I was in the middle of building a gable wall inside the attic. There was no flooring over the joists, and no ceiling over the part of the kitchen directly below my work area. The joists were spaced 32" on center, which left a lot of gaping spaces that my heavy tools could fall through if I so much as looked at them wrong, and I had all I could do to watch out for my own footing. Between having to do this damn job and having to endure my damn in-laws visiting, I guess I was in a dangerous mood to start with. But I didn't find the visit reason enough to interrupt my work. I was already sweltering and shirtless in the heat and just wanted to get the job done.

The one thing I did after the in-laws arrived and before I climbed back up the dropdown staircase was to get right in Raechel's face, with her parents close behind her in the living room, and announce in the strongest voice possible: "Under *no* circumstances or for *any* reason is *anyone* to step foot in the kitchen. I can't be worrying about what's going on down here while I'm worrying about keeping myself and my tools up there!" *It would obviously be extremely dangerous for anyone to be standing below me, especially if I don't like you.* I had given fair warning.

So here I am, banging around in the stifling heat, wrestling another piece of this crazy house into shape, when *it happens.* I watch as a crowbar my right foot just kicked falls through the gap in the kitchen ceiling about eight inches from my mother-in-law, who's stooped over in front of the open freezer. *Damn! Missed.* But if my son had been there at her side, it would have been all over. I don't bother with stairs or a ladder – I just do a Batman and drop down through the ceiling. My boots hit the floor hard and squarely, about a foot from the startled woman, who's just gotten a double whammy of heavy objects crashing down at her and is trying to appear innocent and aggrieved, like none of this is her fault. At the same time, I'm bellowing: *"What fucking part of don't set foot in the kitchen didn't you fucking understand!?!?!"*

I was seeing only red, hearing only my blood pounding in my ears, so I don't know how close Grandpa might have come to slapping me with his glove, but he made the wiser choice of agreeing with his wife's idea that they should leave. Which they did. Though still in a blind rage, I didn't miss their glares of sullen indignation. And then came Raechel's whining. God – I don't remember what the fuck I did then, but I knew I was in no condition to pick up a tool. Any of them could be a lethal weapon. And

153

there was no way I could get back to work. Raechel didn't get it, as usual. *Hadn't I maybe over-reacted?* she wondered aloud at me.

She has no idea. And it's a good thing she's 1,500 miles south of what I'd like to over-react on her right now. Because right now I'm still seeing Jared tumbling down those stairs. And what was his mother doing? Just like *her* mother, she was ignoring what I'd just said to her. She was taking Jared into the bathroom to change his diaper, in the home of a couple of the few friendly acquaintances we had, and I noticed that she had to walk past the staircase that went down to the front door. She would, of course, have to walk past the staircase again on her way back to the living room. It would have been nice if I didn't feel that a reminder was needed, but I felt that it was, so I pointedly said: "Make sure Jared doesn't come out of the bathroom without you. I don't want him falling down the stairs." A few minutes later, I find myself jumping out of my chair at the sight of Jared, alone, toddling toward the staircase. Before I can reach him, he's gone. *Plopity-plop-plopity-plop-plopity-plop.* I feel every bump and tumble. Raechel is just about appearing at the door of the bathroom as I fly down the stairs and scoop up my crying son. I just want to get him out of there, away from her. I rush out the front door and sit with my child cradled in my arms. He's still crying. As am I.

What the hell was wrong with her? Whatever it was, it hasn't changed – she's got some pieces missing. All I was thinking was: I never want her ever to touch him again!

Yeah, and I don't want to have to pee into a bottle, or wake up and find I'm still Earl. But what does that get me? I'm still here and I still have to pee. I'm still staring at the ceiling, and I'm starting to see the fresco I'm painting on one of its plaster canvases. It's a scene from when I was up on the scaffolding, spackling that very section of the ceiling. I see I'm taking a break, having a smoke. But I'm hearing the scraping sound of the spackling knife running across the ceiling. How can that be? Here are my hands, both of them, and they aren't in motion or holding the knife. I look behind me, and there's Jared, thirteen months old, happily spackling away. I have an ever-lovin' shit-fit, right after I'm done having a heart attack. That little rascal had not only negotiated a ten-foot ladder, but had also managed the tricky business of maneuvering from the ladder onto the platform. I'm sure it would have seemed very cute if I'd been watching it on someone else's home video. Am I supposed to be feeling proud of my precocious child, or asking *where the fuck his mother was the entire time it took him to climb up?! Your Honor, I plead guilty to justifiable I-hate-your-fucking-guts!!*

Okay – that's it. *My* guts are twisted in a knot. I can't take any more. Where's the clicker, the remote to this channel I'm stuck on? Shit. Get me out of here! It's like I'm wringing my own neck instead of . . . . yeah, and now, instead, I'm twisting the cap off this damn vial of pills. And it's fucking stuck. God, is there anything out there that's not in conspiracy to make me feel powerless? Is there anything I *can* do? Oh. I've got the top off. Thank you, God. I need a pill. A bunch of pills. I wish I still had Soma. That was some really good shit. I miss it. Soma was my friend. Those little pills gave me the power. I could never have met the contract on that book without them. Another one of Your little jokes, huh? *Let's see how Earl handles this one. We'll get him the book contract he's been trying to get for years, give him a few days to feel good and excited about it, and then put some black ice under his feet and down he goes! Ha-ha-ha-ha. Just to add a little more fun to this chapter of his story, we'll have the publishers – who've already put some of his paintings in their monthly arts magazine – ask him to do a how-to book using a medium he knows absolutely nothing about. And what does Earl say?*

"Have I as much talent in the medium of acrylics as I've demonstrated in watercolor and pen-and-ink? Are you kidding me? I'm a master of all mediums!" (How do you spell 'acrylics'?)

And he strategically adds:

"I wouldn't like to appear to be blowing my own horn, so I'd just as soon not include any of my own acrylic work in the volume." (What work would that be?)

And then the clincher:

"Oh. I have to? And I have to provide a step-by-step demonstration as well? Sure. No Problem."

What was Earl thinking? He was thinking about his experience, way back when, in securing that position taking care of George's dogs, with his brash: "Sure, I can do anything." *Crazy Earl. And how the hell does this shit play out?*

How it played out is – I pulled it off. Me. I did it. Well, me and the Soma. And, yes, Raechel helped. It was no small task. I had to submit a finished outline within thirty days of signing the contract, and a chapter every month after that. To do this, I had to select eleven other artists from the list of a hundred the publishers provided me, which I first narrowed down to thirty who I asked to send me samples of their art and writing. In the four months since the black ice, I had chosen the artists, received their

155

materials, gotten Erik to photograph the product shots I needed, and studied and practiced acrylic techniques, and then it was June and I collapsed in the woods and ended up on the floor. This floor. Where I live. And when the chapters weren't coming in, the project editor started to call. And all I could do was throw her some bullshit – two points for me, bullshit-throwing is something I'm good at – but how long could that go on? I had to throw myself on my good doctor's mercy – okay, I had to take gross advantage of Dr. K.'s trusting nature – and ask him for some meds that would light my fire.

And then came the miracle of Soma. It didn't resolve my pain or mobility issues; I still couldn't use my right arm to pick up a cup of coffee, never mind wield a paint brush. But, since I was abusing the Soma, I didn't know that. Take enough of it and you don't give a shit about how you feel or what you can or can't do. You can't even remember what you did. The Rx was four pills per day, max. I was taking four pills a pop. I can remember medicating each morning, letting it set in, going out to the studio, and standing in front of a white canvas. I'd be laughing out loud, crying: "Jesus, it hurts like hell and I don't give a flying fuck." Then the lights would go out. My brain would be as blank as the canvas. Every afternoon at four o'clock, I would come to – and find myself laying on the kitchen floor with no idea how I had gotten there. Alien abduction, I figured. Evidently, though, I succeeded in completing a painting every three to four days. I didn't understand or even remember what I had done until I saw the photos Erik had taken of me doing it.

Meanwhile, my poor project editor, R.W., was suffering from chronic diarrhea. Ten months had passed and she had absolutely nothing in hand with the exception of the outline and my good intentions. On the other hand, in my hand I had five thousand bucks of their money in advance royalties. I may not have been suffering from a case of the shits, but that's not to say I wasn't sweating bullets. That's when I had to swear off the Soma and drop half my other meds as well, to clear my head enough so that I could work on writing the text and captions. I guess it was lucky that I had only two months left to do it – to write the whole six-chapter book – because to do it I had to spend hours every day sitting at the kitchen table, after a year of only standing or laying on the floor because sitting was so painful.

But I did it. I did do it. Day by day, the handwritten pages went across the room to Raechel, who edited and typed them. It was another kind of miracle, how smoothly our partnership worked when it came to creative projects. How compliant she was, how actually placidly submissive she seemed to be, as opposed to the control freak I had come to expect and dread in our daily dealings. I don't know why this transformation occurred, but it made our interactions a walk in the park instead of a skirmish on the battlefield. Maybe it's because, as much as Raechel could be a bitch of a controller in what she saw as her domain – the home and marriage –, when it came to business, I could be a bastard of a taskmaster. I had not forgotten my apprenticeship at *The Ledger* and what I learned from the Master Bastard, John. I made myself a force to be reckoned with, whether with clients, employers, patrons of the arts – or staff. Even when the staff was in the hospital with a broken leg – she woke up in the post-op room with a lapful of material and a note from me telling her when I expected to pick up the finished product. And she complied without complaint or question. She actually seemed happy to do it.

I keep coming back to this: *I don't understand.* I see her smiling, and in her smile I can sense admiration for me – like I saw that first day at The Art Students' League; she was looking at me – I couldn't have known everything she was thinking – but I had my own feet under me. On top of that image, like a double exposure, I see her pussing up and making her squinchy faces and keeping an eye on my footsteps. Somewhere between the first image and the second, I had surrendered my autonomy – and she had gone through some kind of metamorphosis. Nothing like the caterpillar to chrysalis to butterfly, though. Part of it was the little bundle of joy she was getting ready to deliver. This gave her the idea that I should be getting about cleaning up my act. I had figured out for myself that I had a shitload of laundry to be attending to, some rummaging out and reorganizing the dark corners of my closet, and I was prepared to undertake these tasks. Then again, I was of the opinion that the tasks – involving *my* laundry, *my* closet – fell squarely on my shoulders alone. I had in mind a gentle handwashing of delicates in Woolite. I had no idea that this woman I was now genetically tethered to was going to throw my boots – *my boots!* – into a washing machine. Being footloose was my way of not being disappointed. Where I chose to put my feet, and my boots, was up to me. Things started changing too fucking fast – and bizarrely. Had I been duped? My head is spinning – maybe she threw that into the machine too. All I can think is – what gives? I fall in love with the demure, devoted Lois. I marry the I-will-follow-you-anywhere Raechel. And now I'm living with a person I think of as Kommandant Gretchen, the Kvetch-in-Chief.

Is there a scientific explanation for this? How and why does it happen? Is it a process I didn't learn about in high school because I opted for my boots instead of my diploma? Or is it explained during the man-education that boys get from their fathers? Another *good luck with that* moment for me – but too late. No word about the mysteries of marriage that a man has to deal with was ever imparted to me by that man my mother married. Probably that's for the best anyway. All I've got to go on is what I garnered from my peers' fathers, when I was too young and stupid to know what questions to ask. But I picked up some nuggets like: Don't masturbate – you'll go blind. Wait – what if that bit of folk wisdom is actually a key to the enigma? I think I can work this out logically. *If you masturbate, you'll go blind*. Back then, 'masturbate' meant 'have sex', because that was the only sex we had. Since then, in my reading, I've come across the fact that during the climax of the sex act, the brain releases the feel-good chemical dopamine; excessive releases of dopamine produce the euphoric feeling of 'love'. And it seems to have been established in Classical times that, in fact, Love is blind. Aha! I sure as shit got blindsided when it came to Raechel and her ways. Yeah, love makes you blind. This maybe explains why no one – no man, anyway – knows *how* the transformation happens, and it might be that we'll never know. But I'm still racking my brains about *why*. Lots of whys, in fact.

Sure, when Lois-Raechel moved in with me, the sex was good-to-great, and often. I found myself knee-deep in dopamine, and blinded. But the truth is, I think I was peeking a bit; not everything about her passed even a love-blind inspection, not to mention daily exposure. I kept my mouth shut because I just wasn't willing to cut off my supply of that feel-good drug. But what was *she* making of the scheme of things? She wasn't stupid but, on the other hand, I don't think she was wily enough to be aware of the truth that she had hooked me by virtue of her superior intellect and superlative adorableness. No, I don't think so. And I don't believe that she was either naïve or consciously deceitful in any way. But I do think she knew just how fuckable she was. She had to be aware of the anchor and chain of security she was crocheting for herself through the captivating gift of sex. Me, I had learned to operate on the principle that home is where your feet are. For Raechel, it seemed, home is whose feet are between hers.

158

Why she chose mine, I guess I may never truly understand. That question concerns both her motives and karma's.

I don't know *why*. I don't know *how*. I don't even know *when*. Women are good at remembering dates, right? Men, not so much. I wonder if Raechel has recorded a date in her mind when the Big Freeze started. The Cold War. An undeclared war. One you could try to pretend wasn't being waged. So there could be cooperative efforts, happy alliances for good causes – not the least of which was the shared caring for our son. When she wasn't out to kill him with obtuseness.

There was so much that she just didn't get. And her not getting it got to me. There were things that she flicked off her skin like a little annoyance that fell on me like a big pile of shit. Like, we're doing the cozily-married couple shopping together in the grocery store thing. Life-partners making an outing out of a mundane task. But that's not how it plays out, not if we're dancing to her tune. I choose something and put it in the shopping carriage. She takes the thing out and puts it back on the shelf. *Really, Raechel? Are you getting some kind of gratification by your denial of mine?* No, maybe my wants – and my sense of public humiliation – are not even on your radar. Maybe I'm the little annoyance you're flicking away. The space in your cart is reserved for what *you* want in it. So it's pretty pointless to ask: What happened to sex? On that front, the big guns are out, the barricades are up. The curtains are down: we're in Intermission. That is to say, the battle goes to you.

But don't think you're the only one with a war chest. It's funny – all I really want is domestic tranquility – peace – broken only by cries of passion in the night. But you gals seem to want to see me as a warrior. I'm remembering Olivera – a few lovers back down the line before you – a surrealist. She did a painting picturing me on horseback – naked, except for a Grecian-style helmet and spear – at the bottom of a flooded quarry, submerged, hemmed in by sheer walls of shaved stone. I'm not drowning, or fighting, because I'm a marble statue. So is the horse I'm seated on. Some warrior! And then you, Raechel, came along and, before moving in, presented me with a drawing of me standing on a crag, in medievalish tunic-type garb, looking out over the sea, holding a spear. Freud would have a field day with those images of large bodies of water and upward-pointing spears, don't you think? Your hands on the canvas or drawing board say one thing, and your legs on the sheets say another. No wonder you've got yourself in a fighting frame of mind. I don't really want to fight.

I've adopted the war cry: *Hurry up and run away!* On my horse. With my spear.

Yeah, my trusty charger was beer. My lance – a defensive weapon – was my deaf ear. Both were very effective in beating a retreat. Getting the hell off the field. Not hearing the discharge of the Kommandant's Last Word. Thereby escaping defeat and surrender. Beer, and other booze, armored me with self-preservation. But that only provoked the introduction of a counter-weapon to her arsenal – her hard-to-ignore dissatisfaction and frustration at not being able to deliver the death blow through my liquid armor. The Kvetch-in-Chief might have taken a different view, but my drinking was not an abuse of time but an effective strategy – a form of camouflage, a means of hiding. In my playbook, I was not a drunk but an escapologist.

Anyway, I'm not going to get into a pissing contest as to who holds the high moral ground. Those who are in charge of the battle are those who possess the maps. The high ground would always be Raechel's real estate, at least in her mind, and her thoughts were the only ones that counted. That hasn't changed. I've given up on having thoughts. So what does that leave me with? Memories . . . fantasies . . . or the happy coincidence of the two. What would that be . . . a memantasy? I could use one right now. My body seems to think it's been walking through a mine field. Every nerve and muscle is strained and tensed from thinking too much, and the pills aren't putting a dent in that. I have to take myself someplace else. Out of this Hollow Bushland, for starters. Off this floor. Far from any battleground . . . .

I'm on the Bowery. It's night. I have Tina with me – my last Great Dane – on her nightly walk. Coming down the home stretch, I spot my neighbor Eve sitting on the back steps of The Bowery Lane Theater, where she has an upstairs loft. Actually, *her* upstairs is quite lofty itself. Not to mention it always seems that she has to straighten out the seams of her long staircase whenever I happen to be around. Yeah, I'd say she has the hots for me. But she's just a little too hot – and nothing turns me off faster than a woman who is so solicitous as to show you just about everything in the store before you let it be known that you're even shopping. I get the feeling that the bitch is really truly hungry – and I've already been a blue-plate special and didn't care for it much, thank you anyway.

Across the sidewalk from Eve is this little compact parcel of dynamite. I

160

mean, she's gorgeous and she isn't even trying. Long black hair, dark flashing eyes, sensuous lips – and apparently very well off. She looks so cozy in her lush chinchilla coat, leaning against her Mercedes. You could say she wears the money well. You could say she's the whole package. And I say, I have to consider – what could I be to her but a quick trick. So what? She's sumptuous. I'm tempted.

Oh boy! Our eyes meet and I can instantly read the willingness and playfulness in hers. Some tiny hint of restraint, but not much. I really don't want to take my eyes off her. But I don't wish to appear rude either, so I manage to turn my attention to my neighbor: "Good evening, Eve."

She responds with a friendly: "Good evening, Earl." With that note of recognition acting as passport, the beautiful vixen lets out with a soft but exuberant *"Oh boy!"* and comes off her car and grabs my arm and sucks me into her fur-clad love vacancy, all the while displaying a sensuous smile with both lips and eyes. *Oh yeah, I could get used to this. Why don't you take me home with you and use – or abuse – me. Whatever. Your choice.*

Oops. For a moment there, I've forgotten, but Eve hasn't. Falling back on what memory she has of morals, and knowing full well that I have a pregnant lady waiting upstairs, she quietly murmurs to her friend: "Oh no, no, no." Much to my chagrin, the femme fatale lets go her death grip of me. I'm left to sigh: *Oh! What might have been.*

What might have been. What an original thought – I'll have to write that one down. The sad truth, though, is: a missed chance at a one-night stand is something you can slip into the back pocket of your memory and find it, if it pops up again, more sweet than bitter. What happens if you take a stand – to love, honor, and cherish – that you promise to maintain for all the days and nights until death . . . and, sadly, death hasn't happened yet but you find yourself wondering what might have been, and noticing that only the bitterness is left. Which maybe wouldn't even be so bad, except that you remember that there *was* sweetness, and where it is now is a fucking mystery.

Another damn memory slips out through a hole in my damn pocket – of a day very much like today, when I'm stuck to the floor in pain. That day sticks in my mind, though, because of the tears that were streaming down my face and, brother, it takes a whole lot of freaking pain for that to occur. That day was in the middle of a string of days when I couldn't even stand up and walk; when, after four weeks on the carpet, I had to crawl to

161

the toilet for a bowel movement. I'm on the floor. What could be my state of mind then, at the moment when my dear partner-in-promises, my loving and concerned wife, prances in the front door. She plops down in the chair stationed with its legs alongside my head. The first damn words out of her mouth are: "Let me tell you about my day."

Well, bitch, I don't have anything like a fucking day. I couldn't have felt more alone and isolated in that moment if I had been dead for ten years. But never mind what I wish – God forbid I should be dead! Who could Raechel talk at about her day?

And how is today different? I'm here on the floor. She's not here. No different, really. She wasn't here even when she *was* here, so what the fuck. My back is screaming – probably begging my brain for mercy, yelling: *Shut up, can't you? Stop thinking!* No tears on my face. Could be I've used them all up. What time is it? I need to check out for a while. Put this shit in my head to bed. Maybe something will make sense when I wake up. I mean, if. It's always possible God will be merciful.

Shit. I'm still here, and I'm still me. And here comes my brain, trying to lay it on me again. Maybe today it will enlighten me about something. Make sense out of something.

Here's a thought – I think it was Stalin who said: "When you have someone by the balls, their hearts and minds will follow." Maybe that worked for him. I've got my own little ball-busting gulag going on here, but my mind and heart sure as shit aren't into it. Somehow, balls in the hand during courtship tend to morph into balls in the vise after marriage comes into play. Sometimes I think a marriage is nothing more than a divorce turned inside out – a full circle, like a snake biting its tail, going around and around, getting nowhere. We need to break the cycle. Is that the direction our hearts and minds will follow? A formal parting of the ways? We're almost at that point anyway. I'm already isolated; and can I really fault Raechel for insulating herself from the burden of my pain? I can't even blame doctors for not wanting to know you when they find themselves helpless to help you.

But Raechel – she's not blinking back her tears. She's oblivious. She's so tightly wrapped up in those ribbons of self-adornment, I have to think that somebody wasn't doing their job in adoring her as much as she needed. Those ribbons are about presenting herself as better than she actually is.

162

There must be an adage I let myself ignore – something about being wary of well-wrapped packages.

Well, I accepted delivery. I've gotten past the gift-wrapping and I'm stuck with the contents, no deposit, no return. For better, or worse. Till death – so there *is* an out. If I'm thinking of one out, I can think of another. I went out that escape hatch before, and went on my way. But that was before – long before – I was a father.

What kept my head in the game this time, no matter how the rules got twisted or the field got plowed up, was my child. I had to be – I had the chance to be – Santa Claus. To be building a full-scale urban habitat for my son's Teenage Mutant Ninja Turtles. Showing him where to dig up the Triceratops skull in the backyard. Taking him out trick-or-treating in the creepiest custom-designed Halloween costume. Then – *wham* – I was on the floor, drugged out, out of the picture for him – some alien object taking up space on the living room rug. I know the pain this gives me. What must he be feeling? In the glimpses I get of him, I can see he's no longer a child. Do we even know each other now? I can't think about this anymore. My heart is breaking and there's no pill for that. What can I do?

What I did do over the years was whatever I could think of and manage to do for a slice of sanity. For peaceful co-existence. For the sake of my son. For making his life everything mine never was. And who is he now? What does he think? *Why don't you ask what the Man in the Moon had for dinner last night?*

Dinner. Night. Those are only abstract ideas in Earl's world. Like *time*. Like *life*. Whatever I had of them seems to be in the past. What has my life been since I got off the covered wagon that left me in this town – has it amounted to anything? Have I managed to accomplish *anything?* Not doing much right this minute; I might as well take inventory – maybe Saint Peter will have this on his questionnaire. A list of my good points. Do I have the nerve to open this can of spring-loaded snakes? Another practical joke on me, courtesy of my life? *Well, Good Golly, Miss Molly! Quit yer blubbering. You put it out there. Now, for God's sake, shit or get off the pot.*

Okay. I guess four years turning this Gloria-dump into a house and the garage into a studio counts for something. At least I can lay down my hammer knowing I did the man-job of making a home for my family. Point number two: I am not a burden on society – much as my in-laws (and, I suspect, my wife, and, I know, my own mother and her husband) harbored concerns that I was, or would be. Surprise! I did my part for the community. Served on the board of a halfway house and contributed my energies to a shoreline arts alliance. Started a juried art show for high school students. Put together an arts auction for the benefit of an animal rescue group. Rescued animals. Is that enough to keep me out of reform school, Mom and Dad? And I wasn't a bum, as certain step-dads foretold I would be. Just being an artist is enough to brand me as a loser and a failure, says he. I have worked to support my family, I pay my bills and my taxes. I feed my cats and I don't beat my dog. And let me tell you about being an artist. I admit it's been a can of worms of many colors. But sometimes worms do catch fish.

I painted. I painted because I had to. But did I have to paint *that? Why couldn't I paint happy, pretty pictures – vases of flowers, sailboats, things that go with people's sofas* – my mother and my in-laws never saw a reason to stop asking me. Raechel, at least, loved my art. I'm pretty sure it was her favorite – maybe the only – thing she really loved about me. She wasn't the only one, though. And even if you parental figures could never figure it out, my work consistently won prizes at local and regional shows. Hell, an opaque-watercolor I did was awarded first place in the still life category in a national arts magazine and was subsequently bought by a doctor. I think he was even a Jewish doctor. Nevertheless, my in-laws seemed to be 95% amazed and 5% impressed. All in all, given the costs of the materials, mounting, and custom-crafted framing, I pretty much broke even on the fine-arts enterprise. Maybe I came out a little ahead in what I saved on psychoanalysts' fees.

So – I'm getting the idea that my efforts over the years did amount to something. If it's okay with everyone, I'm just going to rest my bones for a spell in this strange sense of satisfaction, this – dare I think it? – positive feeling. While I'm in this rare mood, let me not forget Little Apple Studio. Our partnership as entrepreneurs. With a logo and business cards and everything. We actually had some years of decent earnings from that venture into the commercial art arena, and – along with working on the acrylics book together – our only unsullied collaborations. Raechel's cartooning and copy-writing talents proved to be a great asset to our free-lance business.

Somehow, when it came to art, there was some wiggle room in the dynamics between us. Even when there was friction, it didn't play out into long-held resentments. Like when I decided to try to introduce Raechel to the business aspect of the Studio, where you have to get out of the studio and deal with clients in the field. In their own territory. That takes some backbone and sometimes fancy footwork to land a punch. I had the feeling that I might come off a little too rough around the edges for the small-business owners, generally women, who we planned to approach with the idea of cleaning up their home-spun logos and lackluster ads. If my style could be too cut-throat, Raechel's, it turned out, was ridiculously demure. She had no presence. She was about as imposing as a cup of Ovaltine. Ironic, I thought, that at home, Raechel was an ass-kicking pair of steel-toed storm trooper boots, but outside her fortress gate, she was little more than a doormat. I sent Raechel in to solicit the business of a couple of women who owned a high-end ladies' clothing shop in a high-end shoreline village. I waited in the car. After quite a while – most of it spent, I gathered, not being paid attention to – she came out, bearing only the footprints of the two bitches all over her face. Not an effective way to do business. To get this point across to Raechel, I expressed it very forcefully, while slamming the heel of my hand into the dashboard – not necessarily intending to crack it, but that outcome did add emphasis and make a strong impression on her. She seemed to – maybe not take it in stride, but accept it as a learning experience.

I guess I learned something too. If I was going to send her into the lion's den again, I had to give Raechel some armor. From my experience, some of the best armor could be forged of bullshit. And, boy, could it be fun to put on. Life lays so much bullshit on you, it's a kick to throw some of it back. Also, it works. I think I might actually be smiling . . . remembering that naughty client with a history of not being timely with payments to their artists, and the secret weapon I cooked up to deal with them: Raechel the Terrible. Over the weeks, while working on their project, I dropped remarks to them about the Boss of Little Apple Studio – this Queen of Horror; I myself was a mere slave to her whims. They had better watch out, because if they got on the wrong side of this one, there would be hell to pay. A word to the wise: you don't want *her* coming in here looking for her money. Your life would never be the same. You would not be able to sleep at night with both eyes closed, ever again. I had their attention. Still, I could see no money was forthcoming. Time to cut the chain and turn The Beast loose, God help them.

I picked Raechel up from the hospital as she was being released, on crutches, with a full leg cast. This handicap actually worked in our favor. What kind of Unstoppable Terminator Superbitch of a woman would come through their front door on one leg?

I stayed out of sight and watched as one of the business owners met Raechel as she was stoically hobbling down the hallway.

"May I help you?"

Raechel played her part exactly as I had coached her. She looked grim. She said nothing but: "I'm Raechel McByrne."

"Oh. *Oh!* Please wait here. I'll just go cut you a check immediately, if not sooner."

And she did.

When we got back to the car, Raechel seemed incredulous at the workings of her power. It was pretty funny, visualizing the scene, and we had a good laugh over it. It still makes me chuckle.   And Raechel expressed wide-eyed respect for my cleverness in concocting this ruse. I hadn't seen her look at me like that since that first day, on the Bowery, walking the dog, when I tossed the plastic-bagged load of dogshit forty feet into an open trash can. *Swish.* And she emitted a soft, slow: "Wow." I guess that was my most impressive facility: throwing the old shit.

Yeah, what a hero. And what the fuck am I now? Where am I? In this goddamn cave that I can't bullshit my way out of – this rabbit hole to hell with a NO EXIT sign on the gate and an inscription over it telling me: FORGET ABOUT HOPE. Why even ask if I'm able to get up off the floor today? Can I haul myself from here to the fucking bathroom? Never mind just today – will there *ever* be a day when I'm not laid out by constant pain and frustration? No one, not one doctor, has told me that there might be. So where the hell does that leave me? Powerless to change how things are and unable to get myself to accept that reality. Desperate.

I'm fucking desperate. Wanting to scream. Or cry, like George did when, yet again, he had to find a new place to live: "I'm too old to be doing this." Shit, I'm not nearly as old as he was then. But it turned out he was able to bounce back, land on his feet. Me, I'm all out of bounce. I'm flat out. Flattened by a slick of black ice. Falling the height of half my body, from my feet to my ass, I'm a fucking cripple.

But falling three stories down off a roof, I brush myself off and walk away – what? Yup. That was twenty-five years ago, but that was me. I can still see the whole thing. I didn't have much to my name that day, but I still had hope. I hadn't even been married yet. I was trying to earn money so I could afford to buy my first house, my first happily-ever-after. I figured I could do carpentry, after the practice I got fixing up my grandfather's house so my mother could sell it.

I got hired. So I'm up on the roof. The gutter beneath my feet gives way. I fall, sort of in slow motion. I don't see my life flashing past my eyes, but I do see a naked woman who had expected to come out of her shower in privacy. I hit the ground about the same time she screams. In the half-minute it takes me to decide that I have come away with nothing more than scratches and bruises, she has a robe on her body and my boss's ear at the receiving end of her yelling mouth.

He probably just wanted her to stop yelling, but she seemed satisfied that she had convinced him that one of his crew had taken a dive off the roof expressly for the purpose of getting a gander at her breathtaking nudity. *No, lady, I planned the stunt in hopes of getting into the Guinness Book of World Records for Peeping Toms. So who's crazier?* Anyway, this got my boss so riled up that, not only did he fire me, but he took the cost of the gutter out of my paycheck – or, rather, the gutter ate my whole paycheck plus whatever I had in my pocket. No beer money. What was I going to tell Dino? My loss was his loss.

Dino, the world-class moocher, a kid destined for ungreatness and having no higher aspirations than that, who showed up every day at quitting time. Maybe he liked me. Maybe he liked my end-of-the-day reservoir of beer, which he helped himself to as freely as if I had invited him.

When he showed up, I gave him the bad news. His eyes got teary as he waited for me to explain how this terrible dearth of beer had come to pass. I told him the whole tale. At first, he looked aghast. Then he peered quietly out at the horizon, as if intently searching for some happier resolution to my day and, of course, his. But he only murmured: "Yeah. Life sucks." Then he paused.

Yeah, Dino, I follow you so far. Life sucks.

After what felt like a very long silence, he smiled and concluded: "But it's okay once you get used to it."

Dino as the Buddha. That's pretty much what The Enlightened One said: Life sucks, but once you accept that, you'll be okay. Dino, tell me how you arrived at Enlightenment. I'm guessing there might be back doors to either side of it, from the angle of insanity or stupidity. It's fine to say "once you get used to it", but please, please tell me – *how do you do that?*

The idea made sense to me that day when Dino uttered it. But that was in a world where you could fall off a roof and walk away – and the worst outcome is no beer that day. You could walk away, with no job and no money, and no thought about tomorrow. Because you trust that, after all, tomorrow is another day. A day when all things might be possible. That makes today a day with hope.

Today I know tomorrow is another day. A day just like this one. And I don't accept that. It's fucking *not okay*.

6 ~ George

We're coming in for a landing now. I guess it's been a normal flight. But then again, what the hell do I know? -- this is only the third round trip off the earth's surface I've taken. It's been dark all the way so there's been nothing to look at. I wouldn't have seen anything anyway. I've been in the dark inside myself during the whole trip. Just fuming. Just fucking smoldering. What the fuck am I going home for, anyway? And, for that matter, what the hell did I just leave behind? I wonder which one is the bigger fucking mess. Can I possibly give a good shit about either at this point? Can I think of one goddamn reason why I should want to go on breathing?

Bam! Wam! Wack-a-doony!

I happen to be staring at the port side wing tip as a point of interest when we're suddenly slammed down on the tarmac, bounced back up and then slammed down again at such a severe angle that the tip of the wing makes contact with the runway, giving off an array of sparks before we're righted again.

Wise-Ass! Yeah, You — You only listen to me when it suits You and appeals to Your sense of humor. Yes, I know I was pissing and moaning about my life. But I didn't put out a request for any particular method or moment of transition to nonexistence, did I? You're just winging it on that, huh? But at least I know

You're listening for a change. I'm sorry I took Your name in vain. It was just a
heat of the moment thing, You know.

I guess that was the wind shear that canceled every East Coast flight
tonight. Everyone's but mine. God must have told someone in flight
control that I was doing fine. *Ha! I'm anything but! God – I'm talking to You,*
now – how apropos if You had *bumped me off during this flight of fancy.* Sort of
ironic. Here I am, returning from my errand of mercy, not to rescue my best
friend from death, but to help him unpack and otherwise prepare for his
last journey. Now he's on his own. But George was always his own best
audience. That is, at least, before I showed up and he was quick to enlist
my youthful eagerness in the service of his ego. Shit, I was young. What
did I know? That was then, back in '67. But George never lets go.

All these years, no matter how stretched or thin the strands got, I've been
stuck in George's web. And now . . . really, what the fuck? I'm stuck on
this runway?? Something about bringing a crew out to check for impact
damage . . . ? *Hey, buddy, don't even think about looking at me for commiseration*
or making some dumb-ass comment about how long do you think we'll have to sit
here. I'm sorry you're stuck with me as a seat-mate, but I'm in no mood to make
eye contact, never mind conversation. Look at me and I might stick your big nose
inside your face. I'm keeping my fists clenched inside my armpits, okay? I'm
planning to brood in silence . . . .

I MEET GEORGE

December '67. Five months out of the Navy. And out of just about
everything else I'd laid my magical hands on – like Midas, except my touch
turned things into dust. My own apartment, a great job on the base – left
in the dust in my rush back to the open arms of my love-want, JoAnn . . .
who vanishes. Languishing in her dust in Pleasantville, I wreck the car
along with the friendship of my roommate and only buddy there. And I
can't quite say I hightail it to Connecticut, because I'm kind of dragging my
tail behind me to take up residence in my invalid grandfather's vacant
retirement house in Norwalk. At least I'm living rent free. All I need is
beer money. Anything left over and I can buy food. My art is once again
paying off -- or should I say, my subjects' vanity is. I have an eye for those
women out there who think that I think that they're attractive enough for
me to stealthfully draw them -- being careful to do it in a manner obvious

enough to pique their curiosity – while they are sitting in my favorite bar at a foo-foo French restaurant. They're intrigued; they're bedazzled; they just have to take a peek. Wowed, of course, they give their dates little choice in the matter. What ordinary woman can walk away from such a delightful homage to her charms? What kind of man isn't going to fork over fifteen bucks to oblige the winsome beauty that he wishes to bed down that evening? If the gents want to get laid, they have to go through me. Five bucks for the drink and ten in my pocket. It's not a bad way to make money, alright, but I could use something with the promise of being a little more steady. You just never know when you're going to hit on a streak of nothing but unarguably ugly broads. It's probably time to take a look at the want ads.

Ah, here it is – tailor made for me. It's a Norwalk address: two hours per day, care for several dogs, with light housekeeping. It's an answer to a prayer, and I didn't even have to pray. I call, and then jump into my modified '37 Ford, which I paid for with the credit of my good looks. Actually, with the thousand bucks I talked my mother into lending me in exchange for agreeing to stay in the same state where she resides so she could attempt to lavish me with my just desserts, drawing from her well of guilt. That guilt, however submerged, percolates its way out of the corners of her simpering smile. That smile, the practiced cuteness, convey the image of a put-upon innocent who could not, in good conscience, be charged with abandoning her only child. With her simper, my mother could look her only child in the eye, expecting absolution. Her virtuoso performance taught me well the art of manipulation. I guess I could say the worm doesn't crawl far from the apple. I'm fully prepared to dip into the bag of tricks my mother bequeathed me. I am going to get this job.

I pull into the driveway and I'm instantly awed. It is a little red cottage/carriage house set on the night's virgin blue snow and surrounded by a Caribbean blue sky sprinkled with frozen stars that hang suspended like tiny icicles. The yellow light from the small square windows shines across the crystal carpet like a path of welcome to the warm interior. The whole scene couldn't be more picturesque if it was a Christmas card.

I knock on the door, feeling half timid and half full of myself. Half, for me, is pretty much a full measure. The instant result is the resounding bark of several animals that sounds closer to an elephant's trumpet than the baying of hounds. The door swings open and I'm immediately engulfed in

171

about a thousand pounds of Great Dane. Three blue bitches tipping the scales at close to two hundred pounds apiece, and a black dog at two hundred forty. I instantly engage them in a prolonged session of smelling, hugging, and kissing, while totally ignoring the presence of the cottage's two human inhabitants. What I know I lack in experience I know I have to demonstrate in enthusiasm. I feel immediately comfortable with the dogs. As for the people, that remains to be seen. In any case, I've already decided that I'm not leaving without securing this position.

Finally, without breaking my contact with the dogs, I look up to confront the two gentlemen. I suspect that my prospective employers will be more concerned about my rapport with the animals than with any skill I may or may not have in social intercourse. The inquisition is short and sharp, with all my answers centered around my love of animals. Some little bullshit, but not a lot. Meanwhile, in the back of my mind, I'm thinking: These two guys have a better chance of putting socks on an octopus than imagining they're not giving me this job. *I mean, I know I don't have any references besides myself and I know we're talking about thousands of dollars on the paw here – not to mention your household items, like your Leakey microscope, the Rembrandt litho, etc. -- but, I assure you, I'm the most responsible and honest, gentle person you're going to find. And if you don't give me this job, I'm going to smash your fucking heads in.* Oh shit -- I hope I didn't say that out loud.

Still slobbering over the dogs and throwing out any answers that seem to be needed, I scan the room, as well as the personalities, to try to figure out who and what I'm dealing with. John, the quiet -- I mean *very* quiet – and distinguished-looking one, I'm guessing in his forties, is seated on a ten-foot-long tuxedo couch done to the nines in black-and-white vinyl-weave hounds-tooth. Not a cheap piece of furniture. George, the half-brother and owner of the dogs and looking in his fifties, is seated behind a French breadboard serving as a desk and backed with bookshelves. The wall treatment is rich crinkled gold foil with washes of color: red, ochre, a little tint of blue. A burning Franklin stove sits kitty-corner to the gable end in which windows rise from the floor to the pine-paneled cathedral ceiling. At the other gable end is a shallow bannistered loft with a rich Italian tapestry overhanging its rail and the stairwell.

All the windows in the room are small and square, and each has a paisley shade in gold-red-and-blue with a red tassel pull. It's a bit whorey, but it works. The floor is gleaming white tile with a black border and a plush red oriental carpet centered to it. The room is sparsely decorated

172

with mostly functional but artsy objects, like the Chinese oil lamp, or some very special piece of bric-a-brac that at one time was functional, like the sword that killed Richard ll. The whole place is overwhelmingly just too, too charming.

Despite the schmaltz of the environment, its occupants are more austere. George has the overall appearance of having been carved. Sharp edges. Rigid. Somehow more fantasy than flesh. His facial as well as his body movements are theatrical, his mannerisms feminine. At the same time, his Germanic precision of demeanor can only be explained by a broomstick up his ass. His voice is edgy and his tone sharp and snappy. John is more handsome than anyone has a right to be, with a full head of black hair slicked back over his lean head to showcase his chiseled features. Lean of nose and lips alike. No wasted flesh. His eyes are piercing x-ray devices. He gives every appearance of being in charge of the universe.

It is more than easy to come to the understanding that both these gentlemen know exactly who they are and what they're all about. Both professionals -- George the head editor of the Children's Division at Random House, and John editor-in-chief of *The Ledger Syndicate*, second largest newspaper syndicate in the country. I know I'm facing an uphill battle in proving my worth as potential guardian of their very valuable property. But, for myself, I have little doubt, being filled with the exuberant stupidity that comes with youth. Of course I am all things. Capable of anything. I have a sudden moment of comeuppance, though, about which rung of the ladder I'm standing on when I spot a Christmas card from J. Edgar Hoover on the desk. *Who* are *these people?*

After being assured that I've made it to first base, I'm further assured that I'm rounding third when I'm formally introduced to the dogs. There's Helga, the fifteen-year-old grand-dame and grandmother, who is nearly blind and a little crippled due to extreme age. Her daughter Getta, who is a little more than crippled due to the dog equivalent of polio. She requires daily spinal injections. Her daughter, Agatha, a dog's dream of a perfect bitch. I don't know, bitches have always been a nightmare for me. But I'm head over paws in love with her from the start. Then there's her first cousin, Hrothgar, who is as deeply if not more in love with her than I am. He is the gentle giant of the family and the most playful and affectionate.

Gratefully, and without having to hurt anyone, I land the job. Was there ever any doubt? Things are looking rosy. Is it possible that I've at long last found my niche? It sure as hell feels like it. Just spending two hours a day in this wonderland would be more than a fair trade-off without the fifty bucks a week I'm getting paid. I almost feel as though I'm taking advantage. On top of that, what a friggin' relief to get some time out of my own digs: five empty rooms – with the exception of my bedroom that is filled with a couch, a TV, a bed, and a whole lot of empty beer cans. Pretty much wall-to-wall. No deposit-no return empties. Aluminum skins. Shells of dreams born, grown old, and passed on. Me, when I'm there, I'm the house funeral director. Having George's house to retreat to is like a daily reprieve from prison. I sure as shit hope that nothing goes awry for the next fifty years.

The dogs are loving me and they're happier yet that I'm spending a lot more than my contracted two hours a day with them. None of us has had it so good. We all become the best of friends; but even the best of friends have their spotty moments. The spot that disrupts the fluency of my relationship with Helga is more like a murky lake. I walk into the house one morning to be greeted by a six-foot-diameter pond of diarrhea in the middle of the floor. I react without thinking beyond the immediacy of my anger and raise my hand in a gesture of exasperated protest. Helga protests back by displaying more ivory than a grand piano. I'm guessing she feels as though I've questioned her dignity and her standing in the house. I have an opportunity to reconsider the matter while spending a long quiet-time shuddering behind the Franklin stove.

With the passage of some months, John starts to warm towards me but, for the most part, George remains aloof, if not downright curt. John is a person of few to no words, so the slightest of comments from him bears weight. It isn't long before he lets on to the idea that he knows more about me than I've ever revealed. I smell my mother's long nose in this. She's been sticking it into my business for as long as I can remember. No doubt she did some snooping the last time she dropped by to "check on her father's house." I wouldn't put any kind of reconnoitering past a woman who would retrieve from the street and tape together the shreds of a note she once saw tossed to me by a girl and torn up by me. No chance to fix things for me is too much trouble for her to let it slip by. She'd better not queer this for me! Evidently, John has caught wind of my art and writing abilities. He's hinting that he might very well be able to put them to his service. In turn, George gets wind of John's intention and throws a shit fit. What the freaking hell did *I* do? I didn't say shit about anything. Suddenly,

174

according to George, I'm some kind of night thief out to rob John. George has a vested interest, he's the Treasurer of *The Ledger.* I start to sweat bullets about my position with the dogs. *Thanks again, Mom.*

I ride the new tide as best I can, but navigating George is becoming more difficult all the time. He's hard pressed, though, to find fault in the performance of my duties and I'm hoping that he's thinking twice about scuttling my boat without a replacement on the horizon. Now John is spending more and more time at home. I discover that, without consultation or a raise in pay, I'm expected to function as a sort of body servant to him – a ragtag version of a valet, I suppose. I care very much for the man and willingly oblige him. One of my new duties is to wait for his morning call, pick up two quarts of vodka, drive to the house, hide one bottle somewhere and help John consume the other over the course of the day until George gets home. Again I pacify myself with the trade-off (the arguable exploitation of my time and effort is offset by quantities of vodka), but this does nothing to keep the peace with George, who lets it be known how very unhappy he is with me. I'm really expecting the other shoe -- I mean the whole shoe store – to fall on me. Somehow, though, it doesn't. I can only believe that John must have some power over his half-brother and that, as long as I'm in his favor, nothing ill will befall me. Whatever and why ever that power may be, I haven't fathomed. But I can feel the tension between the two straining the joints of the house like intractable tectonic plates rubbing each other the wrong way. The house is owned by George. John, I've learned, lived in hotels in the city and frequented the house only on weekends – until the time, while at the local beach, he cut his big toe on a broken clam shell. A case of gangrene and two amputations later, John and his one remaining leg have never left George's domicile. But who knows how deep in their history the roots of their mutual resentment are planted?

As long as I'm pondering unanswerable questions, I'm thinking that there are two Sphinxes in the world; one is in Egypt. The other, here in Norwalk, is just as tight-lipped and enigmatic, more time-worn stone than human flesh and soul – except when he's had too much to drink. Then John will start to sing to himself, old romantic classics, while staring at an elegantly-framed photo portrait of Peggy Hopkins Joyce. Not hard to figure that this is in deference to some persistent heartache over lost or unreturned love. Odd, though – given that the picture is a fixture in

175

George's house. I know that both half-brothers had started out years ago in Hollywood; maybe they kept in their baggage a love rivalry that neither could let go of. Whatever the dynamics of their history, it's hard to be in their presence. As I tiptoe around the house, still an outsider, I hardly know where to set my feet with all the trip wires criss-crossing the shared domestic space.

I OBSERVE AND EXPERIENCE GEORGE – BUT DO I KNOW HIM?

Who are *these people?* What's emerging from the fog, for me, is that John is what John does; and George is what he says he is. George's identity is complicated by the fact that he can really sling the shit. Really, he's world-class – not just in the art of bullshit (from embellishment to chicanery) but in thievery (from petty to pretty grand) . . . I'm not sure which category to put that hatbox full of meat for the dogs in. If you looked up *mercurial* in the dictionary, you'd probably find George – he'd be an exemplar of the element's ability to change shape and elude grasp. Which leaves you without much of a definition – in the case of a person, anyway. These qualities are about the only things that assert themselves over the course of time spent around George.

After some months, I could say that things are running along the rails pretty smoothly . . . but I sense that the rails are running downhill. I mean fast and in a direction I don't really want to go, but I can't quite hit the brakes. John is making more demands on my time and, before I know what's happening, I'm not just driving him to his office in the city; *I am in* the office. How the hell did that happen? I don't think I was ever asked to consider the matter; John just skillfully oozed me on in there. Next thing I know, I'm the Art Consultant. Next day, it seems like, I'm informed of my pending promotion to Vice President. And there's a clause on the next page stipulating my bump-up to President the day after my twenty-first birthday. Come on – what the holy fuck? I'm sure I'm worth every cent of the forty-six thousand bucks a year they've got me on the payroll for as the A.C. But wasn't I the happy little moron kennel boy just last week? I sure thought I was happy. So I make sure to keep one foot stuck in the kennel. If I'm not getting happiness out of my new situation and compensation at

The Ledger, I *am* getting a load of snappy suits to wear to work, a classy new car, and all the wine I can drink, which is a lot. And what is the management getting . . . ?

I guess that remained one of the Sphinx's enigmas for me until the blinders of innocence that happy little morons wear fell off. Sitting here on my not-so-innocent ass on this plane on the tarmac, I know what I heard about how John had bought The Ledger *for the 16K that he got by selling a small plane that he didn't own to a minor gangster. I put this together with other things I've come to understand since that day when I was a barely-post-adolescent minor, and I see the strings attached to that puppet position John was so keen to elevate me to, so it would be my head and shoulders sticking up to take any legal flak coming at the Syndicate. All I knew that day was that, though the lit arrow on the elevator said going UP, my stomach was telling me that the floor of the car felt like a trap door. The rails were running downhill.*

This goddamn plane isn't budging at all.

At the bottom of the hill comes the dark tunnel. A horrible place to be. Especially in the company of George. Having contrived to give some of my scheduled hours to a fourteen-year-old part-timer-in- training, George suddenly calls to tell me that he needs me to move in and take care of things while he flies to Italy to retrieve Agatha, who had been sent over for breeding and is now somehow lost in transit. George ends up being gone longer than he had anticipated due to the fact that, in the search for one another, he and the dog continue to cross paths over the Alps. Finally, after being retrieved and having a safe journey home, Agatha is reunited with her family. All is excitingly happy until Hrothgar takes a sniff of her rear, which informs him that his beloved has entertained a suitor during her stay abroad. The distraught dog nearly collapses on the spot. He never perks up. In fact, from that day forward, he sinks further into depression. Then he starts on the path of self-destruction. He begins chewing his tail and legs relentlessly. His raw appendages are wrapped in tempered-steel mesh. It might as well be paper maché. After a short while, he begins to lose his mind as well; he can be found cowering in a corner with his attention flittering about the floor where he apparently is seeing things that aren't there. For myself, I can't deal with the unfolding tragedy. It's fucking

177

heartbreaking. I'm relieved when George finally has the poor sweet dog put down. That's only after the man is ready to concede that any further measures to preserve the viability of his property are going to be a waste of his time. This concession comes too late, to my mind – but, thank God, at last.

So then what? As it turns out, that was only the first gallon from the reservoir of troubled waters. Shortly after Hrothgar's demise, Agatha dies of complications with her pregnancy, Getta falls down the kitchen stairs and has to be put down, and soon after that, Helga passes due to kidney failure. I don't notice George to so much as blink, never mind shed a tear. In typical Georgian style, George disconnects from the possibility that he just might be serving Fate's perverted version of justice or his own shit karma, and goes right out and purchases an American-bred blue bitch house-dog. Bodine. I have to say, she's a real sweetheart. She almost evokes the affection that I had had for Agatha. Pushing Fate even further, George then acquires another bitch, Fjorgyn, this time of the old family bloodline. I don't get it. She's fully an adult, young but lacking in any sort of personality. Not one I'd be drawn to, but the choice is no say-so of mine. Besides, I'm preoccupied with trying to reinvent my own life.

Yeah, so what's changed? I again – or still – feel like I don't know whether I'm coming or going. Sitting here between worlds. Where – and who – have I been all this time? All these years. How long have I known George? How long has he been eating away at me? And now what? Am I done with him?

Back then, I was just starting. Hadn't even scratched the surface. Thought his aloofness was the worst I'd have to deal with. Really.

So George is treating me with what feels like contempt. At the same time, John appears to be ever growing more fond of me. I'm beginning to feel like a surrogate son in many ways. In turn, I'm finding myself fond of the man . . . although I wonder if my feelings are springing from roots of pity more than admiration. Indeed John wields a lot of power, no doubt; and, in wielding it, has blacked out the word *no* from his receptive vocabulary. But in many ways he appears to be a slave to money, to the wealth that buys power. In that light, I can only view him with pathos, as little more than an abject servant. In his mirror, though, he is always the master. The master of all he surveys and of every situation.

One night, after we had shared a bottle of vodka over the course of the day, John starts to remove his prosthesis and announces the fact that we're going out to dinner. As he is getting his crutches out of the closet -- taking my life in my hands, I'm thinking -- I meekly remind him that it is Thanksgiving Day and we don't have reservations. He gives me one of his no-need-to-speak looks (I think it's Look Number Three); it signifies to me: *I'm an absolute moron for having spoken.* Off we go to a very exclusive restaurant. I'm thinking it just a little bit odd that this dining establishment isn't one that I know John to frequent, but I know better than to ask. Anyway, I don't have to wait very long to surmise the reason for this choice. We walk in and John announces himself in a tone that suggests the fanfare of royal trumpets. The maître d' quickly dismisses us with a half-hearted apology for having no listing in the name of such royalty. So he thinks. I'm uncomfortably aware that our host's dismissal has the ring of the two-letter n-word. I flinch, imagining that John might very well haul off and wallop the sucker with one of his crutches. I'm struck dumb when John, instead, drops his crutches to either side and falls flat on his face. Immediately, he's picked up by a gaggle of wait-staff and, by direction of the headwaiter, we're rushed to the best seats in the dining room, where we repose our dignity with drinks on the house. I guess that showed them.

But life in John's gravitational field isn't all fun and games. I know there's a lot of shady shit going on. Hoover isn't the least of the criminals John is associated with, and there's a lot of capital going back and forth and sideways, including writing me off and paying me in cash. The shoe really drops with a thud when John asks me to carry a gun. Right there, for me, things are getting a little too hairy. The fear starts welling in my gut – and in my conscience: could I possibly become like John? More scary: I'm afraid that I could. It's time to rearrange my ducks.

Shouldn't I know better by now? Yet I find myself pathetically asking: How could anything that started out so good, like a Christmas stocking filled with puppies, feel as though it's going so sour? Why is that sweet stocking smelling more like a sackful of dogshit? At least I do know I'm not expecting any answers. I also know the world is full of puppies and shit. It's impossible to have one without the other. But right now, thinking back on that yellow-lit Christmas-card carriage house with its shitload of

179

whorey trappings inside, I have to say: almost all of the puppies and dogs are dead, and the pile of shit just keeps getting deeper. It's getting hard to see or think about anything else.

I'm more than keenly aware of what John is all about and the lengths and extents he will go to to get those things he wants. I have a pretty good idea of what he will probably do to get rid of – to eradicate – the things that get in his way. The closets where John and George keep their skeletons are beginning to look more like a cemetery. I know, in my heart of hearts, that if I were ever to cross John in any way, no matter how fond of me he is, he wouldn't hesitate in gifting me some small grassy plot of real estate. About six feet deep. This realization makes me consider: just how deeply do I want to get entrenched in John's life and business? That pressing question is beginning to cause sleepless nights. It's John himself who provides the sleeping pill big enough to knock me out. Right out of the picture, as it turns out.

One day, calmly, almost off-handedly, he pitches me an invitation to join an exclusive club of which he is a high-ranking member, a club headed up by no less an icon than his good old friend J. Edgar. The essence of it is that the club is exclusive: Whites Only. Those who do not hate niggers need not apply. At best, this is a low-brow gag in bad taste, right? But John isn't laughing. According to John, Hoover has two things in his vest pocket: the plans of imminent hostilities aimed at the nation's infrastructure, supposedly authored by the Black Panthers; and his own plans for retaliation that would ultimately lead to the extermination of blacks in this country, not to mention the transmogrification of the country itself. With the requisite suspension of the Constitution, J. Edgar would step up to fill the role of self-appointed Emperor of whatever is left. All that will be needed is his version of the SS, John confides. *I hope my mouth isn't hanging open. Not to mention, in no way can John ever find out that just two nights ago I was kicking back some beers with a couple of Panthers.* But that notwithstanding, this imparted confidence pretty much does it for me. Evidently, one of us is crazy – or just a little too white. Or maybe, in my case, not white enough. Either way, it looks as though my decision has been made for me. There's no way, no how I'm taking another step into that pit of quicksand. But it hurts just the same. Thanks but no thanks; I say my goodbyes. To George and the dogs as well. I go out and buy a honeymoon house an hour away out in the boonies. All I need now is to get married. Rashly, I do.

It's the evening of the wedding day and my new wife and I stop at George's on the way to our new home. By this time, I'm pretty well shitfaced. George had given us a very thoughtful and expensive gift of a set of knives. Now, back at his house, he has an afterthought and gives me a penny as a safeguard against severing our relationship. Too little, too late. Yeah. I'm seated on George's kitchen table. I'm reaching for my last beer and accidentally knock it over. I right it immediately, but some has spilled out onto the table. Before I can know what's happening, George grabs me by the back of my neck and, while shoving me in the direction of the bathroom, kicks me in the ass, yelling: "Fucking pig!" I turn on him with murder on my mind and rage in my heart.

After a stare-down, it comes out that George had presumed that I'd been too lazy to make it to the bathroom and had thrown up on his table. With my fist still raised and threatening his face, he meekly – but without a shred of sincerity – apologizes. But it's too fucking late! I can't get past my anger. It's all I can do to restrain myself from hitting him.

While I'm trying to count to ten, I'm seeing flashbacks in the back of my brain. Like seeing stars, only every little exploding star is George's snotty face, looking down its nose at my face. Over and over. Like tonight. Like the night I walked in to find him on the phone to the police, swearing out a warrant for my arrest.

It was a night when John had removed his prosthesis and taken up his crutches – like he always did when he had business to conduct – and required me to drive him into the city, where he would have a steak dinner and stay overnight in a hotel. Along with the steak, John had a quantity of vodka. I left him in the hands of the hotel's doorman, where I also left a $5 tip to ensure John's good care. When I arrived back at George's, I found myself snidely accused of making off with the thousand-dollar roll of bills that John carried in his breast pocket. I was trying to explain to George how I'd seen John fall off his crutches on the way from the house to the car with the result that his money-wad had fallen out of his pocket, and how something similar had likely happened again, when a call came in from John, apparently saying: Never mind, the hotel staff had discovered the cash where it had rolled under the bed, probably when John and his vodka had fallen on the floor. I got the drift of John's retraction from George's end of the exchange. The cops got a call from George to never mind coming out to arrest me. But I never got a word of apology, not even a ruefully raised eyebrow. If George had concluded that an accusation was justified, then the only wrongdoing consisted in my not being guilty as charged. Thus it was still me who was guilty. It was pointless to look at George expecting some expression of repentance. If his face said anything, it was: *Apology? Moi? Sorry (not really), but I don't speak that language.*

I had let that non-thievery episode go. But now, with the non-vomiting incident, which involves not merely sneers and slanders but manhandling, my dignity's dander is up. I really want to throttle the smug, pathetic sonofabitch. I come so goddamn close when he starts yelling: "Go ahead and hit me, go ahead, get it over with!"

I don't. And there we stand. In the rubble of what had passed – in my mind, at least – for some kind of relationship over the last four years. Any bond between us, evaporated. All that's left of anything is the stench.

After a year, my marriage evaporates as well. Whatever it is that I was seeking through the acquisition of a family and a secure home doesn't materialize once I come into a wife and a mortgaged house. I guess, wherever you go and whatever you do, you take yourself along.

And here I am, still hanging out with myself. Still dragging my own baggage around wherever I go. Where am I going now? Running away from something . . . not sure I have something to run to. Not even sure about the leave-taking. I've broken off with George before, and somehow I'm always pulled back.

Not long after my marriage dissolves, here I am -- feeling both adrift and boxed in, trying not to choke on a cocktail of mixed feelings, I reconnect with George. I find a lot has happened in my absence, at least to John. He had hit bottom with his drinking and had checked himself into rehab. Complications had set in with what was left of his left leg. Betty, our secretary at *The Ledger,* who actually came with the Syndicate when John purchased it, now in her late seventies, was looking to at long last get her slice of the pie. She had hated my guts when I came onto the scene, nursing the conviction that the reins should have been passed on to her. Now she was set on grabbing up her entitlement by force. She hired a nurse of dubious credentials and got John hooked on morphine. When he was good and hooked, she held the drug back until John signed over controlling interest of *The Ledger* to her. Betty promptly ran the enterprise into the ground before conveniently dying. John was now a penniless orphan, drunk, and addict.

I happen to be down at George's place on one of my now-frequent Sunday visits. John is there. The sight of him breaks my heart. Physically, there's little left of the man. A collection of bones wearing some dirty rags that used to be clothes as much as he used to be a person. I'm bowled over by the extent of his gladness to see me. I'm wrestling with a great deal of guilt, whether it rightfully belongs to me or not. Even though my brain tells me that no one was responsible for John but John, my heart aches with the sense that somehow I had abandoned him.

I'm really knocked on my ass when John commands George to take a picture of us. John puts his arm around me with tenderness. I'm so freaking overwhelmed – not only by the man's apparent affection for me, but by my guilt, which has just multiplied tenfold. Yet these emotions are displaced by sudden horror when I unwittingly turn to look at John as he smiles for the shot. He has no lips, no cheeks. Just naked teeth that recede into his skull. I'm instantly repulsed beyond bearing.

Whatever you think of God, he's always finally merciful. There is that day in store when your misery, no matter how terrible, comes to an end. That following July, on George's birthday, John's bloated body is found in his hotel room three days after his passing. It's only on account of the stench that occurs with the summer heat that anyone is made aware of John's remnants' existence. A man of great power, great assets, owning so much, doing so much, now reduced to a bad smell.

JUST ME AND GEORGE (AND GEORGE) AND THE DOGS

With John out of the picture, George has the screen to himself. No production is big enough to support two leading men. George takes it for granted that everyone within ear- or eye-shot of him is his audience; but he could never quite subsume John into that role. John had plenty of his own business and theater of operations. It's all quiet on that front now. George seems a little bit less testy, more at ease, as though he's traded in his up-the-ass broomstick for a length of flex tube. There's that empty seat front and center in the orchestra that I can slip into as George does a run-through of his new routine. He's looking for impressionable viewers, and I'm looking for a place to spend some time, away from my house and neighbors who view running over cats as a sport. A partnership made in . . . well, not Walt Disney Studios.

The timing of our reunion couldn't have been better for George. He had decided to breed Fjorgyn, and could use a second pair of hands with the whelping. I just so happen to have a couple of spare idle months laying around, so I agree to commit myself to the labor calendar. Jocko will enjoy the visit as well, having few canine peers in our Bushy Hollow neighborhood. I had taken Jocko on after a year of working with George's dogs, feeling myself now qualified for ownership. Owning a Dane is not something you want to go into blindly. Even so, Jocko could be a challenge. It had taken me two years to train him not to ingest the interior of the house. But there's always a new trick to be reprogrammed. These dogs never stop testing – must have something to do with their sense of humor.

I arrive about a week before the expected delivery date and help with the construction of the whelping pen, a complicated affair that certainly isn't about a cardboard box and some newspaper –   although I think George must have been saving paper for the last three years in anticipation of this event. Then the hour comes and turns into a twelve-hour ordeal, fraught with tension, then relief, and then back to tension with each pup's birth. It all seems to be going well: no breaches among the first half-dozen. And then the inescapable dog curse is back, knocking at the door. The seventh pup is stillborn and the last two don't drop. After facing this ordeal, we can both use a drink. Sorry – no time. Besides, Lady Luckless hasn't sung her last song yet. The following day, Fjorgyn rolls over on one of the pups, killing it. She's such a fucking clutz. It turns out that Bodine is a natural mother – she often gathers the litter up to clean them, treating them as if they were delicate cobwebs.

Pretty much what my nerves are feeling like, but no one's administering any TLC in my direction. Tending to the litter is a full-time, two-months-long workload. There's a limit to what the two bitches can do to help, without hands – leaving the work of cleaning out the pen six times a day to us bipeds – but they do occupy a sizable chunk of George's compact living quarters. This requires George and me to do some fancy footwork, while falling off our feet with fatigue, trying to sidle past one another without too much friction of body or spirit – and with armloads of shitty newspapers.   We're on call for the bottle feedings – preparing, administering, sterilizing – and help with the weaning. There's little time to sleep and, worse, less time to drink. The first time we really have a chance to tie one on is when we bring the little critters home from the vet after having their ears cropped. We set their unconscious bodies out on a blanket on the kitchen floor with a space heater trained on them. We sit there together, witnessing their squirming and whimpering, passing the bottle back and forth and doing our own squirming and whimpering in sympathy and exhaustion.

I stay until three of the pups are sold; George is keeping two for himself. During this time, something strange starts occurring. A supernatural phenomenon, it seems. Every time we leave the house, when we return, we always find cans of creamed corn scattered about the floor. We can tell the cans are empty by the heft and hollow feeling of them. They're empty – yet unopened. We apply a can opener to one of the lids and discover that the interior of the can is as clean as if it had been washed out. Inexplicable. No clue – except for the two puncture holes in the side. Ah! A vampire at work in our midst. What else could it possibly be? The dogs are always left safely contained in their electrified pen. Puzzled, we decide to play spy and see what might reveal itself. There are two large windows in the kitchen that take up almost the entire exterior wall. They give a full view of the interior. We leave the house and circle around back, where we lie flat behind a knoll and wait. It isn't long before Bodine, thinking it's safe, turns off the pen's electrification by means of the switch which is on a wall within the perimeter of the pen. Then, while her sisterhood freak out, she miraculously passes through the wires unshocked and has her way with the canned corn. After polishing the kernels off, she gets back inside the pen and turns the juice back on: *Hee-hee-hee – they'll never figure it out.* For her sake, we pretend not to. Why spoil her fun? Though it does occur to one of us to switch the labels on a can of hot peppers. I'd sooner switch out the contents of George's beer cans with piss. How could you not love Bodine? A sweetie, and a clever rascal too. A real surprise package, the kind you feel is one in a million.

Now comes a day when, out of the blue of a quiet morning, we feel the throb of that Lady's curtain-closing song. It's the young kennel boy who comes frantically running into the house devoid of any blood in his face and unable to speak. He faints dead away on the floor. We look out into the front yard, where the boy had just been playing with the dogs. Someone out for a drive had decided to take a fast detour through the yard and had decapitated Bodine. *God fucking damn it to hell anyway!* I thought they only do this goddamn fucking shit in Bushy Hollow! Turtles, baby ducks, any animate creature on the road or crossing the street is fair game there. I lost every loving cat I had to the depraved sense of humor of the neighborhood trash collector. I heard from a neighbor that she'd seen this garbage man laughing every time he ran an animal over. I can't say he's smiling when it comes his turn to die, unless you count the effect on his expression of that up-curved gash in his throat. Yeah, but that's just my vengeful imagination talking, isn't it. I know if George ever finds the fucking bastard who did this to his dog, there won't be anything left to the imagination! The world was a better place when you could leave such low-life shit dead on the side of the road.

Damn. That was what? – twenty-something years ago? – and that dog still breaks my heart. Bodine is long gone, though. Her pawprints have been filled by the feet of other Danes in George's dwellings over the years. And George is still marching – or hanging – on. I'm putting some space between him and me now. It feels like a matter of survival. Funny – back then, spending time in his house seemed like my lifeline. My refuge, my escape from the pseudo-life I had tried to invent for myself out of some misguided good intentions. Trying to be something I wasn't – Mr. Husband. Mr. Suburbia. And I thought I was finding a better reality in George's domain? It was from there that I was abducted by Shari, then snowed by Robin, abandoned by Milton, and rescued by Don – kind of a crazy ride through Wonderland – to end up almost right-side-up in a two-room in The Village and out of that hell-hole on 16th Street. But back to George. . . . .

George shows up there, at my loft on 16th, on his way to his recently-acquired loft in SoHo, with George The Junior in tow. George The Lesser. A kid a little younger than myself, who I'd first run into at the carriage house in Norwalk – and then never stop running into there. Every time I go to visit George, there he is. Another barnacle-groupie like me. Don't know where he comes from or much about him – except that he's a major dope-head. Hard to understand George's tolerance of Lesser George, given that George is so staunchly averse to any (non-alcoholic) drugs, and the young sprout doesn't rent space on Cloud Nine, he owns real estate – make that fantasy-estate – there. Well, maybe not so hard to understand. George will wallow in attention, no matter where he can get it; but it seems the pickin's are getting slim.

After George and Little George leave my loft, I discover that George has left his briefcase behind. His whole world is kept in it – including, I'm sure, the keys to his loft. I rush to the window and spot his U-Haul paused at the corner. I yell down to a woman, who's crossing the street, to stop him. *Yeah, thanks for your trouble.* As the Georges proceed on down the street, I figure that they'll probably turn west onto 14th and then head south on Broadway. What I don't bother to assess is the extent of my responsibility in the matter. I grab the case and run for the elevator. At this point I realize that I have no shoes or shirt on, just a pair of jeans. There are no phone booths between where I am and where I'm going, so I'll just have to go as I am. I fly out onto the street, capeless.

I run off into the freezing January night, into the sleet and snow that's coming down. I'm skirting Union Square and, sure enough, I spot George on 14th. I quickly calculate our speeds and shoot for what I think will be an interception point. Reaching it successfully, I jump onto the running board of the truck. Some time passes as I go completely unnoticed. Rolling right along, I finally knock on the window as if I was the Avon lady making a delivery. In response, George The Junior turns and stares at me blankly as if I were nothing more than a fixture of the truck, like the side-view mirror. Rolling, rolling, rolling right along, getting some glances from scarved and coated and hatted figures on the sidewalk, angled against the wind as we pass by. Eventually, Young George turns to George and says: "There's some naked dude out there on the running board who looks like Earl." George leans forward for a look, and responds casually: "Yeah, he does. See what he wants." Meanwhile, the odometer is ticking away. When the window comes down, I pass in the briefcase. In exchange, I get one of George's classic comments: "Oh". With no further communication apparently forthcoming, I decide to cut my losses and jump off onto the slush-filled street. I start the bitterly cold walk back to my loft with only the steam of my disdain to warm me. Along the length of my return route, I'm taking the measure of just how much a one-way street our relationship is.

Meanwhile, George's tolerance for his protegé is coming up against a deal-breaker. Young George is not getting the hang of how underlings function in The Realm of George. The kid comes out with observations like: "George, you're out of toilet paper" or "George, you don't have anything in the house to eat" as though he's conveying information that George would appreciate knowing; as though George will be prompted to act on this information, to the benefit of both the Georges. The concept of Georges, of course, is unknown to George. George Number Two finds himself out the door. Maybe surprised but evidently undaunted, The Junior thumbs his way to Spain and shacks up, we hear, with who else but Shari for a while before laying his way across the island. The report of Second George's escapades does take the boy up a peg in George's esteem. George Number One admires that kind of shit. What keeps *me* off his list of admirables, as he's made clear, is that I'm too nice. It's not that I don't use people; I just don't make a living out of it. And that, in *George's Manifesto on Life,* makes me stupid.

No shit – I'm stupid. Didn't I just commit myself to weeks of servitude in that madhouse George calls home? I guess that makes me nuts, too. I proved that by not getting back on the plane the same day I got there. I'm damned every which way. George disrespects me for being stupid; but if I weren't, who was he going to get to put up with his shit? Am I just as stupid for leaving him now? He's probably x-ing me out of his life at this moment and changing his will. Like I give two shits about that. I hope he never imagined he was buying my devotion to him. If he did, then he knows me less than I know him. Is he laughing his George laugh while he's crossing me out? I can still hear that laugh. Not just in stereo – it's like it's in surround-sound. It's the sound track for so many memories, in so many places.

I'm out of my Purgatory on 16th and gratefully nesting in my apartment on Bedford, eager to explore the possibilities of what I envision as a more normal life. I'm having coffee every morning in Don's apartment. I have a makeshift love relationship with Susan, and I'm itching to get into doing some art. Why am I still drawn to George? Still very dependent on his company. Because, I guess, he's magnetic, and I'm a lump of unforged iron. I walk the dogs for him when I can and he needs me to. After my history with the original ones – the canine quartet and their offspring and successors that I met and fell for at the carriage house – I'm feeling gun shy when it comes to investing any measure of love or affection in these latest replacements. I can't help but have some compassion for them, though, knowing as much as I now do about their master.

It's a hot August day. New York hot. The kind of day you spend in an air-conditioned bar holding out until four a.m., when the temperature cools down to a-hundred-and-four. I've just finished walking George's dogs, as well as a Scottie that belongs to one of his friends. We're all on the elevator up to George's loft when there's a blackout (the down side to all the air-conditioned bars) and we're caught between floors. Now in this elevator full of me and the four dogs, there's just about as much room left as you might be able to squeeze an airmail envelope into. Hot? Hell is a skating rink. That's where we are. Where we're all probably going to die of claustrophobia and heat prostration.

Two hours pass, as I periodically let out with a yell which is now nearing something like a scream. I'm soaked. The dogs are drenched and getting very spooked. No one has an inch to move or a breath to spare. This shit we're in is getting dire, real friggin' fast. This couldn't be a better nightmare if it *was* a fucking nightmare. We're almost ankle deep in saliva from the dogs' panting. I don't think this crew can hold out much longer. That includes me. If I don't die of the heat, I'm going to die of boredom. Another half hour passes in spite of the fact that we've all been past our limits a long time ago. Finally, it's five o'clock and people are now returning to the building.

One of the upstairs neighbors -- a friend of George's and a contractor -- comes to the aid of the trapped. He's on the other side of the closed doors on the floor above me. We communicate a plan. I climb up the elevator wall, pull myself through the ceiling hatch, and release the catch to the door. This does little to alleviate anything, especially the heat. But now there's an exit to be had -- kind of. The almost-accessible floor is three or four inches above my head. Well, what needs to be done has to get done whether it's doable or not. We're not talking puppies here. With the exception of the Scottie, we're talking two hundred pounds apiece, not to mention the fact that, at this point, they're not going to be any too cooperative with being manhandled. But up we go. I have to lift each dog in such a way as to get their front feet on the floor above, get a hand under their rump, and push them up. *Are you shitting me?* I weigh one hundred forty-five pounds and I'm already exhausted. But that which needs to be done -- with the help of the receiving neighbor – is done. Now I just have to find the strength to get myself out. That comes close to not getting done. I'm just done in.

Finally free now, I drag myself over to the open window for anything like a breath of air. I see George on the sidewalk cooling his heels after finding the elevator not working. As my sweat is pouring down at him, he asks me, with mild curiosity, what's going on. I tell him. I'm answered by hysterical laughter. He couldn't be more tickled. I'm so glad I made *his* day. Talk about your fucking one-way streets. I wish to hell I had a cinder block, that I might send it one way!

No, George can't really be laughing now. Not in that old George way. Too many things have changed and changed over the years and years. I guess, back then, he knew that his mockery could always rattle me into those impotent fantasies of revenge. He had all the power, because he was imperious and impenetrable, and what did I know except maybe I was *shabby and stupid.*

But things change, don't they. Even my delight in my digs on Bedford Street was pretty short-lived. Between the building's super and the downstairs neighbors, I knew I had to get myself the hell out of there.

The super, in the apartment next to mine, evidently hears me; and I definitely hear the two guys in the apartment below. But all of them are complaining about *me.*

The super, a spinster librarian, complains the day after I throw a little dinner party to celebrate my good fortune in landing this apartment. I'd planned to invite a couple of friends; which would be really great if I had a couple of friends. Even Susan, my lover, doesn't come under that heading. I have to resort to borrowing a couple from George – a sedate married couple well into middle age, who I'd gotten acquainted with back in my Connecticut days, when George always had a houseload of weekend guests looking to escape the city (God knows why – it's such a break from the tepid country). The day after my little soirée, I run into the super on the street. She tells me pointedly: "I hope that last night was an exception and that you don't intend to make a habit of it." The noise, she means; the loud carryings-on. What is she talking about? Granted that between the

190

super and me and the neighbors are walls and ceilings so devoid of insulation you can hear the goldfish next door breathing. But what was Ms Bookshelf hearing through those walls last night – the raucous sounds of forks touching down on plates, maybe the clinking of a glass, or an unmodulated chuckle? If she wants pin-dropping quiet, she should look for space in a library or a mausoleum. I guess maybe she'd gotten used to the previous tenant, my predecessor here, who was dead for a couple of weeks. I think she's being ridiculous, but she scares the shit out of me because I'm an illegal tenant, sub-leasing in a rent-controlled building. I have to worry about being evicted or having my rent skyrocket if she should be inclined to rat me out to the absentee landlord.

But I'm in much bigger dread of my neighbors below, on the other side of my floor – an S&M couple who tend bar at night and have a habit of engaging in roisterous, screeching sex that shakes me right out of bed at 4:30 a.m. If I worked a morning shift in New Jersey, they could be my alarm clock. As it is, they keep me awake wondering if I've been doing sex wrong all these years. Committing bloody murder never entered into it for me. I'm shy about the idea of having an audience, and especially nervous about provoking the prurience of Ms Bookshelf, so I restrict my lusty activities to weekday daylight hours when I can be sure she won't be at home with a glass to the wall. That means no hanky-panky at night or on weekends and holidays, which is a pain in the ass, because who the hell doesn't want to have sex on Washington's Birthday?

With these precautions, I can stay clear of the super; but the brawny screamers below me are another story. The time I accidentally dropped a bottle of oil on the kitchen floor set off a fifteen-minute tirade on the subject of how I was going to die. Now some heavy construction has been going on in an adjacent building. The duo downstairs apparently don't know this and are convinced that my dog has been tromping around, causing things to fall off their shelves. This triggers such caterwauling that I think at first they must be having sex, but why would they be screaming my name? The next day, in my still-undemolished optimism about human communication, I leave a note on their door, explaining that jack-hammer-type vibrations, and not Jocko's (albeit large) footsteps, are creating the disarray in their apartment. In the middle of the night, when they come home, I'm hearing the big guns come out, and that sounds like my cue to beat a retreat. I really have to get the fuck out of here.

I find myself a loft on the Bowery, a pretty raw space – but with

191

eighteen-inch-thick walls and ceilings.

To celebrate the good fortune of having my new abode, I decide to throw a small party. I set out to round up some guests. I'm aiming to come up with some on my own, without having to borrow from George. When I first moved into the Bedford Street apartment, Don had introduced me to his favorite watering hole, The 55. It's a bar for the older set of intellectual drunks. When the old Dylan Thomas crowd split the scene from The White Horse down on Hudson, they splintered into two groups and took up residence in two adjoining bars: The Lion's Head and The '5. The writers with a drinking problem and the drinkers with writing problems, respectively. Having frequented The '5 for the last two years, I figure that there are at least five people that I know well enough to invite to my affair. So I go out and procure a twenty-pound turkey and a ham, along with ten pounds of cheese and assorted breads. A few quarts of booze, a few of wine, and some cases of beer. And two hundred paper plates and plastic forks and knives. I am aware of the fact that New Yorkers are great networkers. I'd invited five, and no less than two hundred show up. Although I was half, if not fully, in the bag all night and could remember little to nothing of the event, I assure myself in the morning that my five invited friends had made it to the party, based on the fact that there are five paper plates and plastic glasses, out of the two hundred used, considerately deposited in the fifty-gallon shit can I had put out for the potential trash.

Yeah, that party. People spoke enthusiastically to me about the event for two months after the fact. Their ravings were always peppered with questions like who was that charming Arab prince or how was it that I knew the mayor of Rome, and so on. Either the U. N. had caught wind of this party or, as I truly suspect, at least half of these intriguing personages were, in fact, George.

The mystique of George. He continued to percolate through my life. But it was about this time that the smoke'n'mirrors surrounding him were starting to show some cracks. At the same time, I was starting to feel, at last, in the groove. I'd made it to somewhere. I had a life and it was flowing right along. I had a place. I'd been going to The Art Students' League for three or four years. This kept me in lovers, and also gave me an excuse to take some time off between them to get into my art. The only distraction was the ever-present lure of the NY café scene. A constant temptation that I gave in to readily whenever George decided to take an executive lunch-hour. That is, an hour that extended well into the evening.

192

I never refuse an invitation to play hooky. We always meet at Joyce's on 2nd Ave, just around the corner from his workplace. We're seated at the bar, as usual, when the mindless course of our usual drivel is interrupted by business. It seems George has to get out of town for a week and wants to know how much I'll charge him for kenneling the dogs. Hell, I can always use some extra money -- but we *are* friends and all, you know. Without thinking, I turn to George – but before I can speak, I see that his mouth is gaping open in anticipation of me putting my foot in it – and his jaws are ready to snap down. I'm about to take a step down the wrong road – that is, the one he's posted a DON'T GO THAT WAY, STUPID police tape across. He's the Stupid Police. He's been trying unsuccessfully for years to educate me as to how the world turns – and, being in charge of it, he should know. Well, there goes my idea of not charging anything at all, as a friend. I wonder what a reasonable rate would be? I turn again to George -- his mouth still open, maybe a little wider, and a playful but devious twinkle in his eyes. Oh, yeah. I feel just like a frog with a snake staring at the back of my neck. *Okay, motherfucker, what would* you *charge?* I have no idea. I blurt out a preposterous dollar amount. His eyes glow. *Congratulations, George! It's a boy!* Judging from the expression on his face, you would think that *he* was the one reborn. I've never seen him happier about anything than my conversion to Georgism.

At long last, he can rid himself of his subconscious burden of fearing that I might be morally better than himself. That fear is the stuff that hate is composed of. Yeah, that hate. I knew it well. I remember feeling it when I was in first grade. It was aimed at Miss Perfect Anne. Miss White Frilly Dress with the perfect ringlet hair and broad white smile of perfect teeth. Miss Straight A-Plus Student. One day the teacher gave her an A-minus; the poor thing broke down in hysterics, you would think she was going to die. She carried on until the teacher gave in and bumped the grade up to an A. God, did I hate that girl's guts! What can I say about human nature? I suppose it's the thing that makes us all shitheads. Now, with my conversion in hand, everything is hunky-dory. Life with George, from this point on, will always (for the most part) be agreeable. Thank God, at long last. No stop signs on this road. If anything, I just have to remember to go on pretending.

That hunky-dory arrangement went on, I guess, until about 1979. I remember that year. I hope it was a good one for wine, because it sure as shit was a turning point, in lots of wrong directions, for George as well as for me. With NY neighborhoods gentrifying as if gritty neighborhoods were going out of style, George was priced out of his loft in SoHo – and out of SoHo altogether. The starving artists had already started crawling out of the woodwork there and migrating toward the newly-dubbed NoHo area, as the Yuppies invaded SoHo like a cancer. George wound up in TriBeCa, still a sort of no-man's land for living situations. The best he could manage was sharing a loft in an office building with three college students. More accurately, co-habiting. With three Yuppie college kids. Yeah, there's a marriage made in heaven.

I'm sure the three sophomoric princes are bowing to his every command. George has to deal with the reality that he is moving down in the world. Even if he doesn't acknowledge it. The ex-Emperor. I know this fate has descended upon other royalty – and George, at least, still has possession of his head and enough theatrics to muddle through. I think. This reality is new for me, too. For the time being, though, I'm safe from invasion by the upwardly mobile, living on the skids and all. On the Bowery. Still home of the proverbial bums. I've got piss in the entryway of my building, and a coal stove for heat. I don't know many Yuppies lining up at realty agencies for the chance to shlep from Manhattan to Brooklyn every winter to bag two tons of coal. Not to mention comb the neighborhood alleys for start-up firewood.

I visit George in TriBeCa only once; I don't ever want to again. That's a first. It's too goddamn depressing. He's living in an office. The building is in a gray canyon where there's no place to get a drink or even buy a pack of smokes. On weekends there's no one on the street – I mean *no one* – and, on the weekdays, no one you want to know. I mean, what's the point? I can see the stress in George's face. That's a first. I can see that George is unhappy. He never says a word. Also a first. I can see this set-up isn't going to last. If I'm wrong on an intuition this strong, that would be a first.

It isn't long, maybe about two months. I'm down in no-man's land again, because George is in crisis. He's getting the bum's rush from his roommates. Big surprise. He hasn't a friggin' clue as to what has happened, how it is that he's not in control, or what the hell he's going to do, where he's going to go. The first thing I do is to assure him that I won't allow him to be on the street. He never acknowledges me. I get on the phone and call all of his friends, looking for suggestions or help of any kind. They don't want to hear it. *Gee, does that sound familiar, George?* At this point, he's crying, another first. That makes about three too many for me to process. I hear him murmur through his tears: "I can't take this. I'm too old to be doing this."

My heart sinks. I'm feeling helpless. I'm feeling on behalf of him and I'm right back on 16th Street. I can't freaking deal with it either. George tells me to leave; he'll take care of it. That's George. If he doesn't want to pay for it, he'll steal it, but he'll get it. Whatever it is.

No sooner said than done. He secures himself the basement apartment of a carriage house in Westport and starts the nesting process all over again. Somewhere along the line he loses Fjorgyn's two offspring. I know not how – I don't remember if he told me and I forgot or if it just was never mentioned. I can't bring myself to care either way. I've had it with the loss of dogs. I just don't want to fucking deal with it any longer.

The hardest thing about '79 is Jocko. When he struggled for dignity and for respite, when he could no longer walk, I have to put him down. Which is to say, kill half of me.

Poor sap that I am – limping along as half-a-self leaves me wide open for the cosmic forces to have some fun hooking me up with a better half. And throwing a few more fractions into the bargain for extra jollies. The first of them is the last thing I'm thinking I need or want – a Great Dane bitch, abandoned and bewildered, left in the dog run with a note on her collar. She's no Jocko, and I've had it with attachments to dogs – but I can't leave her there. She's mild-mannered and finds her place in the loft among the other creatures I've been filling my space with, from all branches of the zoological tree, having two, four, eight, or no legs, occupying aquariums, terrariums, and a couple of cages hanging in the window; the rabbit and cats are free-range. Something is still missing, kismet decides, and arranges for me to get caught with my pants down – or down for too long – with the outcome that my latest Art Students' League lover, Raechel, is about to become my second wife, three months ahead of the expected arrival of my (and her) first child. How many halves have I got now? My personal geometry is getting all out of whack.

195

And if I'm not dizzy enough, the rug is pretty literally getting pulled out from under us – we have to move. SoHo is full, and the overflow of loft-seeking gentry is washing up at our door. Well, at the door owned by the new landlords, who plan to upgrade the building's units along with the rents. Now we're getting priced out of a neighborhood that was, until yesterday, as close to the bottom of the barrel as you could get in NY. And, unlike George, we can't even think about Westport. Not even a corn crib or a chicken coop there. The best we can do is a reverse-pioneering slog back to the backwater Connecticut town Shari had rescued me from. Back into the lap of my mother, who had followed me there during the short span of my first marriage. There's definitely no room for her in the already crazy-shaped polygon of myself. But that's another story.

So, in 1981, I find myself again living in the same state as George. On occasion, when he's in the mood for country-slumming, he drives up for a visit. And sometimes we day-trip down to Westport for a glimpse at how the other half of one percent lives. We keep in touch, but we're in our own worlds.

George's abode is in the world of the rich; and Westport and NY (a commute away) may still be his stage. But, as I was at *The Ledger*, he's standing on the trap door. He doesn't own the ground under his feet. His landlady does. An eccentric old gal who chooses to live in a raw three-story barn, though she's worth millions. There's a large farmhouse on the property where her son and only heir lives. The barn is behind the carriage house in which George occupies the basement apartment – decorated, on a cozy scale, with his usual panache. He seems at home here. He probably relishes the fact that the estate around him is esteemed and coveted as the last undeveloped acreage in Westport. The land is so prime that the realtors waiting in the wings have it priced by the square inch. The cachet of that status, for George, lasts until the old gal is diagnosed with an incurable brain tumor. Bizarrely, so is her son. With both of them terminal, the landlady sells the entire property to a developer and donates the enormous purchase price to cancer research. She does not leave even an outhouse to George. He has about a month to pack up his shit.

George's aura of complacency is dimmed. And I feel alarmed and concerned on his behalf. But George still seems to have the spring-back of a jack-in-the-box. Maybe an old worn-out one, but he doesn't stay down. He's retired now, though, and cost-of-living factors significantly into his search for a new roost. He sets his sights on Virginia Beach. He's pleased

196

with himself because he's found a lawyer who helps him finagle buying a property and declaring bankruptcy at the same time. Nothing tickles George more than choosing the crooked path and getting away with it. Even though there's no one to greet him when he gets off the plane in his new home state, George can chortle all the way down over his devious success.

George would need to get a new dog for his new digs. He'd never allow himself to be without one; and Fjorgyn had been at the losing end of George's most recent quest for a place to live. While he was in Virginia scouting out the real estate listings, he'd left Fjorgyn in the care of former neighbors in East Norwalk. It seems that these people didn't care very much – for example, about where the dog would end up if they opened the door and let her out to do whatever a dog might do. Fjorgyn probably had no idea what to do, as she'd never been in this situation before. I don't even want to think about how, perhaps in the midst of losing herself in the thrill, or the confusion, of her ramble, poor dumb galoot, she ended up across town in the path of a train. All George was able to retrieve from the neighbors was the silver bell I had bought for her collar. Fuck it. If that bell had any luck in it, I guess that was only for itself.

So George took himself to Virginia. Years passed and we barely kept in touch. Somehow, it seems, we managed to carry on – me and George and the dogs. And the wife and the baby. That, I know, was a lot of what kept me *occupied. What about George? If there was any lounge-life down there, no doubt he scoped it out. Or any other venues for hob-nobbing and making his presence known. I remember he did mention getting a membership at the gym, planning to make use of it every day. I can see that. George's vanity is on call all twenty-four hours of every day, and the gym would keep that stoked in two ways, that would feed into each other. He'd keep himself sleek and preened, as he always had, and, while doing that, he could cultivate an audience. What could be better than strutting his stuff in an arena where he could show almost all of it off? If the gym had windows fronting the street, even better. Judging by Raechel's reaction the time she saw him watering the flower garden behind his Westport residence in deck shoes and his boykini, I guess anyone's eyes would be drawn to him. She couldn't get over his bronze-skinned barely-adolescent-looking willowy body which was shocking only because it was topped by his meticulously VanDyked and fully coifed but definitely pushing-sixty head – and because that body had the least amount of coverage a man standing on his lawn could legally get away with. I suppose it didn't need mentioning that the gushing hose he was holding languidly at hip level, watering the flowers, completed the picture. George looked in his glory, well aware of the tableau he was the center of. Raechel's take was that, although this barely-restrained exhibitionism in a man of his age should appear ludicrous, George actually pulled it off. Who knows what George's age actually was – that was classified information. I suspect that he actually let on to be older than he was, so that his admirers would be the more impressed by his amazingly youthful charm.*

While George was presumably drawing a flock in his Virginia Beach locale (but who knows what the sad truth maybe was), I sure was not at the hub of any social gaggle – not even at the fringes. I'm thinking of 1996 now – I'd been back in Bushy Hollow for sixteen years. A lot of water had passed under the bridge – and a whole lot of shit.

SHIT HAPPENS. AND IT HITS THE FAN.

1996. I've spent a lot of it lying on the living room floor. Convalescing over the last three and a half years from a back injury. I'm finally coming out of the prescription drug haze I've been enveloped in – only to find that my marriage has been straining at the seams in my absence. *God, what happened to the good old days – like when I was living alone on 16th Street?* For all my so-called footloose and fancy-free days back then, I had dearly wanted nothing so much as a home that didn't move around and a wife to have a family with. And how has *that* turned out? The whole sixteen years' worth here has been no bed of roses – but I wake up to find someone's thrown me into the briar patch.

At this stage in my life, I'm sometimes slow, but almost never stupid. I know something's up. I figure that that something is more than likely a third party – a three's-a-crowd party who's looking to crowd me out. So I sit my Raechel down for an earnest pow-wow. Right in the middle of her protestations, I have one of my psychic moments: *Oh, shit. I'm in the middle of this crap and, typical of that bastard who has no consideration for my space and time, he picks this minute to have a goddamn stroke. That means I'll have to drop this hot potato in the middle of my living room floor and go down to Virginia and take care of him.*

Sure as shit, the very next goddamn day the phone rings.

"Hi, Earl, this is Nancy, I'm George's next door neighbor down here in Virginia. I'm calling to let you know, George is in the hospital – I'm afraid to tell you, he had a stroke yesterday."

"Yeah, I know, I'll be right down just as soon as I can decide how to get there."

I've only flown twice in my life; both times as a kid, so I had no choice in the matter. Now, given the choice, I'd just as soon not; but a two-day drive would just about destroy my otherwise already-crippled back. I guess I have no choice but to fly. What the hell – the worst thing that can happen is I'll die. Given the present conditions of my life, that isn't a threat, it's a freaking enticement. Before leaving, I secure my wife's word that she'll straighten out her half of our domestic troubles and we'll work together on our marriage when I get back. Off I go into the wild blue yonder. It is, certainly, yonder. Knowing George, I'm sure it will prove to be wild. Can the blues be far behind?

The neighbor picks me up at the airport and drives me to George's house so I can make some calls – like to his lawyer, to see if my power of attorney includes medical or not. The first words out of the lawyer's secretary's mouth are: "I want George's dictionary stand."

Okay, here we fucking go. It's starting already. I'm anxious to get to the hospital to get George, who, I'm sure, is just as anxious to get his dog, a black Dane named Tyr, out of the kennel. As I near the hospital, I'm trying to shake off the secretary's comment along with something I saw which caused me to feel as though I had a knife in the side of my head. It's just freaking bothering me and it won't leave me the hell alone. What I saw was just a bucket of soapy water with a pair of underwear in it. But I just know that it has the potential of growing into something very unpleasant very quickly. Let's just wait and see how always right I am. Yeah. I can wait. The day is already unpleasant enough as it is.

I arrive at the hospital and announce my intent to relieve the nurses of the presence of Himself. A bunch of candy-stripers jump into one another's arms and start jumping up and down, half screeching with delight and crying at the same time. One repeatedly asks in a panicked voice: "Is he really going? Is it true? Is he *really going*?!" I see George is still up to working his magic. Oh, brother, this is going to be good, I can feel it.

We get into his Jeep and he starts to direct me – to the kennel, I imagine. Not. He has me stop at a high-end café. I can see that he knows it well. In typical George fashion, he enters the café's outdoor patio through a gate that has a sign bigger than life on it that reads: EXIT ONLY – DO NOT ENTER. I'm noticing a long line of patrons inside the restaurant waiting to be seated on the patio. Signs, of course, are not meant to include royalty. George finds himself a seat. What choice do I have? I sit too.

A waiter approaches and, with unconcealed brusqueness, inquires of our needs. Rising to the occasion with a haughtier-than-thou manner, George commands a beer. Already short of patience, the waiter rattles off a list of selections. George, in response, states tersely:

"I want a beer!"

"Yes, which beer would you like, sir?"

"I *want* a *beer*!"

"I'm sorry, sir, I shouldn't even be waiting on you after you cut in line."

Uh-oh, here it comes.

"Oh!"

"Now, sir, -- (stiffly) -- what can I get you?"

"I. WANT. A BEER!"

I have to intercede before somebody explodes. "Just say 'very good, sir' and get him a fucking beer."

"Very good, sir."

Well, okay. That worked. Maybe this is going to be a lot easier than I thought it would be.

When we go to leave, I slip the waiter an extra ten with an apology: "I'm afraid my friend isn't himself today; he's seventy-three and he just found out that he's pregnant." This seems to appease the man. I guess he's figured out that his life is going to be so much better with our leaving that he passes on making any comment.

After picking up Tyr from the kennel, we at last can head for home. It's been a long hard day and my friggin' back is killing me. Not to mention I'm mentally exhausted. This whole trip has been dream-like, cloaked in an unsettling out-of-this-worldliness. That's not even taking into consideration those things I know are coming. I could write the book, get it published, make a movie out of it, foretelling every event, before the outcome of the next hour reveals itself. That's how well I know George.

As we walk into the house, George points to the bucket sitting on the kitchen counter:

"Wash those out for me."

I fucking knew it! That wasn't a request. That wasn't a favor asked.

200

That was an imperial command from on high. If I'm half the freaking smart-ass I think myself to be, I'll be on the next plane home, with no reasons or excuses offered. At this point, I realize this is just the beginning, and any shit I find myself standing in is going to be on me. I've lived in this skin long enough to know that my own behavior is not a product of the will or whim of others. If I follow George's dictates, that's my choice. I'm going to have to live with it.

This whole thing can't possibly be fun for George. The reason for his stroke in the first place turns out to be a blood-flow interference caused by a four-cm tumor in his brain. Knowledge of this isn't easy for *me* to live with, either. It comes on top of the weight of depression I've already been under since my arrival here. The moment I walked through the door into this house, a sense of gloom fell on me like a bucket of rocks. It was the house itself – which I instantly recognized as not being George's home. I could see his touches, his attempts to make the surroundings his – all failures. The structure itself is just too modern. All his antiques seem to float like lost souls; they can't find any attachment to the space. It kind of reminds me of some old person bringing some of his things into a nursing home to soften the strangeness; the attempt just doesn't cut it – it just ain't the same place. George had laid tile in the living room and kitchen; that was okay as far as it went – better, at least, than the cheap wall-to-wall carpeting that's standard fare in so many new budget-friendly houses. In the master bedroom, he had made an attempt to replicate the gold foil walls of his former dwelling. He had to have realized he failed miserably. It broke my heart to look at it.

There's just no way that I can bring myself to think that George is in any way happy here. I know he had little choice. After being kicked out of one rented place after another, he needed the security of owning, and this was affordable; not necessarily his preference. I don't think this location was his cultural pick either; apart from the lawyer's secretary – the dictionary-stand coveter – I don't think any of his neighbors even owns a dictionary. If George isn't living a life on the verge of tears, then he has to be a person of superior denial capabilities – although I don't recall him being a Republican.

George keeps me busy with having me chauffeuring him around on this errand and that. He's loving it. The power of it and all. Instead of buying a carton of smokes for the week, it's become my duty to drive him to the deli for a pack every day. I've told him, more than several times, that I can't sit for more than fifteen minutes at a time without incurring great discomfort to my back. That went in one ear and out the other – if it went in an ear at all. I get the feeling that he's rationalizing, writing the daily excursion itinerary thing off as the fulfillment of some obligation to entertain me, as if I were a visiting dignitary as opposed to the friend I had been accustomed to believing myself to be. George and I had always been of the same disposition regarding house guests – we never played host to friends. This apparent change in his policy, or in his inclination towards *me*, makes me feel more distant. Therefore, I imagine, more usable in his eyes.

If George is being a general thorn in the ass, I sure as shit don't need a whole cactus entering the act to boot. Out of nowhere, The Heiress shows up. I haven't the slightest friggin' idea who she is, never heard of her before, but she seems to be a person of great importance to George. This is evidenced by the fact that she has her own guest room awaiting her arrival whenever she makes extended visits from her residence in PA. She comes bearing gifts: a prayer rug. I have to wonder what she's intending to leave with. From what I can gather, she's filthy rich; but I know plenty of those who have more who are always looking to have *more*. Sure enough, it isn't long before this personage and the neighbor, Nancy, are hinting at one another about the probable impending fight over George's eighteen-pelt full-length red coyote coat. *Does anyone mind waiting until George might be done with it?*

Just when you think God can't stack the shit any higher – well, you know. The phone rings one night. I expect it to be my wife again, begging me to come home, again. Wanting to know when I'm going to conclude my business. *How the fuck do I know? Ask God.* She's cold, she laments, and needs me home to tend the coal stove for heat. *You want to know what cold is? You should have been with me today. You want to know what cold is, you should spend time with these two birds. The Emperor and the Heiress.* I have to go through this shit on the phone every night for fifteen minutes at a time. Like I'm having a ball down here. Thank God, this time it's my lawyer, with good news. Well, it would have been great news if he were calling me at home. My court date is set for a week from now. The day in court I've been waiting for for close to four years, to resolve the issue of fault in the

202

case of my back injury. Of course, to appear in court, I need to be in Connecticut.

There's just one little problem. When I had picked George up from the hospital and met his doctor, a very nice and caring man, he was quite explicit about what my being in charge of George's welfare would entail.

"If he goes into the bathroom to pee, I want you there holding his hand. In his condition, he could have another stroke any second. He's never to be left alone."

So now, when I get off the phone, I turn to The Heiress and ask her if she can extend her visit through next week.

"No."

Well, I can't leave George on his own – for a minute, never mind hours or days. Do I really want to put George back in the hospital, rekennel the dog, go through the expense and time of a round trip -- for what? The opposition had already shown their teeth – which is to say, they're willing to do anything they have to do to keep my hand out of their pocket. Lying certainly is not out of the question, right down to their paid assassin of an insurance doctor. What chance do I have? I had requested a judge to hear the case. They got the winning hand by saying No, it would be heard by a jury – which, in the estimation of their lawyers, amounts to a dozen people who weren't smart enough to get out of jury duty and hence can be counted on to be putty in their crafty hands. The only thing I could realistically get out of this would be my satisfaction in having my day in court and maybe exposing the corruption of the insurance system. Beyond that, the assholes are offering me a nuisance-value payoff to go away. An out-of-court settlement of $40,000. The half of that sum that would be left for me after my lawyer's cut, I could put against my still-climbing medical bills that are now at $65,000. That's, at least, a bird in the hand, as opposed to a jury in the bush. It seems clear that it's all the opposition's magic show; they are in possession of all the smoke and mirrors. Why put everyone through this shit? Yeah, I tell my attorney, I'll settle.

No trip back to Connecticut is being planned.

Things just keep getting worse. From worse to worser. I'm losing a lot of sleep because George isn't sleeping at all. He isn't going to miss an hour of life. The trouble is that, between his condition and his lack of sleep, his eccentricities are becoming more exaggerated and more intolerable. One day, he has me drive him, along with the dog, to a large antique restoration shop where, much to my embarrassment, he lets the animal run loose. When the dog leaves a Dane-sized four-pound pile on the floor, I throw my hands in the air and walk away. I walk outside and get into the Jeep. I come damn close to driving off.

I'm sorry I didn't.

Back at the house, George and Company decide they want to run their dogs (The Heiress has a Scottie), and enlist me to take them to the park. What the fuck – doesn't anyone around here know how to drive but me? The park is bordered by a canal with very high grass on the embankment. The Scottie jumps into the grass – which is to say, it jumps into the water. I bend over to retrieve it and go head first into the canal. When I come up, I grab the dog and throw it up on land. It isn't all that easy for me to get out of the water, between the height of the embankment and the tall grass. I obviously can expect no help. George is hysterical with laughter. It's late fall and I'm absolutely frozen. I'm shaking to death from the cold but, naturally, that's my problem, why punish the dogs with a shorter outing than they had planned? *Maybe you should have rather planned for the Scottie's funeral.* I'm feeling that it's the dogs-in-the-elevator incident all over again. *Where the hell is a good cinder block when you need one?*

At some point, I talk George into picking up a copy of *Final Exit.* He spends the night reading it. The following morning, when I ask about it and what did he think? his answer is short and curt:

"I'm not going to die!"

Being that he is George and not just anybody, I believe him. Reflecting further on it, I realize he has to be absolutely right – even God doesn't have that kind of power over him. He then has me drive him to the library, where he takes out six books on the brain and its diseases. "I'm going to show them!" he asserts with obstinate and perhaps theatrical indignation, playing the scene mostly to himself.

That should keep him for a couple of hours, maybe I can catch up on my rest.

Then the phone calls start. Different people who George had left on the roadside some time ago. This just aggravates his bad state of mind; he can't be bothered by dead wood. I hadn't told anyone about George's condition; must be the other one got her little black book out and picked up the phone. The old friends and acquaintances hearing her tale would maybe give her sympathy or praise for being there with George in his time of need, or maybe their recollections concerning some of the choicer items among George's possessions. In any case, this raking through the compost heap of old associations only makes George more ornery.

That night things come to a head. I've just friggin' had it with his shit! And I tell him plainly:

"Look, George, you know that I know that I'm your sole heir. If you think that gives you some license to abuse me, then you better fucking think twice. I didn't put my own life on hold and come all the way down here to safeguard an investment. I'm here because I care and I'm a friend, even if you don't understand what that is. If you can't understand that, then you can take your will and stick it up your fucking ass and I'll still be here to take care of you. I'm not going to wave my sacrifices in your face, because if I did that – or acted in any way like you – I'd be out of here! Then what? You gonna turn your power of attorney over to your lawyer, the one you're so proud of being crooked? Y'know what he's gonna do? He'll replace me with some big fucking fat-ass nurse, like the one Betty put on John, and the first time you crack wise with her, she's apt to throw you upside a wall. So you better get your goddamn priorities together and start treating me like a friend, 'cause I'm giving you fair warning, if I have to leave here, you better believe I'm out of here and gone!"

George is totally silent. He actually looks as though he is genuinely reflecting. It's the most sincere I've ever seen him. God, is there really hope?

Well, today is the clincher. It's been two weeks now, and I have to bring George back to the hospital for a biopsy. How can this be good? I'd settle for it being not disastrous. As we enter the ward from which I had picked him up in the first place, I can't help but notice a hurried evacuation of personnel who all suddenly remember that they have other duties elsewhere. At this point, George demands that I go bring him the chief administrator of the hospital because he just saw the EMT wearing the jewelry that was taken off his neck at the house the day of his stroke. He's in an absolute panic about it. To placate him and to otherwise prevent a riot, off I go. It takes some time, but I finally find the administrator. Getting him to move is another story. I have to fall back on my John and George education and make the whole thing bigger than it is. Just short of a bomb scare. Brother, do I ever feel like a first class idiot when I bring the chief to

George's side, only to have His Highness simply dismiss the whole thing with a placid: "Never mind." *Holy shit!* How George.

Eventually, George is readied for the CT-scan. I'm standing with the doctor when the image comes up on the screen. I can't help myself. I say:

"Excuse me, Doctor, I don't presume to tell you your business, but that looks more like 8 cm to me than 4."

"You're absolutely right. In two weeks, it's doubled in size. Let's go out for a smoke and a little chat."

My kind of doctor.

Before going out with the doctor, I take one last look at George, the kind that feels like the last one. He's on the other side of a huge glass wall. Secure. Separated. Him or us? He's squirming just as the puppies had when we laid them out on the kitchen floor after surgery. They, at least, had been anesthetized. George, of course, had refused any drugs during his biopsy procedure. Now the sight of him like this fills me with a sense of both pity and hate. I can't stand the sight of George looking pathetic. Vulnerable. The doctor takes me out into an alley and lights up.

"I've been dying for a smoke," he says. "What I have to tell you isn't good news."

What you have to tell me isn't news at all. I know you can't go into the brain with a shovel. It's all over – all that's left for you to tell me is the when of it.

The doctor wants to see him again in a week to give him the results. That, at least, will give George some days to continue living his illusions.

For me, the week proves more sleepless. More draining. More cutting. More bleeding. Raechel is becoming more insistent about my return; more demanding. I'm just supposed to give up one friend for the sake of another. The trouble is, I don't see a friend in my wife. At least, I haven't in the last three and a half years of lying on the living room floor trying to survive my never-ending pain, getting small sense of any interest or compassion from her, absorbed as she is in her own separate life. Unfortunately, I'm hard pressed to find any kind of friend in George either. But I'm supposed to be everyone's friend. I'm wanted there, I'm needed to be here, I'm supposed to be everywhere. *You know what? Leave me the fuck alone! You're tearing me apart! You're killing me!*

With Raechel's nightly imploring and nagging, I'm forced to consider my own calendar. Just how long is this absurdity to go on? How had my life become contingent on someone else's death? How much more of myself can I afford to spend? I've already been running on empty for the last week or more. My mind is starting to wander from the preoccupation with mercy to thoughts of the mercenary. I start to compute. What am I going to do with all of George's stuff? It's all beautiful and all that, but we have no room for any of it. How much longer am I going to have to stay here in order to dispose of all this shit? What about the sale of the house? What about the goddamn dog? What about . . . *shit! Did you just hear yourself? You just blew it! You just lost your privileges. You just joined the ranks of the other bedside vultures. You don't deserve any of this shit now.*

All this constant conflict, no combat, leaves me exhausted and reflective. I feel as though I'm stranded on a six-foot island without a single tree for shade. I'm surrounded by two hundred hungry sharks. God, eventually I'm going to have to give myself up to them and there won't even be enough of me to go around. Sitting in my room, the second guest room, I'm absorbing the flavor of my surroundings. It's decorated as a young man's room. Was it for the son George spoke of only once, saying that they were no longer on talking terms? He never elaborated on the subject, or mentioned it again. I never knew if this son had ever existed or was just one more fantasy of George's. I have to wonder if the room hadn't somehow been designed for me, but that's not a question you can ask. Was I expected to act as a son? Or a replacement son?

Son. I am no one's son. I have no son. I lost mine, too. In the last years, while existing in a drug-induced fog, I have few memories of day to day. Two memories I don't want are those from three years apart. The first, I'm flat out on the carpet, my son standing above me. I hear, "Why doesn't Father love me anymore?" The second, I'm flat on the carpet, hearing: "Why does Father hate me?" In my pharmaceutically-detached state, I couldn't speak; just cry. He just couldn't understand my absence from the world he still lived in. I don't know that he ever will. Shit, my fucking world is falling apart. How is it that George gets the privilege of death? He's a lot more in love with his life than I am with mine. *God! You know what? You're a son of a bitch!*

I wake to a normal day – if I were a patient in Bellevue, that is. George wants to go to Stop 'n' Shop. For what, I don't know. With what money, I don't know. He's as free with my money as Shari had been. I'm out, except for the hundred-dollar bill I had safely hidden away for emergencies. By this time, George has all but lost the feeling in his right leg. He's barely able to walk unassisted but wouldn't think of using anything like a cane. We get into the Jeep – that is to say, one and three-quarters of us do. George's right leg is still outside the vehicle. He continuously tries slamming the door shut, which, of course, isn't going to happen with his leg blocking it. I try to intercede any number of times, only to be countered with: "Leave me alone! I'm not a fucking invalid!" This goes on for a good twenty minutes until he finally gets it. Meanwhile, I'm doing a slow mental suicide. Or is it murder?

We get to the store, which is as big as a city block and has a parking lot you could land a 747 in. With George being in the condition he's in, I naturally want to park as near to the store as possible. After passing a quarter of a mile of empty spaces and before nearing a section where any cars are parked, George screams at me: "You always do that! You're passing all these empty spaces!"

That emergency hundred-dollar bill is starting to burn a hole in my pocket.

Once in the store, George decides to avail himself of a senior go-cart. For me, judging from the immensity of the store, I think I'll wait for the bus. Just the vegetable aisle alone would take up the entire space in my supermarket back home; this place must serve the entire state. A nice greeting lady offers her assistance in showing George the operation of the cart. In the process, George rolls the cart forward right atop the woman's foot. The poor thing is howling at the top of her lungs. George looks down to see the problem and, instead of moving forward or back, just sits there hysterically laughing while peeing down his leg. I wonder if they sell airline tickets here?

On the way back to the house, George screams at me once again, this time for not stopping at the deli. He never mentioned the idea that I should. This is fast going beyond the normal twisted head games. *I don't need to wait for a goddamn plane, I'll just keep driving!* When we get back to the house, George demands that I take him and the dog out to a place where the dog can run. Nothing changes – he treats the goddamn dog better than me. I tell him that I'm in severe pain and need to medicate and rest for a while. If he and the dog have to go for a run this minute, his other house guest – who has now returned from her mini-vacation – can take them. George gets out and huffs into the house. He comes out again, passing me with the dog in tow, and gets into the Jeep with a spare set of keys I didn't know he had. He drives off, not very well, not being able to shift or steer correctly. I let loose with:

"That's fucking *it*, man! If you're going to fucking fight me, you can go to hell alone!"

I call the police and tell them what has happened and that George is a danger to himself and the public. I tell them where they can find him. I call George's lawyer and give my notice; I don't want a goddamn thing from the man and I'm no longer going to be responsible for him. I call the airport and book a flight an hour from now and then call the neighbor. *How would you like to make a hundred dollars? Just get me to the church on time!*

The cops bring George back to the house. In fact, the entire police force does. George must have told them he had Hoffa buried under the driveway. Then the whole neighborhood has to turn out as well. George never had it so good – he's the center attraction in this freaking circus. He's in Seventh Heaven. Suddenly he turns toward me and his face turns from sheer ecstasy to something more demonic.

"You and I are going to have words tonight," he rasps.

"Well, it's going to be a one-sided conversation, because I'm not going to be here!"

At the airport, I'm waiting very impatiently for my flight to be called. I am ablaze, I mean I'm on fire with rage, very close to becoming a pile of ash. Anyone capable of seeing auras would see me as someone on fire. A burning coal of hell itself. A young Asian man, who apparently *can* see auras, walks into my seating area. Taking one look at me, he turns white, turns on his heels, and leaves the area hurriedly, while looking over his shoulder. I feel bad. I'm sorry. I didn't mean to scare anybody.

I'm listening to the P.A. system intently. They're rattling off a long list of cancellations due to major wind-shear conditions up and down the coast. Is fate about to prove me wrong? Were my actions too rash? First I abandon John, now George – is there something fucking wrong with me? *Do you realize what you just walked out on? How far are you supposed to bend? Where's the line, the right and wrong of a thing?* Shit, I don't know. Maybe the guy doing the announcements will straighten out all this shit for me. He's the one who's going to decide whether I stay or go. Well, what do you know – mine is the only flight they're letting out of here tonight. That has to be someone's hand at work!

I'm not sure of what the hell I'm going home to, but it can't be like any of this bullshit insanity that I'm putting behind me. Besides, if I wasn't supposed to be going home, they wouldn't have let me out of here. At this point, the only alternative to the fire and the frying pan I'm doing a jig between would be to crash the plane. I get on board and take a seat in the rear. It's a small prop plane, about fourteen passengers in size. Oops, there's that same Asian gentleman. He takes one look at me and I can see he's having second thoughts about taking his seat. I have to wonder if that means anything.

The pilot comes on the P.A., interrupting my stroll down memory lane. The damage has been assessed, the plane has taxied to the arrival gate, we all seem to have survived whatever turbulence we encountered in the air and the near-calamitous touch down. It's now safe to disembark. As I stand up, I can see the pilot and co-pilot having a heated argument in the exposed cockpit. Apparently, they're arguing about who is going to pass out the luggage to the passengers. The co-pilot loses. As I approach him, I can see a very large wet stain running down the length of his pant leg. Which probably explains his reticence about subjecting himself to the gaze of the deplaning passengers. I can only assume that the pilot's stain is more egregious. I don't imagine either man knows just how lucky they both are to come out of this journey carrying with them nothing more burdensome than fear or more permanent than excreted stains. Fortunate to be feeling relieved, if red-faced. As opposed to weighted down, and scarred. Like me.

7 ~ I Didn't Mean To . . .
Yeah, I Guess I Did

My damn back feels as though I'm going to fold over backwards and snap in half, the muscles in my gut are straining to hold me erect – in a matter of a few more panicked moments, one or the other will give way. Then what? Is it going to kill me? Cripple me? The freezing cold – it's like a thousand shivs penetrating my skin; my body is a pin cushion full of icy needles. I climb the bars in an attempt to get closer to the ceiling heat, if indeed there is any; the air up there just has to be warmer than this Arctic blast down here on the cell floor. But, in stocking feet, the iron bars are conductors of the cold as opposed to an escape from it. In desperation, I try hanging by my hands from the crossbars, but that just results in cramping my arms and chest. I feel like a monkey at the Central Park Zoo, only there's no kind old lady to sneak me a lollipop. I'd give anything to keep my feet off that frozen cement, but the only other alternative is the steel bench and that seems the coldest of all. No blanket, no pillow, I'm not even allowed to keep my jacket. Oh, wow, they didn't deprive me of a roll of toilet paper – must have been an oversight on their part. Maybe these cocksuckers are more considerate than I thought them to be. Oh – ha, ha, the joke's on me. There's no way to use the fucking toilet – it's already clogged up to its rim with paper and shit. *Right. Where did you think that stench was coming from?* Gee, I wonder why those assholes chose this particular cell to put me in, with all the others being empty. I'm sure as shit glad that over the years I've developed a good relationship with these cops, especially Lt. Chaplin. I'd hate to see how they might treat me if they had the feeling I didn't like cops.

Which right now is closer to the truth. My brain just got bent when I asked to have one of my spiritual books, that I might gain some comfort in reading it. The grudging answer was: "I suppose it's alright for you to have a Bible." *But I didn't ask for a Bible, did I?* So much for freedom of religion. It just makes me glad all over that I once put my life up on the block for the protection of this country. I don't remember seeing any of these jerks around the base. In fact, this particular cop I remember from way back when I did my first stint in this town and was driving a school bus. I was five years out of the service then, he was still in high school. As he was getting off the bus one day, he called me an asshole under his breath; I guess that made him a bit of a disrespectful little twit. Not much has changed in all these years, except he's a little bigger.

Here I'd been thinking that cops were supposed to enforce the law, not make it. And these dickheads have stretched their job description to include doling out punishment as well. What the fuck am I guilty of in the first place? I know I used some naughty words on the phone. But absolutely no one has spoken to me about charges or even read me my rights – like I have any. I was brought here to the station, unscheduled, from the funny farm where I spent my initial two-week incarceration; not even my wife knows where I am. I wonder if she has realized yet that I'm not around.

When I asked for a phone call to let my lawyer know where I was, the Super-Pig Assistant-Chief Schweinz refused me. I reminded him that I have rights. Ha! – that didn't seem to ring any bells with him. He made a throat-clearing sound, and I could hear a cop in some old movie saying: "Yah, tell it to the judge."

Well, you know what? I think that's just what I'll do. My ass is so numb with cold that it won't know the difference now if I sit myself down on this metal bench, one step removed from a slab in the morgue. What the hell. No one here has paid me any mind when I've tried to get their attention, so I doubt they'll take any notice of my conversation. If they do, so what? They already think I'm nuts. And I expect The Judge is going to be the best company I'm likely to have while I'm in here.

----- So, Your Honor, I appreciate your interest in my case. My apologies for the lack of amenities in this cell, but I hope you'll be comfortable. You ask what brings me here. Damned if I know. I'd say a paddy wagon and a bunch of over-zealous officers, but I don't want to offend your dignity with a lame attempt at humor. I seem to have had some sort of breakdown. I guess I did – because someone decided that I should spend some time in the psych ward at Yale New Haven, and I was okay with that – as okay as I've been capable of being with anything for a while – not that I was given any choice about it. I suppose you surmised as much.

So your question might be: Why? What happened? Well, there was the alleged hostage-holding of my family and wielding of deadly weapons – a whole arsenal I supposedly had stashed in my studio – and maybe some disturbing remarks on the phone to the police. That's the part the cops will tell you – their version of it, anyway. But before any of that, there was the wrecking of my back, the years of pain and incapacitation and drugs – the Rx kind, Your Honor – that, I think you could agree when I plead my case, wrecked my life. On top of that: the frustration and anger, frustration and anger – you can hear it in my voice right now. Because there was liability. Because the hope of healing and moving on hit a brick wall; and seeking compensation for my losses – that was another brick wall. So I looked for a lawyer.

The lawyers that I had met before finding Atty. John A. in Hamilton, CT were of two ilks: either "I don't handle slip-and-fall cases" – like that was some kind of contagious disease or something – or not really interested in whether or not my injury was real, but – did it have the potential to be a real piggy-bank buster? In which case, as you know, you have to show damages as a result of the accident, like not being able to make love to your wife. Uh, which way is this lie supposed to go? I'm confused.

Well, in any case, *my* piggy bank was busted; along with my back . . . . You're not in any hurry, are you, Your Honor? I think it might help my case if I could tell you the whole story, and try to get across the idea of how it all fits together and makes sense. If it does. I'll let you be the judge of that.

----- Yes, I know you are. Sorry. Let me present the facts of the incident in question. There were no clouds in the sky the day it happened. It was a

213

beautiful February morning. Clear, sunny, and unseasonably warm. I stopped to gas up the car at the Shell station down the road from my house, thinking that I might take advantage of just how beautiful the day was and shoot a couple of rounds of archery. I was a bit reluctant, though, it being a weekend and therefore Raechel – that's my wife – being at home. She might be offended at being stuck in the house alone with no car for three hours or better. Little could I have understood at that point in time that she might very well have enjoyed the reprieve. Or that it wasn't only my back that was on the brink of being fractured, but my marriage and my life.

I had no sooner stepped out of the car when both my feet went flying out to the right. I went down, but my left arm was hung up on a tail-fin, so the upper half of me could not follow in the flight path of my legs. I heard a loud snap and felt a deep, sharp pain in my spine. And I hung there until I managed to turn myself towards the car and slowly lower myself to my knees. It took me quite a while to gingerly pick myself up from there. As I did, I noticed a man, at the pumps on the other side of the lot, starting toward me. When he saw that I was now erect, he went back about his business. I remember thinking it was nice of him to take notice of me just the same. It took me a minute to catch my breath and I sure as hell wasn't moving like I was just a minute ago. Or thinking about archery. It was all I could do to maneuver myself into my car.

When I got home, I winced my way into the kitchen where Raechel was standing with her back to me, washing dishes. I told her: "I just fell and I think I hurt my back real bad." If my life had been depending on a response from her, then I was a dead man. She didn't even bother to turn around and look at me. I stood there for a moment, as if I were waiting for something to change. But nope – I'm still alone.

This little event changed everything. I was now unable to draw a bow, which up until then, Your Honor, had been almost a daily practice. In fact, I was pretty much unable to use my right arm for anything. When I attempted to use it, a panic attack would come upon me. I mistook these attacks to be some form of anxiety. I was never one to rush off to a doctor at the drop of a hat unless there was a corpse under it; I just continued on my merry way, and suffered that which I had to suffer. Alone. On top of everything else, my plumbing had given up the ghost as well. That got Raechel off the hook about any guilt she may have been suffering over the infrequency of conjugal relations – but I doubt she felt any pangs to begin with. Anyway, she no longer needed to worry about her two-day-per-year

214

obligation, for the time being. Also, at the time, I had been engaged in remodeling our house, and that would have to be put on standby as well; but that was really a moot point since we were a long way off from ever having the minimum of six thousand dollars we'd need to start work on the bathroom, which was next in line for a makeover. In a way, though, the injury served as a blessing. It removed all distractions and let me buckle down and get to work on the acrylic painting book I had just contracted to write – as long as I could find a balance between writing and medicating.

So, you see, I'm not looking to make a case for loss of marital intimacy or inability to work.

But speaking of meds, Your Honor – would you excuse me for a moment? I can hear some of the good ol' boys down the hall. My state-appointed caretakers.

"I need my meds! I need my meds!" No sense going hoarse over these assholes – I know they can hear me yelling because I can sure as shit hear every word they're saying in a normal voice. They're just having their fun by ignoring me. Shit, I'm trapped in some kind of medieval justice system. These jerks are the jailers of the dungeon. No different from those damn lawyers that are the guardians of the realm's gold. Those that comprise the Inquisition that's set up to set me straight as to what is what. I'm finding that their "what" is not in the dictionary of the world according to Earl. This is a totally different world, where everyone else knows how the wheels turn but me.

----- Sorry, Your Honor. I'm afraid I'm being rude. Let me stop gritting my teeth and clenching my fists before I continue to address you. Thank you for your patience.

At the time of my fall, I had no lawyer; I didn't realize that I needed one. Yet. I thought it would count for something that I had always been on friendly terms with the gas station's owner, Brian. Here's what happens: I approach him outside the business one fine day in the end of June.

"You know, Brian, as you're aware, I fell out there last winter," I say politely, pointing over to the pumps under the still-leaking canopy. "Since then, I've come to realize that the extent of my injuries is far greater than I first realized. I wonder if you'd be willing to pick up the excess medical bills, after insurance."

My query is met with laughter and: "That's why I pay insurance."

I inquire as to who the insurer might be. Allstate, the good hands people, I'm told. So I call the people with the good hands. Good hands – yeah, around your throat. I make the same inquiry of them. I'm met with the same laughter and: "That's why we pay our lawyers."

Yeah, let's avoid doing the right thing here, no point in making this easy. I'm guessing they're just hoping I go away; but if I'm stupid enough to oppose The Force, then they'll be glad to show me just how many ways they have to fuck me over. *Bring it on.*

Oh – excuse me, again, Judge – you can see I'm still dealing with some frustration and anger.

----- Thanks for understanding. I'm not sure this chat would work for me if I had to watch my F's and U's.

So, I find my lawyer, John, in the eleventh hour – more like 11:59. Immediately, he seems to be a man of ethics. I'm feeling greatly satisfied by the fact that he doesn't contract with me until our fourth meeting. I'm sure he's taking the time to be certain that I am real. But that's where reality stops.

Some time passes before I receive a letter from Allstate telling me that I have to report to their insurance doctor – or else. Or else, I can forget about leveling any sort of claim ever again. *Paging Dr. Steller, paging Dr. Steller.* Holy shit! A surgeon? What the hell do *they* know about tissue damage, much less about its cure? Their job is to cut it out, not to heal it. The deck has been stacked, though, and I have no choice but to meet with him.

"Good morning, Doctor, how are you?" *You fucking paid assassin.*

"Keep your mouth shut, Mr. McByrne, unless it's to answer my questions." *You stupid fucking pigeon.*

This is going to go well. It's easy for him, he never asks any questions. And though I'm here for a back injury, he never bothers to examine my back. If he were to do that, he would find a golf-ball-size bulge on the right side of my lower spine. *Fore! Yeah – duck! Good. You missed it.*

I had no way of knowing it then, but he had scored my toe/heel-walk test as normal. He totally overlooked the fact that I went down in flames of screaming pain every time I attempted the walk. How forgiving of him to give me a high score. Was this a prelude of the type of treatment I could look forward to? I mean, this jerk was nothing more than a carnival barker. The Big Show was yet to come. *Hurry, hurry, hurry, step right up into the big tent. If you dare.*

I know you probably can't come out and say it, Judge, but from the way you're nodding, I get the feeling you know what I'm talking about.

Atty. John and I drive to the office of Shell's and Allstate's lawyers for the first of two depositions. The stack of chips is in their favor, two against one, plus they're not beyond the stretch of ignoring the truth I tell them in favor of the lies of others. Starting with Brian's declaration during his deposition: "Mr. McByrne called me at home." *Sure, on his unlisted number.* "He said, 'I'm suing you, and how do I sue Shell?' "

In point of fact, I never knew until that moment that I *was* suing Shell; I had no idea that they had a dog in this fight.

Upon entering the office and getting down to business, I'm informed that the two lawyers had watched me cross the parking lot to their office building. *This means what to me? Did you see that I was having an ever-loving shit-fit about all the goddamn ice on the pavement out there?! Black ice is why we're here, you know! Assholes.* I'm guessing that ice-sheeted parking lot is some kind of red-carpet welcoming. It was a much smaller piece of black ice at the Shell station that brought me here: about one square foot – but even that was big enough to be catastrophic. The pump's canopy's drain system was apparently not functioning properly and the accumulated water was dripping down onto the apron by day and freezing by night.

At last, we're seated. Let the show begin.

"Let me ask you, Mr. McByrne – how do you get along with your mother?"

Are you friggin' shitting me? That's your first question? Either they're interviewing the wrong client or they've done their homework and are testing me right off the bat as to whether I'm willing to lie as effectively as their witnesses.

"I don't!" *That should set them back a peg.*

It just gets stupider and stupider. They even try to talk me into the fact that it was my car who assaulted me and I should go after *my* insurance company. Oh, that doesn't work? Let's try: You didn't fall at all; yeah, that works for us. They can't seem to make up their minds. After all, I had no witnesses, and everyone knows if a tree falls in the forest and there's no one there to hear it, then the tree never fell in the first place. Of course, they have their own witness who saw me not fall. One of Brian's flunkies who's a psychotic dog-killer who wasn't even there that morning; but I'm willing to concede that, if the truth be known, yes, on every day he *was* there, he didn't see me fall. After more than two hours of this bullshit, it seems

217

they're far from running low on crucifixion nails.

The second meeting is at my lawyer's office. It isn't going much better, except the for fact that we're dealing with only one oppositional brain this time. I'm guessing they felt they had me under control enough that one of their side's lawyers could be excused. The lawyer who drew the short straw goes on asking me trick questions that I don't let get by me. After almost every answer I give, he comes back at me with accusations that I couldn't possibly have knowledge of this or that, because I never attended college as himself had done. It's not my fault he wasted his money in school instead of in bars, like me. My education was just as good, but a lot cheaper. I can see that his smart-ass tank of superiority is down to the fumes of desperation. I begin to feel sorry for his frustrations. Maybe I should cut the guy a break.

Then his last question: "Before we conclude, do you wish to say anything?"

I stand up and clench my fists. He looks at me warily.

"Just this," I say. "I will not, under normal circumstances, allow myself to be self-justifying. I am not now – nor have I ever put myself -- above the law. But today, if I could wrap Brian, the doctor, and you fucking lawyers up into one person – I would kill that man!"

I start to violently tremble and break out in tears. The lawyer just sits there, apparently stunned, with his mouth hanging open, as is the mouth of his stenographer. I hurriedly exit the room, but not before hearing the secretary gasp: "I've never heard anything like that before."

I go out onto the back fire escape to have a smoke and calm down. John follows me out.

"I'm sorry, John, I didn't mean for that to happen."

He puts his arm around me and pulls me in to him and kisses me on top of my head, murmuring: "I wish the other idiot had been here to see this."

The Judge is nodding sagely when my train of thought is shaken off its tracks by the sound of the outer door of the station slamming shut. This is followed by the rise of almost hysterical laughter and the words: "*There's* someone Earl wants to talk to!" Then more laughter.

It must be that Lt. Chaplin just walked in. I'm thinking that crack I just heard was somewhat cruel and unwarranted. But then, look at the source. To my mind, these idiots just painted a portrait of themselves as being nothing more than the bunch of easily-entertained country bumpkin yahoos that they truly are. Now, apparently, they're reflecting back on that night of nights, just two weeks ago, when I engaged Chaplin on the phone for some hours in an attempt to forestall my suicide just long enough to enable me to unravel the reason why. *Why am I bothering? Who the fuck cares?* But here I am, and I don't see anyone upstairs in uniform perceiving my tragedy of a broken marriage and consequent rage-filled events that got me here as anything but comic. It brings to mind something that happened not very long ago and within their own ranks. I had heard that this cop took a long walk off his roof with a short rope around his neck. The reason being that his wife had announced that she no longer loved him. Brother, these yo-yos must have been rolling in the aisles for days over that one if they find this kind of thing to be funny.

Chaplin was someone who I felt I had something in common with from the start. I felt a deep warmth towards the man although it probably wasn't for the healthiest of reasons. The first time I ever laid eyes on him was in a grocery store. I immediately saw something in his eyes that opened my heart to him. It was as though I was looking at myself. I saw in him a very lonely friendless man; one who had more problems than picking out the right brand of ice cream his wife had demanded he bring home. I'm thinking he must have recognized something in me as well because, as total strangers, we had no problem joining in conversation. Not something I readily do. We ran into each other several times that way before I learned he was a cop. Then, over the years, I became comfortable enough with him that I would visit him at the station.

He may very well have been a leader of the gang, but I never felt as though he was truly a member of the club. Too much brains, maybe a little too much earnest caring for others outside his circle. In turn, I was always very open with the man, almost too trusting perhaps, but that's on me. For the amoral life George led, he was seldom wrong in his advice, which included: "Never befriend a cop." I guess he wasn't wrong there either. But, like I said, that was on me. At some point in time, I had confided in Chaplin that I was cortisone intolerant. That must have scared the ever-loving shit out of him because, as I came to understand from one source or another, his wife suffered from that condition as well and could be a real straitjacket case at times, or so I was told. Yeah, I knew that feeling; I'd been there a few times myself, especially since '93, with my never-relenting pain. If I didn't keep it well medicated, it was off to Psycho Land I went.

But then there was that day, while paying him a visit at the station, when

I let the cat out of the bag. I was confiding in him about my adventure of the previous night, when I had been planning to do great harm to a neighbor I was having trouble with. In telling my tale, I let on to the fact that – although I hadn't realized it at the time – I had been under the influence of my body's release of cortisol, which makes me psychotic. I also mentioned that, when you're in a state of psychosis, you feel perfectly normal, and therefore abnormal acts such as murder seem normal as well. I wasn't so hung over that I didn't recognize a look of great disturbance come over his face. I took to heart his advice to go home and medicate and get some much-needed rest. By all rights and logic, he should have – or, at least, could have – arrested me on the spot. But what are friends for? Maybe George was only half right.

I wonder where The Judge went. Guess I've been talking to myself for a while. What's new.

I wonder where Chaplin was that night when I went off my nut and told the dispatcher that I would only engage with Lt. Chaplin and no one else. I wonder if he was even on duty or not. Whatever, wherever, it must have crossed his mind to wonder why he had to know me in the first place. I'm sure he must have had better things to do than to deal with my shit. It's not as if I really went out of my way to inconvenience him or anything; but then again, that night I was giving little consideration to anyone's considerations. As far as I was concerned, this was my last night on earth and if anyone found me to be inconvenient to a few hours of the rest of their lives, it was just too fucking bad. *What do you want from me? Guilt?* Okay, I feel bad all over.

I wish I could say that night started out normally, but I can't, because I had long since ceased to understand what the hell normal was. There certainly was no element of sameness to it. Besides, I'm now a different person. It's not like I was reborn or anything like that, it was more like everything that had composed me had died and left me without definition. That night . . . yeah, I've had plenty of chances to relive it over the days since it happened. I wish it would stop replaying in my head . . . but, of course, here it is again . . . .

I've just arrived back from my insane stint in George's Realm, Virginia, but I've hardly escaped the toxic fumes of guilt for having run for cover. And that shroud of shame that my psyche has woven for me is doing little to protect me from the resurrection of guilt from years before over my absence at John's ending in that NY hotel room. I mean, how high can you stack the shit? That and I'm so friggin' physically exhausted from being sleep deprived for the last three weeks. I just have no tolerance for being in my own skin at this point.

The plan of the moment, however, is to not just get by – although that in itself would be just as much as I could comfortably handle. No, I'm going for the whole nine yards. Yeah, as usual, I'll cook dinner. Afterward, I'll celebrate my homecoming, under the sheets with Raechel – not so usual. In anticipation of that internationally-noteworthy event, I forgo my pain medication that dulls not only the pain, but all other sensations as well. And it's already been some years that I haven't had the use of that particular sensation I hope to experience tonight, so I don't want to fuck it up now.

The hitch is the danger of a cortisol release. That trigger for the emotional bomb that I am. *Watch out -- here it comes!* I open the mail that includes the phone bill; as usual. *Wait for it!* In the bill, there appears a number that had been called repeatedly every night of my absence, showing calls of an hour in length. As usua . . . no, maybe not so. Gee, I wonder what it is I could possibly be thinking? No, I don't want to go there; that would not be a good place for me right now. But could it be true? The uneasiness tugs and tugs at me until I can't stand it any longer. I step into the mine field with a loaded question.

"Raechel, what's your best friend's phone number?"

"Um -- I don't know off the top of my head."

"Well, don't you think, if you dialed it every day for three weeks, you'd have it memorized?"

She's tongue-tied. The self-incrimination of her silence, as obvious as it is to me, must be mortifyingly blatant to her. It seems we're committed now to jumping on a sled and going downhill from here with no brakes. It's apparent that, in my absence, Raechel has been continuing her wayward thing with that married deviant friend/coworker. A sexual chase game that brings up all-too-familiar images of our own beginnings. Before my leaving for George's, Raechel had promised faithfully to end the nonsense. When later questioned, she told me she had. Whether I like it or not, I think the fat lady is about to come on stage. You can hear the thumping of her footsteps. Or maybe that's me, letting all hell break loose.

I throw an ever-loving fucking shit-fit! I throw a few other things as

221

well. Like dinner on the floor. *Fuck it – let them eat cake.* Then I throw a few choice words and follow them with the death-by-smashing of my most prized possession, a fine-art ceramic-iguana tea pot, just to make sure the degree of my angst is understood, and then, in case there is any further doubt, I commit my wedding ring, along with a diamond one that George had gifted me, into the burning coal stove. *Now do you understand that I'm pissed off? By the way, it's over.* With a barrage of darkly colorful words and female-specific epithets, I point to the door and growl: "I want you the fuck out of here in two days!"

I guess I didn't make my point clear – she lunges at me as if to lovingly embrace me with out-stretched arms and hands. I act on my immediate reaction of repulsion and, with absolutely no forethought, slap her hands violently as if repelling an attacking lioness. Just as quickly, I'm sickened by the harshness of my physical response.

At that moment, Jared appears at his bedroom door, bristling. "Did you just slap Mother?" His tone of vengeful displeasure suggests that he's threatening to kick my ass. That's it, brother! There's no way I'm going to allow this to escalate into something that I've always been incapable of engaging in. I'm not going to be turned into a cowardly brute! No how, no way. I'm not going to let this fucking bitch push me over the line. I retreat to my studio and lock myself safely in.

Fine; I've expended my volatility and drunk myself to near oblivion. When I wake, I'll realize this was just the nightmare that it must be. This can't possibly be reality because I only have one life, and this can't possibly be it. All is right with the world now; the monster sleeps.

But – shit! – the maddening dream won't stop. There's Raechel kneeling over me with her incessant pleading. She's in the studio? What the fuck? Did she pick the lock? What has to happen for this everlasting insanity to draw to a close? That's it! I know. There's only one way to go now that's lock-pick-proof.

I stride through the surreal pre-dawn darkness, back to the house and into the kitchen, with Raechel still firmly attached. I pick up the phone and dial the police. Calmly, I adhere to polite protocol and give my name and address followed by: "I'm holding my wife and child hostage with multiple weapons." Then hang up. My hand isn't even off the receiver yet when the dispatcher calls back. She asks if my wife and child are free to leave the house. I answer in the affirmative. She asks if she can speak to my wife; I hand Raechel the phone. I don't hear both sides of the conversation, but I gather from what Raechel says, she's being asked to get out of the house, if she's free to go. *Fine! Go already!*

So go! She's not moving. I tell her, if she's going to stick around for the game she better get our son and get safely into the bathtub because the bullets are going to be fucking flying just about any minute now.

It's now my intention to leave my mark. In this case, in blood and guts. I happily envision Raechel on her hands and knees, scrubbing up the gore off the floor for the next two weeks. What better revenge can I possibly visit on the Queen of Neat Freaks? The fantasy seems well worth the price of death. I'm now armed with my target bow and half a dozen arrows. This doesn't frighten Raechel, but hopefully it will scare the cops enough to draw their fire. In reality, cops have less to fear from me than flies do, and I can't remember the last time I sent any flies to the cemetery.

Raechel and Jared leave. Now it's just me alone with my thoughts, although I have few that are not regrets. I suppose that, even in the last moment of life, I'm not going to be able to divorce myself from regretting that this too is just the last painful moment on top of the past three and a half years of pain. Shit, as long as you're alive, you can't get rid of it. In all my years, I have to say, I was looking for something a little less hurtful in the end than being shot to death. But such is the sacrifice one makes for the love of revenge.

You know, if I was dealing with a brain trust here instead of a bunch of boys in the wood who probably relish the idea of playing cowboys and Indians -- I mean, what chance do they get around here to use their guns except to clean them? -- chances are this whole fuckup would simply run out of gas. *Oh – speaking of gas – there's Corporal Agarn, standing right out in the open.* I don't know whether he's ever made the connection, the recognition of me as that school bus driver, or not, but twice since I've come back to this town, he's insulted me as well as assaulted me with that smug puss of his. I guess he's just the type of wise-ass coward that, *in a uniform*, feels safe from the ass-kicking he could use. Now here he is, just a mere hundred feet away. Little does he realize I'd have no trouble putting an arrow right through that little shiny tin heart on his chest at a hundred yards. Hell, if I was going to shoot anyone, it would be him.

I call Chaplin and tell him to get his little flunky out of harm's way. I see the headlight beam of a car flash the wise-ass – then, apparently, he's waved in. That was stupid on Chaplin's part. Now I know exactly where he is. Just on the other side of my neighbor's house. No matter, though –

he's safe from me.

Well, they're not going anywhere and neither am I. I'm dog-tired and I need this to come to some kind of resolution. I'm beginning to think that perhaps I was too rash; everything unfolded so quickly.

I call Chaplin up once again, hoping to find some rational voice that I can't seem to connect with in myself, that line being busy. Chaplin reminds me that we're on open mic. Yeah, I'm sure more than half the busy-bodies in town have their ears glued to their police scanners. Shit, it's a great melodrama for the poor of mind. Hope they're enjoying the show.

I vent for quite some time: a lot of nonsense about my past, my guilts, my crimes. I'm pretty much keeping the personal stuff, about my wife and all, in my vest pocket. At some point I do want to put it on the table – I mean, how it is I got here and all – but not over the public airways.

I invite Chaplin to come in and sit down with me and perhaps work something out. At least get to tell my story to someone before leaving. He flatly refuses.

Some more time and conversation have passed, but not my frustration for some type of resolution one way or the other. Again I extend the invitation, again it's refused. What few strands of reality I have left to clutch at are fraying, and I sense that the final curtain is being readied to fall. I begin in earnest to measure the options that might still be available to me. The greatest obstacle to considering the option not to die is knowing that I will be at the mercy of my neighbors. And knowing that they have no mercy. I know the ways of their wagging tongues all too well, and I know if I survive this night, I will never be able to endure their unrelenting gossip. The shunning and finger-pointing they won't bother to disguise. Life on The Shoreline would never be worth living again. God! It's hard to imagine that it could be worse than it's been up to now.

It's ironic, but everything the police are doing – or not doing – is just pushing me further into the corner of no return. They are actually forcing me to do harm to myself. I have perhaps an exaggerated fear of incarceration, but it's a dread that's real to me nonetheless. And then there's the tune-up to look forward to. I've seen it first hand from a local state cop and, on top of that, Schweinz has a reputation for putting the hurt on people and enjoying it. Anyway, I'm having a hard time trying to imagine what they think their purpose is out there. Maybe they're protecting the rest of the world from me. Yeah, that has to be it. Otherwise, it would just take one good cop to end all this. I feel myself sinking deeper and deeper into my aloneness. I'm finding, at the bottom of that pit, there's no one to keep me company or reassure me of anything. The inner-self, my go-to person when I'm in trouble or need, appears to already be deceased.

That's it. When you're this fucking alone, there's nothing left to consider or argue with. I've given myself more than adequate time to back out of this shit. Enough time to consider the alternatives. Which are? At this point, as they say, it's time to shit or get off the pot. This brain constipation isn't going to get us anywhere. I can't think of one goddamn good reason to continue this lunacy. *You're going to die someday anyway.* Yeah, but I was kind of hoping God would surprise me, not let me set it up myself. *Shit! Let's do it and get it the fuck over with already. After all, it isn't like dying is going to be any more painful than the pain you've already survived.* Holy shit – if that isn't an oxymoron, then I don't know what is. But hell, I'm not sure if I know what *anything* is.

I take a deep breath. I take one last peek into my mind to see if I've forgotten anything that might be a lifeline. Nope, the file cabinet is empty. I take up my bow and nock an arrow. I take one last deep breath, thinking I'll be able to exhale the incoming burning pain I'm about to encounter. Somehow that will make it hurt less. And, what the fuck, can you really realize pain if you're not there to remember it? I'll have to send someone a post card with the answer.

I violently fling open the front door and jump out onto the walkway like Robin Hood confronting the Sheriff of Bushy Hollow. An hour-long second passes. Too long. Then another hour. Way too much long. I can't hold my breath forever. A long vicious growl permeates the air I'm not breathing. It's coming from behind a large tree not more than ten feet away. *Shit, I've been given the Great Green Weenie! Fucked over!* I instinctively run back into the house, slamming and locking the door behind me. Trembling with anger and the sense of betrayal, I call Chaplin.

"You son of a bitch, you've got dogs out there! I can't shoot a dog. Besides, they're police officers."

"Well, Earl, you said you'd shoot a cop."

That was a threat, and I can't threaten a goddamn dog – they're a lot smarter than regular cops! I'm fucked!

I hang up the phone and, without so much as a thought, run over to the cabinet by the kitchen sink where I keep my meds. I throw handfuls of the

225

shit in my mouth, followed by a swig of Scotch. After about the third mouthful, I start to retch and bring everything up. I don't let it daunt me. I just recycle. So does my stomach. I can't keep anything down any better than I can think of an alternative. Cutting myself? No! I remember Collin too goddamn well. Besides, it takes too long. Besides, if I had the guts for that sort of thing, I wouldn't have relied on the cops to do this thing for me. I guess there's nothing left to do except to surrender. What's the worst thing that can happen? What – are they going to kill me?

It's well past dawn now. I step out the back door with my hands on my head. What the hell is that sound? Still silence. No birds. I mean this is the kind of silence that comes when the earth stops spinning. Where the fuck are the birds? Do they know something I don't? Are they holding their breath in anticipation? I count off ten seconds. Nothing. I start walking slowly towards the center of the yard while counting to ten again and stop. Still nothing. It's so quiet, you could hear an atom bomb go off – I half expect one to, at least some sound louder than a cap gun. I stand there for another ten count, then drop to my knees. Nothing. Is someone playing head games with me, or did everyone just get bored and go home? I count to ten again just before I ready myself to lay face down. Then the shock of a human voice finally splits the deafening silence.

Well, almost human. I immediately recognize it as belonging to a state K-9 cop who I remember from a few years back when I witnessed him tear the door off a Jeep to get at a suspect. Barney Miller he wasn't. He commands me to lay face down. I know the drill. Yeah, too goddamn well. Uh-oh, here comes the tune-up. Sure as shit, he drop-kicks me, which is to say he drops his three hundred pounds of mean out of the sky, landing squarely on the very spot of my spine that I have devoted close to four years to trying to heal. Someone must have supplied him with a map. I guess he felt that wasn't painful enough, so he then takes my right hand and proceeds to see how many revolutions he can get out of it. I offer no resistance, but that makes no difference to him. He's set on the idea of causing me pain. I have to laugh at the whole friggin' thing because this is the bozo who's facing brutality charges in the case of the guy in the Jeep. It was my eyewitness deposition that got his bacon out of the fire. Now he's got me in his pan. Ain't life funny. After about the fourth revolution, the cop on the other side of me, probably a local, yells at him: "Hey!" And the jerk, at least, ceases his torment. I guess, like my wrist, the brotherhood stretches only so far. I'm cuffed, then thrown in the back of a car and then into a cell, without being booked. Schweinz asks about the human skulls I have in my studio – which, evidently, they've entered (with a warrant?). I tell him: "They're legal, I purchased them in city shops quite legally; they were all people who were already dead." *How would you like to join the collection?*

At least that cell had a working toilet, not that I was any too conscious of my surroundings that morning, with all the drugs and booze in me. I know there was heat because I remember that I wasn't freezing like I am now. As I recall, there was someone else in the block as well. The heat was probably for him, seeing he probably wasn't a cop-killer. This cold is killing my freaking back!

"Hey! Hey! I need my meds! I'm having a medical emergency!"

I know those cocksuckers can hear me as loud as a bell. I'm glad that I must be serving as some point of amusement for them. To think I used to feel high esteem for cops – but, then again, we're talking city cops, who are professional in the role, not these cowboys with control issues who are playing at it.

"I'm having a medical emergency! I'M HAVING A GODDAMN MEDICAL EMERGENCY!" Maybe if I'm disruptive enough they'll pay me some attention.

I hear the door open, finally. The custodian pokes his head in, not too far, and looks at me as if he's trying to figure out which one of us is doing all the yelling. Must be me, 'cause I'm the only one here. Now, with that info, what the fuck of it? Maybe, he was just checking to see that the pipes weren't bursting from the cold.

"Would you tell someone that I'm having a medical emergency? PLEASE!"

The head of one son of a bitch pops out and another one pops in. Schweinz himself this time.

"What kind of medical emergency are you having?"

"I need my medication."

"The nurse at Yale gave you medication this morning and gave no instructions for any other."

"What the fuck are you talking about? She's not my goddamn doctor. She doesn't know anything about my condition. I want my phone call that

227

you never bothered to tell me I was entitled to, so I can call my lawyer so he can get me out of here!"

"When did you talk to him last?"

"This morning at Yale before I was picked up."

"Then you don't need to speak to him again."

"What the fuck are you talking about? He doesn't know I'm *here,* nor does my wife. He can get in touch with my doctor, because I know you're not going to bother checking with him. I need my meds. I need to talk to my lawyer!"

"That's not going to happen."

He disappears behind the slamming door.

I wonder how long that nice cop who sat over me at the Yale emergency room lasted in this Gestapo outfit? The good cops I've run across from time to time never seem to make it more than a year, if that, before moving on to greener, or more realistic, pastures. I remember that one at Yale looking at me with what seemed a great deal of caring in his face as I lay handcuffed to the gurney. I thought at any moment he might have to fight back the tears. I must have looked pretty near death. That was the last kindly face I would see in the next twenty-four hours. Even so, I'd put myself back there in a heartbeat. Or a mind-blink . . . .

The E.R. nurse hands me a cup of black oozy shit and tells me, like it or not, to drink the whole thing.

"What is it?"

"Charcoal."

"Am I being used for a cookout?"

"It will clean all of the drugs out of your system." *To the extent that, if you were black, you'd become a white guy. Maybe vice versa too.*

I drink it. I actually prefer Scotch.

I'm now transferred to a psychiatric evaluation and holding tank. I'm put in a fish bowl. No one looks at me. No one speaks to me. Good, I'm invisible. Maybe I can just walk out of here. I'm absolutely clueless as to what's happening; what's supposed to happen. The only attendants I see are in their own fish bowl and they're not paying any attention to my being here. I wonder if I really could just walk out of here. I guess they're one step ahead of me – they know I'm not going anywhere but the john. The charcoal has set in and I've become my own port-a-potty. God – what do I

228

do? There's no toilet in this glass case. Am I allowed to leave it? Well, two police forces and two police dogs didn't stop me from doing what I wanted to do – I don't think these guys are going to. I'm not going to wait and see. I scurry to the men's room. Man! Mt. Vesuvius has nothing on me. That was some wicked shit they gave me. I'm shitting my tonsils out, and talk about gas -- I've got enough methane going that I could power a race car.

Between gastric attacks, I'm transported to Yale Psychiatrics proper. My particular ward is kind of a Holiday Inn for the mentally displaced. Not necessarily the insane, just those that aren't coping well. Attempted suicides, drug abuse, having to live in Bushy Hollow, that kind of shit. My consciousness takes a short reprieve. I wake to find myself tethered to a padded board someone is trying to pass off as a bed. This is supposed to be my twenty-four-hour quiet time. Not too quiet, I'm still shitting my guts out. The aide is overseeing me while I'm on the john. If anyone here is that paranoid that they think I might use the toilet as a vehicle to escape through, then they have the wrong person in restraints. After my "good time" is up, I'm let out and I can now join the free population of the confined.

This is not a bad place. The staff all seem very pleasant and easy going. I get to smoke twice a day. The food is above average. I really can't ask for more. It beats the hell out of jail. In fact, it beats everything about my life as I knew it in the last month. I wonder what the hell that says? Do I ever really have to go home again, I wonder.

At last, I finally find myself in peace – how goddamn refreshing. I haven't felt anything near this in almost two decades. I'd forgotten that anything like this kind of feeling existed. No anger, no frustrations, no burdens, and best of all, no nagging! Does it get any better than this? I mean, it's so surreal. I'm actually having a hard time imagining that I'll ever have to leave this place. I hate to admit it, but this may very well be the best I've had it in all my life. What the fuck does that say? I'm no longer a citizen of the Outside. I don't have any of the baggage or burdens that come with ownership. Having discovered this place, as far as I'm concerned, the world can go to hell for all I care.

Out there is where all the real fucking nuts are. I haven't run into an unkind face or word since I got here; I sure as shit can't say that for the Outside – not even my own home. In here, I find nothing more than very decent people who have been handed, or beaten with, the wrong end of the stick. The luckless, sometimes the ill-fated, the ones who made bad choices, if indeed they had anything to choose from in the first place. There's one young lady who has my heart. She attempted suicide when she learned that she had contracted AIDS. So what's her crime? Or should I ask: which? Then there's my roommate, who I really like. He's hooked on whatever friggin' shit the street has to offer. I know that street; I've visited it from time to time but somehow always found the means to escape it. Sometimes dumb luck; probably more being white than anything else. Everyone knows there's no such thing as a black guardian angel; I guess that comes from God being white and all.

This kid reminds me of my best friend from back in my childhood: very good-looking and very bright, but not white. The only reason his family was able to buy a house was because his father was a career criminal; you know, all those "nigger type" things. Drugs, the numbers. At about the time we were both twelve, my friend told me that his big ambition in life was to become a "bad nigger." Seven years later, after not having seen him in all that time, I dropped by the old neighborhood to visit him. He took me into his room and pulled half a dozen gators out from underneath his bed and proudly proclaimed: "See, I've made it, I'm a bad nigger!" He lucked out. He dropped dead at thirty. I can see in this roommate my old friend. I can see that the world, or at least our society, hasn't changed all that much from my childhood days: I'm sure this kid will go far. As far as being black will take you. Enjoying his company is one of the few things here that sadden me.

Now being in the main ward, I have the privileges that come with it, like use of the phone. I get to talk to Raechel. She tells me I made the papers.

"This isn't news to me," I answer, not really giving a shit.

"No, I mean you really made the news – not just the police blotter, but the front page. And not just the local paper, but *The New Haven Register* as well. Do you want me to read it to you?"

"Sure, why not."

Well, they got the quote right as far as my call to 911 was concerned, but then the yellow journalism kicked in. I'm talking 'yellow' as far as pissing on the public's leg. Not to mention my character. I just love the part where I was "apprehended while running to his weapons shed."

After I stop laughing myself near to death, all I can say is: "Where the fuck did they come up with that goddamn fairytale?"

I just knew it – let the game of telephone begin! I can just hear all those beakers flapping now. By the time I'm out of here, I'm sure I'll be Charlie Manson's first cousin. Even though Raechel wasn't in the house at the time that I did to her all those things people are going to claim I did to her, apparently she's forgiven me my brutality and visits me on what seems to be a path of reconciliation. It won't be long now before my insurance runs out and the powers that hold me here will forgive me as well and release me back to where I can further be bothered by those things that bothered me in order to get me here.

Wouldn't you know it, just before the ward is to go out for their morning smoke break – something I've been looking forward to for hours – the cops show up to remove me from heaven and bring me to what new purgatory. Isn't it just like them? Isn't it my luck that one of them is one of the D.A.R.E. officers and just happens to be Corporal Agarn as well. Useless as it may be, seeing that once upon a time this gentleman went out of his way to tell me that he hates people who smoke, I beg him for a moment to have a quick one. I'm answered with that ridiculous smirk of his. *That's okay – I hate people who abuse power.*

Just before getting into the car, I spot my young lady with AIDS in front of the hospital. I yell over to her: "Remember, you're the most important person in the world!" She looks over and gives me a wave and a big smile, which immediately sinks when she sees me cuffed. The other cop says to me: "Looks like you've done some good work while you've been here." Brother, do I ever want to tell him – *I'm the same fucking asshole you dropped off here!* But I think better of it. Gee, maybe I really *have* improved. The old me would have told him to go fuck himself. Nah, I haven't improved much – I just tell him under my breath.

We pull into the station. It's been an agonizing forty-five-minute ride for me, sitting on a hard bench with my hands in back of me. This ride has pretty much stolen years of repair from me on top of what the state cop did. I give the smoke thing one last shot, hoping there's some tiny grain of mercy in this dickhead's heart. Nope, no such thing. Just that friggin' smirk again.

Now they finally book me and throw me into a cell. The time passes. The battle of the cold. The battle of my rights with Schweinz. . . .

At this point they bring someone else into the block who's crying and whining. Judging from his voice, he sounds to be not much older than a teenager, if that. When the cops get back upstairs, I overhear them talking about the kid. Apparently, this is his second trip here in as many weeks for the crime of stealing.

The kid's hysteria soon gives way to utter frustration and regret. He starts to bang his head against the concrete wall in earnest. I mean, this guy isn't holding anything back. The loud thuds are sickening-sounding. For normal people, I suppose. They sound as if someone were taking a sledge hammer to a watermelon. It brings back the too-vivid memory of back when I was a teenager and standing at an intersection one night, with some other kids on the way home from a school dance. It was a T-intersection and a car had run the light and t-boned another car that was passing by us. The passenger in the car that ran the light, a teenage girl, came through the windshield and slid beneath the car that was parked in front of us. She came to a sudden stop when her head met the curb. *Thud!* The car she had been in rolled and hit the parked car which then rolled over her head, *pop!* You never want to see so many young people all doubled over puking their guts out. I don't think the girl was feeling any too good herself. That's what I'm hearing now and my mind's eye is seeing. As for the boys upstairs hearing these goings on, all they can do is to laugh hysterically and joke about having to pad the cell someday. I guess they don't get to witness enough tragedy around here or something. Like I said, all the wrong people are in cells.

I hear the door to the block open again. Don't tell me someone is actually going to intercede in this crime.

"Earl, your lawyer's here."

Well, I guess one crime is going to come to a conclusion anyway. John is shocked at the sight of me.

"Why is my client blue?!"

"Ah, uh, ah."

"Earl, why didn't you call me?"

"Because they wouldn't let me."

"Why the hell were you holding my client incommunicado?!"

"Ah, uh . . . ah, uh, ah."

Suddenly the cops are aware of me. "Earl, can we get you something to eat? We can go to McDonalds."

I answer with one of their wise-ass smirks, and: "Coffee."

"Is that all you want?"

232

"Yeah, I've had enough."

John and I get to talk in a small room. Small – it's a good thing someone must have been using the mop and broom, otherwise there wouldn't have been enough room for us all in there. The long and the short of it is that my bail was set at fifty thousand dollars, the same as it is for people who go around sticking knives into other people.

It will only cost Raechel five thousand bucks to get me back. That's a little more than the bag of chips I wanted that Raechel put back on the shelf at the grocery store. She's going to spring for it. She must really love me. Yeah. They say bars make not a prison; but very often a marriage does.

8 ~ Glory, Glory, GLORIA

Every time I find my mind is blank, I know I'm thinking of my mother. Why I have to go over to see her, I'll never understand. Doesn't anyone get it by now? But Raechel says I have to, so I guess I have to. Something about Mother's Day or something. Fucking *Mother's Conspiracy Day* is more like it! A day of socially-sanctioned child entrapment – there ought to be a law against it. Hell, I have no business setting foot in that waiting-for-the-funeral community she lives in in the first place; my mother said so. That's fine by me. Ever since that incident with the police that night. That did it. I suppose everyone in this subsidized retirement complex had their ears attached to their police scanners, leaving every elderly busybody scared to death of me. Everyone with the exception of the only one that counts. The only one who might very well have reason to fear me. But she still imagines I'm the reincarnation of Jesus – and people think *I'm* the nut. I pull into a space in front of her unit; I see everyone peering out from behind the safety of their shades. *Boo!* It's a normal day.

As I approach her unit, I can see that her front door is open, so I know she's expecting me. I knock on the screen door and wait with about as much enthusiasm as I'd muster in meeting the hangman at my execution. I can hear her oxygen compressor running in the back room, so I know she's in. I wait impatiently. I mean, I don't even want to be here, let's not drag this damn thing out any more than we have to. I knock again – nothing. "Mom!" Nothing. After waiting more time than I would bother to give anyone else, I try the screen door, knowing full well it's locked. It always is, even when Raechel, Jared, and I are in there with her. You'd think the two-room apartment was a bank after hours.

The screen door isn't locked. *Shit, this isn't good.* I walk in. "Mom?" Her pet, Tiny, a rat in dog's clothing, peeks up over the top of the couch, shaking and obviously in distress. I come around the couch to find my mother laying on her back with a small square pillow balanced on her face. I take her pulse. She has none. It *was* a normal day.

The TV is on, but there's no programing – just static . . . how appropriate. I turn it off and take up a seat in a chair across from it, staring at the dead screen. Sort of a drab gray-green glass portal. How little it's changed in all these years. I remember, back on Stevens Street, in the old Victorian where we lived when I was between the ages of four and nine. The dormant one-eyed God looked just the same then. My mother on the couch. Me sitting there on the floor, alert with anticipation. Then the magic moment would come and the God would awake. Afternoons spent in front of the TV with my mother were some of the best few hours of my life. There was John Nagy for the artist-in-training of me and the frustrated artist of my mother. Then there was the Liberace show, my mother's heart-throb for the frustrated housewife of my mother. And then there was the holy of holies, the Mickey Mouse Club! I vividly remember the day the mail came and there was a package addressed to me. I ripped the wrapping open as if it contained all the Christmas mornings I had ever known. It was now official. There were my ears and my very own membership card! This couldn't have meant more to me than if I had been a solider being awarded the Medal of Honor. This was the very first time in my life that I ever felt as though I belonged to anything. Of course, as it turned out, that was not a normal day.

All of that occurred back in the golden time when we were living at the Victorian, which I referred to as Grumbly's; to this day I don't know if it was because that was the landlady's name or because the woman did little other than grumble. There was still magic in those childhood years – but also the start of the eruptions and dysfunctions that would make *Life With Mother* an R-rated show.

I was about four then and, when Mommy was in a playful mood, she would delight in playing "Motor Boat" with me. She would lay on her back on her bed – the bed being in a room that was normally off limits to me by order of my step-dad made it all the more special – and she would have me balanced on the pinnacle of her bent knees, extending her arms and hands upward to hold mine. She would rock me back and forth while making a noise like a boat motor. I would gleefully join her in mimicking the sound. My perch on her knees was precarious, and had the thrill of the possibility of falling – but my Mommy wouldn't let me fall, I trusted. It was a real balancing act on her part, yes it was. But much scarier to me than me swaying atop her kneecaps was watching *her* teeter between her apparent roles as sometimes-savior and sometimes-executioner.

At that time, I had two pets: a parakeet named Dicky and a little green turtle named Oscar. Dicky pretty much had free range of my room, which was open to both the bathroom and the kitchen without the benefit of doors. One day, Dicky flew out into the kitchen, with me in close pursuit. I saw him turn left into the room but, upon entering it myself, I found no sign of a bird. Then I saw it – the open window next to the sink. I panicked and ran to the window, breaking out into hysterical crying. Dicky was gone forever! Out there somewhere in that unfamiliar vastness that I myself was so deathly afraid of. What was a poor little bird to do? How would he survive? How was I going to go on living without him? I could not be consoled. I saw my mother go to the window in some vain effort, I thought, to look out – for what? Suddenly she reached down into the sink, where I could not see, and plucked up a greasy, wet little bird who had come very close to drowning in a soaking stew pot. My tears instantly turned to ever-loving joy! The bird had apparently flown into the upper closed portion of the window and had fallen into the sink. The hand of some winged and feathered guardian angel at work, no doubt. Any which way, Dicky was safe, and my mother had acted as the Great Savior.

But, then again, there was that day when, while cleaning my room, my mother let out with a terrible scream, which caused me to believe the floor had fallen through, leaving me suspended in midair waiting to drop. Then I saw her bend down to retrieve some yellow-and-green squishy stuff that just moments ago had been Oscar. *No! That smushed blob can't be him!* I didn't know then that my mother would later save Dicky, whose loss would have been even more terrible to me than Oscar's ending. But even though my mother seemed crushed as I was, and even though Oscar had arranged his own death by running away from home (a shallow plastic

236

container), I couldn't stop my mind and heart from being flooded with the black notion that my mother was somehow a monster.

The seed of this notion had been planted by a not-so-distant memory of a night when I was about three and the two of us were living in my grandfather's future retirement home. I had just been put to bed when I screamed at the sight of a very large beetle on the floor at my bedside. My mother grabbed a tissue and squished it against the floor . . . light blue creamy stuff pushed out of the bug's hard shell. It was like a cream-filled candy, the blueness in it almost glowing – which made me feel that the bug had been happy, all filled with this pretty stuff. Now it looked sad, like something I wanted to not look at. I had cried out, I guess, because I felt terror at the first unexpected sight of the black alien creature creeping so close to my bed – but nothing like the terror I felt at what my mother did. Terror and shock. And guilt. I had meant the poor thing no harm, I just wanted my mother to catch it and take it away. Whether she was acting on her own revulsion for the insect or because she imagined that smashing it in front of me was what I was wishing her, as my mother, to do – this was something about her I never could come to forgive.

The blur of confusion over whether my mother was Savior or Executioner didn't stop with the simple matters of life-or-death. It spilled over into the mundane choices of everyday life – especially after her life-changing decision to marry my step-father, which kept my head spinning, watching her balancing act between being a mother to a son or a wife to a man with a step-son. That wasn't quite as easy as playing Motor Boat. I'm sure the warning lights were flashing from the get-go. Apparently, someone was wearing blinders. The question would eventually have to be asked: Was the blind sight intentional? Was she innocent and unprepared for what she had gotten herself (and me) into, or did she know exactly what she was doing?

My stepfather's sudden arrival on the scene when I was four was world-busting. But the first tremors to rock my faith in goodness and mercy struck on my third birthday. It's odd, but up until that very day, I have almost no memories of my mother. I have to wonder why. In my first years of life, I formed many memories of my grandparents and their Yonkers home. I even have a memory of my father – and he left us when I was two. I have as many memories as I have photos of my mother and me together, but these are not memories of *being* together. Even in the photos, she's never very physically close to me. They all look as if they were a Gloria shoot. In every shot, she's wearing this particular smug smile, the kind that beauty pageant winners wear. It's obvious she really loves being in the spotlight, rendering me almost invisible somewhere in her shadow.

But my third birthday – *Earl's Birthday* – a day with my name on it. Oh boy – the glow of the idea of it lights up the inside of me. My special morning . . . . it's a bright, clear January day with the crisp snap of clean cold air in my nose. I'm out in the back yard, which is actually a side yard to my grandparents' summer weekend home. I'm not wearing a jacket because I don't wish to hide my Sunday best: a white shirt with blue-and-white striped short overalls, and white socks and sandals. I have a clear view of the street from here, and nothing but nothing is going to tear me away from this spot. This spot where my birthday present is going to go. I stand here all day – at least it feels like that to me. At last – there it is! A big bright-red square truck turns onto the street. It looks as though it belongs to a circus. But it must be here for me! This is a dead-end road, there's no other place it can be going! It's here to deliver my birthday present from my grandparents. My very own swing set! I wish my Grandma could be here right now.

It takes the two men almost as much time to assemble the swing apparatus as the time I spent waiting for it to arrive. It takes a fraction of that time, though, to realize that fun on a swing set really isn't fun when you're alone, as hard as you try to pretend that it *is* fun. But I'm spared any length of time to consider this let-down. Mommy calls me in to have my birthday celebration with her. I'm so looking forward to my chocolate birthday cake. Of course it will be chocolate – Mommy knows that's my favorite, and before, when she asked me what kind I wanted, I told her chocolate. Instead, what I see is my *least* favorite: a white cake with white frosting and, at least, some pretty blue trimming. But what about the candles? I had been so excited about turning three, because that would mean I would have *three* candles on my cake, like a big boy, because three is bigger. Three is more than two. But no, there's only *one* candle, shaped like the number 3. Why only one? This grand day isn't turning out to be at all what I was wishing for. Mommy seems happy though. I sit here at the kitchen table pondering the white candle with blue trim and wondering how adults are able to figure out which side of the candle to put the trim on; after all, the number three looks exactly the same, no matter which way you face it.

238

Who knew that turning three meant coming of age? Which means what? Not that bad things had never happened to you before, not that you never got hurt or disappointed before – but you've turned a corner now where you're *aware*, where you see and feel things – and you *ponder* them. And you remember.

This is hard. But the days after my birthday turn out to be even harder. Since I had become a young man, the man of the house must be me – there isn't any other here. And now I find out that I have to lose my precious sandals in trade for my very first pair of manly shoes: Buster Brown lace-ups. I feel as though I've been threatened with having my feet cut off. I never realized just how much I loved my sandals until now that I know I will never see them again. I cry over the loss and add buckets more of tears over the next hour, spent in learning how to tie the new ugly torture devices. I hate them! The stupid laces – my fingers don't know how to make them into a bow but Mommy makes me do it over and over and is not nice to me. She keeps being mean even though I'm crying. I hate her!

As a special bonus and extra penalty for having become a man, it was time to leave home and make my mark on the world: I was enrolled in nursery school. This was my first real sense of abandonment. And how could I have known – the best was yet to come. The institution was run by a witch, a character who I thought only existed in books that my mother had read to me. Was my mother aware of this person's true identity? Did she care? She was always warning me about what happens to bad boys – is that why she sent me here? Had I been bad, or did my mother grow tired of me and now hate me?

The one good thing about this scary place is that I made my first friend here – Doug. But very soon I lost him. When I ask why Doug isn't coming to nursery school any more, I find out what happens to little boys whose mothers hate them – Reform School! Now when my Mommy gets mad about something, she tells me, with a mean face and voice, "I'm going to send you off to Reform School, just like Doug's mommy did!" This makes me very sad and scared. I don't want to be taken away and not be with my Mommy. But how can I make myself not be bad?

Yeah, how could I, when I didn't have a fucking clue as to what I had done to make her angry – or was it just me that made her angry, made her hate me, just for being there. Apparently, being me was bad. I don't know how my three-year-old brain handled living with Mommy Who Loves Me and Mommy Who Wants to Get Rid of Me; but I do know that this was the beginning of the push-pull tug-of-war over how I perceived my mother.

That year passed as the others had, being just shy of a century long. Then I turned four, which I don't remember – probably because I didn't get a chocolate cake. That was the year my mother met my stepfather-to-be. That came out of nowhere, and should have stayed there . . . but we're talking my mother here. *Never pass up a chance to wreck your life* is her mantra; and while she's at it, why not take me along for the ride?

They met at their place of work, a factory. This stranger approached my mother and asked her out on a date. Without much thought, she turned him down, thinking that he had cruel eyes. Afterward, another co-worker asked my mother if she had turned the guy down because he had an artificial leg. My mother hadn't known this and immediately felt sorry for the man (and maybe for having made herself appear callous) and relented. He came over to the house one evening and watched a couple of hours of TV, at the end of which he asked my mother to marry him. I guess he didn't have TV where he was living. I don't know if she said yes that night, but at least the line had been drawn in the quicksand as far as Meeting the Parents was concerned. His parents came first.

His parents lived in a very small house, down on the river and on the other side of the tracks. I recall his father as a shadow of a man, haggard and mute. Looking at the mother, there was little doubt, even in my young and inexperienced mind, as to why. Poor man – his wife has a cane that looks like it's used for anything but walking. I'm careful to stay its length away from her. Her hair is snow white and I bet it hasn't been combed in the last ten years; judging by the smell of her, it's been at least that long since she's bathed.

My future step-dad takes me down to the cellar and entertains me with some sparklers while the interview with my mother is going on upstairs. It isn't my mother who has to pass muster with her prospective in-laws, though. Step-dad's mother tells my mother emphatically that no one should marry her son – not because no woman is good enough for him, but because no woman should have to be afflicted with him. He's cruel and spoiled and has been that way since he was fourteen and lost his leg to an infected injury from a skating accident.

When it's her parents' turn to meet the intended groom, my mother's

240

mother gives her the same advice for the same reason – her alarm at the cruelty she senses in the man.

Of course, I wasn't made privy to any of this at the time, when it was in my mother's interest to pass herself off as innocently and earnestly looking out for my interests by providing a provider and protector in the form of a husband and father. I was only told, years later, when it was in my mother's interest to impress upon me the sacrifice she made by enduring such a cruel husband so that I would not be deprived of a father. Once again – thanks, Mom.

Maybe the concern expressed by the two elder wise-women was not just on your behalf. Possibly the two grandmas had a thought about how a small child would fare under the thumb of Lord Jim – I'm pretty sure mine did. But you weren't listening to anyone. Your thought was for your own security which, you thought, only a man could provide. And you were burdened with a four-year-old, so what other prospects did you have? You had your lines out, you hadn't had any other bites, and this one was on the hook – had leapt at the chance before you even had a chance to take his measurements. Why weren't you willing to bide your time and wait for the possibility of a more suitable catch? Maybe it was because you knew your father was set to retire in less than a year to his retirement house and we'd have to move out – to where? A little fact you kept from your future husband. A little less TV and a little more conversation might have saved a lot of trouble for everyone – huh, Mom? But you didn't see it that way.

My nursery school teacher brought me to the wedding. As my mother and her soon-to-be husband passed me on their way to the altar for the tying of the noose, I realized that I wasn't gaining a father, I was losing a mother. Brother, wasn't I just as smart as new paint.

On our two-day whirlwind honeymoon to see my uncle at the upstate asylum and my great-aunt at the women's shelter down on the Bowery, my new step-father wasted no time launching what would be my ongoing education about failed lives and how I was destined to be among them. My mother just perched there in her glory and never murmured a word in my defense. If I had any imagining of a soft-feathered wing of maternal protectiveness, I was all too painfully aware of its absence.

Maybe my mother was in for an education as well, but she had taken the primer course taught by her Victorian tyrant of a father. She was far from stupid and knew all the tricks; she'd get along just fine. It might take

241

a little conniving and juggling, and what if she dropped a ball now and then as long as it was me – starting with dropping me outside the church door. This place of worship had always been *our* church, the one I attended every Sunday with my mother. Now I was left on the steps of *Earl's* church like an orphan, while she and my step-dad drove off to the Catholic services at his. To add to my misery, Step-Dad dictated that I must sport a fedora to complete my Sunday attire. Why? No other child could be seen wearing one; was I being molded in his image, expected to follow his example? Ha. My step-father had never worn a hat of any description in his life. He just had a knack for devising new ways to make me feel like an idiot and a misfit.

Sunday was what I had to look forward to after surviving the Saturday morning visit to the dentist and the weekly enema on Saturday night. Every day of the week, the enema bag hung in plain sight of my bed, on the door of the little shed that housed our toilet in the bathroom; Mommy made sure I got to ponder the event all week long. On the weekdays, going to school provided no respite or escape – just another opportunity to feel like a misfit and an idiot. Constant knots in my stomach and bouts of diarrhea kept me out of class, sometimes out of school – and that kept me from earning passing grades.

Any kind of quality time spent with my mother was getting more and more scarce. I could see her slipping over to the Other Side; not that there should have been one. But, at the same time, seeing her sporadic attempts at making an effort to be a mother to me just became more and more confusing. Her kindness could turn without notice and become a threat. Reform school was ever present in her vocabulary, with the vivid example of Doug hanging over my head. My mother harped on the idea that Doug had been a bad boy. What I understood was that Doug had gotten in his mother's way.

I knew in my never-settled gut that something was terribly wrong with my life. But it was the only life I had experienced – so how could I know in my head what was normal? I knew the feeling of love and happiness and belonging, as long as my Grandma was alive. The year she died, we lost our home and Mommy married that man. Step-Dad. When he wasn't around, she could be and act like my mother, willing to share her time with me, whether in drawing and painting or a game of checkers. When Step-Dad was on the scene, she went missing. She might be in the same room, but not as my mother.

242

Wake up, Earl! She's in the same room with you right now. Or maybe I'm in the room with her. It's her apartment, isn't it? Am I in it as her son? – whatever the hell that means. I'm staring at her desk next to the TV. I wonder if she ever found the twenty-dollar bill I hid in her papers. She was always finding money that God sent her way by one means or another; all she had to do was ask and Poor Gloria's prayers would be answered. She had a really great God; he always provided for her, like her Personal Banker. If God didn't provide what she needed directly, He could always drop me a hint. And time after time, I guess I fell for it.

One of those times, she was whining that she didn't have enough money to get a new roof put on the house. She pointed out that the responsibility fell on me if I were interested in protecting my investment – the one I'd been making since she'd asked me to come up with the monthly mortgage payments for her, in exchange for having my name added to the deed. This was on a property that had been mortgage-free twice in its seven-year history. She just loved milking the property for all it was worth whenever the need for money arose. God knows what she spent it on. I can't ever recall her having any medical bills or any kind of serious need at all, for that matter. Her ticky-tacky décor, however abundant, couldn't have used up those two self-created windfalls. It beats me how she blew it all.

Well, I didn't have money to pay a roofer either, so I guessed it was falling on me to put the roof on myself. I boarded Jocko, rented a car, and brought my lover of the time with me up from the city. To avoid spending time around my mother, I made arrangements with a neighbor, a dear old sweet thing in her nineties, for a place to lay our heads at night – which turned out to be a feather-bed that must have dated back to the old lady's grandmother. When you got into bed, you sunk down three feet into it – not so great for my day-laboring back, but less painful than the havoc my nerves would wreak on me if I were cooped up in my mother's house with Herself. I couldn't stand the company of that woman, and I took my aversion as far as bathing in a river at day's end and eating every meal out.

Several days into the job, my mother inquired of me as to how I was enjoying my ration of liquid cheer, a half-pint of vodka that she was daily leaving on the old lady's porch for me. *What vodka?* I asked the old lady if she knew anything about these missing bottles. "Oh! I'm so embarrassed" she admitted. "I drank them. I'm so sorry, I thought God had left them there for me." *Who is this God?* Must be a neighborhood deity or something. Such a generous and thoughtful Celestial Being, I don't understand why he couldn't provide my mother with the ten dollars I needed to buy a tool for my partner, who was also working for nothing. When I asked my mother to spring for the tool out of her own pocket, I thought she was going to break down and cry.

Then the last day came, thank God, and there was nothing to do but pack up and go. As I backed my rented car out onto the street, my mother came running out of the house like it was on fire. The smile across her face was so broad, it bordered on laughter. She jumped into her car and sped off without so much as a wave good-bye. What the hell was that all about?

Before heading back to the city, we stopped at an antique store. I found something I wanted to buy, but had no money. My girlfriend had her own car, so it was little trouble to return the next day to purchase the antique piece. I don't know what possessed me, but I decided, as long as we were here, to drop in on my mother. That little voice in my head again. Well, that pocket-sized voice broke out into some heavyweight swearing. There it was, in the driveway – a brand new shiny car. Poor Gloria's fifth, to my memory. Shit! She's the richest poor person I've ever known. I kept my goddamn mouth shut, but that's not to say I didn't have a strong desire to kill her. Maybe I could hit her upside the head with that ten-dollar tool.

If the jury wouldn't find me innocent on that one, then maybe they would side with me on the next round of shit. It wasn't long after the Miracle of the New Car in the Driveway episode that she wrote me a letter telling me how she had no choice but to take matters into her own hands. I guess there are some things that even God won't dirty His hands with. Enclosed was a sample of my forged signature and a note that read: "Pretty good, ha." The letter went on to explain that she had taken all her assets – the ones, I suppose, she cried to me last month that she didn't have – and put them under my name so that she could defraud the state and go on welfare. So this time God, with clean hands, doesn't have to worry about going to jail; just me.

That wasn't the first time that Gloria saw me as the instrument of her financial security. She nosed out the scent of potential funds the minute she discovered that I might be eligible for Veterans' Compensation. I was not long out of the service and really lost, floating between drinks and jobs. . . .

My mother informs me that she's made an appointment with the VA on my behalf. *You can leave my goddamn behalf alone, thank you. I don't give a shit!* Needless to say, I don't go. She makes a second appointment. I still don't give a shit. I don't go. She goes right ahead and makes a third, the last according to the VA. I let her know that I still don't give a shit. Well, she does. She can smell money, like a shark can smell blood. Yeah, here we go again with Poor Gloria, she has a drunk for a son who can't keep a job. Yeah, that somehow entitles her to money. Her mind is set. She'll find new stones to turn over, if she has to, to get me there.

The morning of the appointment comes and I'm sleeping in, my mind being set on not giving a shit. There's a loud banging at my front door that stirs me – to anger, mostly. I answer the door naked and pissed off, thinking it's my mother. It isn't. It's a pair of very large, muscular Italian men with broken noses and a shared shocked expression on their faces. They're there to see to it that I make my appointment. *Yippee, I'll play your silly little game.*

I go to the VA. After a short interview, I walk out of the hospital as a Disabled Vet. *Yeah, I already knew that. So what?* So now they throw money at me like that's some kind of cure. It proves not to be.

My mother has an ever-loving shit fit: "What do you mean, *you're* getting the money?! That money was for *me*!" Poor Gloria, no money in it for you after all? How can I help? I can always shoot you, if you like. I don't know if anyone will give you money for your pain and disfigurement, but I'll be glad to do it.

The closest I've come to that kind of enjoyment was the dream I had, about eight years ago, in which I got to kill the bitch and then chop her up into little pieces and throw them into the marsh for the crows to feed on. God! I remember how relieved and happy I felt as I woke up – best friggin' dream I ever had! I was able to do, in virtual reality, that which I couldn't in life. There's some kind of goddamn unwritten law in American culture that you can't hate your mother. It's like, by virtue of being a bio-birth unit, any bitch gets to walk away with some kind of gold Certificate of Holiness or some bullshit like that. Hell, why not? We have a whole industry built around mothers. Between candy, flowers, and cards, the powers-that-be would have every other Tuesday Mother's Day. Maybe that balances out in somebody's world – but, in mine, the best I could say is that *one day* of homage is equal to the total number of hours, over the course of the year, that my bio-birth unit has actually attempted to be something like a mother.

245

That leaves all the other misspent hours rolled up into the other three hundred sixty-four days that entitle me to despise the flaws, failings, and pain that she funneled through me and then arranged to be my personal property. Hell, she had no more business posing as a mother than as a realty agent.

I have to wonder who she was posing for that day when I was a toddler and she let me out of her sight or, at least, far enough out of her reach that I ended up falling down the two flights of stairs along the outside of my grandparents' house. I got to survive – and to bear with life-long pain. Which, throughout the eternity of my adolescence, was in the form of severe leg cramps. All those years, it wasn't as if it wasn't obvious that, when I walked, my left foot would dramatically swing out. Yet this wasn't brought to the observation of a doctor until I was thirteen. Step-Dad wasn't a big believer in doctors. His approach to correcting my odd gait – which was probably an embarrassment and an irritant to his sensibilities – had always been to yell at me to keep my foot straight. Where was my mother? If I was looking for her to be my voice, to tell him that I couldn't help it, I'd still be waiting to hear it. Or any acknowledgment from her of what I might actually be feeling.

I guess this doctor they finally took me to wasn't being paid enough, so he didn't know what the problem was; he sent me to a foot doctor, who also wasn't being paid enough. Both these doctors had their offices in the poorest section of town. Maybe I'm being cynical or maybe that's as far as their skills would take them. They could see – anyone could see – that I had a leg that was all out of whack, but they couldn't figure out why.

Nothing changed until thirteen years later, when I was out in the world on my own, and sciatic pain started to kick in. In other words, things got worse. But I hung in there – what could I do? I hobbled on, the years kept passing, and the pain kept getting worser. A year into fatherhood, my pain had become a full-time resident, along with my family, 24/7, no let-up. But the search for a town where better doctors had set up was in my hands now, and I found a few who were able to put two and two together: *It's your mother's fault!* The probability of getting this diagnosis might account for her apathy in seeking one – one that might suggest that the probability that a life's-worth of pain could have been stopped at the gate if my mother had given half a shit. I guess the excuse that she simpered at me all my adult life was her get-out-of-jail-free card: "Your grandmother said that, as long as you were crying, you were all right." My mother was a big believer

246

in what mothers said. Except when mothers' words went against the grain of what she wanted.

But I'm not going to demonize her. After all, she wasn't the problem. My stepfather Jim was. My mother told me so, every second Wednesday since she left him. The problem was that *I* wasn't big on believing mothers. Who the fuck chose Jim in the first place? *Oh, shit – that would be me.* That story was told to me every third Thursday: "I married him so that *you* would have a father. I did it all for *you*. It was a great sacrifice for *me*, to be sure that *you* had a secure home."

Then there was Sunday's tale: When my mother walked out on Jim, she threw me to her brother and his family, then to my god-parents, the whole time having to work a second job to be able to support me at the cost of the dollar a day she paid to my keepers. She worked in a bank by day and as a hostess and book-keeper at a restaurant in the evening. According to her story, all the waitresses at the restaurant *prostituted themselves* after hours in order to have enough money, as single mothers, to keep their sons with them. I guess they hadn't heard about the dollar special.

I heard this story over and over throughout dear Gloria's life. I would have had no reason to know or even suspect that other mothers were doing such a thing, but my mother went out of her way to inform me, because of the point she wanted to make: "I was far too virtuous to lower myself to do anything like that – so that *you* could be proud of me." Yes, again it was all about me.

It never occurred to her that the words I was hearing the loudest were: *to keep their sons with them* – the words that were thrown in offhandedly in her virtue-focused narration. No clue that I could be feeling such a thing as hurt – the furthest thought from her mind. If I should be so reckless as to try to communicate such a feeling to her – for example, if I said "It hurts me to know that" – she would hear it as my sympathy for her ever having had to even pass the word 'prostitution' through her head in connection with herself; and maybe as a bit of righteous pity for the boys with wanton moms. If I were so bold as to say "It hurts me that you wouldn't try to do anything you possibly could to keep me with you (like the mothers who actually loved their sons)," she would explain to me that I *couldn't* be hurt because how could I think that she was hurting me when her actions were prompted entirely by her determination to spare me from hurt.

By about the twentieth time I was reminded of her virtuous devotion to my moral and emotional well-being, I was flushing not from pain but from

247

fury. Which she interpreted as an indication of my questionable mental health, and could only wonder what had made me such an angry person. Oh, right – it was Jim. Living in hell all those years with that devil is what left me filled with such rage. She understood, because it was worse than hell for her, since she was suffering doubly, on behalf of both of us.

When I heard the opening words of the I Would Never Lower Myself to Prostitution story for the fiftieth time, I was ready to kill her just to get her to *shut the fuck up*. Now it looks like I'm not going to get that chance. Except in my recurrent dreams.

Wrapping herself in her snow-white virginal cloak, like a little girl playing dress-up in front of a mirror, my mother could not see that she wasn't an adult woman who had grown into a station of virtue, but rather she was stuck in the fantasy of a juvenile mind that had never matured. Apart from her self-centeredness and penchant for make-believe, her childish qualities included the temperament of a spoiled brat. I witness it even now, when she's seventy-three going on ten. But I remember instances going way back into my childhood. Like that time, when I was actually about ten . . . . my mother is in my room, in the midst of punishing me for God knows what. Her impulse to vent her anger and frustrations on me is at its peak, but she seems unsatisfied with the effect of her rantings and flailings. I haven't started bawling my eyes out, I guess, or melted onto the floor in abject defeat. I'm still holding my breath, hoping to get off with no more than what's come at me already. At the last moment, as she's exiting my room, she spots a treasured model airplane. In answer to her as-yet-unresolved chagrin, she picks it up, with an exultant smirk on her face, and slams it down on the floor, smashing it beyond repair. I'm crushed beyond belief -- that model was my pride and joy. My accomplishment. Something that I loved. *What is wrong with her? What gives her the right to do such a thing? How can she take so much pleasure in hurting me like this?* I don't know how she ever came to be in control of my life. All I know is that, every year, she makes my life more and more miserable. It's like the older I get, the more she hates me. Sometimes I think she'd rather see me dead. That would probably be better than the way she's making me live. This can't be my life! I don't feel like it's mine – I don't want it! I really hate her. She always seems most satisfied whenever revenge can come into play. I think she feels it as her only true power.

248

As time went on, though, I began to feel that my mother had been taking power lessons from my step-father. Or maybe a mind-meld had taken place between them which imbued her with a new brutality and deeper disdain for me. I could see in her eyes the ghost of Christmas past – the Christmas morning, years before, when Jim got a load of my joy as I unwrapped a gift that delighted me – Heaven forbid – and he smacked me; and then, as though that smack and my tears had put all right with the world, he declared, "I was never that happy at Christmas – I'll be damned if he'll be." There was something brewing in my mother that I couldn't have defined then – a perverse sense of righteousness mixing dangerously with her frustration and spite, and taking shape as resentment of me for existing. My existence had been an impediment to her quest for security for as long as I could remember. And now, I knew, I was a pebble in the family shoe. Sleepless nights, I would lie in bed listening to the screaming and arguing over me, and wondering which of them would be the first to break into my room and kill me, ridding themselves of the encumbrance of me. . . . Now my mother seemed almost to look for a reason to put me in the bathtub, so I couldn't get away, and whip the shit out of me. Fear was the breath I drew. She found her chances, and the regularity of the act increased. The broadening smile on her face as she lashed out was, to me, an expression of demonic gratification that wiped out any memory or hope of having a protector in my mother. I had nothing to protect me at all. What about Jesus? I found no comfort in that thought. I knew I wasn't nearly half as good as Jesus – and they crucified *him*.

Pretty much the only device I had to beat a sword into a plowshare was my art. Maybe my mother garnered some sense of vicarious satisfaction through my artistic creations, or perhaps – truer to form – she was happy with the attention that came to her as the proud mother of such a gifted child. She could feel that she was adored, like her sister-in-merit, the Virgin Mary. I did my first oil painting at the age of six; when I was nine, my mother bought me my first set of paints, and by the age of eleven I was selling my work – at first to relatives and neighbors. Then, when I was thirteen, my mother was hanging my paintings in the bank where she worked. Every piece that hung sold. I even took commissions. But above and beyond her pleasure at having money put into her hands, I'm sure my mother relished the many hours of public attention and admiration that

249

came her way.

There was yet one more harvest Gloria reaped from what I created. My work acted as catalyst for my mother striking up relationships with two famed artists – one of whom purchased one of my works and the other, Ed Georgi, expressed to her his perception that I was a genius. ("Imagine that! *Me*, the mother of a *genius*. *I* gave birth to him, you know – he gets his talent from *me*.")

Some little bird must have whispered in Mr. Georgi's ear that I was between homes, my uncle having declared that I was no longer welcome in his. Mr. Georgi decided to unofficially adopt me and have me live and train under him in his gracious home in Silvermine. As I think of the two of them arranging for this, I imagine my mother disingenuously observing that Mr. Georgi might need a live-in housekeeper or something like that. Leave it to my mother to hook her claws into anything, or anyone's life, if she smelled a free lunch. Or, in this case, a mile-long gravy train. It doesn't matter now. Nothing came of it anyway, through no fault of anyone or anything, except the premature death of the generous man. At least I had the pleasure of meeting my future benefactor the day before he died.

Oh, shit! I forgot. *She died.* She's dead. What a day. I'd better make sure, though – I don't want this to turn out to be just a great dream or something.

I walk over to her and check her pulse once again. Nope, nothing, she's gone. I look down on the pillow that's on her face. Nah, I don't ever want to see that face again. Yeah, leave well enough alone. And thank God. I thought this day would never come.

I pat the poor, still-quivering dog on the head while picking up the phone to call the unsuspecting police. I hope no one jumps out of their skin when I give my name, recollecting the last time they heard from me.

Yeah, it's me and I'm at her apartment and she's dead.

"How do you know that, sir?"

"Because she's no longer living."

"How do you know that, sir?"

"Because she's dead."

"How do you know that, sir?"

"Because she hasn't been breathing for quite a while."

"Are you saying she's dead, sir? Are you a doctor?"

"Look, Bozo, I've been here for well over a half hour now and she hasn't mentioned Jesus once, or professed her lack of guilt about anything, which means she's dead! So why don't you send someone over."

"Where are you, sir?"

Oh, brother! I can see this is going to be another fifteen minutes of questions and answers. Now they want me to stand out in front of the building so they can more easily find me. Right – out of five buildings, like this is a freaking city. They probably want me in clear sight to make sure I'm not armed. After all, I probably killed the bitch. *Ah, I do wish I could take credit.*

I go out on the stoop and take up a lawn chair. The daylight seems to be lacking something. Yeah, that's what it is – the daylight itself is shrouded. Not a sound, either. Like a dead theater with no play, no audience. No one about, not even the sound of a bird. It's like I'm sitting in dead space. I'm just a product of my own imagination, imagining that I'm sitting here imagining that the body of my dead mother is lying in there imagining herself to be dead. It's almost become boring. I mean, how many abnormal days in my life have come to feel normal. It seems as though there should be something wrong with that.

Wrong! What wrong? What the fuck did I ever do? *I don't know – who's asking the question? You or your mother?* I am! Now I know how my poor stuffed toy chimp felt when I almost daily beat the ever-loving shit out of him from the youngest age – like, right after my stepfather came on the scene. I had no idea at the time what was causing my behavior, somehow it just seemed normal. I'm sure that little stuffed chimp sure as hell didn't understand why *he* deserved such treatment. Shit, if he wasn't on that big rag-pile in the sky right now, I would profusely apologize to him. That's more of a reconciliation than I ever got a whiff of from either my stepfather or – especially – my mother. According to Herself, she never did a wrong thing in her life. Therefore, she caused no harm. That was the blanket story that covered me, along with everyone and everything else. She could never come to understand the delusions I was suffering under – such crazy, muddled notions of my suffering and distress under her hands – or where they could possibly have come from. She could only conclude: insanity.

To my mother's thinking, my diagnosis of insanity meant: Great, another cross for Poor Gloria to bear. What a shame, her only son, how painful for her. But the idea of me seeking the road to wellness – well, that's another story. God forbid! That would ruin everything. Even worse, the idea of me going to a therapist – that would be like burning her at the stake. Lo! Witness Poor Gloria of Arc! She tried to explain: "It's a

251

therapist's job to make you believe that there was something wrong with your mother. You can't believe anything they tell you!" Over the years, she never gave up exhorting me to discontinue seeing one. They were all mother-haters.

Yeah, for more years than could have been healthy, I lived in that house of denial. The residence of choice for both my parents. That's one thing they didn't argue about. Of course, they were in denial that they were in denial – my mother in her head, my stepfather in his house/man's castle. The layers and layers of their self-defenses made for some very thick fortress walls. Those walls started cracking the day a truant officer showed up at the door, wondering where I had been all this time. Where I had been was in a state of chronic diarrhea and abdominal cramps. That visit was the beginning of something that no one ever saw coming. The next thing that anyone knew, the principal of my junior high school called my parents in. This was my second year there, repeating the 7th grade. I was present for the meeting and got to see, to my amazement, what looked like my parents being called on the carpet. Nothing short of reading them the riot act, the principal put them on no uncertain notice, as if he were chastising a couple of his students, that he was taking a personal interest in me that wasn't going to conclude with the ending of this meeting. There were just too many disparities between my high IQ and my continuing academic failings.

This was the first time I ever saw my parents looking sheepish – especially my stepfather, who had no blood in his face; it was all in my mother's. She was dying of embarrassment and he of terror. I was feeling very smug and shouting in my head: *How the fuck do* you *feel, feeling like me for a change?*

This was also the first time an adult had ever taken an interest in my interests. It was a far cry from the "little boys should be seen, not heard" philosophy, which is all I ever had shoved down my throat all my life. As I left the office, I felt as though I was living in a new skin. I was important to someone; that was new. I had a funny feeling, though, something that felt really strange and foreign. I think it was hope.

Imagine that. Hope. Hope of what . . . ? There were still so many unanswered questions then, and so much time stretching out ahead of me . . . time to figure out what the questions were and which ones I might go out into the world in quest of answers to. Open-ended hope. At that moment, though, it was just the hope that something in my life would be different. Possibly, even – reassuring.

And suddenly, that miracle began unfolding. Someone was actually asking: *I wonder what's wrong with Earl's leg? I wonder what's wrong with Earl's stomach?* While I was feeling heartened, I think my stepfather was feeling absolutely terrified by the prospect of anyone sticking their nose into his business and asking The Why Question. There was an unwritten law in our house, enforced under penalty of death, a daily indoctrination that nothing that went on in that house was ever to be revealed outside the locked doors of Jim's very private castle. I had to wonder what was going on in *his* stomach. And his steely mind.

On the next page of this new chapter in my life, I was placed in the hospital for a week's observation to find out what was up with my chronic diarrhea – a condition nine years in the making. Maybe I could hope to get some relief at last. But I would have to spend my thirteenth birthday in the hospital – not that it would have been better at home. As one of my birthday gifts, my mother brought me one of those fortune-telling 8-balls that answers questions with stock responses printed on a floating cube inside it. My stepfather was playing with it during their visit to my room. Suddenly, he let out with a deep belly laugh, a sound I had never heard come out of him before. I was so startled, I forgot myself for a moment – my despondency at being confined to a hospital bed, even the stockpile of vengeful thoughts I normally harbored against the man – and, in that unguarded moment, I felt my heart leap with joy to hear his joy and, for a moment, this connected us. Something was evidently tickling him – and my mother, also boggled by this unaccustomed outburst, asked Jim what he had just asked the 8-ball. Still rollicking, he crowed: "I asked it if Earl was crazy (haw-haw-haw) – and it answered YES!"

My heart, my body, my soul, all of me instantly sank eight feet into the depths of my hospital bed. I was engulfed, crushed, with a knife deep in my heart, a knife that couldn't have been bigger or sharper. My mother's response was a short glance of disapproval aimed in my stepfather's direction. Not much of a motherly defense of her son, but even that much cheek on her part was unheard of. She dared it because my mother had a secret that gave her new courage; she could see the light at the end of the tunnel. Unknown to anyone, she already had one foot out the door.

253

She was the master of deceit, the queen of sneak, the mistress of fabricated truth. "If you didn't see me, I wasn't there. If you didn't see me do it, then I didn't do it. If I say this is the way it happened, then that's the way it happened." And that's the way it was, even through my entire adult life. My mother forever chasing me, often clutching my arm with her fingernails to be sure it hurt, while trying to reinvent history to her bent. That's the way it was, and is, according to Gloria. Pain included. No extra charge.

Jesus. She's got me clenching my fists again. Wait – Jesus is *her* Daddy/Hubby, not mine. And she's dead. Maybe out of respect for Him, I shouldn't be sitting here thinking ill of the dead. Especially one of His pets. What can I say to her credit? Let's see – to back up her version of history, there were, I'll concede, a few facts that she could summon in support of her self-description. Starting with her claim that she's my mother – which I'm sorely moved to dispute – she is, in fact, in possession of my birth certificate. I'll have to trust the State of New York as to its accuracy. So that's one.

Other facts that may be in her bag of tricks might come to me if I sit here long enough. But meantime, I'll give her credit where credit is due. Once, although late in the game, she did beg my stepfather to play catch with me for at least ten minutes. Not that by his own nature he was willing, but I have to hand it to him, in this case: he gave it a try, which lasted all of four throws. My dad's efforts came to a sudden close when, while trying to catch a wild throw, he caught a seven-inch shaft of wood up his forearm, when his arm collided with a four-by-four support to the porch's roof. I'm sure he was sorry for having put in the effort with me and the ball, but maybe not so much for the pain it caused him, which he seemed, as a habit, to relish. He never got Novocaine at the dentist's, and he flatly refused any anesthesia when he had to have a scope put up his urethra.

Ah – I've thought of another instance of a bona fide fact that my mother defends – or uses in her own defense – in her historical narrative. She absolutely did lavish me with things I wanted. But – caveat, Mom! – she never examined her motivations, such as buying me things as a way of resolving her guilt for those other things she should have been responsible for providing. Like a safe environment, an education, an understanding of adult responsibilities – little things like that, which don't cost a goddamn thing.

On the other side of the parental coin, there was my step-dad who – on a good day – actually showed some genuine parental qualities. There was the time that he taught me how to clean a fish and, more importantly, how to clean up after myself. Whereas my mother never taught me anything at all about being responsible. Where the hell in her would that have come from anyway? I think, in the course of those few times that he interacted with me, Jim was earnestly trying to be fatherly. But I don't think he had any clue about how. The significant difference between the two was that he was, at least, willing to reach outside his comfort zone. I could see that, and – as rare as those visible efforts were – it meant the world to me. Yes, Mom, as incredible as that may seem to you, it did. Let's bring Jesus back into the discussion here. It was something he said when he observed the rich putting their gifts into the offering box, and he saw a poor widow put in two small copper coins. Jesus pointed out that the rich gave a bit, out of the abundance they possessed, but the widow gave all that she had. Well, Mommy, you're the daughter of a minister. Do you remember that story?

The simple truth is, whatever my mother had to say about herself, she never did anything that didn't benefit Gloria. Period. When she didn't get her way, there was shit to be paid. And, yes, Step-Dad doled out the shit, too. But the vulgar profanities that came out of Holy Mother's virginal mouth, as well as the physical and verbal threats and punishments she spewed, all were followed by an air of smug satisfaction. Whereas, in my Step-Dad's case, his harsh outbursts, his cruelty, were followed, at least, by some evidence of remorse. And as for my mother's acts of kindly treatment or even gift- giving, those served an ulterior purpose: the resolution of guilt or a means to keep me out of sight so as to keep the pond that her boat was on mirror-smooth. Like, oh, the two years of Saturday art classes she thoughtfully enrolled me in at the Silvermine College of Art. The cost of those Saturdays was covered by no longer sending me to day camp. During the rest of the week, I guess, I was no longer of an age where anyone had to care for me.

There must have been something lacking in my mother's education at home concerning self-reliance. She therefore had nothing in her bag of tricks to teach me – or, if she did, there were none she was willing to share with me. Any such useful things she may have figured out would have been her exclusive property for her exclusive use. I'm pretty sure that, very early on in life, she learned the ability to hide in plain sight while, like any

255

puppet master, manipulating the strings of anyone within the scope of her little marionette theater. All she had to be was a cute little girl. I entered the scene as little more than a paper doll that served some purpose in gratifying her wish for a plaything, up to a point; and, beyond that, seemed just as expendable. I, unfortunately, made the mistake of imagining that this little girl, as my mother, would be there to prop me up. To support me.

But support was a one-way streetcar for my mother. She would pick up any passenger who seemed willing to pay the fare – the currency being ample attention or material comfort.

When I was thirteen, I was failing in school. My mother seemed unfazed by this, which suggested that either she didn't much care or she thought I was stupid. Yeah, I guess she thought I was too stupid to figure out, or even notice, what she was up to. She was good at seeing only what she wanted to see – and imagining that seeing only what she wanted them to see could be put over on other people as well. For sure, I saw more than I wanted to.

That year, my mother was working some evenings in a restaurant as a bookkeeper. One night, I had occasion to be in the back seat of the car when her boss, a married man, was driving her home from work. It was in his new Cadillac and, brother, was she eating it up. Oh, she could get used to this, her smug little smile revealed as she cozied up in the corner of her seat while showing a little leg. And her boss's smirk was speaking to his own yeah-I'm-okay-with-this-ness as well. I felt sick to my stomach, and furious inside, seeing clearly that the two of them either expected me to play the part of a dummy or assumed that I actually was one. I was also not clueless about a relationship she had going on with an officer of the bank where she worked. He, too, was married. Which didn't appear to be an obstacle to my mother's possible availability.

She certainly wouldn't let a little thing like a marriage certificate – not hers or anyone else's – get in the way of her security. A birth certificate, however, presented a problem. From day one of her marriage to Jim, she saw me as an impediment to securing the world she was seeking. I was a mere by-product left over from her first investment gone bankrupt. Now I was threatening the second bond. One can only tolerate so many crashes. When I became more of a deficit than an asset, it was time to cash out. As soon as I turned eight and was eligible for enrollment, she started pressing me with the idea of how much happier I would be in military school. A big roadblock to this scheme of hers was the fact that Jim was very frugal and his hard-earned money was going to further his own education to enable him to advance in the workplace and raise his standard of living. Like having a house, and a car that wasn't yet another junk Studebaker.

That was the pathetic reality of it. My mother wanted me out of the way, convinced that my absence would afford her a more secure life with Jim, but he wasn't willing to pay the price tag for the pleasure of it. I mean, this was a man who bought his clothes at Robert Hall's, where the store itself was so cheap as to not even put carpeting on their cement floor. If he could have bought used oil for his car, he would have. My stepfather was a no-frills kind of guy. He wasn't going to spend a dime more on anything than he had to. I'm sure he was counting the money he had saved on anesthesia.

I can see now how all this explains my mother's increasing brutality over the years. She was acting out, as any spoiled child would who wasn't getting her way. And it was little Earl who was the worm in the apple of the world as the world should be according to Gloria – the world of Gloria, fashioned by Gloria, for Gloria. I was the thorn in the side of her dreams; if only she could tweeze me out, she could rub the wound with vanishing cream, and no one would be the wiser. The fact that I existed as this massive, unbudgeable boulder on her path to glory is something that should have been addressed *before* the fact, in sex education class. But since such classes were nonexistent in my mother's day, the task would have been left in my grandmother's hands. I'm sure Grandma gave my mother the same advice her own mother gave her: "Now that you're getting married, you're going to have to allow your husband some depravities. Just lie back and think of God in Heaven surrounded by angels." Grandma was proof that the ordeal could be survived as many as five times. Somehow my mother managed, miraculously, to get by with never. Maybe *God*, instead, was the one lying back, thinking of *her*.

As for the angels – my mother's alter-egos, a whole chorus of them. But the most special one was the winged and haloed figurine suspended over the bed of the Christ Child in the Nativity scene my parents set up every Christmas, a hallowed family tradition, in which my mother always performed the crowning glory of hanging the angel over the manger herself. I can still see her cherubic smile as she gazed upon the banner unfurled across the span of the angel's outstretched arms: it was inscribed with a triumphant word – not *GLORY*, but *GLORIA* – written in her distinct hand. What an angel she was.

257

Maybe she was caught up in seeing herself as an adoring angel all those times, in the past decade, when I would catch her staring at me with a ridiculous smile on her face. This performance of hers did nothing for me but make me squirm. I'd give her a sidelong look through narrowed eyes, as if to ask: *What the hell is up with that?* And she'd respond, in a demure rapture, how much I looked like Jesus. That would be, of course, the Western European Jesus, who – though I was already years older than he had lived to be – I may have resembled because I had fair hair and a beard. And a chronically anguished look, which I'm pretty damn sure she never noticed.

Of course, her observation might have been not so much about me. If I was the image of the Son of God – or the Second Coming of Christ – what did that make *her*? What did she say to me one year . . . ? "If you want to get me a Christmas present, you can get me a very simple cross on a chain, something that can hang on a sweet virgin breast." Right – even her breasts are virginal. Probably another reason I'm so fucked up. I can only imagine how gently she shoved the bottle into my infant mouth. She has all the maternal instincts of a guppy. A cold, cannibalistic little fish. God, that brings up another image I don't want to see again – the time she was leaving my house . . . . she's on the front walk, and her dog is still inside, on the other side of the doggie-gate that she has just hurdled. She has a bundle of something in one hand, and the end of the leash in the other. She's focused on the problem of what to do next, and she's not aware that I can see her. She looks down at the hapless little Chihuahua with a petulant tilt to her head, and then she yanks on the leash and hoists the dog up by his collar like a fish on the line – or a condemned innocent at the end of a noose. Now she glances up and realizes she's been caught in the act – but only for a second, because now reality changes. The simpering smile, set at full power, shows her to be a little girl – maybe a slightly naughty little girl – but so adorable and sweet, really, that all is instantly forgiven – and forgotten. 'Nuff said.

Maybe she kept her mouth shut at the end of that little performance – but how many times has she twisted my ear with her protestations of her virginity. What? I guess that makes me the product of an immaculate conception. In that case, why am I not worshiped and revered as divine? Ha. What about just being recognized and cherished *for who I am?* That's the way I've always felt toward my child – and I know for damn sure how he got into his mother's womb.

258

How is it that my mother doesn't recognize me – has never seen me for who I am? She never gives up trying to herd me into the parameters of who she says I am, and giving me my life history as recorded in her diary. Reconstructing my past is one way to polish her halo and give proof of my waywardness and ingratitude. And, of course, instruct me in what my memories actually are. So every time I hold my Furies in check and agree to sit down at her table, she's serving up roast beef and chocolate cake, because those were my childhood favorites. Hell, I was lucky to see a roast once a year as a kid. And chocolate cake? Yeah, I remember hoping for it quite often in those days. Whose childhood is she trying to resurrect, anyway? She sure as shit hasn't come to terms with what *mine* was. Or what it wasn't. Jesus.

Oh – sorry. But speaking of You again: You – contrary to your will, I imagine – are another item on the menu of what she keeps trying to shove down my throat, on the pretext that You've been in the freezer, just waiting for me to find You again, after I left you on the table at the last house I lived in with her. Don't take this personally, but if she's on her way right now to the Heaven she's always trying to sell me on – believe me, that's the last place I want to end up. I'll take my chances with Your Dad's ex-right-hand-angel any day before I'd look to meet up with that woman again, no matter what feathery disguise she might be in. I've had more than enough of her phony evangelizing.

Jesus, thanks for listening but – sorry, again – I have to go now. Here come the cops. Great – it's Schweinz, my favorite, leading the pack.

I go into the apartment with them and answer a few routine questions, like why I believe my mother is dead (in case they didn't get the word from the dispatcher). More important, I point out a few facts, like the pillow on her face (in case they overlook it). But even more important than that: the fact that I found the door open and unlocked. I go to great lengths and detail about my mother's history of rape-phobia and how the only way that that door could be found unlocked would have to be because my mother was dead when the last living person left that apartment. They aren't buying it. I could have admitted to killing her myself and they wouldn't have believed me. They're sticking to their guns that it was a *natural death*.

Yeah, if I had killed her, it would have been. But I didn't, so it wasn't.

Either they don't share my sense of humor or they just don't get my logic; they ask me to resume my seat outside. They have an officer look

259

after me while they peruse the apartment looking for twenty-dollar bills that God may have hidden about the place. So I bite my tongue and sit back in my chair again.

Biting my tongue was something I've had to practice a lot around my mother in the later years. It was too embarrassing to try to meet her on her ground. God knows, it was impossible for her to meet me on mine. She could never come to realize that I existed outside the frame of the fantasy portrait she had painted of me. Somewhere along the line I had become corrupt. I had matured. I had grown up. Out of her presence and her shackles. I was no longer the child she remembered. The one that never existed in the first place. The one that she had manufactured in her own mind that could reflect back to her just how perfect she was.

It's okay now, Mom. You're in that Big Manger Scene in the sky. You've got your wings . . . you're looking down at the dear little Christ Child – or me – whichever – we look almost like twins, right? – and you're ecstatically blazoning that glorious banner: GLORY, GLORY, GLORIA!

And me – thank God Almighty – I'm free at last.

9 ~ The Life and Times of a Splinter

Her gracefully curvy frame, all of five foot tall but heightened by spike-heeled boots and long windblown blonde hair, is silhouetted against the waters of the bay. Her absolute stillness suggests that her fixed gaze is burning a hole in the horizon. She couldn't be more lovely, couldn't more perfectly convey the essence of loneliness if she were a Hallmark card: "Missing You Eternally." Suddenly, she breaks from her rapt concentration and steps over to the Harley. She swings her leg up and over the bike and straddles the "bitch seat" like an old-time pro, ready to ride. That's no bitch. She's my wife.

We hit the road to our Sunday haunt to have our riding nightcap; then home for dinner. Uncharacteristically, Sandy dons her nightgown and slips into bed, where she'll have her dinner, if you please. Her favorite TV program will be on in minutes. I ask what she'd like to have, and she shocks me with: "noodles and cheese." Not the gourmet fare I'm used to preparing for her, but so be it, if that's truly what she wants. I serve her just as her show comes on. She expresses her appreciation with: "Yum, yum." I don't share her taste in programing, so I distract myself with little things to do about the room. Behind me, there's the usual tap of the headboard against the wall as she settles back in the bed. I think little of it.

A couple of minutes pass and I redirect my attention to her to inquire how she enjoyed her meal.

I'm mortified by the sight of her – her mouth gaping open, blue lips turned inside-out. Her eyes glazed over by milky shades. She resembles something closer to road-kill than she does my beautiful Sandina. I panic, which is to say, I totally ignore the DNR in her living will. I get real friggin' selfish real quick. Fuck it! I can't think of living without her, she's not going anywhere! I jump on her and do the Heimlich, thinking that she may have choked. She doesn't respond. I check her pulse – she has none, nor is she breathing. I start CPR on her and then check her vitals again. Her breathing is very shallow as is her pulse, but it's a start and gives me an opening to call the cops.

I run to the kitchen and phone 911. I'm hoping to God that I don't connect with that same asshole I dealt with when I called from my mother's. Thank God, I connect with another asshole – who apparently doesn't get it.

"Do you have my address right and are you rolling a bus yet!?"

"Can you stay on the line, sir?"

"No, she's in the bedroom and I'm in the kitchen, I have to go and resume CPR!"

"Do you know CPR, sir?"

"Well, why the fuck would I say I have to go do it if I didn't know how to do it!?" *Do you want to revisit how I knew my mother was dead, shit-head?*

"Can you hold on to the phone while you're doing CPR, sir?"

"I just told you, she's in the fucking bedroom, I'm in the fucking kitchen with Dinah!" *Would you like to take a break from what you're doing and sing along with me?* "Do you have the right address and have you got a bus rolling yet!?" *You fucking moron.*

"Yes, sir, can you stay on the line?"

Fuck this shit! I hang up.

Agonizing hours pass in the next two minutes as I'm brutalizing my wife's chest. I don't think that I'm even aware of the sirens of the eight vehicles that are stacking up in front of the house.

Suddenly, there's a flood of uniformed humanity gushing into a twelve-by-ten-foot room with almost all of the floor area taken up by furniture. With each body that swells into the inadequate space, I'm pushed further and further back on the floor that's quickly falling from beneath my feet, ever and ever closer to its edge where there are no walls to prevent me from falling into the abyss. It's all just a stage for this horrible cosmic melodrama. I'm breathless, I'm boneless, helpless as I grasp for a reality that just isn't there. This sure as shit can't be happening, it has to be a nightmare I'll wake up from. I'm ordered to get out of the room by one of the cops. I obey, almost as a matter of welcome escape. They wheel her out of the room, then out of the house where there are about twenty people, whose faces I don't recognize, their mouths all gaping. Who the hell are all these people, and what is this, some kind of fucking circus?!

In the next five hours, my own life support system seems composed of stolen single breaths and heartbeats. One borrowed moment of life to the next moment. I see it now. Our lives are suspended by threads held by the great Indian-Giver and can be rescinded on a whim. We truly ride the wind until God becomes breathless, then we drop without thought or notice.

Between the house and the emergency room, I think Sandy's heart stopped a total of eight times. At what point does this shit become ridiculous? Now she has bags and tubes and machines and every other modern medical knick-knack coming and going, in and out of every orifice and exposing and degrading her every modesty. I'm embarrassed on her behalf. I've totally, up to now, ignored the tipping of the scales that are measuring the questionable quality of her life should she remain on life support. Fuck this shit. It's all so fucking stupid. I really don't need to hear it from the doctors. There's no question, when I bring myself to look at her – she's gone. She's the color of ashes, her fire is out. I honor her soul's wish – I have the plug pulled. That leaves me the only player in the farce. With my hand gently gracing her chest, I share her last earthly breath. The shell of myself leaves the hospital. The shadow of myself gets into the cab. When the cab pulls up to the house, it's empty.

I awake to the familiar and secure blackness of my bedroom. My body is still trembling violently, still engulfed in the unthinkable terror of terrors. All I desire is to shake off the terrible sense of loss and loneliness I felt in my dream – in my nightmare – when I got out of the cab realizing full well that she wasn't home and that I would never see her again. Jesus. That was without a doubt the worst fucking nightmare I've ever had in my life. I never need have another, because nothing could top the mind-fucking of the one I just had. Anyway, I don't think I could have lived through this one much longer. I'm still shaking, still breathless, my heart still pounding through my chest, and wishing that my mind could take a long vacation from itself. I turn in the bed to put my arm around my beloved wife. I so much need to feel the living warmth of her. I never knew exactly the all-consuming power of my love for her until this moment. I wonder if she would mind if I wake her. I hate to – I know she has to get up for work in a few hours – but I so much need her to comfort me. I think she'll understand if I tell her what I've just been through. How grateful I am, how blessed I feel to hold her close to me. Maybe it will even make her smile.

I reach over toward her, and my arm falls from where it expected to find her shoulder, down onto the vacant cold sheet. A panicked wave of emptiness hits my gut. My eyes strain into the darkness. She has to be here somewhere. *She just has to be!* my head is screaming. *No, she doesn't. Don't you remember? – she's dead. She died two weeks ago, exactly as you just dreamed it. A perfect minute-by-minute playback.*

I shoot up in the bed with a vengeance. Fuck You! What kind of fucking God are You anyway! Is this Your idea of a fucking joke or something? I fucking hate You! It's not bad enough – I mean, the cruelty of taking her from me in the first place – but *this?* To have me believe that this was only a bad dream? You must really hate me, and I don't even know what the fuck it is that I've done! I'm knocked down all my life, and then I find her in answer to my life's last stupid hope . . . then You take her, and now – *this* shit! Are You fucking kidding me? You Motherfucker, let it be known that, at this point, You're on my shit list – I'm talking the very top of it! How do You like that shit?

Well, despite Your warped sense of humor, at least she's escaped Your web of cruel game-playing. By Your intention or not, she's now seated as an honored guest at the table of the Feast of Fools. She now gets to taste the divine qualities of mercy, doesn't she. Yeah, go ahead and have a good laugh at the fact that You've left me behind to wash the dishes. I get to scrape off the left-over pain and anguish of what was her life into the garbage pail You've designed me to be. I guess, by now, You might be thinking that I might be feeling pretty empty, violated, and eviscerated; well, don't give it another thought. And, by the way, don't hold Your breath waiting for a Christmas card from me. And another thing: there's one thing You can't take from me – my memory of her last moments of life. She lay in still peace with not a trace of stress or bother, but a hint of a sweet

264

knowing smile. In short, she died happy. Happy. As were her final years, with me. Alright, I'll give You that. For that much, I thank You. But don't go thinking that I'm ever going to talk to You again.

Today may be the point of no return. God knows, this shit has been going on longer than seems possible. The pendulum of my brain's clock has been swinging back and forth from dreams and delusions to physical torment and agony; from night to day; from shit to shit. After ten days without food or water and not a whole lot of what could be called rest, I can no longer distinguish the sunset from the sunrise; where my body ends and the iron yellow-pine floor – my open-air coffin – begins. All I know is that my bones are in screaming pain and just want to vacate my fucking flesh! But the body's torment, at least, has been able to distract me from the brain's nightmare of dreaming of dreams. What a trip to hell that is. But I'm far from being out of the burning hole, laying here in a pool of my own piss. Having released gallons of it into the floorboards, I can feel the planks under me conspiring to eject me – an orphaned splinter. I'm forsaken again. No bonds to anything or anybody.

I think I've felt splintered off from just about everything for just about the entirety of my life. Somehow, I briefly believed that all that had changed when I found Sandy, or we found one another. The answer to my bedraggled hopes. She was it! I didn't give up my world to be in hers, I gave it up to be hers. To be but a person of service, a lover, someone on vacation from himself, especially from his history. Hoping to transform his future. Or, at least, his present. But sometimes the act of turning yourself inside out isn't enough to disguise yourself in an effort to escape Fate. It's still your skin you're in – inside out or not, there's no escape.

I wonder what Fate truly is. Does it possess a sense of irony, a sense of humor? With nothing else to do these last ten days, I've been playing with the numbers game of Fate. Fate by the numbers. It took only forty-eight hours to meet and fall in love with Sandy and have her move in. Five hours for her to die. And yet I've been suspended in this purgatory, this death-process-on-hold for two hundred sixty-four hours, if you count the first day when I first realized that something was wrong. The dawn of that day – eleven days ago – was not significant. Just as boring as the last nine hundred twelve had been. Maybe a little more so, come to think of it. That was the first day in two and a half years I didn't have a drink. Well, the words 'a drink' hardly cover it. I should say, that's the first day I didn't get up at 3 a.m. and pour myself a tall one, then another, then another, until I poured myself into bed in preparation for the next dawn. There was only one purpose to my drinking. I needed a different reality. Either Sandy had to rejoin me, or I had to join her. Somehow my plan fell through, although it wasn't for lack of effort. That morning was different. I woke late. My head said: "Do you want a drink?" I answered: "Nah, this isn't fucking working." I could have saved myself a lot of trouble if she hadn't been cremated. I would have just gone and dug her up and brought her home, where she belonged.

Too late. I couldn't dig up an earthworm today. I feel like I've been steamrolled over. But that's nothing new – that's how I was when she found me. I was flat out then, but I could still be remolded. Now I'm flat out and there's nothing left in me. *No shit – you're flat out and you're lying in your piss.* Yeah, it's been leaking out of me for ten days, and nothing's been going in. Not even my meds, God knows. Or air? The scarcity of it might explain the fraying of my mind. I'm seeing things that aren't here – aren't I? Times with Sandy – but different times, in the same place. My head is spinning, and the voices in there – coming at me from different directions – aren't helping. Where am I going with this . . . ?

We're in our favorite bar one night . . . Sandy brings it to my attention that some really ugly and weird guy down the bar is staring at her . . . . That's funny, that's exactly how *we* met. . . .

The Cycle Of Life Goes Round And Round. As I Always Say, Not Much Changes.

. . . How we met: At that time, I had an antique shop in The Hollow. Sometimes, after closing, I would stop by a friend's shop that was an after-hours hangout for the other dealers. Occasionally, I would accompany the crew to a local bar for a brew. As kismet arranged it, I always found myself seated next to the same couple – the man to my right, and his ever-loving gorgeous wife to his, turned on her stool to face him. This meant she was also facing me; so I couldn't not notice her long beautiful blonde hair, her figure that wouldn't quit, and her general drool-worthiness. A first-class

266

head turner, the type that other women hate on sight. Assuming that she was married enabled me to squelch any fantasies of her before they could take root.

Squelch? I Think Not. Your Brain – And Everything South Of It – Was Dancing To That Primal Drumbeat. Let Me Tell You, My Boy, You Can't Turn That Music Off On A Whim. Buh-Bum, Buh-Bumba. Voluptuous Temptress, Knuckle-Dragging Mate. Sex, And Violence – There's *A Story. Let's Get Back To That Weird Ugly Guy At The Bar.*

Apparently, this guy down at the end of the bar isn't allowing our wedding rings to stand in the way of *his* fantasies. When I look down the bar, I can see his head craned over in our direction. I recognize that face immediately. I'd seen it on the news years ago. Not a face you easily forget. He was wanted for the killing of his girlfriend. I remember, at the time, how strange I thought it was that they couldn't find this guy. I ran into him almost every single morning, right here in town. I would usually catch a red light at this particular intersection – and, nine out of ten times, he'd be stopped there too, heading in the opposite direction. So what was so goddamned hard about finding this jerk? Three hundred yards up the road, he had to drive past a Dunkin' Donuts – and there were no cops around? Eventually, I know, they got him and put him away. And he did his time in that institution of higher learning where he was supposed to have learned his lesson; but now he's out, evidently no better educated, and sporting that look that guys have when they get out of the state's college: like they'd be willing to fuck a bale of barbed wire.

Smartly Said. Yes, Violently Sexy.

or, one could say, crude and barbaric. let's move on. the civilized *story is in the tender – not vulgar – recollections. paying attention to propriety – that's what's kept us from being stuck in the ranks of the knuckle-draggers. love, pure and chaste from afar. fantasies of romance . . . .*

Romantic fantasies – where was that going to get me? I was in the presence of a goddess who was seated with a mortal clod, and I naturally assumed that this was a married couple by the way the man smoothly ignored all his partner's connubial attentions. *Good God, throw it my way, and I'll sure as hell pay attention!* Naturally, I didn't really take direct notice of any of this shit, because, as the gentleman I considered myself to be, I wouldn't have been looking. Or, at least, wouldn't have gotten caught. Oops. I was getting caught far too many times. Goddamn it, I couldn't help myself. There was something so soulful about her eyes – like bottomless wells filled to the brim with love's torment. . . they would have been tormenting me, if I had allowed myself to gaze directly into them. *Maybe I'd be better off staring at her cleavage* was my lame attempt to keep my impulses in check. I just knew the thought of her was going to keep me awake at nights.

You Had No Fucking Idea About Sleepless Nights Back Then, Did You? Live And Learn. And, As I Recall, You Were About To Learn That Ugly Jerk A Thing Or Two About Ogling Your Yummy Wife . . . .

Clearly, this joker is no gentleman and his gaze is making Sandy very uncomfortable, which she naturally brings to my attention. She need not say more; I'm painfully aware of what's now expected of me, knowing Sandy's history. From the age of thirteen, she had told me, she had ridden for years with the Diablos. Every member of that club was her protector. One day, she was tending bar where a few of the crew were patrons. In walks some dude, slumming, and having the poor judgment to pass a comment about how good Sandy must taste. The only thing he got to taste was the asphalt of the parking lot that he met teeth first.

Now here we are, I'm Sandy's crew, and I'm supposed to straighten this new asshole out; to do that, I suppose, I'm expected to put on my bad-ass biker-dude skin. Unfortunately, I had left that particular item in the cedar closet when I walked out on my first Harley and that lifestyle years ago. Besides that, there is the pesky factor of my damaged back. Not to mention an oath I took to God, on my son's birth day, that I would never ever raise a hand in violence against another human being again. So now I'm as helpless and about as threatening as a ham sandwich. And I'm supposed to put this creep in his place? Well, if I think about it, rare was the time when I ever had to get physical to win over an adversary. On the other hand, when you ignore knowing better, you're flirting with defeat before you even get started. I have to think – and quickly, too – of doing that which I have never done before.

ah, but you've done that before – many times – even when you first met sandy – and you never forgot about being a gentleman then, did you? if a person couldn't come up with a civilized, clever, and rational approach to a situation, we'd still be knocking stones together, wouldn't we.

All true. After closing shop one night, I did something I'd never done before. I went to that same bar without my drinking buddies. Alone. There was no one else there, which was almost a relief. What the fuck could I possibly have been looking for, anyway? I sat down at the end of the bar where there was a large package of food to go, waiting to be claimed. Who suddenly appeared to collect it but that beautiful vixen herself in the flesh -- all of it; and all of it being just . . . well, just being. Then I did another something I'd never done with a strange beautiful woman: I said hello. Now I felt like a total jerk. Where did I get off? She was a total stranger, unless I considered that we had already met many times with our coy and stealthy eye to eye exchanges. Now that I'd shot my mouth off – did that mean we were engaged?

Yeah Yeah Yeah Blah Blah Where's My Violin? You're Not Sending Any Morse-Code Messages With Your Eyelashes To That Neanderthal At The End Of The Bar, Are You? Open Your Eyes. The Meek Shall Inherit The Earth – I Think Not. The Meek Won't Live Long Enough To Inherit Anything. Get Up And Walk, Like A Hominid.

walk like a man, he means. or he would *mean, if his brain had evolved past the stone age. now, which is more the essence of manliness – out-slugging an opponent, or out-thinking him?*

Okay, Sure. Outwit The Guy. I'm Okay With The Sound Of That – It Has The Ring Of The Sparring Ring. An Undertone Of The Devious And Slithery. I'm All Ears Now.

I'm staring sidelong down the length of the bar. I could use a minute to collect myself. Once again in my life it feels like something's been set in motion and I'm being swept along, like a leaf at the end of a hose-spray in a gutter. Then again, it feels like I've got too much time to think before I get to the end of the bar, more time than I really want to contemplate the unknown outcome I'm heading toward and whether it might be based on seeking pleasure or avoiding pain (and are those the only choices?).

I get the shivers. How did I get into this shit? I hadn't realized that I was signing on to a lifestyle I had left behind. Or did I? Either way, I don't recall kicking ass or getting your ass kicked as very much fun.

The shivers were sure running up and down my spine that other night, too – when I was emboldening myself, not to defend the goddess's gate, but to knock at it. It was impossible to ignore the fact that this beautiful lady was allowing her food to cool in trade for engaging me in conversation. I finally brought that fact to her attention, figuring it might give one or both of us a way out. She dismissed my concerns and kind of put a different slant on what was cooling and what was hot. Yeah, it was getting hot in there. But we kept talking.

Somehow the topic of marriage came up. Of course it did, which made it obvious which way the conversation was headed, especially after we discovered that we had something so important in common – we agreed energetically that marriage was a stupidity never to be committed again. But then – where could the conversation go from there? I figured things were winding down when, out of nowhere, she leveled me with: "How would you like to take me home and have wild, unbridled sex?"

Out Of Nowhere? Really? Hoo, Boy, Where Have You Been? Leveled??

I was knocked off my stool. That invitation came at me fast, even by city standards; I'd been used to expecting to wait a decent amount of time after meeting a woman– at least twenty minutes. And another crazy thing: like me, she'd been married twice – *and she still wanted to have sex.* Brother, I missed that boat – *twice.* I had to collect myself before I could say anything. Then, without a whole lot of thought, I shot back: "Well, I'd rather get to know you as a human being first, if you don't mind." I came damn near having to jump off my seat to catch her jaw before it could hit the floor.

I Heard 'Wild' And 'Sex' And 'Hit'. The Rest: Blah Blah. It Sounded Like 'Manners.' What Does Manners Sound Like? Sniveling. Tiptoeing. Pretty Please. Wise Up! If You Want To Get In – You've Got A Strong Shoulder, Put Your Weight Behind It And Use It, Sissy.

it just kills me to hear 'wise up' coming out of a wise ass. my ass knows more than you ever will. what you understand about manners is less than a chicken knows about plato.

Hold on – I think there's a meeting ground between delicate manners and skull-bashing aggression we can all agree on. It's called chivalry. That's where I'm called upon to defend My Lady's honor, lest it be trampled on the floor of this bar (and I be trampled on the bedroom floor when we get home).

Yes. Trample.

If trampling comes into it, I'd prefer to be the one on the dishing-out end. But fists are no longer my weapons of choice. This Mexican standoff calls for a little brain work, I'm thinking.

270

I start with a glance down the length of the bar, an eye-signal that says: Acknowledged – we're both killers, Sir. Where do you want to take this shit? I sure as shit can't back down in the eyes of my wife. *(Mind you, I wouldn't be throwing my gauntlet at you if my wife had more sense – or her priorities in the right places. Like not seeing me end up dead, or in jail, over a wanton look. But, hey – I married her.)*

I exhale and slowly mosey on over alongside the dude. I buy him a drink. That seems friendly enough, for a start. Then, politely, I offer him some advice.

"You look like a nice enough fellow. I just came over here to give you a friendly warning. You staring at my wife is causing her to feel real uncomfortable."

"Yeah? Whaddya wanna do about it?"

"Well, that's what I came over here to talk to you about. You see, it wasn't that long ago that I was up at the courthouse in Middletown – I had just gotten off, my second time being charged with a violent offense. That's when the prosecutor grabbed me, before I could leave the court building. She said to me: 'The next time I see you, you're going to be a three-time loser, and I'm going to send you away for a really long time.' Well, you know, I believe her. She's probably the same bitch who sent you up, so you know she means business. That's why I came over here to warn you. I can't see why you should have to come to any harm unnecessarily . . . but if you keep staring at my wife, I've got to tell you, she may, at any second, sashay on over here and kick your ass. I've been there – and, believe me, you don't want that to happen. So, I'm just cautioning you that, if what I just described comes to pass – well, what with the DA's threat hanging over my head, there isn't a goddamn thing I can do to try to protect you from her. I'm just going to have to step aside and helplessly watch. I just thought you should know. Enjoy your drink."

And that was that.

Yeah, and this is this. I've been reduced to being a part of the friggin' floor!

Well, How Is This Any Different? Welcome To Your Life.

Yeah, you're right, I'm back to square one. Back on the floor and back in more pain than what I hoped might be behind me. Back then – let me see . . . it was three and a half years of sometimes agonizing convalescing; then –

271

my big reward – I get well enough that I can get back into bed with Raechel. And that lasted all of about two weeks, until the remnants of our faltering marriage finally defaulted. Then it was back on the floor again for the next two years, the first of our formal, but still co-habitational, separation. God! She took enough goddamn time in getting out. I hope she wasn't too freaking inconvenienced in the process. Yeah, just like a floorboard, my life had been reduced to something flat, narrow, and straight. I'd become almost resigned to the idea that my path would no longer have any ups and downs to it. Over time, I just developed a fuck-it attitude.

Well, La-Di-Da – But You Weren't Doing Any Fucking, Bucko. That Was A First In Your Adult Life. Let's Face It, Man, You Have Become But A Splinter Of Your Former Self.

Is that you, Catfish?

Well, Who The Fuck Do You Think It Is – Ralf? The Subject At Hand, I Believe, Is Sex – Not Exactly In Young Ralf's Bailiwick. He's More Of A Head Guy.

Sure, but at least he doesn't try to think with his little head; he uses the one with the brain in it. He sometimes succeeds in keeping me out of trouble. I do have to give *you* credit where it's due, though, and thank you for small favors. I'm sure you're responsible for lighting up those full-body fireworks the first time I laid eyes on Sandy – and you kept them sparking long after. I can't blame you for that.

Of Course Not. It's Only Natural.

But, if I am going to get into the blame game – what Ralf did is another story.

Once Upon A Time.

He got me thinking – well, fantasizing – about romancing her. You pulled me to the edge of the fiery pit, and Ralf shoved me over into it. It's clear to me now – I was set up by the two of you and taken unawares. Like: *Hey, I've got a great idea – why don't the three of us go down to the beach, lay down and take in the sun, and just relax for the rest of our lives.* Fast forward three seconds: *Whoa – didn't see that tidal wave coming.* What the hell do you call that? I set foot on the sand, I lay eyes on this blonde siren, next night we're dining out, night after that we're making love, she showers me with gifts of gold jewelry, and never leaves. I look around and find myself out at sea riding the waves – shit, I might have settled for the sex and a bag of chips. But you two gave me no choice except this or another hole in the head – and I think I ended up with both.

who're you trying to kid, lover boy? when the princess said: "i had to kiss a lot

272

of frogs to find you," you know we couldn't have been happier at the prospect of the ball and chain.

We? Well, I guess we're all here now, Ralf. And you're right. I won't try lying to you – I know better. But, I have to tell you, I would have much preferred it if she had ridden in on a normal high tide. I think Catfish was in charge of the tide charts that day. On top of everything else, I had to deal with the flood of Sandy Stuff washing over my threshold and deluging my well-established and comfortable living space. To me it was an incursion; she saw it as inoffensive nesting. That brought some squalls into the picture. We had to navigate – sometimes through ripples, sometimes raging gales of sacrifice, compromise, and disappointment – on both sides.

When the tide finally receded, the house was pretty much back on an even keel, and mostly unchanged on the outside, but with the inside transformed into a virtual hothouse by all the new green pets it had taken on board. I love the natural world and – though I imagine it as existing outdoors – Sandy's affection for houseplants was hard for me to argue with.

As Long As You Didn't Mind Using A Machete To Find Your Way To Bed At Night.

Never mind your snippy comments, Catfish. A jungle in my house was the least of my worries. I had a giant anaconda as a permanent resident, and I'm the one who brought it in there. When a snake sets up in your Garden of Eden –

There's Trouble In Paradise. We've Always Known That. The Mouth Of Every Cave Had A No Snakes Sign Across It. But Your Friend, Mr. Goody Two-Shoes, Told You It Would Be Noble – Generous, Gallant, Very Good Manners, And All That Crap – To Take The Old Lady In. Whether She Wanted To Be There Or Not. Whether She Even Knew She Was *There Or Not. Whether Any Man In The Long History Of Stand-Up Comedy Would Even Dream In His Worst Nightmares Of Wanting Her Living In His House.* Your Mother-In-Law?? *A Person Who, In Fact, You Had Never Met. And Stupidest Of All, You Idiot, You Never Checked It Out With Your Wife. No – Stupider Yet – You Weren't Even Married Yet.*

Yeah, it *was* Ralf's idea. After I brought the woman home, he went incommunicado for a while and left me up to my knees in the shit by myself.

That's probably one of the reasons why I was in the men's room of the church, chugging from a bottle of scotch with my best man before the ceremony. No matter, it was the best goddamn wedding that either I or my bride had ever attended. We laughed all the way through the ceremony

– we even got the minister into it.

bravo – transcending life's adversities by sharing in a spirit of joy is enlightened and commendable.

Bullshit. You're Only Saying That Because It Gets You Off The Hook For Leading Our Boy Down The Path Of Wrongishness And Abject Selflessness: Oh, Look At Me, I'd Give A Crotchety Old Hag The Last Hair Off My Chest. As For Their Silly Laughter, They Had Enough Liquor In Them To Float The Spanish Armada. That Poor Sap Minister Joined It Because There Was No Way He Could Fight It. So Much For Your Lame Ideas Of Joy. Cross The Great South Bay Alone In The Stormy Gloom In A Sunfish In Three-Foot Swells. That's When You'll Feel Joy.

That's interesting. At the time – almost thirty years ago! -- I thought I was feeling the line between life and death in my grip on the lines and the tiller.

Exactly.

I could ask myself why I set my course for Fire Island that night instead of turning back up the Patchogue River estuary when I saw that holding myself taut at a horizontal angle was the only way to keep my boat's keel in the water; I had to know the crossing would take hours; and, with the swells, I couldn't see a blessed speck of the land I was making for. I guess I had to decide which would be worse – pitting my untested sailing skills against a storm, or facing Hobby's ridicule if I turned tail and had to swallow my bravado.

the jury is still out on that one. but as for "rowing the rescue boat" out to sandy's mother –

That. Oh, Yes – Dear Ralf Will Tell You How Heroic That Was.

You don't have to bitch-slap me, Catfish. I know a self-made sucker when I see one in the mirror. The one who could really have smacked me down for my Don Quixote impersonation was Sandy. I could ask myself, didn't I know I was walking the line – or putting my life on it – by trusting that my wife would be fine with the going-behind-her-back part of my derring-do – she'd forgive me for that, I imagined, when she was greeted by the wonderful surprise I delivered to her doorstep.

You Were Hoping For A Pat On The Head And A Lollipop?

I'm lucky I still *have* a head.

Much Good It Does You, That Evolved Brain You're So Taken With.

he believed he was rescuing eleanor from the violent clutches of her other daughter's husband. i applaud that.

274

Of Course You Do. And How Did That Work Out For You, Son?

How the hell – did *I* know the two of them hated each other? I knew that Sandy had been picking her mother up every Sunday and taking her out to lunch or dinner. I thought that everything was hunky-dory. And maybe it was, as long as out-of-sight, out-of-mind prevailed for the rest of the week. Absence makes the heart grow less in danger of ending up with a knife through it. In any case, bringing excess baggage into a newly-cohabited household already overloaded with vegetation – I had to be out of my fucking mind. Well, if I thought *I* was nuts, Eleanor brought a new meaning to the concept – her baggage was packed with a case of advanced Alzheimer's. In response, I became an advanced drunk. That was okay, I was just catching up with my wife.

Well, what the hell. There we all were. We ended up finding and settling into our respective stations: Eleanor on the couch in her nightgown, wearing my oriental carpet to threads in the spot where she permanently planted her feet, was referred to as The Black Hole; I answered to Oh Lover Boy, and Sandy was called Yes Dear. It was working out very well, actually. Eleanor notwithstanding, we understood our places and how to fulfill each other's needs, without either of us having to ask for anything. No one needed to keep score or weigh each other's doings on a balance scale. In the cold-sober light of day, things could not possibly have been better.

But . . . ? I Smell An Uh-Oh Coming. And Something About Balance.

The night times.

No Shit. What A Shock. But, Do Tell.

That's when the spooks and evil spirits of the past slipped their shackles and came at her, showing their teeth. Every hobgoblin of times, things, and relations that had gone unresolved in Sandy's past were poured out in the fourth drink from the bottle of neurosis. Two or even three drinks would take her as far as a dreamy smile, a contented murmur: "I think I'll go to bed now." Nice and peaceful. A bit early in the evening, though – it left me alone for some hours. That was fine.

I Said, DO TELL.

Alright – it left me lonely and pissed off. But God forbid she got to that fourth drink – that's when the light would really friggin' go out.

Let's See . . . That Left You Lonely And Pissed Off – Or In The Dark With A Madwoman. My – Whaddaya Call It? – GPS Puts That Somewhere Between A Rock And A Hard Place.

That's where my Advanced Drinking credentials pulled me through.

But watching the light of rationality and sanity go out of her eyes still sucker-punched me. The chaser to drink number four was always psychosis. I came to fear the dark-fall. When the drinking started, I never knew what was going to come out of the bottle – angel or devil.

But, shit, who am I to say anything about her drinking. When we met, I was damn near dry, or as dry as I get, a couple of beers a week. Nothing will put you on the path to drinking every day faster than living with someone who drinks every day. But that was my decision to make. I figured that it was a lot easier to deal with the crazy-making if I was a part of it.

And now, after two and a half years alone spent trying to kill myself with the shit, I've finally put myself on the cusp – one good bump and I'm off the cliff. I hope You're happy now, Asshole! I wonder how much longer I'm going to have to wait? *Shit* – I forgot. I'm not talking to You.

i'm *here for you.*

Great. You've been a big help. What the fuck do I do now? Think?

Now, eleven days after jumping back on the wagon, leaving behind my passport to oblivion, I find myself teetering around the rim of death's abyss; now the tipping point will come by natural causes as opposed to by design. Nature will take its course. But *when?* What goddamn power has been keeping me from further, or mortal, harm? Is there some kind of backasswards design to this shit? Am I supposed to survive? Why? For what purpose? If I wanted to stay alive, I could have dialed 911 right off the bat. But I didn't. I couldn't find cause to. Besides, if I have to be responsible for my resuscitation, how the hell could I afford myself? The medical Powers That Be borrowed Sandy for a mere five hours and, after not bothering to return her, charged me well over twenty thousand friggin' dollars not covered by her excellent insurance. The heartless bastards billed me just like the White Star Line billed the family of the *Titanic*'s band leader for his drowned uniform. So me, with no insurance? Yeah, right – I'd be paying off the debit of myself for the rest of my unwanted life. But, wow, I must really be important to the world or something. With everyone missing me and all. Not even the mail person has knocked on the door to ask why my mailbox is so stuffed that the shit is falling out of it.

I know one thing. I can't take this freaking floor another second. I'm breathing better now and the cramps in my legs, and especially in my feet, have eased up. I wonder if I can walk.

276

I pull myself up, clutching the side of my desk. I push off a little – nope, not yet. But I'm willing to bet that I can probably crawl more than five feet now without totally losing my breath to the point of near fainting.

God, those first days on this floor were the most flat-out I've ever been – the closest to being a coating of dust on the pine boards. But not as peaceful. Dust doesn't imagine it should be able to regroup itself into a form capable of motion. Dust is content to lie there not breathing and is not scared shitless by the feeling of its chest heaving in and out and not pulling any oxygen out of the air. Dust doesn't feel the impulse to scream and not have the breath to do it, till its head wants to explode. Dust doesn't panic; but I damn near did. I envied the dust – I was waiting to return unto it. Dust probably has more patience than I do.

That first day – the morning after the day after I quit drinking and I couldn't get anything to stay down my throat, even water – all I did that morning was get out of bed and down I went like a sack of rocks. *Help! I've fallen and I can't get up!* That old TV line that I laughed at because that would never happen to me, and I'd never say anything so lame. Well, now it's my chance to find out. And yeah, I find I have my own version: *I've fallen and I don't give a shit.* What else could I tell myself to believe? I couldn't move, let alone get up. I was trying with whatever focus I had left to do one thing – breathe. I was doing what one, by habit, does, but without the expected results – nothing's happening, and it's not like you have the power to make it any different than it is. I'd never felt that kind of helplessness in my life.

And I guess I'm living to tell about it. Even if I'm the only one who hears the tale. I agree with myself that the first thing I have to do is take a real long painful piss. I start crawling towards the toilet.

I've gone about five feet in the last five minutes. I stop. I have to, or I'm going to die.

Fifteen minutes pass. I start to move again only after I've gotten the rhythm of my breath back – which is to say, I'm slightly less breathless than I was fifteen minutes ago. The toilet is somewhere on the horizon. I can't hold it any longer, the pain is just too goddamn excruciating. I release the wicked flow. I know full well that I'm shortly going to have to go again. That, and I'm probably going to have to take a shit as well. I resume my pilgrimage to the toilet. The journey is the most painful and remarkable one I've ever made to the bathroom. It isn't one I'm considering making twice.

I manage getting onto the toilet – which proves to be the easiest of the feats I'm faced with – using my still-intact upper-body strength to swing myself up by grabbing the toilet and the side of the tub and yanking my body off the floor while twisting myself in midair and landing on the seat. That's fun. They should do this trick on game shows. The problem is, how the hell do I get down from here? I have plenty of time to figure it out, all the time it takes to catch what little breath I'm ever going to recover. And then free fall. That's the only way. But, brother, I'm not going through this again.

Eventually, I make it back to the bedroom. I have this really stupid desire to be back in bed. I don't know why, do you? Some kind of sense of comfort and protection, I'm figuring. Yeah, well, good luck with that. For every little movement I make, I have to take that fifteen-minute break. It's amazing how much time is being eaten up by doing the least little thing.

It's been eleven days – I wonder if I shouldn't try to get some water into me. Maybe this dying business has played itself out. Shit, I don't even know where the absurdity begins and ends. This whole warped pageant of finding love, losing it to death, now this twisted melodrama after the theatrics of being a drunk for two-and-something years. If it all wasn't so goddamn tragic it would be comical. Or something.

But, at the end of it all, where am I?

Not Dead.

I guess not – but no thanks to myself. I think I had really given up – quit trying to make sense of myself or of what my life was supposed to be about. I was ready to be absorbed into another, to be a function of her being. The walking dead plugging into someone else's battery. Fucking even that up with drinking and thinking like a drunk, stumbling around being noble. Being my woman's man. After she was gone, just stumbling around. Then crashing. Squatting, like a homeless derelict, on death's doorstep. And not ending up dead. Why? It seems that no matter how much I try to fuck things up for myself, there's always an unseen hand at work protecting me from my worst devices. Like now.

My body is showing an inclination to go on living. Is my spirit on board with that? Is there any point? More of the same shit?

things do change.

Some Things Change, Some Things Stay The Same.

it could be some different *shit this time. something you can sink your teeth*

278

into.

If Not, You Can Still Always Die.

I don't know . . . . But, yeah, things do change. Like my colossal fuck-up that made Eleanor a permanent fixture in our living room – for weeks, months, two tense years – I could see the calendar pages stretching to infinity, like a long gray cloud over the cavern of purgatory we were living in – and then: reprieve. It came with a blitz at our front door, and left us on a cloud of newlywed bliss and privacy we had never yet gotten a fair chance to enjoy . . . .

Sandy's daughter volunteers to take the old baggage off our hands for an extended weekend, threatening (I think she said 'promising') to return her Monday night, but probably Tuesday. *Thank you, God.* This weekend, Sunday night falls on the anniversary of the death of Sandy's father. She always celebrates the occasion with a bottle of champagne. Tonight we giddily retire to our candle-lit bedroom with two bottles of wine. We snuggle down on the bed, me in the nude and she nearly, in her best scanty negligee. I'm pouring the first glass, when our front door is struck by cannon-fire, causing me to spill some of the wine. For a practiced drunk such as myself, this is intolerable, and unforgivable. *What the fuck was that!?*

Before the question can fully get out of my mouth, Sandy is fully out the bedroom door. Before I can ask myself what the hell she's doing, she's out the front door in full pursuit of her fourteen-year-old grandson, the offspring of her son and his wife. From my station, all I can hear is the sound of screeching tires and the high revs of the car's engine, followed by the frantic voice of the young man screaming: "Mom – wait! Don't leave me here! Wait, Mom! Help!" What I can't see, but can picture in my mind, is Sandy's daughter-in-law speeding away backwards up the street, her son chasing her – with Sandy in hot pursuit, barefoot and bosoms popping. From the fact that it is the *daughter-in-law* who seems to be stuck with the dirty work of bringing Sandy's mother back to our doorstep, I have to surmise that the *daughter* is not unfamiliar with the fearsomeness of Sandy's wrath. The display of that fearsomeness at this moment causes the mission to be aborted and the delivery vehicle, with Eleanor still in the back seat, to disappear around the corner, still in reverse.

The following morning, I answer a banging at the door, a smaller cannon this time. It's Sandy's daughter-in-law, in the company of a very tall cop. I've never met her, but I presume that's who it is from the clues of her snarling face and her curt introduction: "I'm here to pick up Eleanor's

279

stuff", as she rushes past me as if breaking a tackle. "And," she asserts, "you're not getting her back!" Oh? This must be some kind of reprisal, I'm thinking. Well, in that case, let's drop the formalities. Oh, we already have . . . well, then, I'll just stay the hell out of your way, while you go about your business, and I'll talk to the cop. You're not going to hurt my feelings any.

I crane my neck to look up and engage the officer: "I didn't expect to see you here today." He smiles, as if he'd been here before; yeah, him and the entire force.

"I'm just here to see that there's no trouble," he reassures me.

I smile back. "No problem. She's in the bathroom. She doesn't even know you're here."

After everyone is gone and Sandy eventually emerges from the bathroom, unaware that anything has occurred, I inform her about our loss. She becomes so overwhelmed with relief and excitement that she rushes back into the bathroom to redraw her eyebrows inasmuch as she has none of her own due to a terrible over-waxing incident in cosmetology school. The current expression on her face is all wrong for the occasion – she has to adjust it to something far more joyful. The wonders of makeup – a formula that can make a happy woman.

For me, it's not that easy. A more dynamic mood-lifter will be needed. For the next two months, I'm still haunted by the old woman's image every time I walk into the living room, the horror of the witch is that ingrained in my mind's eye.

But, *for every door,* and all that. Finally, in came the rush of fresh air our marriage needed. Seated in tandem on that two-year-old Harley we treated ourselves to, we rushed into the wind and never looked back. As someone said, you never should – something may be gaining on you.

Here we go down the road. *Eeerrk!* Sandy presses her knees into my ribs, hard; her signal for me to hit the throttle. I do, hard. The front end of the bike jerks up from the sudden thrust in power. Sandy's turned around in her seat swearing at someone as we miss our turn. We also just missed getting rear-ended. I know I used the bike's signal, and I know goddamn well Sandy was watching our asses with her hand signal, all of which counted for absolutely nothing to the dumb bitch behind us who was too busy on her cell phone to take notice of anyone else in the world. Fuck her! (if Sandy hasn't already said it).

But such occurrences as this were the moments that added quality to our lives. There's nothing like the bond that comes through riding together. In the back of our shared minds, we were always aware of the fact that we might very well die together, and that's okay – it beats old age all to hell. This minor incident could be added to our great track record. On average, our lives were threatened only once a year. That was something to be grateful for. As an added bonus – for me, anyway – riding again picked up where I left off back when I bought my '54 hog, which was the first thing I did after getting out of the service. It was a part of my rebellion back then against everything, as it was now against the stagnant lifestyle I had fallen into before meeting Sandy. I was 'all that', again.

Yeah, that 'all that' ended eight hundred twenty-five days ago, but who's counting. The referee packed it in long ago. I guess it's up to me to decide if I'm down for the count now. This is not the first knockout punch I've taken. I can look back at my history of them as training to stand up to the greater shit to come – and, sometimes, even as a blessing. Another opportunity to reinvent myself.

I remember Susan telling me that I was the luckiest son of a bitch she had ever known. I didn't have the slightest idea of *wot the 'ell* she was talking about back then. Somehow, looking back over everything, it's making some sense to me now. At this point, I think, I owe it to my guardian angels to give them some material to work with – they can't be expected to do everything on their own.

I start by slowly crawling to the kitchen, taking care to not cover too much ground too fast. This proves to be relatively easy. I pull myself up to the sink and drink a small amount of water. Then I raid the freezer for a little ice cream. I'm careful not to overdo it – I don't want to shock my system. I have to be patient. I'll repeat this regimen tomorrow, adding a little more effort and intake. I think I can tell myself I'm over the hump – providing nothing new and unexpected steps in and trips me up.

Every little step – a movement forward, or a trip-up. Who pulls the strings on the moves and the slips? After our release from the indwelling of Eleanor, the happily-ever-after path of our marriage was impeded by the big pink elephant in the room – Sandy's drinking. But, in that third year of our union, something or somebody smiled on us. Sandy had fallen into the habit of staying in bed on Saturday mornings and getting drunk before ten-thirty a.m. Up until then, I had been able to count on our daylight hours together as time spent in heaven. Where the fuck did this new little slice of hell come from?

This particular Saturday, the miraculous intervention we needed came with the sudden, unannounced visit by Sandy's best friend. I think she simply showed up when she did because there was some kind of connection between them that told this friend when she was needed. This was manifested in their history, on a day two weeks before Sandy and I met, when Sandy had given up all hope of anything ever being good in her life. Her gun was in her mouth when her friend called. She was there that day to tell Sandy: "Don't worry, honey, the good times are coming." Now, here she is again.

She and I are seated in the kitchen, talking about what to do with Sandy, when there's a loud crash in the bedroom. Sandy is falling-out-of-the-bed drunk, taking an antique glass lampshade with her. She's so goddamned embarrassed, mortified, in front of her friend, that she actually gets her act together. For her, that translates into never drinking in the morning again, and never, ever having more than three drinks in a day. As if a benign spirit had taken up Eleanor's place on our couch, from that day forth until the day Sandy passed from life, not a rude word passed between us. We had, at last, found our sure footing in heaven.

I think I can give myself a little pat on the back for my part in that happy outcome. If ever I perceived even the smallest hint of trouble brewing in her mood and about to spill over, I pre-emptively countered with: "If you're looking to have an argument, you're going to have to have it with yourself." The result was always the same – she would smile, and the gunpowder would fizzle out before a shot was fired.

How did I arrive at this perfect stratagem of passive resistance? I'm no dummy. I gleaned that cue, and others, from my marriage with Raechel. If you want to be happy: don't listen, and keep your freaking mouth shut as well as your ears, and, above all, remember that it's not necessary for anyone to know that you're happy. In retrospect, I can say that my marriage with Raechel was something like the Nevada proving grounds. Which confirms that, as Hobby taught me: "Nothing is never for nothing."

✳ Epitaps

Don't ever tell anybody anything. If you do, you start missing everybody.

It's enough to make you nuts. George, for instance. I've broken off with George before – how many times? -- and somehow I'm always pulled back. Even after he's dead. I uncorked my last bottle of him – what's it been, almost twenty years now? And I'm still hung over. I had my last hair of the dog, I thought, a couple of months after I saw the dog for the last time. The hair that would cure me, if anything could. But when is it ever that easy?

I turned tail on George the day I jumped a plane out of Virginia in a smoldering fury. You'd think the heat of that rage would have immolated every other fleck of feeling, burnt them to a crisp, leaving a swath of scorched earth in the places where George used to get at me. But – hell, no. After my departure, the things not yet done or said were like a hair on the tongue. A freaking maddening hair – no matter how hard you try to find it and dispose of it, it remains impossible to lay your finger on it. After a while, it takes on the obtrusive size of the Empire State Building, so how hard can it be to locate it and finally rid yourself of it? I guess it's about as easy as exonerating yourself from guilt, warranted or not.

283

Off the plane and back in Bushy Hollow, CT, there seemed to be plenty of guilt to go around. Back in the same kettle of connubial fish I had left behind when I flew off, capeless as always, in response to the summons from George's neighbor Nancy. Why should I be surprised that Act V, scene-the-last would open with another call from Nancy. . . .

This time she's calling from George's bedside in the nursing home where he's been confined since his inevitable loss of any capability of movement. He can't move, but he's bound to the bed by restraints that guard against the oncoming loss of his sanity. His neighbor is suggesting that, if I have any final words for him, this would probably be the last chance to communicate them. George was wondering, she says, why he hasn't heard from me for weeks. I could wonder how he communicated this to her, since he had also, she said, lost all capability of speech.

"I've been a little busy," I tell her, "getting arrested and hanging out in psychiatric lockup and dealing with a domestic snakes'-nest. But, hell, put him on the phone."

Nancy says, okay, she'll hold the phone to George's ear.

I haven't rehearsed this scene. What am I going to say? George is off-stage, with no speaking part. Maybe that makes it easier to ad lib my lines – but also a little surreal.

Well, no one taught me the art of bullshit better than George, so maybe it's poetic justice that I serve him up with a goodly portion of it now. Starting with me pretending that everything is as it's supposed to be. No allusions to anyone's exasperation with anyone's imperiousness. I give it my best effort and try to tone down the sound of curtness in my voice. I'm laying it on a bit thickly. The spirit is righteous, though, even if the content is a little embroidered. I speak of the infusion of his life into my own and, beyond that, the future extension of his life into my own heir. Yes, George will go on living forever through those who will follow after.

Of course, I can't hear how George is receiving this. Before the call ends, Nancy thinks to take the phone and tell me that George is nodding and seems at peace.

I guess I hope that he is. That would, at least, make one of us who's found relief, and some sort of tidy finality. Twenty years, almost, the curtain's been down. The end of the long run of *George* hit me a lot harder than I would have expected. For all his seemingly-immutable presence, there's little trace of evidence to show that someone had once walked the trail. All that's left are vague clues, like the powdery residue of butterfly wings just discernible in the disturbed geometry of a spider's web. You

284

know that something has occurred, has passed through, but you're not really sure what. All there is is the lingering aerosol of memories.

What's real?

What I told George about his immortality through me and my posterity was pretty much the bull. I didn't tell him that not even my *own* life experiences had managed to drip down to my own son, who was already estranged from me. I guess sometimes the sap doesn't flow down the family tree. The sap. Yeah. That would be me.

10 ~ Pidge

So the kid is now living on 16ᵗʰ and Park, right across the street from where I got my NY start. Although I guess I can't call him a kid anymore; he's a lot older today than I was in my yesterday of living where he lives now. Shit! That's a real head-warp, if not a time one. I have to wonder why the ex let that little tidbit out of the bag. Yeah, it cut – did she want to see if I bled? She knows full well that I don't want to hear anything about or concerning him. I've been trying to keep him buried in the graveyard of my psyche for decades now. There's not even a blank stone to mark the spot. Just some nondescript weeds protruding through the ground mist that's almost indistinguishable from the eternal gray sunset. No one, especially me, trespasses on this lot; not even the ghosts of other loved ones gone. This is exclusive real estate, the kind where you dispose of the victims of the plague. Is it an appropriate grave for my only child? I guess I could better answer that if I knew who buried him there in the first place.

If there's anything more beautiful than being pregnant, then it's looking at the naked belly of the woman who's carrying that cherished little package. It's funny that you can love someone as much as you do before you even know their gender. Apart from their sex, there really isn't anything, identity-wise, to know and love, beyond your own projections of that person-to-be. So much of that *to-be* is to be formed by what you *are*. You and your mate. Parenthood can be a second coming or – as it was in my parents' case, me being the package – a criminal event. I'm guessing our role will fall somewhere in the middle. I know for damn sure, without even consulting with God, our child will not be shadowed by the latter. He will know he has value and is cherished.

I guess there's nothing more life-changing than bringing a new life into the world. If that isn't so, then it shouldn't be happening in the first place. I'm only too well aware of being born to the wrong parents, having to spend almost my entire life getting over my entire life. As much as I love and agree with the ways of the ancient Spartan culture, I think they may have gotten one thing wrong. As the descendants of evolution, we can do better: instead of examining children for defects at birth and exposing the unfit to the elements, we should be exposing a few parents-to-be here and there. With that mindset, and having the character to put my money where my mouth is, I have no fear of such a practice. I may not be it all, but I think I have a pretty good handle on how to expose it all to my little sponge.   To assist in any way I can in the absorption of it. If I were to believe in God to any degree, then let my child be shown to it and be recognized as the blessing of it as I feel in my heart!

11 ~ Conversations in the Garden

Click-clack goes the little door in the big door. Clang bang goes the lock. Eeerrrrck goes the door as it's opened; not too hasty, using caution. There stands Nurse Rita (no surprise), glowing in her white uniform – well-starched, of course, like her personality. She can stand there and glow, with that demure simper on her face -- she's backed up, as usual, by her ape Otto, the Observer, who always lets us know by his hulking King Kong pose that he isn't going to tolerate any monkey business. Letting his hulk do his talking. Words are Nurse Rita's province.

--- *It's time for your medication, Mr. O'Riley.*

--- I don't give a shit!

--- *Now, Mr. O'Riley, you know, if you don't wish to co-operate, Otto will be more than glad to help you.*

--- Well, at the risk of breaking Otto's rice bowl, I guess I can see my own way to taking whatever you're dishing out today. Oh – same as yesterday? And last Tuesday? Yeah. Fine. So I'll get my garden privileges today?

--- *I don't see why not; I'll mention it to Dr. Z. I'm sure, if you continue to behave, there shouldn't be any problem.*

--- Right, no problems. The only problem is – I shouldn't be here in the first place. Otto's the one with anger issues. And another problem – who did the decor in this resort? Someone should have told those jokers that wall-to-wall carpeting is supposed to be on the floor, not on the walls.

To humor everyone, I gulp down my pills, mugging delight, sticking out my tongue in Otto's direction to let Ms Rita check out the hiding places in my oral cavity where I might be stockpiling my meds for later resale.

Clang bang goes the door. Alone again – that's as good as it gets in this Hilton, apart from the occasional visit to Dr. Z's office. And time in the walled garden-- a few hours a day of air and sunshine. If I behave. Behave at what? Do I really have any choice? There's always a camera trained on me, whether in my cell or out in the garden. I wonder what it is they think they're going to learn by watching me? I'm often tempted to take off my underwear and turn it inside out and put it back on. That would give them something to talk about for at least two months. At least the garden isn't bugged and I can get away with talking to Ralf and Catfish. But they know that I do that, because I never made RAL. and CAT.'s existence a secret. I suspect my past shrinks came to be as comfortable with their goings on as I am. Either that or they were great at pretending.

Looking forward to garden time is a mixed blessing. The reward of being out of this hole speaks for itself; it's the waiting that's the killer. Most of the time spent here is no-waiting time because there is nothing to wait for. Nothing changes. Like, for example, what they call food around here. When it comes to that shit, you do something like *anti*-waiting. Maybe except for Thanksgiving; Otto always sees to it that I get a turkey head for dinner.

A small slice of eternity seems to have passed. Click clack again. The little viewing door opens and there's Nurse Rita's eagle eye poking in, probably to make sure I haven't got a shotgun lined up aiming at the door. Clank; it shuts. Now the waiting game begins. Another scheduled peep-show, or the first step to a temporary reprieve? They'll give it a couple of minutes to keep me guessing. They love head games.

The door slowly opens and, sure enough, there's Ms Rita and Otto, with the addition of young Axel, Otto's right-hand chimp-in-training. Probably a mere apprentice because he doesn't have a black belt in ka-nut-te. He gets to carry the restraints in case of an outbreak of common sense, like not wanting to be here. They usher me through several locked passages and then release me into the great outdoors – or, at least, a delimited little portion of it, seeing that they have learned to constrain even space itself.

It's alright boys, we're alone.

The sky is simply blue, the sun simply yellow, and the air simply fresh. Everything beyond nothing is complicatedly simple. The longer I grow old here, the more simple my wants become. It's almost like growing young. If I get any more juvenile in my thinking, I'll be wearing diapers again. Yeah, life is getting as simple as my childhood was.

RAL. Whose childhood are you speaking of? I know I was a late-comer into your life, but I certainly don't remember any of it as being simple.

CAT. Damn it all, Ralf, you little upstart. You're always looking to make trouble where there isn't any. And you're right, you weren't there from the beginning, so why not let the lad have some fun. I assure you, *I* can stir up some childhood memories that're quite a hoot. Sidney -- I might call you Sidney, mightn't I? -- as everyone seems to around here. Do you remember the first time I came into your life and endowed you with marvelous powers of manipulation? I'm not speaking of early on, when I taught you to cry to get your way; that will only take you so far. No, I'm speaking of the time when I trained you in conscious decision-making to milk a situation for all – for *far better* than -- it was worth. If your memory fails, allow me to enlighten you. It was in upstate NY, while visiting your Uncle Stuyve in the state nut house (no offence), when your brand-new stepfather of two days got pulled over by the highway patrol for speeding. That's when I first stepped into your mind and began your education, and you were smart enough to pick right up on it. You started bawling like a little baby, hysterically pleading with the officer not to take your new daddy to jail, knowing full well nothing like that was going to happen. Clever tyke.

290

Junior, did you turn it on! I think you got the copper so worked up that not only did he not issue a ticket, he ended up apologizing to your stepdad for having pulled him over. And what's more, you were loving it. My boy, you had discovered the art; and I was your Grandpappy.

RAL. Catfish, you have the memory of convenience. I noticed you failed to mention how proud his stepfather was the *second* time you tried manipulating a situation. That ended in the first beating that little Sidney had ever known in his life. I don't see you jumping up and down begging for credit for that one. Let's play fair here.

CAT. I think I know of which you speak. And I don't feel guilty in the least. I did my part. And give the kid some credit; he did his best as well. It's just that all the parts didn't fall into place as either the lad or I supposed. I remember it well. Little Sidney was in tow when his stepfather was looking for work. They were seated in a room with twenty other men looking for the same job. This didn't escape the little rascal and, after some forethought which was of *my* doing, Sidney pronounced in as loud a voice as possible: "Daddy, what's the problem? Won't they hire you, because you have a wooden leg?" I thought he was brilliant, knowing how such attention had succeeded with the cop and all.

RAL. Yeah, it was an attention-getter all right. I remember every man in the room turned and stared at his dad. Everyone but the person who was doing the hiring, who wasn't even in the same room. You might have taught him to look before he leaped if you're such the great educator. God and I know, not to mention poor little Sidney's bottom, how much Daddy enjoyed that kind of attention.

CAT. Ah, get off it. If I sat on the right shoulder of God like your little ass-kissing self, then I'd be as near perfect as you profess to be. Ahem. If you'd take into account the region I come from, you might afford me a little more consideration regarding my occasional miscalculations.

SID. Wait a minute, guys. Let's not get into a battle of egos here. We're all in the same cell together. More like a box . . . yeah, like a box of Cracker Jacks. Ralf, you're the gooey carameled popcorn, Catfish the nuts. That leaves me as the prize -- the booby prize, I'm guessing. But I can't find fault with either of you guys. You're both necessary. Together you compose the whole of me. Just try to keep in mind that I'm the meat and potatoes in this stew. Ralf, you're the heavenly aroma and Catfish, you're the shit that sticks to the bottom of the pot. Try to accept your stations for what they are and we'll all get along a lot better. After all, I'm not blaming either one of you for the plight I'm in. Any time I fell on my ass was because I foolishly gave one or the other of you too much say and power, too much rein. Ultimately, the fault's with me. And if I can resign myself to accept my responsibilities, or lack of, then you assholes can certainly own up to the reality of what you are without getting all defensive about it!

CAT. Well! I mean, certainly. I'm willing to play along, as long as Ralf recognizes my seniority. I've been around since man has been conscious, Ralf has only been on the scene since man developed a conscience; that gives me an edge of some hundreds of thousands of years.

RAL. Well, maybe some of us need a running start. Some of us are slower learners than others.

SID. Boys! Keep it civil! Like I said, I don't play favorites. I recognize that you both have your equal importance in evolution. Every force, be it positive or negative, has to be met with an equal opposite force to maintain balance and stability. Without that common meeting, you have chaos . . . oh! -- that would be me. Hey – *shh!* Axel's coming this way.

The little goon has a strolling gait that exudes purpose. He's about twenty-three or so, but seems somehow prematurely withered. It must be having to carry that heavy load of self-assigned importance. Even the surrounding flowers seem to shudder in awe of his overwhelming majesty. He gives one last nonchalant look over his shoulder as he nears his exit. I give him a coy smile of recognition. That will hold him for a while. He's now earned some small portion of his paycheck. In secret, we all feel more sorry for him than we hold him in disdain. After all, we all come from the same shame. It's called youth. It doesn't get any more ignorant than that. What are you going to do? We all have to go through it. The reward is in coming out of it undamaged; whole. Or at least as close as possible. Ah, looking around here, I can't say that we made it.

RAL. Well, Sidney, I'd like to think that I brought something to the table when, in your youth, you were indigent and hungry. I feel as though I did everything in my power to ease the burdens you were born into -- with the exception of picking your parents. Sadly, that was out of my hands.

CAT. Alas! Boo-hoo. Ralf has his limitations. I thought, by the way you strut about the stage, that you were practically divine. It's refreshing to hear you admit to the possibility of a shortcoming. Perhaps you're indeed more fallible than I ever heard you confess to before. Maybe, dear Ralf, you're more akin to *me* than you would like to think.

RAL. I am, yes. It's true – we're very closely related. I've never distanced myself from our bloodline. However, we are different blood *types*. I'm a donor and you're a bleeder.

CAT. That was cold!

SID. Hey! Give it a break already! Ralf hit on something when he said he wasn't responsible for who my parents were. In fact, we can all consider ourselves blessed in being able to exonerate ourselves from that great guilt. I wish to God I did know who to blame; that sonofabitch is owed a class A ass-kicking. But it's all a crap shoot anyway. You might as well say, if my parents had had more money, they might have been able to own a TV and then I wouldn't be here. What the hell -- even so, there might have been a blackout one night. There's no winning. That said, I do appreciate all you did for me in my formative years, Ralf. Not that I'm taking anything away from you, Catfish -- your talents stood me in good stead later on, when it became necessary to navigate through the displeasures of adult reality.

CAT. Thank you, Sidney. I appreciate your sensitivity toward my feelings. My job has never been easy. A great many weighty responsibilities, you know. I have to support the more earthy demands of mankind's psyche -- and let me tell you, Ralf, it ain't easy. Dirt weighs a ton. I'm down in the trenches, while others I know are drifting about on clouds polishing their halo.

293

SID. If I might interrupt, Catfish – there's no need to be defensive. Or offensive, either. As I said, both of you have been necessary. Ultimately, it was up to me to handle the juggling act, to walk the tightrope, balancing between the two of you. Even if I were blind and stupid, I'd realize that I failed Circus 101. I was always prone to giving more weight to one of you or the other. As my grandmother used to remind me: Moderation in all things. But in trying to be what I thought Grandma meant by moderate, I often ended up leaning too far to the Ralf, which eclipsed my vision of the whole picture. Ralf's middle name, as I now know, is Naiveté. And looking at your surroundings only through Ralf's eyes, you end up running headlong into a brick wall that you didn't see on account of being told it wasn't there to begin with. I've learned to make adjustments to my vision. But it's a challenge. We're all born blind to the delusions that one day we come to see and then have to do battle with. Eventually we come to some point where we have to settle the score of no longer believing in everything we believe in.

CAT. You mean Santa Claus?

SID. Damn, Catfish! Every time I lapse into complacency on the question of your true temperament, all you have to do is open your damn mouth and your cruel streak flies out. It seems it's in your nature to bring out the combativeness in me. Maybe the shame of that falls on *my* head. Perhaps your normal inhumanity is nothing more than Nature itself, and I truly believe that Nature cannot possibly be wrong in its nature. Regardless, you annoy the living shit out of me! Your fault or not, reality is a depravity and you are the eternal messenger of bad tidings. Hurt feelings aside -- you can consider this an ass chewing!

CAT. That's some fighting spirit! Work with that, my boy.

RAL. I hope you're not going to turn the blame-game guns on *me*, Sidney.

SID. You're no more guilty than is Catfish. I take it that it's my responsibility to deal with accepting or resolving any disparities in your natures -- though there was no official assignment to that task, any more than there was an educational program showing me how to negotiate the caverns that lie between fantasy and reality; nonetheless, any failure to sort things out so they make sense belongs to me. On the other hand -- maybe it *is* Nature that's truly insane. A mistake that meanders with no real aim or purpose.

RAL. A wondering minstrel?

SID. Yeah, and I willingly followed, prancing and dancing and singing. At least for the first three years of my life. The spotlight was on me and it seemed as though mine was the only act on stage – especially for the two of those years when my grandmother was my audience and her home my playhouse. At that point in time I only had tunnel vision and was blind to the fact that both of you were stage hands controlling the ropes that bind. I wasn't an actor, I was a puppet.

CAT. Hrumph! I take umbrage at your veiled aspersions on my character. You are indeed still blind and ignorant – or still dancing with Ralf to that minstrel's ditty that you hear with only one ear. I hear your words between the lines – you suggest that I cut in to your sweet childish song-and-dance, as the perverse rapist of the innocent. I tell you in the strictest confidence that the concept of innocence is no more real than the idea of the Devil himself. Of that I give you my personal assurance. Yet you defame me as the ravisher of something that has never existed; this is the thanks I get for my brutal honesty. God, in his wisdom, has endowed me with those properties of mindfulness that assure the continuation of mankind, and it is a position I am proud to hold and maintain. I can't give a tweet for the sugar frostings that your dear ally Ralf goes about sprinkling on everything that fate brings to your table. He is a diminisher and, for the life of me, I do not understand my own tolerance for being housed with him, or with you, for that matter. I'll have you know that I have given guidance to many a substantial personage who, in turn, rose to fame and fortune under my tutelage.

RAL. Hitler comes to mind.

CAT. I resent your impertinence. To think that you would imagine me so crass as to be a name dropper. I'll have you know, I am a gentleman in every respect, down to the last detail. Even in the least of things, I cannot

295

be considered boorish -- why, I even remove the band from my cigar before smoking it so as to not give hint to my wealth or appear in any way to be flaunting my superiority.

RAL. Pardon me, Catfish, but I have to say -- Who gives a shit? (Something, I might add, that you're already full of.) We're all too well acquainted with your immortal qualities that are instinctual and therefore necessary for survival; but what I can find no shred of in you – and which I myself spare no effort in affording humanity – is the quality of mercy, or any attribute of the heart which --

CAT. Don't even go there! *Heart. Mercy.* Folderol! Superiority is the name of the game – *Survival of the Fittest* the catch phrase on which I hang my hat. The only reason you have a platform to expound from in the first place is because I, in my wisdom of knowing reality for the quagmired labyrinth that it is, provide the course, the path that assures the forward movement of all living things. Without that motion, all things would cease to exist. Life would decay and rot with stagnation. And where would you be? Not even a flicker in God's imagination.

SID. Okay! We're all duly impressed. I think we all understand our places. Maybe not our purpose, but that's a flaw inherent to all living things. I doubt trees contemplate their knots or skunks their stripes. But, above all, they don't go around spraying their pontifications in the faces of the disinterested. Catfish, you, most of all, know all there is to know about the nature of Nature. You should make more of an effort to mimic Nature's wavelengths – which, apart from their undeniable strength, are generally silent; perhaps with the exception of big winds.

CAT. I shall not pay you the courtesy of appearing to be insulted.

SID. Think nothing of it. God only knows I have to spend enough time overlooking your arrogance.

CAT. How diplomatic of you. I do believe you have softened over the years -- which is to say, you have stiffened against my touch. I might even suspect that you hold me in disdain. It was not so many years ago that I slept soundly with the assurance that my chokehold on you was unchallengeable. Now I suspect that, through the accumulation of time spent with Ralf, you have become tainted, corrupted beyond repair. I fear next you'll be sporting a Betty Crocker apron. You are not the man I knew, sadly, not the child I raised. When your stepfather got his grasp on you, you at least learned to be cruel and dogged, my kind of boy. A man's man in the making. However, you were not the best material I had to work with. I think you were too well born. Those pesky genes, you know, they can get in the way of my best efforts. I was proud of the work I did, notwithstanding.

RAL. Even a dog will turn. Notwithstanding.

CAT. Ralf! I have done my damnedest to avoid direct contact with you, as it could only be confrontational in nature. I bow to the obvious. To any interested party – and, I assure you that, beyond us, none exists -- it may appear that you have won a soul, to couch it in the most childish of terms. But that doesn't mean that at any time or place have I displayed a white flag. White for me is always out of fashion. As is anything plain and clear. One of my greatest powers is to let my adversaries wallow in the false sense of security – but, uh . . . to say any more would be to show my hand. That being said -- or not -- I shall content myself with the fact that the fat lady hasn't finished singing yet. And . . . and by the way, Ralf . . . um . . . *your mama.*

RAL. Hmmmmm . . . .

SID. Children, children, will either of you ever be satisfied? You know, it might be something to consider that both of you – independently, of course -- take a hike. I mean, a vacation. I'm sure that neither one of you can remember the last century you took a day off. Believe me, the universe isn't going to cave in on itself in your absence. In fact – I'll say it -- I could use a break as well. That's not to say I'm not fond of your company or unappreciative of the fine work and effort that you have both extended in pulling me this way and that as if I were taffy. It just might be that I've simply outlived your usefulness.

CAT. I daresay, you couldn't possibly live without us. Oh! I do beg your pardon -- I didn't mean to step on your wing, Ralf, of course you can speak for yourself. As for my interests as well as yours, Sidney, you might as well consider stopping the blood flow to your brain. The very idea is absurd. You simply cannot amputate a portion of your history that you feel inconveniences you. Things are what they are, whether you like them or not. God knows, as long as I've lived, I've had to deal with the most abhorrent of things, not to mention never-ending time itself that at times feels as though it's crawling on its hands and knees. As a lad, I had only reptiles to amuse myself with. I speak with vast experience when I tell you that spending millions of years doing little more than chewing on vegetation was not only the acme of boredom but a black hole in time that prompted me to better myself that I might achieve the better.

RAL. Speaking of boring, is this story going to take you a million years to tell? I'm fresh out of carrots to gnaw on.

CAT. As I was saying, can you possibly imagine my excitement as I came into my teen years with the advent of mammals, especially the meat eaters. And as far as the birth of man was concerned, I could not even begin to exaggerate my exuberance. Best sex I ever had. Mm.

RAL. I just knew, when you got started, this was somehow going to end up in the gutter. I'm not sure you've ever risen out of it.

SID. Ralf, equal time for all. Isn't justice and equality your thing?

RAL. Sorry, you're absolutely right. Please, go on.

CAT. Very good, Ralf. Remember to use your nice manners, as long as you're on a mission to shove them down everyone else's throat. I was about to say that the passage of millions of years has afforded me an education. One that is far more steeped in worldly experiences than can be expected from the likes of a novice moralist Johnny Come-Lately, like our Ralf. His sole purpose in life, it seems, is to be the gatekeeper of the Pleasure Palace of Fantasy – that is, to keep the vaults of its treasury always open and the stream of fool's-gold flowing out. Wishes, pipe-dreams, speculations, superstitions, airy beliefs, helium-filled hopes – the currency of fools. I tell you, it does not stand with me. These trinkets cannot be self-supporting in the natural and healthy course of evolution. In structure, they are too

298

flimsy to withstand the force of a spider's breath. They are nothing more than a childish web of false security. In the evolution of a healthy psyche, I maintain, Fantasy has no business mingling with Reality!

RAL. You have proof of this?

CAT. I confess that I am far from being a scientist, but I am certainly not ignorant when it comes to understanding the model of evolution. Been there, done that. For millennia. Indeed, I have the advantage of knowing the structure from the ground up. There's not a brick, sill, or wall that I'm not on the most intimate terms with, down to being on a first name basis with the termites.

RAL. Not a scientist, just a know-it-all.

SID. Ralf, I swear sometimes I think your role is more like the Devil's advocate than the confidante of angels.

CAT. Gentlemen, if you please . . . I am merely laying out the case that my importance is far from being self-declared, as *others* might perceive it to be. While I imagine that it must be exhilarating to stand on the highest rung of the ladder, Ralf, I cannot claim that privilege for myself – *but,* needless to say, you need all the ascending steps to support the highest one. With regard to maintaining that lower weight-bearing structure, I hardly need blush at taking my credit. Personalities aside, you must consider the facts in the light of reality. These are the facts: All of life was founded, and is still grounded, in the basest of functions and principles. *All of life* includes the self-exalted race of *Homo sapiens. Sapiens* – in reference to their marvelous brains. This brain, of the most advanced design, is equipped with *three* functional compartments, rated from lowest to highest. Yet all are rooted in one primal process, unchanged by time and just as valid today as it was three hundred thousand years ago. Hence its functions. The cranial nerve: I shit. The cerebellum: I know where to shit. The cerebrum: Thank God I know where to shit.

RAL. I'm not surprised. I knew you were full of shit!

SID. Please, I think he's trying to make a point.

299

RAL. Yeah, I know. We grow up and we all enjoy taking a good shit.

CAT. I'm simply stating that, in the structure of evolution, the cellar floor supports the attic roof. In any given time, in any given level within that structure, not a lot happens beyond one living thing eating another living thing. Eating, of course, ends in shitting. A to B. But -- with the advent of the higher chambers of the brain getting into the act, something new came into play: emotions and perceptions -- such as cruelty. Now we have a faculty that supersedes the mere act, that goes beyond the simple function of excreting what you've eaten. A faculty that must contend with perceiving, remembering, thinking, and feeling. Processes that make the creature newly vulnerable. In need of self-protection. I've been on this from the beginning, and I've risen to the task. In short, my friends, of the three of us, I am the most superior. The armor that protects the living breathing id from harm. I am the experience that quells harmful emotions. I block out the emotional sewage that causes instability. I am the fortress strong that protects you from the beasts of emotion that wander through the darkness of your subconscious. You sleep better for the sake of me.

RAL. Thank you, I'm almost asleep now.

SID. Damn, Catfish -- you almost had me going there for a moment. I started to believe in the idea that you've truly nurtured and protected me. Brother! What a crock of bullshit. My memory isn't that fraudulent that I'm ready to take anything you have to say at face value. I think you're sneaky and crafty -- and I'm borrowing my euphemistic politeness from your nemesis. What you've touched on may have some merit and credibility, but not nearly enough to move me to feel gratitude – much less to fall down and worship you. These things you mention as benefits you've bestowed are more like accidents, by-products, not intentions. If I shit on the grave of my enemy and the grass grows better for the act, does the act become good in its intention? I might well see you as the personification of evil itself, owing to your ability to bend facts while glorifying yourself in the process as if you weren't a serf to God like the rest of us. And that pronouncement comes directly from my experiences with you. Then again, that's a matter of memory, and memories are manufactured in the present moment, as opposed to being a tape on playback. On the off chance that

300

my memory may, at this point, be biased, I'll refrain from giving you the lambasting I'm so sorely tempted to level you with.

CAT. You are too kind, sir. Let me add that I think, for the moment, we must mutually indulge one another's whimsies, if for no other reason than that we have been judged to be not in our proper collective minds. There is no reason, at this point in time, to judge each other too hastily.

RAL. Oh brother, I think I'm gonna be sick.

SID. Come on, Ralf, let's not get melodramatic.

RAL. If no one minds me putting my two cents in, I'd like to buy two minutes of air time – if you and Catfish can spare it. *No reason to judge each other*, he says – but I'm sensing that, in some covert manner, I'm being faulted in the performance of my job. I have a handicap to overcome -- I'm an extension of Catfish. I'm an outgrowth in an upward direction, toward higher power -- but my feet are of the same clay, molded of the same earth you and Catfish are so grounded to. I'm the higher end, not the hired hand. Whether you recognize it or not, I'm always working independently for the benefit of you.

Sidney, the first three years of your life were my bailiwick. Unfortunately, I admit, I was too nearsighted when it came to my guardianship of you in presupposing that you were in the good hands of your angelic grandmother, who was one of my biggest fans. I fell on my ass in overlooking your mother's ignorance, if not selfishness, in hitching your star to the likes of your stepfather Jim. He himself was the personification of Catfish, and Catfish owned the house, and I wasn't even allotted closet space.

SID. There's no reason to reproach yourself. If things could have been different, they probably would have been. You enriched me for those few years, and there's more substance to those memories than just being memories. They are the bricks and mortar of my foundation. Why shouldn't I have found my footing in the rich soil of fantasy and its magic, where you and my grandmother planted me? What were adults otherwise doing right? At age three, I could not have been more grateful for having been born a child as opposed to one of the Big Ones. Even then I detected a friction in their lives that I had no understanding of. You led me to wonder if their history would predict my future. For the insight and guidance you gave me, I'm indebted more to you than I am to Catfish.

CAT. In defense of myself as well as my dignity, I take the greatest affront at the criminal mystique I sense in the mention of my name. I would have thought --

SID. I apologize for any hurt feelings. In no way do I wish to malign you unintentionally; if anything, you do that better than I could every time you open your mouth. No one is asking you to change your spots. I may not like you, but that doesn't mean that I disrespect your value. I fear you may be judging me as being judgmental. But, if you're so inclined to better yourself, as you've professed, then shut the hell up for a minute that you might better listen to your betters. Are you capable of doing that?

CAT. I'm – I'm humbled. Please . . . continue.

SID. If we are to continue as cellmates and maintain any sense of good neighborliness, then it's imperative that we understand where we stand. I'm feeling ill at ease with the perception that both of you are acting out through some sense of failing on your respective parts. You, Ralf, seem far too apologetic, and you, Catfish, seem overly defensive, even for you. It's as if you suspect that someone has discovered your underbelly. As B. Franklin once said: A fish smells from the polite manners down. Such politeness among family, methinks, doth protest too much. It doth suggest that someone's got something to hide.

CAT. Dear boy, I wouldn't be me if I didn't.

RAL. Not being you sounds like a great idea. And by the way, whatever you're hiding, I don't need to see it.

SID. Let me tell you both – your incessant bickering could drive a teacup to drink. Nevertheless, I have to admit to being rather fond of both of you.

CAT. Oh, ta-ta.

302

SID. Therefore, I can't help feeling sorry for you two for being so fond of your separate corners. But I'm not sure it's a good idea to introduce a sentiment so potentially destructive as pity into our conversation.

CAT. Pity? At last! A dish I can relish.

RAL. Just a minute! That's a nutriment for the better -- you have no right to lick your chops!

SID. Aha! I think at last we have reached an un-impasse. You are on the border of realizing what the problem is between you. When you come to understand yourselves as well as I do, you will realize that you're the same goddamn stick, just opposite ends that both refuse to recognize the other end. God! You're two of the oldest children I've ever known, with your sibling rivalry.

RAL. Nonsense!

CAT. Ridiculous on the face of it! Sidney, my boy, I fear you are once again attempting to wriggle out of your conditioning – your programmed perceptions, responses, and reactions -- which I labored so hard to custom fit for you. The very idea --

SID. Catfish! Are you so incapable of keeping a secret? For God's sake, surreptitiousness is what you're all about, isn't it? You're slipping, buddy. I'm only too well aware that conditioning is your stealth weapon of choice, your hook, line, and sinker. You should realize by now that an educated consumer such as myself is going to check out your references before buying into your shit. I put in a call to the Better Up-Yours Bureau some time ago. That said, there's nothing you're selling that I'm wishing to buy. But – damn it, I'm digressing. Or maybe you sensed a comeuppance coming, and you contrived to change the subject. Point scored to you, Catfish.

Actually, I brought the subject of pity up because it provides the perfect illustration of how our threesome works. The two of you come in force against one another in a common cause and butt heads, with me squarely in the middle. The sizzle you hear is the result of me being the pancake caught between the griddle and the spatula – which represent the two faces of pity, one worn by each of you. That wonderful gift of being able to feel pity, no matter which of you was the presumed donor, came into use, I remember sharply, in my seventh-grade homeroom, which was also the music room. It had wrap-around bleacher seating. Seated directly across from me was a fat ugly blimp-shaped boy who looked very much like the back end of a garbage truck. Catfish, I think you know who I'm talking about.

CAT. Indeed I do. Since that time, he and I have spent many a year in the calaboose. In fact, the lad had harbored me from the beginning. I am exceedingly proud of him.

SID. As I was saying, the poor misfit was sixteen at the time and apparently too stupid to know how to drop out of school. He was the favored fodder for the teacher, who delighted in ridiculing him at every chance that arose. The class would be kept in stitches, and the blimp would nervously giggle too, more out of defensive embarrassment than the ability to laugh at himself. Ring any triangles, Catfish?

CAT. You have my fullest attention.

RAL. Catfish, I think your pride is shameful.

SID. Not so fast, Ralf, you're knee-deep in this as well. It was by means of your good intention that you bestowed the capability of pity in me, which, in turn, I demonstrated by not laughing at the loser. That pity was commiseration born of my own sense of pitifulness, having been subject to that same type of ridicule by assorted others at different times. In my heart, I was putting myself in the fellow's place. Then our eyes met -- and my lack of snickering, coupled with the P-word conveyed by my glance, quelled his laughter and turned his face into something that might resemble Catfish's ass. I was trying in earnest to lend him some support, but I don't think he saw it that way. Have you ever stopped your car to remove a snake, who was sunning itself in the middle of the road, to keep it from harm? I know you don't drive, but I'm trying to make a point here. It bites you! It simply doesn't understand your good intentions. Only that you're fucking with its serenity. Well, this two-hundred- pound num-nut chose to bite me every time we crossed paths. Once, he one-handed me around the throat and slammed me into a concrete wall. Another time, he came up from behind me and kicked me in the ass just as hard as he could. It hurt! But not as much as when he turned to his buddy and said: "I hate that kid! I don't know why." I didn't either; not for many years. Then one day, while pondering the enigmatic events, I realized it was because I had dared to pity him. He himself couldn't tag the feeling for what it was: an offer of kindness. He just knew that I was fucking with his serenity. So you see, my fellow creatures, no matter your intentions, whether they be maniacal or full of grace, they corrupt me. You are each what you are and I'm the center of where you both meet. It doesn't leave me with the dirty end of the stick. I *am* the dirty stick.

CAT. I fear you become insufferable when you allow Ralf to wag your tongue for you, Sidney. I do not in any way wish to aspire to become a target for the darts of sympathy. I lose all patience with you when you start smelling of that upstart Ralf.

SID. And what does your nose tell you when it comes to the fact that Ralf is your offspring?

CAT. Before I point out that such matters are none of your concern, I would say that one cannot pick one's children. In matters of love-making, it is first of all essential to not be in love. I never marry my lovers or, for that matter, have anything to do with them after the fact. As the highly-adulated 20th-century Germanic leader noted: The unmarried demigod (or demagogue), admitting of no peers, is more readily worshipped and unquestioningly followed.

SID. Before you go further, let me say -- and this brings Ralf back into the picture again -- because of the balancing act that I have to pull off every time my mind takes a deep breath, it would be so much easier for me to decipher the incoming load of bullshit if you would just drop the pretenses. I didn't just get out of bed. I've been awake for some time. And yes, your relations are none of my concern any more than Ralf's are. But it is through your reactions and interactions to one another that I draw my behavior. Would you have me replicate your doings without first watering them down with Ralf's piss? And you need not answer that. I'm simply bringing it to your attention that I am fully aware of the fact that you are very well educated -- it's just that your IQ is somewhat in question. You are indeed crafty, without a doubt. You are a master of deceit, the king of supposition, the top of the heap when it comes to emulating. For myself, I'm grateful. These talents that you have exposed and rendered to me have been of the greatest use to me in the most dire of times. But that's not to say they didn't contribute to the direness to begin with.

CAT. May I applaud you, and therefore afford myself a small pat on the back. Your compliments are warmly received. I cannot tell you how often my efforts are overlooked. It is unreasonable to think that civilization would have gone further than crawling out of the swamp without my contributions. Just the skill of emulating is one of the most essential faculties endowed by moi. Children would never have become adults without mimicking. How would they know that they were supposed to stand and walk and run so as to not get eaten? Can you imagine a race of crawlers?

SID. I don't have to put too much effort into imagining. Some of my best friends have been night crawlers. As far as mimicking goes, I've always held you in the highest esteem for your agility. The chameleon abilities that you bestowed on me were worth their weight in forged passports.

RAL. Well, if the two of you are going to start kissing, I'm sure there must be somewhere else I'm supposed to be with something else I'm supposed to be doing.

SID. Relax, Ralf, you're losing sight of the fact that we're all equal partners in all things. Though, God knows, I don't always see the equality myself; how many times has Catfish taken me out for drinks and then he's nowhere to be found the next morning to share the hangover. But it's not surprising, he's full of disparities.

RAL. Well, he's full of something.

CAT. I am not here.

SID. He's such a kidder. Look, Ralf, you two are always facing off, but I've been around back and seen CAT.'s other side – the lighter side of his darkness. He's got quite the sense of humor – a wellspring that I've drawn from many times myself in the darkest of moments. There's good in everything if you're willing to dig deep enough.

RAL. Fine, let me know when you've dug deep enough and I'll help you bury him.

CAT. I'll be damned if I'll stand for any more of your impertinence! Here Sidney is trying to bridge the distance between us and you're continually trying to burn it down before it's ever a blueprint. I myself have taken steps forward to meet you halfway, although I don't give a tinkle for those codes of society that you represent. You are so high up that you have lost sight of the fact that you were born into a softer world than I. Furthermore, you ignore the fact that it was through my diligence and sweat that you were given the cushy landing pad for your unblistered candy ass to land on. And what is my thanks? You squat on my domain and erect fences of the new world order and outlaw me as if I were the rustler of the two-legged cattle you refer to as deserving, if not somehow divine. I am closer to God than you might believe and I'm sure he would judge you as I do. *You* are the alien! Before your presence and agenda graced the world, only the strong survived. There was reason for disease. Through God's wisdom, the weak perished. I furthered the cause by giving mankind the aptitude to make war so that the last man standing could set and dictate the standards. What have you brought to the fold? Democracy? What has that wrought? Social Security, welfare, food stamps, free hospitalization for infants who had no business being born in the first place, pension plans for the tired? For the weak, I declare. God! How I long for the supermen of yesterday. The Spartans were my superlative disciples, bar none. The world was orderly because people were subject to order, plain and simple. For the life of me, I cannot find a level plain on which to meet you!

SID. I am that plain. I'm the fulcrum. You two keep hanging your butts out off either side of the see-saw, trying to weight it down to your own side. Here's a sample of how that strategy plays out. When ol' Stepdad Jim came on the scene, it seems he parked himself on your side of the board, Catfish, a champion of the good ol' status quo, defended by the willful mind and the strong fist, both closed. Setting himself up as the stalwart paragon of righteousness for my callow self to emulate. Quite a challenge for you, Ralf, to hold your own ethereal weight and keep me from sliding into Jim's lap.

CAT. Yes – getting back to Jim – please prattle on.

SID. I'm too calloused for the memory of my stepfather to cause me to cringe -- but I'm too sensitive not to. Score a point to each of you, CAT. and RAL.

CAT. Point taken. Do continue.

SID. Jim was seething about the news that the Jew family across the street was moving out and had sold their house to a bunch of Coloreds that was moving on up. Moving up was what Jim had supposed our household had done when, in the natural order of things, he had gotten us out of the dirt-poor white trash neighborhood and into a version of the American Dream. Now here "they" were, unAmericans who had no entitlement to dreams. As the family across the street were packing their last belongings into their car, my stepfather and two other neighbors were seated curbside on our lawn yelling obscenities. *You dirty kikes! You nigger lovers! You sellouts – burn in hell!* Catfish, you must have been -- excuse the expression -- in seventh heaven. But, for every fish you catch, another gets away. Ralf, was that you tipping the scales? Under Jim's very shadow, I came to be more comfortable among blacks than whites. And over the years, most of my lovers, not to mention my second wife, were Jewish.

CAT. Sidney, you love to hear yourself talk – blah, blah, blah – a big tub of sentimental slop.

SID. Speaking of slop, here comes His Majesty Axel . . . it must be lunch time already. It's time to go covert now and continue this little chat later.

--- *So, Mr. O'Riley, guess what time of day it is.*

--- I was rather hoping you might have forgotten, you know.

--- *Not a chance. I just love the opportunity of serving you.*

--- What's the shit of the day?

--- *Same old, same old: used-to-be-meat, used-to-be-vegetable. If you're a good*

308

boy and lick your tray clean, I'll see to it that you get dessert. A nice little Dixie cup of sand. That should cover all your important food groups -- animal, vegetable, and mineral.

---   You are kinder to me than words can express, you are truly among God's chosen deviants.

I'm being escorted through the same puke-green-colored halls which I'm sure are meant to heighten my sense of appetite. Ah, and yes, yet another reprieve; I get to eat in the common room to ensure that there's room for everyone -- my herd of Florence-Nightinmares: Nurse Rita and Otto and Axel. It takes the whole crowd to make sure I don't stab myself in the eye with my plastic spoon or beat myself to death with my fiberglass tray. I'd settle for just beating off, but I'm camera shy. I wonder if this tray would fit up Axel's ass? It's too bad I licked all the grease off it. It would be fun to try anyway.

Trays, yeah, trays. What I'd like to do . . . yeah, I did. I remember it was one of those days. One of those big days. That day I traded in my Ralf Get Out of Reality card for a charter membership in the Catfish Club for Wayward Worms. Every worm has its day, the day the worm turns.

It was back in seventh grade again and I was in the cafeteria. I was returning my empty tray when I observed that the few people ahead of me were being tripped by the deftly-placed feet of one of our other sixteen-year-old two-hundred-pound sit-ins. As with all bullies, he had adhered to him his bevy of minor thugs who would applaud with resounding laughter every time another hapless patsy and tray would go flying.

I was suddenly seized with enlightenment, although this condition was as perishable as ice cream in August, but somehow it was finally a square peg actually fitting into a round hole. I had a flashback of the very present past: my mother had me strip and stand in a dry tub, then commenced to whip the holy living shit out of me with a belt. A pronouncement, I'm guessing, that she was taking a leave of absence from her station of being my mother and joining the Jim–team. I thought without a doubt that my own screams would be the last thing I ever heard on earth. Kind of like hearing angel wings, without the euphoria. Lots of without.

With my grey matter being displaced by something closer to walnut matter, I came to the conclusion that this was it. No more, brother -- not from my mother! Not from anybody! With all the brain capacity of a worm or a nut, I instantly formulated a plan. When it became my turn to return my tray – and, sure enough, there were those protruding thirteens (the shoes, not the IQ, which was smaller) -- I allowed myself to be tripped and, in great melodramatic fashion, fell towards the perpetrator and emptied my tray squarely on his chest. In a Catfish moment, I had to wonder if I had ever done a more stupid thing in my life, about to end. No, this was it. Unlike the response to the victimizations that went before me, no laughter arose from the crowd. As my heart vacated my body in search of some other better place to be, I stood there helplessly awaiting my fate. Then the assailant began to rise, and rise, and rise -- the time it took him to erect himself could have been measured on a sun dial. Suddenly his trashcan face broke into a broad incongruous smile and he reached out and shook my hand. From that day on I had no trouble; the edict had been passed on down. I was someone to be respected. Catfish has his moments.

--- *Come on, Mr. O Riley, let's go to the little boys' room and do our business, daylight's burning. If you want to get in another hour in the garden, you better move it, let's move it!*

Jesus, I hate those grating words: little boys' room. I spent almost my entire school life in that room. That was on the days that I was not-so-ill, so that I could go to school in the first place. Diarrhea was the name of the game. Other kids got to play dodgeball. Other kids got an education. I got to study plumbing. But my 'dad' taught me that doctors were for the seriously ill, like those who suffered from death. My mother told me to pray and everything would work itself out. It didn't, it projectiled its way out. After nine years of this shit, someone in the school administration must have threatened my parents with a charge of dereliction, probably the school janitor who had to clean out the toilets. I spent my thirteenth birthday in the hospital. Diagnosis: nerves. Yeah, the nerve of some people. The ingrate who showed his gratitude by reacting adversely to the honored station of whipping boy, and that station was conferred on me at every opportunity that I was in arm's length.

310

As I plop down on the cold seat, I reflect on what it was like to be in the hot seat. That would be my chair at the kitchen table to the right-angle of my stepfather. It was his throne, from which he could serve out his brand of food for thought. No generic brands there. It was all in the name of Me and Mine. He brought to the table that taut thin line that made eating as pleasurable as shitting. He always started his meal in the same old fashion, not with prayer but with taciturn meditation. He sat quietly and willfully, staring at me through the corners of his eyes that were as grey as steel and just as cold. With all the anticipation of a spider waiting for its prey, Jim would patiently wait for the smallest infraction of etiquette, such as a spilled drop of milk or a pea gone astray. Excuse enough to backslap me across the face. If my mother didn't wish to be a part of the drama and exited, that was acknowledged with yet another and more brutal slap accompanied by: "See what you've done to your mother *now?*"

RAL. What was the first thing? Was she expecting someone else at your birth?

--- *What's that you said, Mr. O'Riley?*

--- Nothing, I was just talking to myself.

--- *Well, that's as good a reason to be here as any. Let's hurry it up there, the less time you spend is the more time I have to do more important things.*

RAL. Probably reading *Mein Kampf.*

--- *What's that you say?*

--- Will you keep your goddamn voice down!

--- *I wasn't yelling. Yet! Let's go!*

--- By the way, have you got a toothpick or a stiletto handy? I think I have a pebble stuck in my teeth.

Tra-la, tra-la, it's off to the garden we go.

CAT. Don't the two of you ever tire of sitting around in the fresh air and sunshine when you have the cozy primal dim and dank cell to enwrap yourselves in? Ah, it so brings me back to the days of cave living. Back before man strove to distance himself from me. Those indeed were the good old days.

RAL. I can speak to dark and dank, back in the days when I occupied a dead body for more years than I wish to account, waiting for a new host.

SID. And I can speak of boring, which coincidentally coincides with Ralf's tale. It was the same place, the same time. Although both of you have been with me from the start -- or I should better qualify that by saying the *indwelling spirit* of you has been with me from the beginning but the *selves* of you, the *manifest sprites* themselves, came to me at a later time. The place that I'm recollecting is where I came to discover Ralf's consciousness, which had been gnawing at my interior to get outside myself and manifest its purpose. You, Catfish, on the other hand, have just been gnawing at me for little reason that I can discern -- beyond the primal art of survival, anyway.

CAT. I stand on my record. You're still here, aren't you? You've been enough trouble to me that it might have behooved me to cut the strings long ago. I certainly wouldn't object to the idea of having a little more free time. In fact, the idea of joining Axel in his reading is a thing I might very well enjoy.

RAL. I love the open-endedness of the word 'thing', I wish you would get lost in it.

CAT. Not that I should wish to lift the focus off myself, but Sidney's tale might be slightly more of interest to me than your feeble attempts at dull and insulting witticisms.

SID. Well, I'll tell it then. It was the best of ages, it was the worst of ages. I was fourteen. I had finally come to the understanding that, though I had been born a child, I was not destined happily to remain one; but, for all my experience, I was not yet a man. I had been born into a family and had lost it. I had been conscripted into another family and had lost it. I had been loaned to another family and had lost it. Now I was on an installment plan (soon to end) with yet another family.

CAT. Did you ever stop to think that families aren't your thing, or are you still looking for stop-loss options?

RAL. You know, Catfish, sometimes I think your head is up your ass; but, personally speaking, I've always had a difficult time telling them apart in the first place.

SID. You guys want to hear this or not?

CAT. Shh!

RAL. SHH!!

SID. As I was saying, falling through three families – on top of losing my grandmother the same year my mother married Jim, when I was four – during the summer when I was fourteen I ended up on the doorstep of my mother's sister and her family in Michigan. At that point, the walls of my psyche weren't much thicker than toilet paper. It didn't seem as though I could handle much more out of the ordinary. It was okay, though -- my aunt and uncle were super extremely ordinary. No shit to be had there. *Zzzzzzzz.* What was to become of me after my arranged six-week stay, no one could say or seemed very concerned about, including my mother, as long as it didn't cost her any money. The first two weeks went by relatively quickly without too much to complain about. The family (which included two cousins) took me out every day, rain or shine, for 18 holes of golf, their long-time passion and my first introduction to the game. That abruptly ended when, on each of the last two days, I sank a hole-in-one on the same green. That's why it was the last two days. My family, who had played all their lives, being older than me, had never accomplished the feat even once among them. I think they held the expense of having to purchase new clubs, to replace the ones they broke while gnashing their teeth, against me. But through my Jim training, I was already acutely aware that whatever fault might be discernible in anything was, by cosmic consensus, my fault.

RAL. You know, maybe it's time you let that kind of shit go.

CAT. What! You would take the bread and butter right out of my mouth? Think of the years of conditioning you are willing to throw right out the window. What are you thinking -- I work for nothing?

RAL. I think your work *is* nothing.

SID. Gentlemen, if I might be allowed to continue.

RAL. Of course.

CAT. By all means.

SID. The door to my budding career in golf having snapped shut, I found the portal to boredom now flung wide open. My aunt's household, as I mentioned, held nothing to engage a 14-year-old imagination for five minutes, let alone another month. The house squatted in a new subdivision on erstwhile farm land where, I think, the main crop had been tedium. What could I do? I took to wandering restlessly into the neighboring fields, each day farther afield into the flat vastness. One day I found myself walking in a treeless sea of endless grass which resonated with an irritating buzz. It might have been the sound of vegetation baking in the sultry summer heat, or maybe the simple communication among insects: *Is it hot enough for ya?*

RAL. When you start hearing bugs talking, you don't know what to expect might happen next.

CAT. I'm waiting for *something* to happen.

SID. I'm just getting to it. I was blazing a path through an unexplored stretch of meadow when, seemingly out of nowhere, as though it had been dropped into the tall weeds at random from some other place, there was a small derelict time-worn shed. As it sat there adrift in the waving grass, it looked to me like a tiny Dixie cup bobbing on an expansive ocean. To my parched imagination, this find was like tripping over a full canteen in the middle of a desert. I relished the mystery of it. My senses engaged, along with my curiosity. The structure was in sorry shape -- the few slats of siding still hanging, out of habit, on the skeletal framework had seen better days, the sun, wind, and rain having taken their toll. The only hint of color was the blood stains of nails that Nature had extracted from the weathered

314

boards. There was an opening where a door had once hung. But the interior was shadowed by the decaying tin roof. I paused at the threshold, wanting a better look at what was inside.

RAL. Go in! You're seeking something. Maybe you'll find it . . . .

CAT. No! Under no circumstances should you enter. You're looking for trouble, young sir. You're crossing the line.

SID. Well, there *was* a tug of war in my brain, between my selves. One of us won, and I went in. The shed was filled to the rafters with things that were hard to identify, objects that had fallen into the mold and cobwebs of organic despair and human neglect, tools that were vested in a future gone awry. No less organic, or neglected, were the remains of a human being, evidently once a man, lying supine on an otherwise unremarkable rustic table, and somehow no more startling than the quaint and enigmatic implements reposing around him. He seemed to have been lying there inert for a very long time, not missed enough for anyone to have come looking for him, and now not much left of him.

I was drawn, by more than adolescent fascination with the macabre, to examine and ponder what chance had put before me. First, why was this man lying here? How did he meet his end? No pitchfork protruding from his chest, no cause for his demise that I could see -- just that he looked tired. Who was he? I stared at the remnants of his face, which looked more like a featureless withered leather mask. I could just see well enough through the vacant eye sockets to realize that the brain cavity was empty but for an abandoned mouse nest. Eyeless, tongueless, deprived of sight, sound, and thought. I found myself choreographing feelings and emotions and maybe even dead dreams, and projecting them into the hollow. I suddenly felt on the cusp of -- what? Was I on the edge of a dream? Was any of this real? Me, for instance? I felt I had been lifted to a higher plane. A level above myself. Beyond myself. Somehow, in some way, I had ejected a great lump of my selfish core. Now I perceived a rending in my chest that I fully recognized as an illusion, but as real nonetheless. Out through the rip emerged the manifested substance of a higher self. Though we hadn't been formally introduced, I recognized him as Ralf -- the real-live baby-sitter as opposed to the walkie-talkie monitor version. He had come into his own at last.

RAL. What a moment that was, Sidney!

CAT. Personally, I suspect it was a recurring bout of diarrhea.

RAL. I suppose *your* coming-out party was closer to resembling the Second Coming.

CAT. No, nothing so garishly radiant, certainly nothing as dramatic as your revelation. I guess you could say I just sort of oozed on out.

RAL. In other words, you just got too big for your britches and could no longer contain your grandiosity – of both mind and body. You outgrew your hooded sheet.

CAT. Please allow me to ignore that. It's true, I would have much preferred to remain in the dark recesses of the interior, undetected. That's how and where I do my best work.

RAL. That's how vampires operate. They too prefer the dark.

CAT. It was through God's wisdom that I be stealthy by design; no one, but no one, ever pays attention to the obvious. Unfortunately, back in 1973, our host had come to recognize me. You might recall the day. You and I were arguing about whether Sidney should spend that beautiful day out and about or stay in and drink so he could better wallow in the melodramatic shit du jour. That's when he suddenly realized that the fault was not in his stars. There had to be more to himself than what he saw when he looked in the mirror. He sought *me*. He found me. But he's never conquered me.

RAL. If I remember that period correctly, it's hard to pinpoint that exact day. They were all pretty much the same. That's probably why I don't have your birthday marked on my calendar.

SID. It's okay, Ralf, all this nit-picking isn't going to make water any wetter or less muddy. I was grateful for his coming out. At last I could see the enemy as it was. I knew I always had your light as a weapon, but I never understood what direction to wield it in. Of course, that never made anything better. That was the battle of the windmills. It's taken all this time to realize that the battle plan all along should have been one of tolerance and compromise. Not blood and guts. I am. You are. We are. I am the skeleton, Ralf the muscles, and you, Catfish, the nervous system. In reality, there exists no tipping of the scales when balancing light against dark. Tipping can only occur when you put the thumb of unknowing on one tray or the other. Until that day of reason, I spent my time hiding from the self who was then chasing me, not knowing if it was you or Catfish. Scared knows no reason. I got so good at hiding that the idea of hiding got hidden in the hiding. Back then, my choice of hiding places was beer. A case a day will keep reality away.

CAT. I remember very well. The gent at the liquor store actually shed a tear when you told him you were moving away. Knowing Ralf's influence on you, I'm surprised he didn't talk you into telling the poor chap that you would be willing to commute for your daily supply.

SID. I have to laugh. It's not as though I didn't give the idea some consideration. Poor guy. I really hate committing any action that causes harm to another.

RAL. Sometimes, Sidney, I think, you think with an intoxicated brain. And, you know, mush begets mush.

CAT. Ralf – making cautionary remarks about mush? The earth will tilt off its axis if hearts and flowers and sugary sweetness are deleted from your cup of tea.

RAL. No need to reach for your seatbelt. I was referring to the sludgy thinking begotten by a headful of sodden sponge. It's been known to interfere with a person's sense of direction, and good intentions don't come with a map.

SID. You may not be far off the mark there, Ralf, but booze was tonic to me –

RAL. I think you mean *toxic*. But please continue.

317

SID. Yes, as I was saying, my pickled state went a long way in helping my first marriage to self-destruct, and – to my own peculiar way of reasoning – made my second tolerable. As to my third, drink came close to acting as the executioner – but I was not the one who wielded the ax.

CAT. Ralf, you need not be staring at me out of the corner of your eye with that ridiculous smirk of yours whilst Sidney is phonating his self-described dilemmas that may or may have not been attributable to his over-use of beverages. Such doings were his choice, through his own free will. Yes, his free will – that faculty you so boastfully lay claim to, Sir Ralf, as adorning one of the exalted upper branches of our family tree, where you hold sway. *His* free will, *his* choice, to look for an alternative to reality inside a bottle. Tut! – hold your tongue. I won't hear a word – not so much as a whisper – suggesting that I have ever had a hand – not even a finger – in pointing any soul toward seeking oblivion – and certainly not by means of a bottle, a vial, a needle, a sniff, of any substance, legalized or illicit. No, that chicanery is entirely in your bailiwick, oh noble, self-congratulating Sir Ralf. Enticing fools to believe that not only are they *entitled* to attain to a higher power, but that they *can actually achieve it* – even if only through resorting to agents of delusion. That's your department, Mister.

My business is all about the striving – the energy in motion, the doing – that bears no false promises. The action, the effort *is* the attainment. Such a blank stare and furrowed brow, young Ralf. Let me put it plainly for you: it's about running, not about getting there. No – speak not, dear boy. I know your bent of thought. One strives toward the better . . . *attains it!* Ah! And then sees above him the shining light of the better still. There's always better still. But where is it? There's a world where Father Knows Best and all problems can be tidily dusted up in thirty minutes, minus commercials. And oh, those commercials – in thirty seconds or less you have no debt, no pet odor, no depression/arthritis/heartburn/diarrhea, no streaky countertops, but a really fast car and plenty of sex. You've been promised that your sins will be forgiven. Santa will fill your stocking, and blah blah happily ever after. What happens when Santa shows up as a skinny guy with a padded belly and a fake beard? When the shiny world is turned off with the click of a remote? Is there a Heaven? A lottery that you actually win? A happy sit-com marriage? *What?* I'm shocked. Embarrassed. Defiled. If I'm one of your silly protegés, that is. If I were, I would naturally

318

seek solace in the alternative reality I now see, not above me or around me, but in the bottom of a bottle. Ralf, don't you dare place those poor saps on my doorstep. If they fell down anywhere in my vicinity, it was you who placed the trap door in their path.

Cat got your tongue? Let me go back to the bigger picture. I myself am merely the lower bowels of evolution, not the sum total. Ralf picks up where I leave off. Please blame God for the design. I just work here. As for me, I'm far too politically correct – or should I say, prudent – to voice an opinion over flaws in the Divine Design. Lightning bolts protruding from my derrière would not be a good look for me, fashion plate that I am – as you couldn't possibly have failed to observe. If you wish to challenge God's blueprint, by all means you should – but outside of my company.

RAL. I'm beginning to understand why I find myself confined to this place we're in – sometimes I actually start to believe that you almost make sense. Although I have to say that the very thought of agreeing with you goes against my grain.

CAT. Tut-tut, I beg of you, no flattery please, it does not sit atop my digestion well. But now, Sidney, do tell us more of your experiences with the beverage, and especially the bits involving your wives. How did the sex figure in? I presume there was sex, surely.

SID. Booze in any form seemed to me a gift from heaven – or, if not, at least from a celestial suburb. Booze was the prime number (silent b), the divine anesthetic, the optimal alternative. It conferred on me a sense of being there without having to be there, feeling the emotion without it being heartfelt. It was great while it lasted. Ultimately, though, it proved to be some wry cosmic joke that never let you know the punch line: that you yourself are the joke. That's pretty funny. Of course, there's much more to it than that, but I don't want to get us lost in the forest of true lies that springs from the bog of inebriation. I was already deep into that woods at the time of my first marriage – which was actually quite fortunate, since I didn't really want to be married. But why go into all that? You guys know more about that shit than I do and you've never deemed it necessary to reveal any information to me – so why open that can of worms? I will say, though, that taking my bride to Bushy Hollow, CT did me or my marriage no favors. Being stuck in that so-called community just added another

319

layer of unhappiness – like moving a person with a raging case of poison ivy out of his leaky tent into a hornet's nest. My wife couldn't get out of there fast enough.

CAT. Not before you partook of the connubial pleasures inside the tent, I trust?

SID. No, there's not much connubial involvement when you marry your best friend.

CAT. What did he say?

RAL. No sex.

CAT. Oh.

SID. But before she took off, the Mrs. had more to contend with than my drinking habit. Early into our marriage, I became homesick for my old territory and the lifestyle that went with it. I started to stray.

CAT. At last! Is this where the sex comes in?

SID. Sorry – no. My straying was just from the tedium of Bushy Hollow, on my weekly Friday drive down to my old stomping grounds in Pleasantville, two hours south, where I would kill the afternoon and night drinking and playing pool. This was something my wife certainly didn't deserve, never mind have to tolerate. Not only did she put up with all of it but, more often than not, she would make the trip too, just to spend some hours with me. God knows why. To make a long drunken episode as short as it deserves to be, our marriage ended with a whimper.

CAT. You did mention that you married three times; what about your second? Surely you didn't make the same mistake, and there was some sex involved, wasn't there?

SID. I was coming to that. But before I tied the knot in the noose again, I took the time to have a few drinks – a few years of drinks, and as many rounds of lovers to go with them.

CAT. Ah, lovers.

SID. But I'm not one to kiss and tell, so I'll get back to your interest in my next marriage. One day, when I was sober, or nearly so, I met my second wife, Gretchen. Due to a lack of common sense or booze, I found myself roped into a longer relationship than usual, for me, which is to say, one that lasted longer than thirty days. This led to the added complication of getting pregnant. Of course, this all happened in NYC, where I had been living very happily and thought I would go on doing so forever. But, for the sake of the new wee one, we moved to the country. That bizarre hinterland, exactly where my first marriage had landed me.

CAT. There's no place like home, even if it is hell.

SID. I don't want to mislead or excite you with the idea that this will be an unfolding tale of horror. I mean, the move was only a part of it. The story of my second marriage doesn't start where I left off telling. Actually, that's where it came to a close – when my wife got pregnant. Suddenly, she had forgotten the process that got her that way in the first place.

CAT. So – no sex.

RAL. Our boy was a saint.

CAT. He suffered torture for his faith.

SID. If I had any faith I could turn to over the next sixteen years, it was the liquid kind, as the marriage slugged and sloshed on and on. We slept in the same bed, out of habit and lack of house-space, but we were peas under each other's mattress. Quite often, our mutual irritation was not so discreet as that. We kept the sparring gloves handy and, by the end, we were getting into round six-hundred-and-two. But never mind about winners and losers. The truth is that, looking back, I regret the time spent by Gretchen in having to combat me. However, it was a two-way street; I was constrained to do battle with her sense of entitlement, under which any pleasure, however small, had to be dispensed from her throne. My battle gear usually came home in a brown paper bag. It could break me out of any siege so that, without my ever having to leave the house – or, rather, my studio out in back – I was gone. Yes, indeed, I became quite the escapologist. An excellent one. So good, in fact, that at last I was able to escape the marriage – though that isn't a credit I'm due; that was Gretchen's doing, more than mine.

CAT. Ho-hum. Are we done there? Moving along to your third marriage –

SID. – to Barbie – yes, Catfish, there was sex. Lots of it. So much, in fact, that after the passing of these ten years, I'm still exhausted by the memory of it.

CAT. But such an exhilarating exhaustion, is it not? For all the so-called enrichments that Ralf touts as state-of-the-art contributions to your well-being, is it not the more primal satisfactions that are the most rewarding and memorable, after all?

RAL. Oh, Catfish, you think with the mind of an antique dealer. Everything has to be old, tested, and over-used to be any good. If you had your way, you'd have poor Sidney running through the forest grunting primal noises and clubbing animals to death.

CAT. And you find the sight of him standing in line at the A&P, clutching preprocessed shrink-wrapped cow, grunting *please* and *thank you* an advancement?

RAL. Your world view allows for no growth. You openly despise any betterment of the original. I think you would have been content with the idea of Sidney never getting off the bar stool. God knows how you used to revel in his inebriation. He served as good company for you in your primordial swamp. I, on the other hand, have made available a higher order of mind and the capability to create from that platform. A host of creative endeavors, Art not being the least of them. In short, Catfish, I think you suffer from fossilphobia, the paranoia that comes from the fear of being left behind in the dust.

CAT. Sir! Your insults become more and more intolerable by the

322

moment! You speak as a lawyer does, deliberately deleting key facts of evidence. You out-word me with your hot air, which you use to inflate your façade of white armor – which, to my mind, is nothing more than tin foil. You, sir, are nothing more than an over-educated upstart. You have no history to borrow from but from my humble self; your feet begin where my head ends. Furthermore, you dare to speak to me regarding the nobility of Art? Why, I would have you know, my fine, kind, well-meaning pinhead, I am the Grandfather of Art.

RAL. You know, Catfish, should it ever come to pass that Sidney and I are given the opportunity to be released from this place, you might give some consideration to remaining behind in hopes that someday you may be cured of your self-serving fantasies. Speaking of which, your boasting begs the question: When is the last time you stood in back of Rembrandt? I myself can recall being present in his studio; I don't remember seeing you anywhere about.

CAT. Perhaps I haven't framed my credits in the clearest of lights. All that I am in the cycle of evolution is analogous to all that I am in my love life. I am a lover, not a husband. I am a creator, not a father. You, sir, are the babysitter for my prodigies. Art was one of my greatest achievements. Being the forerunner to language, it assured the advancement and welfare of mankind. With some stick- figures and bison-shapes dabbed on the cave wall, father could teach son how to hunt without getting killed himself. You, as the mere child you still are, Ralf, have advanced this skill to the height of that which you're so proud of: creature comforts and toys. Whereas, with all my projects –

RAL. You know, I'm fast wearying of your tone of supremacy. Again, you are skirting the issue. I ask you once more – how do you see yourself as the Grandfather of Art, pray tell.

CAT. To make my answer clear to you, it is necessary, as it is with all the achievements in my portfolio, to reach far down into it, back many hundreds of thousands of years, before you were not even a twinkle in God's eye. God only knows that I myself was so young at the time that I could not even conceive of the appearance on the stage of a spoiler such as yourself. I shan't trouble you with the details that unfolded over the course of two million years but, instead, will mark a time of four hundred thousand years ago for convenience's sake.

RAL. If only there was something convenient in having to listen to you.

CAT. At this point in time I speak of, man had long since used fire to his advantage in various ways, one of which was the cooking of meat. This, in turn, expanded his attic, allowing me more living space. I think your ancestors, Ralf, must have been vegetarians. Now man's brain could think in abstract terms. Prior to this period, Barney and Fred had been sitting around the cave on cold rocks, contemplating why they had had the piles for millennia. One evening, after having consumed a lovely mammoth steak, Barney and Fred sat before the fire, Fred watching Barney experimentally tying two sticks together. *Poof* – Fred instantly had a torch moment. A brilliant image popped into his illiterate mind. But how to convey his idea to Barney? There was no language yet. Fred, inspired, pulled a charred stick from the fire and drew a picture on the cave wall. The sketch was primitive, but the concept was there: a chair. That breakthrough was an end to having the shits and the beginning of everything man was to create from that time on. Nothing man makes, to this day, can be created in form without first appearing as a drawing. And you, my friend – how have you been able to bastardize this gift? You have naturally expanded on the comfort level of the man cave – you've designed The La-Z-Boy! A chair. Is a chair. Kind of gives new meaning to the old meaning of things never changing.

RAL. I am hopelessly speechless; or is it that I'm speechless at your hopelessness. After listening to you for any length of time, it's almost impossible for me to tie two words together correctly.

SID. Hey! Numbskulls! Can we shut the hell up already? God, what does it take? What is it with you guys, anyway? Every time we sit down to have a pleasant little sing-along around the campfire, it has to erupt into an operatic forest fire. What was it that Rodney said? *Why can't we all just get along?* You idiots just don't seem to get it – we're not just on the same team, we *are* the team. Remember my story about Charlie, and why I went into the service? At the age of seventeen, I wasn't willing to let someone else go to the fight and perhaps die on my behalf for my sake. On top of that, if my body counted against the numbers-game slot and filled the space where Charlie would otherwise fall, then all the better. I would gladly go in his stead. Now, fifty-some-odd years later, if you asked me if I'd be the one to go fight, I might very well say: "If *you're* stupid enough to go, be my guest." Now I ask you – is that to say that, back then, I was a 'hero' and now I'm a 'coward'? For God's sake, I'm still the same *one* person. I'm just standing at two different poles separated by time. Don't you assholes get it? I can see from your combined blank faces that the wheels aren't turning.

Remember when we had that pleasant two-week stay in the mental ward of the VA hospital? Do you remember that poor semi-unconscious fellow who was strapped to his bed, next to ours, for twelve hours? He never shut the fuck up, the poor guy. All he did was to assault our weary ears with his unrelenting and merciless screams of: "I chose life!" We didn't need a psychiatrist to fall on us to realize that this tortured human remnant was suffering from survivor's guilt. He was caught squarely in that ongoing raging battle, that eternal internal struggle that occurs in a normal psyche that is trying to find the middle path, having failed to achieve hero status by not dying, but not without having been awarded the patriotic stigma of being a coward. His fate was one of a life saved, but of having, in turn, to live in a state of remorse and shame, as opposed to being dead and beguiled by posthumous honor.

So I ask you – if you're both so keen to be separate from one another, which of you wishes to be the scabbard for the sharpest of blades: righteous morality? Think about it. Marking the line between 'right' and 'wrong' requires acuity. But the cutting edge becomes dangerously sharp when it's wielded as a weapon. It's that very double-edged sword that's wounded me and caused my inability to walk the middle path between Catfish's primal ways and Ralf's civilized ones, leading me to seek medical treatment in this place. When my sense of well-being is raped by those who, willingly or otherwise, reside beneath Catfish's roof – those, for instance, who find some kind of warped joy in running over my pets but are protected from my wrath by the laws that are set in place by the adherents of Ralf – for some reason, I'm not allowed to answer Catfish with Catfish, in kind. I'm not allowed to run the fuckers over and leave them in the road for the crows. It's enough to make me fucking nuts!

CAT. Hold up – I see Axel coming.

325

SID. Great. Just when I thought I might be getting through to you guys.

RAL. Lucky for you, Catfish, you truly are blessed. I was just dying to hear your retort.

SID. Shut up!

Axel approaches with his usual swagger, his habitual smirk that loudly boasts: "I know more than you do about something; just about everything." Yeah, then there's that twinkle in his eye that speaks as well: "Maybe I'll tell you and maybe I won't. I have the power."

--- Yeah, so what the fuck do you want? Is there something I can do for you? Don't you know you're interrupting my quiet time? In short, you're invading my space.

--- *Well, Mr. O'Riley, I just came out to inform you that you have a visitor. But, if you prefer, I can pretend that I didn't find you. But if you are interested, she's in Dr. Z's office as we speak.*

--- She? What the hell are you talking about? She? What?

--- *I don't know what. I just heard someone refer to her as your wife what. The Dr. is interviewing her now, while I'm playing ring-around-the-rosy with you.*

--- Her who? What do you mean, being interviewed? What? What? She where?

--- *Relax, it's policy. No nut can be seen by someone from the outside without them being checked over first. We can't take the chance of someone being a nut cracker. You know what I mean. Come on, let's get a move on. By the time we get to the office, the Dr. should be done with your wife.*

--- Wife? What wife? My *wife?*

Somehow, I find myself in the office. Sitting. Dr. Z comes into focus.

--- *Good afternoon, Mr. O'Riley, I'm glad to see you looking so well today – it's been a while since we've had a chance to talk. How are you feeling today? I just had the pleasure of speaking with your ex-wife moments ago. She's waiting in the next room to see you. However, I just need a few minutes of your time before I can allow you to meet with her.*

I'm pretty sure I'm dreaming. It's been years – five, six, maybe seven – since I've been here, where there are no wives, I'm sure of that. What's this about?

--- *You seem a bit tense, Mr. O'Riley. Let me get you some water. You can just relax for a few minutes before we talk.*

SID. Talk about my ex-wife? She's here? *What* ex-wife? It can't be what's-her-name, the first one – we haven't spoken since just after our divorce. By now, she wouldn't even know where I am, never mind care.

CAT. Maybe it's simply a matter of old business – you know, unresolved issues. Perhaps she has been thoughtful enough to bring you that can opener she walked out with.

RAL. Excuse me – what the hell are you talking about now?

CAT. Oh, my, have you no head for history at all? Don't you recall – when his first wife left him, she took everything with her that wasn't nailed down. All but a single pot and a can of soup. But she didn't leave the can opener. I'm sure that, after having realized this, she felt very sorry and it has been preying on her all these years. Yes, I rather think that is what it must be.

RAL. Good God, I can't help but hope such things are well behind everyone – everyone but you, who so dearly loves sticking your head up the behind of history. That's the only concept of behind you understand. For God's sake, why don't you give it up? Sidney, who do you suppose your visitor might be?

SID. Well, it can't be Barbie. I seem to recall her passing away at some point. At least I do remember the grief of the occasion. Of course, it may be that I myself have died and she's simply looking me up. But I can't think of any unresolved issues there. I certainly gave her more than my all. What could she possibly want of me further? No, I'm sure it's not her.

CAT. Well, that only leaves one choice, I'm afraid. What the hell's her name? You know, the one whose name you never could remember. You know the one, the one that was in the middle, the one with three names and as many faces. Remember, she used to constantly make squinchy faces all the time. Yeah, every time you did something that didn't meet with her approval. If I remember right, she had to get a face lift because she squinched up so many times, it froze on her. Her mother always warned her about that.

RAL. Come on, Catfish, you know very well her name was Gretchen and she wasn't half as bad as you would make her out to be. As I recall things, she was always supportive of the important matters in our Sidney's life, like his Art, for instance. And even after the absence of six years – of not communicating during the six years of his marriage to Barbie -- who was it that came to support him when he fell apart after Barbie's death? During and after their own marriage, she was always the lighthouse in the storm, doing her best to shine the way towards his betterment. An anchor in rough seas.

CAT. Yeah, well I would have cut anchor just as soon as I had been ignored when it came to the welfare of my son. I can hardly forget the time when Sidney instructed her not to walk with their son near the back end of a certain pickup truck: "I don't want the tailgate falling on Jared's head," he said. And *Bam!* What the hell good is ESP if no one bothers to benefit from the warning given? I can't help but think that your so-called advanced mind of man still has some kinks to be worked out. But getting back to that one, that middle wife, I'm still restricted in my sitting abilities due to the ass kicking afforded me when I indulged with Sidney in the simple pleasures of smoking and drinking. Not to mention I came ever so close to being blinded by that eternal squinchy face. Yes, if I had had more say, I would have jumped ship long ago.

SID. I'm sorry, Catfish. You have a point, but Ralf is right too. Gretchen has been very supportive of me these last ten years.

CAT. Perhaps it's nothing more than her love of nagging you and making squinchy faces at you.

SID. Goddamn it, Catfish! The more you defame her, the more reason I find to defend her. It's coming back to me slowly now – how and when I was walking around in a coma, there was Gretchen, encouraging me to get back into my art and writing. Helping me to clean up my house. Supposing that I might be ready to take on the responsibility of caring for another life in the form of a cat in need of rescue. And the really big one – the mission impossible – going to the VA, to reassure me of my good health. Countless boons that any man would give his right arm for in – guess what? – a wife. You know, I'm beginning to catch on to your ways. Your idea of winning isn't winning anything at all; it's seeing to it that no one wins. I swear to God, I think you suffer from Sand Castle Syndrome.

CAT. What the hell is Sand Castle Syndrome?

SID. It's when a small child builds a sand castle on the beach, then, out of spite at the idea of the sea taking it, he destroys it himself. No winners – you get it?

RAL. I couldn't agree more. All things move forward in my sphere of influence. In your little world, Catfish, I would hardly expect you to grow up. If, at your age, you don't get it, then I doubt you ever will. I'd advise you not to meddle as much as you do. Try to let go of the reins of the past and let things evolve at their natural pace. Try to relax. Maybe we should all join hands and sing a chorus of *Cumbaya*.

CAT. I think Sidney's going to have to talk to the Dr. first.

SID. Yeah. Keep it down, both of you.

--- *Well, Mr. O'Riley, I had a very interesting little chat with your ex-wife, she was most informative. However, I'm just the least bit disturbed with some*

329

small discrepancies that arose in our conversation. It would appear that there are a few disparities between our records on you and what your former spouse has revealed to me. I wonder if you might wish to shed a little light on the subject. Why don't you tell me, in your own words, how it is you think you came to find yourself with us. I have to profess my ignorance; I'm afraid I've concerned myself more with the records of your stay with us than with the vehicle that brought you here. If you're quite comfortable in doing so, why don't you tell me what you yourself perceive as the trouble and when you think it first may have occurred. I haven't forgotten the material concerning your childhood that we discussed in our last session together. To what degree do you consider your early history to play a part in your self-proclaimed inability to cope with the world as you see it?

--- The question almost answers itself. The key phrase: "How I see it." What I saw was something that never ever matched what it was. Yeah, I knew that back as early as when I was four. Too early, ha? A four-year-old can't understand anything like that, right? Well, relax, I'm not so delusional as to think I *knew* that things didn't match. That would be as stupid as asking if I thought, as a child, that it was unfair that my childhood was destroyed. It wasn't. Nothing was taken from me. Because I never experienced the difference in anything. The *used to be* or the *could have been* of it. Not that long ago, children had to stand at the dinner table and be thankful for what scraps came their way. They were basically property born into the family labor pool. The point is that things are only different after they change.

--- It has become self-evident that you're very intelligent and, despite your lack of formal education, you've felt compelled to educate yourself. Did you do so with any vision in mind? What were you hoping for, in terms of your life?

--- To survive it.

The doctor chuckles and bends his head forward to better look over the top of his glasses. He's evidencing the hint of a smile and is using this pause to measure the level of suspected leg-pulling. The doctor is all of five foot eight and of a portly stature, especially about the midsection. This suggests that he enjoys good food, as do his dark-stained teeth allude to his taste for red wine. With his uncombed white hair he also sports a long gray mustache that overhangs his lower lip – a soup wick, no doubt. He wears

330

a three-piece tweed suit that's frayed at the cuffs and worn at the elbows and smells of mothballs and pipe tobacco. His brown shoes don't seem to have been polished since the day his wife purchased them. His voice is low, gruff, and calm. He's slow to be moved by wit, having to first measure it before taking the joy of it.

--- *Is that it? No aspirations? No ambitions?*

--- Wasn't it Wilde who said: Ambition is the last refuge of failure? No, I never had ambition, I never had to gain or possess more than the next guy. Nothing to prove to him either. But, deep down, I really hate the next guy. Every time someone asks you to sacrifice something, it's always for the next guy living tomorrow. How is it that I lost my place in someone else's tomorrow? Why is it that I'm always here today? Really, I'm not trying to shit you; I really do believe surviving is an art, especially when you do it without expense to another.

Are you expecting me to complain? I'm not going to, you know. To me that's about as useful as sitting around having a conversation that begins with "remember". Whatever it is that's so damn important to remember in the first place probably wasn't sitting around and saying "remember".

--- *No, somehow, I wouldn't expect you to complain. However, I understand that, when it comes to engaging the staff, you can be most irritating and complaining, which is quite natural, if not expected here. Understanding aside, I do find it somewhat odd that you've apparently never found it in your interest to complain to me, where it might do some good. I'm very suspicious of the idea that, in fact, you may very well seem comfortable here. I find some degree of confirmation in that idea from my little talk with your ex-wife. Let me come right out and ask you this: Are you hiding here?*

Sidney shifts in his chair as if it were the electric chair. He crosses his arms and legs. He stares straight at nothing on the floor; he's trying desperately to achieve Clam Mode.

--- *Come now, Mr. O'Riley, I've always been open with you, haven't I? I've complimented you on your intelligence and education. Perhaps you can pay me the same courtesy of at least pretending that you recognize the fact that I may very well be as smart as you think you are. Right now, your body language is telling me that you're trying to hide from me, or from something.*

CAT. The jig is up!

RAL. Come on, Sidney, it's not going to hurt to spill the beans now.

--- Well, Doctor, I do believe in the open book policy; I just don't want anything that comes out of this session to turn around and bite me in the ass, you know.

--- *Come now, Mr. O'Riley, I think you know by now that you don't have to be gun shy with me. I think you understand that I wish you no harm.*

RAL. Go ahead, Sidney, you'll feel better for it.

CAT. Yeah, like an enema.

Sidney uncrosses himself and leans forward in his chair, looking the doctor in his eyes.

--- Well, Doctor, it's complicated as all hell. I hardly know where to start, or even the order of things, for that matter. It sure as shit involves a lot of people and events. I'm just not sure how to separate and map out all the pieces so that it makes any sense.

--- *I'm a patient man; I'm quite capable of dealing with the abstract, if not the obtuse. Why don't you give it a shot?*

Sidney starts to quiver a little and appears to be having some difficulty reaching for the next breath.

--- Okay, here goes, but I'm not sure that I can promise that I can put the whole crazy mish-mash in any kind of order, but here goes.

RAL. Come on, kiddo, you can do this.

CAT. That's right, my boy, you have both your fathers standing behind you.

--- Well, if you put all the kid shit aside, not to mention the dysfunctional young adult that came out of the ass-end of that tale, I guess the shit really hit the fan when Barbie died. For two and a half years, I tried drinking myself to death; I was in a walking coma, to put it mildly. That meant I pretty much ignored my pain medication, almost altogether. That was living dangerously. Not keeping my pain in check is like a death sentence – for someone else's death. At that time, I had so much shit piled up inside myself, most of which was deposited by a couple of my neighbors. I spent years of wishing them great harm and, to my way of thinking, they deserved anything that might befall them.

--- *Does this bring your cortisol intolerance into the picture?*

--- In spades. It had gotten me in trouble twice, which had ended with me being arrested and committed. Believe me, and I don't like telling you this, but there were quite a few more times when I should have been put under one lock and key or the other. It was only a matter of circumstances falling or not falling into place that prevented trouble. Sheer shit luck! But how much can you count on that? Perhaps the booze itself had something to do with keeping me from going over, I don't know. But when I got around to getting sober, I found myself in more pain than ever and more deeply depressed, to boot. I was becoming a real keg of dynamite with an ever-growing-shorter fuse. I don't want you thinking that I'm quick to temper; like, when it came to my neighbor Joe, it took years of accumulated shit to trigger an explosion.

CAT. Shit, if I had had my way, I would have done the creep in years ago.

--- That fuse started burning back in '79, when the asshole put poison out for the birds that my mother used to feed. He really didn't go on in an effort to endear himself to me after that point. In the early '80s, he illegally sprayed his lawn with pesticide and, the second he was done, jumped into his car and took off for his other residence, leaving me and my family to sicken and poisoning my pet rabbits to death. Those animals were the peace in my soul.

RAL. The bastard!

--- I could give you a laundry list of things he's done, one worse than the other, but what would be the point? Then there was my other neighbor, Blarny the Cop; you know what that means, I'm sure. Below IQ and above the law. You have to understand that my backyard was not just a garden to me, it was a sanctuary for Nature's animals. It was our shared Eden. These critters knew and trusted me; they knew they were safe there with me. They were familiar enough with me that I could hand feed and pet them. We're talking raccoons, skunks, and possums here, that, after feeding, just like to hang out and take in the peace of the night, lay on their backs and play with an empty peanut shell. To me they were like domesticated pets. Then that cocksucker Blarny took to shooting the animals when they left my place to cross his on the way to the marsh. Later he put out leg traps –

RAL. & CAT. The dirty son of a bitch!

--- In one night, within fifteen minutes, he caught three 'coons, who chewed their own feet off to escape. Right back to me and my safe haven. What the fuck could I do? It's against your law to aid or abet such animals. The enemies of the people –

CAT. The people. We could use a few less of *them* around, if you ask me.

--- I was left helpless and torn apart. I had to stand by and watch as those poor things took two weeks to die. Did I want to kill that cocksucker? You're goddamn right I did! The hell with the consequences – could they be any worse than what I was already suffering?

--- *How concerned were you that you might very well act out on your feelings?*

--- Well, I'm in here, aren't I?

--- *Tell me, did you ever consider an alternative action, as opposed to confrontation and/or violence?*

334

--- Yeah, I'm sure suicide would have been an answer to all concerned.

--- *Has either Catfish or Ralf ever offered up such a suggestion to you? Are you content with the two of them living in your head and offering advice?*

--- Is this a roundabout way of verifying that you're in the business of killing off the Ralfs and Catfishes of the psyche? To my mind, that act is pretty much mindless, amoral, not to mention – guess what? – legitimized murder. That's what your society has accused *me* of – although they omit the 'lawful' designation. Nonetheless, to my way of thinking, it was. Eminently justifiable.

--- *Well, I'll ask you again: are you happy with the two of them living in your head?*

--- They *are* my head. It's not like they pay friggin' rent, you know. Nor are they exclusive to me. They are simply the high and low archetypes of personal evolution. In short, they are my holon. And brother, if you dare ask me, as all your predecessors have, what the hell is a holon, then I'm going to suggest that you go back to whatever institution of higher learning you got your degree from and ask for a refund!

RAL. I think you can be very proud of your boy, Catfish.

CAT. Not at all, I can see clearly how he takes after you; it is you who should be proud.

--- *You'll have to forgive me if, at this point, I break a confidence – or, rather, I should beg your ex-wife's pardon. In my conversation with her, she led me to believe that you have, in the past, complained about having to live with these inner entities being in conflict with one another, yourself included. I'm just wondering why you become so defensive at the idea of ridding yourself of the problem.*

--- One could say the same for a wife. So you leave her dead on the side of the road? There's a problem? Conflict? What the hell do you want? To sanitize the world? My three-way tug-of-war is a mere microcosm. The universe is composed of conflict. Push – pull. Gravity vs. repulsion. All things in Nature are a contradiction in conflict, and there exists nothing in

Nature that isn't natural – and nothing exists outside of Nature. Catfish is nothing more than the primal consciousness and Ralf the hybrid blossoming of conscience. I simply give them free rein to walk about in the open daylight of my mind. That's not to say I have holes in my head, just a picture window. If you and society don't get it, it's just too bad. Meanwhile, we collectively would appreciate it if you all would get on up off our collective backs.

   --- *I feel a need to apologize, I had no intention of offending.*

   --- Think nothing of it. More often than not, I've found people such as yourself to be educated stupid.

   CAT. You know, the more I listen to him, the more sense he makes.

   RAL. Well, you know, he couldn't have become who he is without your influence. I think you've done a great job with him.

   --- *Well, Mr. O'Riley, I think we've pretty much worn out the welcome mat of polite evasion. Perhaps at this point you might wish to enlighten me as to just how you manipulated your way into our little sanctum. I do suspect it was through manipulation, was it not? You appear to be just a little too bright to allow yourself to be a victim of the system. Am I right?*

   --- Well, you're half-ass right, but I am a victim nonetheless. A victim of my own fears. Oddly enough, my fear of incarceration. But when all was said and done, it came down to something like being eligible for the draft. You can take it upon yourself to choose a branch of the service and join, or you can wait to be drafted and they choose the branch for you. I was the one to make the choice of spending my time on your farm now, as opposed to taking the chance of doing time in a prison later.

   CAT. Sidney, my boy, you might be making too much sense. Give the old Dr. a break. Are you sure you want to let the whole of Ralf out of the bag?

   --- *Yes, I understood that you pled guilty to a plea bargain in order to get yourself in here. I really have little to no interest in the mechanics of the judicial system. I'm far more interested in the peripheral evidence I was able to garner from my little chat with your ex-wife concerning your mind- set in total. She was very fervent about the fact that, at least in her opinion, you are emphatically incapable of hurting anyone, never mind murdering anyone, as you were accused of having done.*

--- Not capable! *Not capable?* Gretchen is speaking from her heart, for the love of me – from her own warped sense of the word 'love', anyway! That doesn't necessarily mean she knows what the hell she's talking about!

--- *If you're admitting to the fact that you are indeed aware of that love, then you must realize, also, that her name is Raechel.*

--- Leave her the hell out of this! She has no business sticking her nose in my business. She and everyone else who's ever been in my life have been overthrown by Ralf and Catfish, who have known me *all* my life. Gretch- . . . I mean, Rae- . . . *that woman* has only known me for thirty-some-odd years and she abandoned me, the same as everyone else had, so what gives her any rights? Shit, the only thing I've ever had of any lasting quality is my Sanctuary Garden and my two Serpent Daddies. At least I can have an intelligent conversation with them. What's the old joke? "The last time anything intelligent was said in the White House was when Jefferson had dinner alone." Well, that's the way it is with me.

--- *Could we not consider the idea that you might have been making an attempt to hide from the world? The argument could be made that you are continuing to do so now, in this place, as well. Were you not in a state of hibernation after your wife's death?*

--- Do you get paid by the goddamn word, or are you just trying to justify your paycheck? Either way, I don't give a good friggin' shit. What the hell difference does it make to anyone regarding my reasoning to be alone with my selves in the peace of my own making? What, are you fucking jealous or something? As long as I can remember, I was always different: more sincere, more caring, more sympathetic, more sensitive, empathic – you name it. What did that ever get me? It only made me so different that other kids used me as a target of ridicule, and to throw rocks at. I wasn't a part of the mindless clan. Then I spent my entire adult life

337

attempting to be as good as or better than everyone else, just to eventually realize that I didn't really wish to fit into everyone else's thinking as to how the world was supposed to be. It turns out that everyone else was just the same gang of kids in adult skins. In short, I never became 'socialized', thank God. And who's been my boots and my umbrella? Catfish and Ralf. And what was my protective castle wall, but my home and garden that I created out of my mind and with my own hands. The one thing I didn't suppose was an invasion from the outside. That's why I neglected to construct a drawbridge with a moat, and let's not forget the boiling oil – Oops, excuse me. For a moment I slipped into the norm of misinformation: no one defending a castle tossed away oil, it was far too expensive; what was used was actually boiling water. All this means is that I've gone through my life not fucking with anyone and, foolishly enough, expecting the same in return. If indeed I've killed anyone, it hasn't been a matter of revenge, as supposed, but rather of self-defense.

--- *As I understand it, that's more than you ever said in court. From what little I've been able to glean of the case, I would have to conclude that you basically allowed yourself to be railroaded. That is to say, you allowed the proceedings to go against you without a fight. Was there some method to your madness?*

--- You're goddamn right there was! After more than twenty years of fighting pain – and that, in turn, meant fighting this battle with the cortisol shit, and that being a constant and present threat to the security of my freedom – I knew something had to be done. Nearing the end of these years, it became more and more difficult to keep my pain under control and, likewise, to keep a check on the resulting psychosis. I found myself daily threatening Blarny and Joe under my breath. Exactly what I would love to do to them and why. As soon as I would catch myself thinking these wonderful thoughts, I would realize that I was in trouble and take more medication. But that was becoming more and more often, and what about the big one? What about the day I didn't catch on to my 'wrong thinking'? That's easy to happen. It's happened before, when I've slipped over the line – and, once you're there, you have no realization that you're doing or thinking anything wrong. It's sure as shit a real dangerous place to be. I used to ask myself constantly, how long do I want to take a chance on living like this?

The more and more that I thought about it, the more I toyed with the

338

idea of having to commit myself, for the sake of all involved. I'm not a mean-hearted person, you know. In the cold stark daylight of my sanity, I'm far closer to being a lover than a killer. Yeah, I could commit myself – with what money? Then, by chance, out of nowhere, the goose that lays the golden egg nests right in my backyard. Some idiot knocks off Blarny. Now my contempt and hatred for the man is well known, and my flirtation with psychosis is also well documented by the police. Naturally, suspicion fell on me. The volatile gossip that developed about me being some kind of wife-and-child-beater didn't help my public image any. Even the prosecutor couldn't get it out of her head that I was some kind of violent nut. She apparently had her own issues, because no one – I mean no one, including my wife or son – ever accused me of violence or wrongdoing. People had made up their own stories about me based on one single fact that was in the papers: that fact was that *I said*. I *said* something about holding hostages. Not that *I did;* whether or not I *did* didn't matter to anyone. Then there was the cops' lie about me "running to my weapons shed". I wasn't running anywhere, and the 'shed' they were referring to was my studio. That information morphed into the 'fact' that I had a lot of *guns*. First I knew of it. So you can see, it doesn't take much to put a kangaroo court together. But that public eagerness to judge that had made me a pariah for years now took the form of opportunity knocking at my door.

When I was questioned, I didn't deny my love of the idea of killing the son of a bitch. I may very well be some kind of nut, but I'm certainly not *nuts*. In fact, I supplied the final nail for my coffin when I allowed the prosecutor access to my VA psych files. They were just chock-full of hatred and veiled threats against the man. It used to terrify my shrinks something awful; though, eventually, I think they realized who I truly was. But those records put me closer to the shadow of the gallows. So they came after me with a lot of circumstantial evidence. But knowing that the bitch DA wanted to nail my ass to the barn door for the acts she already assumed I was guilty of, I didn't want to take a chance on this shit going to trial, and ending with me going to prison. So my lawyer and I put our heads together and came up with the money- and time-saving idea of pleading no contest in exchange for a life sentence to your little twinky farm. And at no cost to me. Everyone is happy.

Dr. Z has been listening attentively but, before he can articulate any response, Raechel rushes through the door of the adjoining room, through which she has been listening. She's firing, with both barrels blazing, in an outburst of exasperation.

--- Is that what you wrote?! You know Blarny's not dead. You know none of this is real! Is that how you go about healing yourself in the story? By lying and hiding? Is this your idea of revelation? This is how you end your story? This is how you end your life? I encouraged you to sit down and write your life's story because I supposed that you could find a way to healing yourself through facing those things that so deeply troubled and hurt you. Not for you to cop out on the last page! I was so hoping that this could serve as a venue to get out of your sense of victimization – not commit yourself to it.

Sidney panics. In terror, not knowing whether to cover his eyes or ears, he breaks from the room through the nearest exit available, the French doors that open out onto the garden. A garden ringed by a green hedge. Earl's garden. In Earl's backyard. In his vision, blurred, as if by tears. A sudden intake of breath fills his brain – a submerged man, propelled upwards, he breaks through the surface of the ether. Into the garden air. Dr. Z's voice . . . Raechel's voice . . . . fade into vapory echoes.

Ralf?

Catfish . . . ?

No answer is forthcoming, nothing to disrupt the peaceful solitude that is the garden.

About the Author

Earl Grenville Killeen is an artist and the author of *The North Light Book of Acrylic Painting Techniques.*

He shares his home with two rescue cats and his garden with hummingbirds and butterflies.

Made in the USA
Columbia, SC
10 February 2018